Face of
the Enemy

Books by Joanne Dobson

The Maltese Manuscript
Death without Tenure

The New York in Wartime Mysteries
(with Beverle Graves Myers)
Face of the Enemy

Books by Beverle Graves Myers

The Tito Amato Baroque Mysteries
Interrupted Aria
Painted Veil
Cruel Music
The Iron Tongue of Midnight
Her Deadly Mischief

The New York in Wartime Mysteries (with Joanne Dobson)
Face of the Enemy

Face of the Enemy

A New York in Wartime Mystery

Joanne Dobson and
Beverle Graves Myers

Poisoned Pen Press

Copyright © 2012 by Joanne Dobson and Beverle Graves Myers

First Edition 2012

10 9 8 7 6 5 4 3 2 1

Library of Congress Catalog Card Number: 2012936473

ISBN: 9781464200311   Hardcover
9781464200328   Trade Paperback

Poisoned Pen Press
6962 E. First Ave., Ste. 103
Scottsdale, AZ 85251
www.poisonedpenpress.com
info@poisonedpenpress.com

Printed in the United States of America

Joanne Dobson dedicates this book to
Shea McKinley Dobson

Beverle Graves Myers dedicates this book to
Keegan Monica Myers

Acknowledgments

Joanne and Beverle would like to thank the following people for their help and support: Madeleine Burnside, Dave Dobson, Kit Ehrman, Robert Fish, Kathy Gibson, Naomi Hirahara, Kate Lombardi, Lawrence Myers, Thelma Myers, Katherine Priddy, Beth Reid, Damaris Rowland, Nell Taylor, and Sandra Zagarell.

Special kudos go to the entire staff of Poisoned Pen Press for their assistance in bringing this book to publication.

Chapter One

November 29, 1941: Saturday, early evening

"Shall I, Robert?" Masako held the green silk kimono by its wide sleeves. Fresh from her bath and smelling of jasmine, Robert Oakley's wife turned the kimono this way and that between her slender, naked body and the full-length mirror in their bedroom. Outside the tall windows the glistening panorama of Riverside Drive on a wet evening unfolded: rain-glazed yellow taxis, red tail lights, green and blue umbrellas shining in the glow of street lamps. December's early dusk had fallen over the Hudson, leaving the room in a melancholy gloom only partially relieved by the peach-colored walls and the hanging silk scrolls with their glowing brushwork of bamboo, chrysanthemums, and waterbirds.

"Why not?" he answered, heart thudding even after seven years of marriage to his Japanese wife. It wasn't simply that she was beautiful—golden skin, silky hair, the exquisite tilt of her dark eyes—but also that he never tired of the wry intelligence with which she faced the mixed nature of life's blessings. Take tonight—they were dressing to attend the opening of Masako's first solo New York art show, but the timing of that show, at the prestigious Shelton Gallery of Contemporary Art on Fifty-seventh Street, couldn't have been worse.

Yes, for almost a decade he and Masako had found a tolerant welcome among Manhattan's artists and intellectuals. But now that the country of Masako's birth had gone mad, the long-term friction between Oakley's two beloved nations threatened to burst into flame. What would he and his wife do when it caught fire? Where would they go? How would they live? Where would she would be safe?

Oakley shook his head, gave a deep, rumbling cough, then rubbed his brow. His hand came away damp. Every muscle in his body ached, but he wasn't about to ruin his wife's gala opening by letting on that he was sick. "Why not wear the *houmongi*? It's a garment suitable for any festive occasion." Damn, he thought, I sound just like the fusty old professor I am—lecturing the love of my life on Sartorial Practices of the Far East!

He was, after all, a professor of Asian history; perhaps his specialization made him oversensitive to the looming threat. The politicians could yet find a way to avoid war with Japan. War with Hitler's Germany seemed certain—but Japan? It was so far away. Across a greater ocean than the Atlantic.

As he fumbled with his shirt studs, Oakley forced a smile for his wife, who continued to study her image in the mirror. He gave himself a swift mental kick in the pants. Gloom and doom be gone! Tonight Masako's artistic triumph would take center stage.

But yet…yet. Even as Arthur Shelton, the gallery owner, had been picking through the paintings in Masako's Bleecker Street studio, feverish rumors were spreading about Japanese subs in Hawaiian waters. Frenzied news commentators speculated that Japan intended to gobble up Pacific islands, just as they had Chinese ports and provinces. What would be next? San Francisco?

By the time Shelton had actually mounted Masako's canvases on his bright-white gallery walls, Japan's special envoy to Washington was making a public mockery of Roosevelt's efforts to forge a diplomatic solution. Oakley could only hope and pray that tonight's event wouldn't elicit any displays of Jap-hatred from New York's high-strung art patrons.

Masako finally turned away from the mirror, gathering the glowing silk between her small breasts and granting him the half smile of the indulgent wife. "That's not what I meant, Robert. I know my *houmongi* can double for an evening gown."

Oakley left off efforts to knot his bow tie and injected his tone with more confidence than he felt. "Well, and, of course your work transcends nationalistic fervor. This crowd knows that." Professorial again—damn. "No true art lover will think twice about the kimono."

One corner of his wife's mouth lifted in a fleeting smile; he must have gotten it wrong again. "No, Robert. I'm asking if I have the right to wear this garment. Given how long I've lived in the West, Japanese people might consider it offensive and others a cheap pose. You understand, don't you? Given that it looks as if I've turned my back on my native land."

Oakley crossed the bedroom in long strides and cupped his wife's chin in one hand. "Do you want to wear the kimono?"

She nodded, grey-black eyes questioning him silently.

"Then wear it, darling. For me. I love you in it."

"Oh, yes?" she replied, reaching up to release the crooked bow he'd made in his black tie. Her eyes glowed with mischief, with invitation, but he looked away. Oakley didn't know how he was going to make it through this gala shindig tonight—he felt sick as a dog.

◇◇◇

"Tell me the truth, Bob. Do you understand this modern art?" Oakley's friend Dr. George Wright tilted his head, pencil-thin moustache twitching. Arthur Shelton had positioned Masako's signature painting, "Lion After the Kill," so anyone coming up the circular staircase into the large center room of the Shelton Gallery would encounter its vibrant images right off.

Oakley studied the painting, trying to see it through his friend's eyes. A jagged outline in dark yellow contained, but barely, a lurid green circle and a swath of crimson that both radiated and dripped. Inked calligraphic figures danced down one side of the canvas. Stifling a cough, Oakley explained, "It's this way, George. Only Masako understands Masako's paintings. The viewer merely experiences them."

The doctor snorted. "Well, I must say I experience this one as...unfeminine."

"Unfeminine?" Oakley raised an eyebrow.

"Yes. Bold and a little wild."

"Wild? Of course, don't you see it? Masako may be small and delicate, but her spirit is fierce...with passion. That's what drew me to her in Paris years ago. That's what attracted Shelton to her work."

George Wright gave "Lion After the Kill" a puzzled second look. "Well...if you say so." He scratched his head and glanced around the crowded gallery. "But, anyhow, the paintings must be selling. Look at Arthur—he's almost walking on air."

Arthur Shelton, his hair shining like a golden helmet, flitted from group to group as his patrons admired the haunting canvases. Smoke trailed from the long cigarette holder he waved in the half-moon arcs of a stage conjurer. Oakley watched him weave his magic. First a joking interchange with a fat man sporting a *pince-nez*—James LaSalle, the *New York Times* art critic. Then a slap on the back for that scrawny young Rockefeller— was it Nelson?—who was such an avid art collector. A courtly bow for Lillian Bridges, Oakley's colleague at Columbia. Then a wicked kiss of the fingertips blown in the direction of another professor, Lawrence Smoot.

Arthur was certainly bold tonight—but, then, it was no real secret about him and Lawrence.

Oakley nodded at Wright. Manhattan's art lovers did seem to be giving Masako's vibrant work a warm reception. His fears about the evening began to evaporate.

Then a shrill giggle cut through the animated chatter. Guests paused in their conversations, turning to gape. A tall woman in a white satin gown stumbled up the circular stairs. Raindrops glistened in her sculpted blonde pompadour. She posed there at the top, an over-age ingénue in a Broadway musical, gloved arms extended at her sides, as if she were expecting applause. Then she giggled again, even more piercing than before.

George Wright put his mouth to Oakley's ear. "It's not like those Fifth Avenoodles to use drugs, but either that broad's on something or I don't know my narcotics."

"Who is she?" Oakley frowned as the woman snagged a glass of champagne from a passing waiter, but he didn't listen for the answer. Rather, he experienced a sudden, piercing sense of anxiety. Where was Masako? The blonde disappeared in the crowd, but Oakley heard again the sound of that maniacal giggle. Shrill. Jolting. It made him shiver. For some irrational reason it made him fear more than ever for his Japanese wife.

His gaze swept over the art patrons crowding the reception. Suddenly he felt feverish and disoriented, almost as if he were lost in one of his wife's abstract paintings, weaving through colors and shapes and textures, searching for that one swath of green that always anchored her compositions. Then a deep cough forced its way up his windpipe, and he clapped a handkerchief to his mouth. Damn Plato's balls! He didn't have time to be sick; Masako might need him.

"Bob, are you all right?" George Wright narrowed his eyes.

"Of course."

His doctor of many years tapped him on the chest with an insistent forefinger. "I don't like the sound of that."

He shrugged. "It's just a bad cold."

George gave a professional squint. "Look, if you're not better by Monday morning, drop by my office—I want to give that chest a good listen."

Oakley replied with a grunt and left his friend studying a series of Masako's smaller paintings. The gallery air was a poisonous fug of cigarette smoke; that was all. He would *not* be sick. He coughed again, and waved away a waiter offering canapés from the Russian Tea Room. Arthur Shelton had done things up brown.

Spotting Shelton coming nearer now, he raised his champagne glass in a congratulatory toast. The elegant art dealer responded with a wolfish grin and jutted his chin toward James LaSalle, who was twirling his *pince-nez* on a silk ribbon. LaSalle was smiling, too. Excellent! Masako would be thrilled—her avant-garde oils reviewed in New York's leading newspaper!

Oakley halted at one of the arched windows that ran the width of the gallery's second floor. He rested his burning forehead on the glass. Ah. Cool at last.

In a secluded alcove a jazz trio played "Dancing in the Dark." For a moment, he relaxed. Then—damn—another cough. Gathering himself, he again plunged into the crowd, eyes peeled for that flash of green kimono. Ah, here was Masako now—joining Arthur for a shared photograph in front of "Lion After the Kill." Oakley stepped toward his wife, this diminutive beauty, shiny black hair piled high and pierced with *kansashi* in the traditional style.

Now Wright was beside him again, and they were pushed back with the rest of the crowd as the photographer cleared a space for his tripod. The professor could only watch as the art dealer slipped his arm around Masako's waist.

Damn! Oakley sucked in his stomach and tugged at his too-tight vest, precipitating yet another painful cough. Shelton's beautifully tailored tux fit him like a second skin. The dealer really could be a bit of a twit, Oakley thought as flashbulbs popped, but, over the past several months, Arthur had stood by Masako as more casual friends had disappeared like pebbles with the tide. Oakley had to hand him that—the professor and his wife were hard-pressed to know whom they could trust anymore.

Once again, the scene seemed to swirl before him. He was ill, no denying it. He should go home before he collapsed. If that photographer would just finish up, he would tell Masako that he was taking a taxi back to the apartment. She'd understand. One of his friends from the university would see her home. Probably good old Lillian. Or George, if he didn't have any late-night rounds.

Oakley turned to the doctor, but once again the giggling blonde distracted him, suddenly rolling into the photographer's field, as if she meant to have her picture taken, too. Shelton looked annoyed, Masako dismayed.

"Who *is* that woman?" Oakley asked George Wright.

"Like I told you—she's Mrs. Gregory De Forest. Tiffy to her friends. A…" the doctor shrugged. "…socialite, I guess. You see her name all over the society columns."

"Never read them." Oakley noted the sturdy, silver-haired gentleman in formal garb who'd been shadowing the blonde's every move. "That her husband?"

The doctor cleared his throat. "No," he said meaningfully, "that's Nigel Fairchild." At Oakley's blank look, he continued. "America First?"

Uh, oh. Now Oakley recognized the name. This was the Jap-hating, Jew-baiting demagogue who spearheaded the New York chapter of the isolationist America First organization. Nigel Fairchild—who saw himself as a candidate for vice president in a future Charles Lindbergh presidency.

No, by God—not the racist America First! Not here. Not now. Waves of clammy nausea washed over the professor

"George, we've got to get Fairchild out of here." Oakley felt a sense of impending crisis in the air, a tight, inaudible vibration, like the thrumming of an electric wire. "Who knows what kind of grandstanding that Nazi-lover has in mind? I wouldn't put it past him—"

The blonde shoved between Masako and Shelton, intent on mischief. Oakley staggered in the intruder's direction.

Dr. Wright grabbed his arm. "Let Shelton handle it—it's his shop."

In the instant the professor hesitated, the blonde shrilled, "I can't believe you're showing this Jap crap, Arthur. You're a filthy traitor! Someone needs to shut you down."

That's enough! Oakley dove forward as Tiffy grinned malevolently, grabbed a glass of red wine from the nearest bystander, and hurled its contents. Oakley saw the dark liquid arcing toward "Lion." A woman screamed. Masako's voice.

He was almost there. One more step. The professor yanked his wife sideways just as the wine hit Arthur Shelton square in the face, then splashed across the canvas behind him.

Desmond Cox, Shelton's assistant, grabbed Tiffy De Forest by the arm and hustled her through the astonished crowd. Oakley could see the snide grin on Fairchild's face as he trailed behind. Coward, he thought, sheltering Masako under his arm. Getting a woman to do your dirty work!

Arthur Shelton, of course, handled the situation with grace. He turned to his guests as if nothing awkward had occurred. "Looks like that was a No Sale, folks." Everyone laughed. He made a small comic show of pulling the handkerchief from his pocket and mopping at his face. The jazz combo launched into an upbeat number.

Crisis averted, Oakley thought. But no—what was this? Suddenly the floor was tilting. His head was spinning. Oakley sank to his knees. His fingers brushed the soft fabric of Masako's kimono, and then he was flat on the floor.

"Bob!" George Wright knelt beside him.

Masako knelt on his other side, a vision in green so bright it hurt his eyes, her beautiful face transformed by shock and fear.

"Robert!" He saw her mouth form the word, but his ears were ringing so loud he couldn't hear her voice.

Oakley took her hand and whispered her name. After that, nothing.

Chapter Two

Sunday afternoon, a week later

"Jimmy Datillo bet me two bits a Kraut dies faster with a bullet in his head. I say his gut." The dark-haired boy pushed his white paper hat forward and leaned over the counter of the Brooklyn candy store. "Who's right, Miss H? You're a nurse. You know this stuff."

"What a question!" Louise Hunter squirmed on her stool. "Yes, I'm a nurse, but right now I'm off duty. I came in here for an egg cream, not to talk about shooting people."

Gus Voskos frowned. "I gotta know. Jimmy and me, we're gonna enlist soon as war's declared. Well...Ma says I hafta graduate high school first."

The marble counter was sticky with dots of cherry syrup. Louise eyed the crimson stain on the sleeve of her baby blue dress. Oh, swell! Then she lifted her gaze to find Gus chewing his lip, staring at her intently. Behind him, chrome seltzer spigots gleamed. Louise wanted her weekly chocolate egg cream, and she wasn't about to let war talk ruin her treat. Three months ago, fresh off a train from Kentucky, Louise had never even heard of an egg cream. Now she was addicted to them.

She'd hardly even heard of Brooklyn, either, but, surprisingly, its brash vitality was beginning to grow on her.

"If I sneak some ice cream in your glass, will you tell me?" Gus spritzed seltzer into the milk and chocolate syrup. His teasing manner was creeping back. Good. She didn't want to think about this friendly soda jerk trading bullets with German soldiers.

"No, thank you. No ice cream. Just regular is fine."

Cute kid, Louise thought, as she took her first sip from the foaming glass he'd slid across the counter. But why did boys that age have to be so keen on guns and blood?

The bells over the heavy glass door tinkled, and three girls pushed their way through, chattering and giggling. "Helllllooo, Gussie," cooed the one with the polka-dot hair bow perched in her golden curls.

Suddenly, killing Krauts seemed to be the last thing on soldier-boy's mind.

Sipping slowly, Louise tried to relax the tension that had gathered into a knot at the back of her neck. She'd been on a private-duty case since Wednesday—four nights now—a crusty old Columbia University professor. Robert Oakley had driven his previous nurse away with his irascibility, but Louise had set him straight immediately. When his wife ushered her into the bedroom the professor had been smoking a briar pipe. Imagine. A pipe! With pneumonia! She'd plucked it from his mouth and doused it, hissing, in a basin of water.

"You have a subconscious death wish, Professor?" she'd asked him.

"You read Freud!" he exclaimed.

"Well, everyone talks about his theories. I was curious."

Her patient had been a pussycat from then on. Mostly. Super-Nurse, Louise Hunter, RN. She chuckled briefly, stirring the remains of her egg cream with the straw, then she swiveled her stool a quarter turn and looked out the plate-glass window. Already a week into December, but sunny and pleasant. Her mother had gone on and on about New York City blizzards, howling winds, two feet of snow, but on a day that sparkled like this one she knew Mom had just been firing another blank in her relentless campaign to scare Louise back to Louisville.

The Sunday-afternoon sidewalks were busy. A snappy green roadster pulled up to the curb; a soldier in dress uniform got out of the passenger seat and leaned over to kiss the girl driver. It was a long kiss. As she drove away, she blew him another. Instantly Louise felt a hunger in her heart that was almost physical. Dr. Preston Atherton—damn him. Damn him and his snooty family. The dark-eyed cardiology fellow had enticed her to New York—and then had second thoughts. Seduced and abandoned. It was an old, old story.

Louise tossed her head, the honey-blond hair flying, and returned her attention to the street. She was done with Pres. She wouldn't waste another thought on that worm. Right. She'd be just fine on her own, thank you.

Across Flatbush Avenue, a Hasidic man came out of the kosher poultry shop with a plucked chicken, its head dangling from carelessly wrapped butcher paper. He went out of his way to sidestep an olive-skinned woman with long dark hair who was balancing a white cardboard baker's box in the crook of her elbow. She shot him a Brooklyn sneer as she shepherded two little boys across the street. Just outside the candy store, a fat, red-faced man in a worn work jacket ambled past with a big portable radio balanced on his shoulder. The door tinkled open again, and Louise heard the radio blare the score of the Sunday afternoon football game.

What a city! How could her mother expect her to scoot back to pokey old Louisville when this whole new world lay at her feet? Every time the boarding house phone rang, Louise flinched. Calls from home ended with hysterical pleas for her to hop the first train south. But, no, she wouldn't. Louise nibbled at a fingernail as sidewalk dramas unfolded before her eyes.

Outside, the man in the work jacket had stopped dead in his tracks, pressing the radio tight to his ear, an unreadable expression paralyzing his suddenly pale face. He looked ill. Louise half slid off her stool. Was he having a stroke? Did he need help?

The man stood stock still, as if there had been a hitch in time. For a second or two, people pushed around him. Then he shouted several hoarse words Louise couldn't make out, and everyone else on the sidewalk froze.

"Gus? Do you see—" Louise pointed outside, then people started running, the door crashed open, and all hell broke loose.

"They're bombing us!" a boy's cracking voice shouted. "Turn the radio on! The Japs are bombing us!" When Gus stared at him, motionless, the boy with the cropped blond hair scooted behind the counter and twisted the big Bakelite dial: Howie Schroeder, her landlady's teenage son.

A squeal of static blasted her ears, resolving into an announcer's solemn tones: "We repeat: This just in from Washington—The Japanese have bombed military bases at Pearl Harbor—"

"The Japs?" Gus exclaimed. "Jeez, everyone thought it would be the Krauts."

"And where the hell is Pearl Harbor, anyways?" someone asked.

"Out on Long Island," squeaked the girl with the blond curls. "Hey, I bet we could see smoke from the roof."

"It's in Hawaii, you blockheads," Howie snapped. "Shut up and listen."

Everyone clustered around the end of the counter. Howie stood at attention, as if he were reciting the Pledge of Allegiance. The report crackled on, announcing the unthinkable. Air attacks, wave after wave of Japanese planes, Navy and Army bases taking heavy fire. Hundreds of servicemen killed.

Hawaii. Louise pushed her soda glass away, suddenly sickened by the sweet smell, and glanced at her large-dialed nurse's watch: 2:33.

2:33 on a sunny Sunday afternoon, and nothing will ever be the same.

Mr. Voskos clattered down the stairs, sleeves rolled up to his elbows, Sunday comics crumpled in his hand. Jamming the front door open, he yelled at Gus to turn the radio as loud as it would go. People poured into the small store to listen. Most of them were stunned into silence.

"How the hell did Japs get halfway across the Pacific?" asked a man in a neat double-breasted suit.

A woman in a plaid jacket grabbed her husband's arm. "Bill's over there, isn't he—Sadie's boy—in the navy." The man nodded, face drained of color.

Gus' dark eyes gleamed. "To hell with high school. I'm enlisting tomorrow."

A hand squeezed Louise's arm. She whirled to find Cabby Ward, her boarding house roommate, clinging to her as if they were the best of friends—instead of two thoroughly mismatched women enduring each other because of the prevailing housing crunch.

Cabby never seemed to stop talking, and her Bronx accent grated on Louise like fingernails on a chalkboard. If the girl wasn't recounting every sorry detail of her latest date, she was droning on about her editor at the *New York Times* who insisted on assigning her fluffy "women's" pieces instead of the real news she aspired to report. And why the girl went by Cabby while she carried the perfectly lovely name of Catherine Joan, Louise had no idea.

Cabby must have entered the candy store with the crowd from the sidewalk. In her round, dimpled face, under that hacked-off mop of dark curly hair, her eyes were wide with shock. For once her mouth was shut. Louise covered Cabby's hand with her own, reminding herself how young her roommate was. Just because the girl had somehow, incredibly, landed a reporting job for the *New York Times* fresh out of college didn't mean she was actually a grown-up.

"We're in it for sure now, Louise," Cabby responded. "You know that, don't you? This means war."

Louise nodded, barely breathing. If the enemy now flew across oceans, New York could easily end up like those devastated European cities newsreels showed before every film. War meant aerial bombing, U-boat invasions, sabotage at home. Maybe even fighting in the streets. What would happen to all these people? Images invaded her mind—brownstones in flames, Italian frame houses with their carefully cultivated rose gardens blasted to smoking rubble. What would happen to boys like Gus and Howie? To girls like Cabby? To her?

"Filthy Japs!" It was Howie at Louise's elbow, feverish with excitement. "I'm gonna get me a bunch of those sneaky little, squinty-eyed rats."

Louise gaped: how could a young boy spew so much venom? The only Japanese person she knew was Masako Oakley, her patient's wife. And Mrs. Oakley was such a nice person.

"Howie, you're fourteen years old!" Cabby exclaimed. "They won't let you enlist."

Gus sneered at Howie from the other side of the counter. Obviously the blockhead remark still stung. "Yeah, Squirt. You don't know onions about war!"

"I'm almost fifteen! But I—" Before Howie could say more, his eyes popped. "Ma?"

"Vy you run out the house like that?" Helda Schroeder's usual carefully modulated English slipped as Louise's landlady pushed her way through the crowded store. "I vant you home vhere I can keep an eye on you—time like this! *Ach du lieber!*"

"But, Ma!"

Helda grabbed him by his collar. In spite of her agitation, the stiff blond curls that surrounded her plump, pretty face remained unruffled.

"Ma! It's war! Don't you understand? It's war!"

"*Jawohl*, I understand—all too vell. And I vant you home now!"

"Yeah." Gus was leaning over the counter. "Run on home with your mommy, little boy. Us men'll take care of the Japs. Go on now, shoo."

Howie glared, hands balled into fists.

Cabby slipped her arm around the younger boy's shoulder. "We'll all go, Howie. No place like home on a day like this." Five-foot-two with a curvy figure and a sassy mouth, she could almost have passed for a kid herself—almost, except for a certain wounded expression that occasionally crossed her face when she thought no one was watching.

Surprised by her roommate's tact, Louise slid a dime onto the counter. Not waiting for change, she followed Cabby and the Schroeders out of the candy store onto Flatbush.

It was a whole new world, one that had abruptly taken on a somber hue.

Chapter Three

Something's wrong with Helda, Cabby Ward thought, something even more than the staggering news of the bombings. Her landlady was gripping the edge of the kitchen counter so tightly her knuckles had turned the color of bone. Her eyes were unfocused, and she didn't seem to realize she was muttering. "War comes…that devil Ernst…who knows where…vat to do…vat to do?"

From her seat at the long table beside Louise, Cabby shot her gaze around Helda's roomy ground-floor kitchen. Late afternoon sunshine slanted through the windows over the sink, bright red cherries dotted the looped-back curtains, and the smell of the midday pot roast still hung in the air. Except for the shock on the faces of the women clustered around the white-enameled tabletop, it could have been any ordinary Sunday.

But today was different. The world had been set on its ear, and most of Helda's boarders had been drawn as if by some magnet of despair into the kitchen. What were they seeking? Simply the quiet comfort of their own fear reflected in another's face?

It would be different at home. Cabby knew exactly what obscenities her father would be bellowing at the radio in the cramped Bronx apartment. He hated Japs. But, then, he hated Jews, and Italians, and the Irish—and Eleanor Roosevelt and FDR. Let's see—almost three o'clock. He'd be emptying his second quart of Schaeffer and reaching for his third. Her mother—well, her mother…She'd call her mother tomorrow—when the s.o.b. was at work. Right now, Helda's kitchen provided all the comfort Cabby could hope for.

She glanced back at the landlady and was relieved to see her release the counter, take a deep breath, and let it hiss out slowly between her teeth, a good, long, expressive hiss. Good. Helda was back in charge.

"Coffee. Coffee. That's what we need." Helda smoothed her apron. She reached for the empty pot and whirled around to face her assembled boarders. "Coffee strong enough to walk on its own. Strong to buck us up, *jah*?"

Several women nodded, but not even the perennially polite Louise made a move to get up and help. Cabby recognized something in her friends' expressions—the same weary, haunted look as in wire photos of women driven from their homes by earthquake or flooding.

Or bombing.

I feel it, too, Cabby thought. After that first rush of terror in the candy store, her legs, on the short walk home, had turned to lead. Even if a Junkers 88 made a direct hit on Ebbets Field a few short blocks away, she wouldn't be able to run now.

Snap out of it, she told herself, stabbing fingers through her short curls. Look on the bright side; the men will all enlist and the *Times* will need every reporter they can get. Even the girls. Surely they would give her hard-news stories now? Yes! No more covering Women's Club teas and bandage-rolling parties for Cabby Ward! She knew she should get herself uptown to the city room right now, but somehow she remained rooted to her chair and could only watch wordlessly as Helda bustled into action.

The landlady filled the pot at the sink, dipped her measuring scoop into the coffee canister, and called to her son, "Howie, bring more cream from the ice box. Get moving now!"

The boy, who'd been sitting in sullen silence at the table full of women, hitched up his dungarees and slammed out the door to the back porch where the old ice box was kept.

At the other end of the table, Mousie was the first to stir. "What should we do?" she whispered. Her beady gaze skittered from face to face, settling with a frown on Helda's tight-lipped mask. "We can't just sit here." She was the new girl, the one who'd moved in last month, with straight dun-colored hair and a wardrobe right out of a home economics classroom. Cabby and Louise had dubbed her the Mouse, because neither her name nor her personality had yet registered.

"Maybe we should go to church," said Ruthie Boyle, chewing a painted fingernail. The brassy red-haired stenographer toiled in some big bank's steno pool.

Alicia Rosen snorted. Built along the lines of a clothes hanger, but tough all the same, Alicia was a hard-driving law student, even more ambitious than Cabby. "Church? You?" She and Cabby had heard Ruthie bragging about her plans to snare one of her gray-suited, sex-deprived bosses. Get herself pregnant. He'd have to marry her, wouldn't he? She'd be on Easy Street for the rest of her life.

"Why not? We could all go down to Holy Innocents." Ruthie turned to the Jewish girl with hands on hips. "Light candles for everybody who died in the attacks. Would it kill ya?"

"Everyone can pray for peace," Louise murmured from behind a flowered hankie, her sleek fall of honey-colored hair nearly covering her cheeks.

Now it was Cabby's turn to snort. Talk about holy innocents—this transplanted Southern belle might as well skedaddle straight back home—too naïve for big-city life. Where was it she came from—Memphis? Or was it Nashville? Louisville, that was it. Louisville, Kentucky—where they ran that big horse race.

Cabby jumped to her feet, finally roused. "We don't need prayers, Ruthie. We need information. Try the radio again." Astonishingly, no further news had followed the report of the attack, only the usual Sunday afternoon programs.

Ruthie turned the dial, squealing through all the New York stations. With a frustrated sigh, she paused at the Philharmonic broadcast.

"Just leave it there," Cabby ordered. "That's CBS. They'll run the news as soon as they can. How's that coffee coming, Helda?"

As the German woman mechanically transferred cups and saucers from the cabinet to a tray, she seemed to have retreated to her own world once again. Over the lush music, Cabby was able to pick up a few agitated whispers: "...trouble for Ernst... trouble for all of us...knew this would come...."

Cabby could only imagine the landlady's state of mind—a German immigrant, alone in this alien country, war with her homeland inevitable. She shook her head. She'd always liked Helda, a comfortably built woman who was willing to let the rent slide a day or two in an emergency. Was there a Mr. Schroeder? Helda had never mentioned Howie's father, and there were no photos of a man anywhere about the house. Was he the Ernst she was muttering about?

Worried, Cabby tried to catch Louise's eye. If Helda collapsed, at least the nurse would know what to do. But her roommate was wringing her dainty handkerchief, lost in thought, chin on chest.

What a charming little heartbroken Southern pose! From the moment Louise moved in, Cabby had read tragic love affair all over her. She'd followed some sweet-talking charmer to New York, and the jerk had left her flat. Try as she might, though, Cabby hadn't been able to wangle any particularly juicy details.

The back door slammed open, and Howie burst in, *sans* cream bottle. "A plane! Flying low. Betcha it's German...a Heinkel bomber!"

Helda slammed the loaded tray on the counter. Everybody jumped. "Is that why you dawdle around on the porch? I need your help and you look for airplanes?"

"Maaa!" Howie protested.

"German airplanes? For god's sake!" Through the butler's pantry, a woman in a swooping hat made a grand entrance, her voice jumping a dramatic octave. "First Japs? Now Krauts? The bastards are attacking us from all sides!"

A minor commotion broke out around the table. Alicia jumped to her feet. "Marion—" she warned.

Cabby was closer. She grabbed the newcomer's arm. "Can it, Marion. Howie's just overexcited. Show some sense, for cripe's sake." She finished with a small jerk of her head toward Helda.

"Ooohh." The way Marion Sutherland said it, that wordless articulation ran to three syllables. As she pulled off her gloves, she crossed the faded red linoleum. "So sorry, Helda. I didn't mean you, of course. You're almost like a real American."

"*Jah*." The German was back, through gritted teeth. Helda's usually good-natured expression was a mask of anxiety, the round, rosy cheeks now pale and drawn, the generous lips pressed together in apprehension.

"I mean, you've been in our country how long? Fifteen years? Well, there you see," Marion said airily. "Might as well be forever. You're a good German. Father would never have let me move in here, otherwise."

Father was old money from Cleveland and Marion, his stage-struck daughter, an exotic creature with a reed-thin figure, exquisitely tailored suits, and sculpted raven bob, who'd come to Gotham, as she insisted on calling the city, to study thea-tuh.

The Mouse spoke up in a quavering voice. "But what if the Germans really are coming? The Japs did." Her wide-eyed gaze was on Helda.

The bubbling coffee pot filled the kitchen with a homey sound and aroma, but it couldn't calm the rising tension. Ruthie, too, glanced suspiciously in Helda's direction.

"Now wait a minute," Cabby said. "Let's not panic. No bomber exists that could make it all the way across the Atlantic. We ran an article about it just last week," she intoned as if citing Holy Writ. She might have a running feud with the editor who refused to take her seriously, but the *Times* was still the best damn paper in New York, and she was proud to be on their payroll.

"Maybe not planes, darlings, but what about U-boats?" Marion retrieved a cup and saucer, turned off the heat under the bubbling pot, and helped herself to coffee. "Submarines can go anywhere there's water." She looked extremely knowing. "There might be a whole fleet of them right off Long Island this very

minute, just waiting for the signal to launch a Nazi invasion."
She blew on her steaming cup and assumed a Noble Expression.
"We must all be vigilant."

Howie smacked his fist in his palm. "The Coast Guard!
That's it! I'll join the Coast Guard. I'll get those Krauts, every
last one of 'em."

Cabby shook her head. Howie was an all-American boy
wrapped up in comic books, the Dodgers, and model airplanes.
But given his last name and his mother's native land, many
Americans would consider Howie to be one of the very Krauts
he wanted to exterminate.

"Krauts?" Helda bustled over, grabbed her son's ear, and
pulled him toward the big, walk-in pantry. "Krauts? You don't
know what you say, and no son of mine is joining any…"

The sounds of a palm smacking flesh and blubbery cries of
"Quit it, Ma" came from the pantry.

The women traded uncomfortable looks. Cabby brought the
coffee pot to the table and began to pour.

"So, Louise, you'll enlist, won't you?" Alicia Rosen asked,
poking at her unruly bun of thick, dark hair. Alicia, Cabby
knew, considered beauty parlors a waste of time and lipstick a
frivolous indulgence.

Louise tensed visibly. She stared at Alicia with a guarded
expression. "Enlist?"

Cabby stifled a snort. She couldn't imagine the dainty Louise
tending shot-up, bloody men in some makeshift battlefield
hospital.

"You know, join up." Alicia's eyes glinted behind silver-
rimmed glasses. "The military will need nurses—that's for sure.
If I were a nurse, I'd go."

Ruthie had draped herself over the white-tiled counter.
"Yeah, you gotta join up, Louise. To take care of our boys. It's
your patriotic duty."

"My mother would kill me," Louise stammered. She gave
a dry laugh. "I expect my brothers will go ahead and enlist…
they'll lose their student classification. Mom won't be able to

stop *them*, but she'll want *me* home for sure." She sighed and ran a hand through her sleek hair.

"There's a lot more going on than enlisting, girls." Marion had been silent for the past few minutes, sipping at her coffee, but now she plowed on. "When they announced the bombings, I was at the theater with my gentleman friend. The management stopped the show and told the audience to get home as quickly as possible. My friend does something important down at Foley Square." She paused. Everyone leaned forward, holding their breath. "You know? Where the federal offices are?" She lowered her voice to a whisper. "G-men?"

Oh, she's good, thought Cabby. The money Daddy's forked over for drama lessons hasn't been wasted one bit.

Marion bent toward her audience. "So, he's very knowledge-able. Don't repeat this to a soul, but my friend told me that they're going to start rounding up Japs any minute, just as soon as war is formally declared."

Louise threw her handkerchief down, suddenly pink-cheeked. "They can't arrest people without cause, can they?"

"Oh, yes they can," Alicia answered grimly. "And they will. In wartime, civil liberties are suspended."

Marion nodded and put a finger to her carmined lips. "It's been in the works for months. All very hush-hush. Next they'll come after the Italians and Germans."

Helda, just returning to the kitchen, stumbled, and caught herself against the Frigidaire. "They come after Germans?"

Alicia, who studied at Brooklyn Law School daytimes and worked at a Jewish legal-aid organization in the evenings, continued, "Professor Pritzker says they can do anything they want with enemy aliens."

"As well they should," Marion shot back. "We can't have people with divided loyalties running around loose. Not at a time like this."

Helda's cheeks flushed bright red. Her back bowed, and she pressed a hand on the counter for support. Cabby expected an outburst, but just then the phone rang in the front hallway, casting the group into uneasy silence.

The *Times*, Cabby thought.

She sprinted through the butler's pantry. Not the *Times*. She plodded back into the kitchen. "For you, Marion. Some guy."

Louise and Marion both rose.

"Where you off to?" Cabby asked Louise sourly. "Catching the night train for Louisville?"

Louise drew herself up. "If you must know, I'm on duty tonight. I have to iron my uniform."

"Scooting off home tomorrow, then, are—" The music from the radio abruptly changed to an announcer's baritone.

Ruthie turned up the volume and froze like a department store mannequin, elbow crooked, hand raised to the knob.

A foreboding voice filled the white-tiled kitchen: "—from Japanese Imperial headquarters, by proclamation of Emperor Hirohito, Japan has formally declared war on the United States of America. A declaration from the government of Germany is expected at any hour."

Chapter Four

Masako Oakley peered around the edge of the apartment door, her dark eyes wide with an expression Louise couldn't quite decipher. She had stretched the security chain to its limit.

"Mrs. Oakley?" Louise asked. "Are you all right?"

The brass chain rattled and fell with a clunk. Louise's employer pulled the door wide. "Oh, Nurse Hunter, you cannot know how happy I am to see you. Such a horrendous day—and this he-bear I am married to, he is trying to kill himself."

Professor Oakley's wife was a lovely woman, whose tilted eyes seemed to find a charming absurdity in much of what the world had to offer. Until tonight. Now Louise was alarmed to see dark circles smudging those eyes and stoop-shouldered weariness altering her graceful bearing. Usually so elegant in dress and grooming, Mrs. Oakley had scraped her hair into a limp, disheveled ponytail, and the poppy-flower-print hostess pajamas she'd worn the day before were now crushed and stained.

"Nurse Hunter—thank god!" The he-bear staggered through the oak-paneled foyer dressed in a wrinkled plaid robe and leather slippers. His cheeks were flushed, lips tinged with blue.

"You see," the professor's wife whispered, quick to relieve Louise of coat and uniform bag.

"Professor! You're supposed to be in bed." The nurse grabbed his thick wrist; the pulse pounded under her touch. She felt his forehead: burning up. "Let me get you to your room."

Brown eyes hectic, he pushed her arm away. "Never mind me. Masako's the one in danger. Tell her she must leave this city and leave it right away." Robert Oakley coughed and then winced in pain. "After that…unconscionable air attack in Hawaii no… Japanese person will be safe in this country." More rapid, wheezing breaths. "The radio said a man from Kyoto was…beaten on Forty-sixth Street…an engineer—it will only get worse."

Mrs. Oakley spread her arms helplessly. She seemed as near collapse as her husband.

The nurse slipped an insistent arm around Professor Oakley's waist and steered her patient down the long hall toward the bedrooms. Mrs. Oakley preceded them in a fluster. The professor veered suddenly, knocking a large celery-green vase off its pedestal table. The elegant object crashed in shards on the parquet floor. Louise winced. It looked ancient, but neither of the Oakleys seemed to notice the damage.

The tiny woman grasped her husband's other arm to help Louise support him. The professor rambled on, "If she won't listen to me, maybe she'll listen to you. Masako must leave New York…find a safe place…hunker down until saner heads prevail."

"Shush. Shush," Louise said, as if she were speaking to a child. "Nothing will happen to Mrs. Oakley. This is a civilized country." Alicia's dire words concerning enemy aliens she pushed firmly to the back of her mind. "Now, calm down, Professor. If you keep this up, you'll be no good to your wife at all."

He shook his head weakly. "Nurse Hunter, tell her—she'll listen to you. She says you have a profundity—what did she call it? Oh, yes—a heart wisdom unlike any she's seen in American women."

Heart wisdom? Given the excruciating blunders she'd made with men, Louise could hardly call herself wise in the heart department. Puzzled, she glanced over at the Japanese woman shouldering her husband's bulky arm. Her face was pale, eyes expressionless.

The sickroom at the end of the corridor smelled of stale sweat and fever. The only light came from a torchiere illuminating the ceiling and encouraging ominous shadows to clump in the corners of the large chamber. The exquisite hanging scrolls that gave the room a distinctly Asian beauty had retreated into darkness. Louise eased Professor Oakley across the room and onto the bed, where he collapsed against the feather pillows. His wife knelt to remove his slippers.

"Cool water, Mrs. Oakley, quick." Louise handed over the enamel basin from the bedside table and stripped off the professor's robe and pajama top.

"Yes. Yes. Whatever I can do." The smaller woman scurried into the attached bathroom.

"And a washcloth," Louise called. After donning a protective gown, she began to mop her patient's face. Then she gave him the first of several sponge baths. After a half-hour's ministrations, the professor was cooler—and finally asleep.

The Japanese woman, curled up on a slipper chair at the foot of the bed, breathed a relieved sigh. "He's too much for me, Nurse Hunter. I must accept it—the attack in Hawaii has him all…*bouleversé*, and then, the final straw, a mob of boys stormed down the street chanting…hateful things…and he got like… like he was when you came."

Her English was fluid and precise, with an occasional charming inconsistency. Her accent, when Louise detected it at all, was more French than anything else, with only an intermittent clip in the intonation that must be the influence of her native Japanese.

Louise removed her soaked gauze gown, folded it, and bagged it for the wash. Finally she could change into her uniform. "What were the boys yelling?"

"Kill the Japs! Get Tojo! Young boys—some of them not yet in their teens—screaming Bombs over Tokyo! It was nightmarish, like those dreams where even the most innocent—babies, kittens—turn into demons. That's when I ran to put the chain on the door."

"Have you been alone all day?"

"I might as well have been. Lillian Bridges, one of Robert's friends from the university, stopped by with flowers after the

attacks were announced." She fluttered her hand to her chest.
"What good are chrysanthemums at a time like this? And then
my maid called and, how you say, fired me? Now, the super, he
won't answer my calls. I was so frightened that you would not
come."

"I would never abandon a patient." Louise was indignant.
"And as for the others, well…I don't know about the maid,
but…" Louise recalled the name engraved on a brass plate in
the building's lobby. "The super's name is Kaiser, isn't it?"

"Yes. I know. He's German…he's terrified, too. But…tell me
the truth, now, Nurse Hunter…have these horrendous bombings
turned me into a monster?"

"You're not a monster to me," Louise assured her, as they
moved toward the kitchen. The previous four nights, while the
professor slept, the two women had talked over cups of steaming
tea unlike any Louise had ever tasted. Green tea. Jasmine tea.
The flavors of earth and of blossoms.

Mrs. Oakley, a true citizen of the world, was the most
sophisticated person Louise had ever met. She'd been born in
Tokyo, but, as the daughter of a senior Japanese diplomat, had
grown up in the embassies of Moscow and Paris. Her manners,
speech, and dress seemed more European than Oriental. After
studying philosophy at the Sorbonne, she'd alienated her rig-
idly traditional family by refusing to accept the marriage they'd
arranged for her. She'd remained in Paris when her father was
recalled to Japan, and she'd heard nothing from them—even
after her whirlwind courtship and marriage to Professor Oakley.

Imagine, Louise thought. Just imagine such a life—sounds
like something from a book.

And Mrs. Oakley's recollection of meeting her future husband at a Montparnasse gallery had seemed like the height of
romance. "Seeing him now, so ill," the Japanese woman had told
her. "You wouldn't believe what Robert was like when he first
complimented one of my canvases. The vitality of him. That
gleam in his eye. I was galvanized. I felt exactly what they call
un coup de foudre."

Yes, Louise thought, remembering.

Tonight, the two women again settled in at the scrubbed-wood kitchen table, and Mrs. Oakley said, "Robert insists that I leave the country—but I don't want to. In every way but on paper, I am an American. I bless the fate that brought me here—to freedom."

"Not an American?"

"No. The leaders in Washington ban Asians from citizenship by law. You didn't know that?"

Louise felt her jaw drop. "No…even if you marry an American citizen?"

Mrs. Oakley nodded slowly. "Asian exclusion, they call it."

Louise shook her head. "Is there no way to get around it?"

"Well…Robert could petition his Congressman to seek a special exception. It would have to go before the full Congress, and they don't always vote yes. We've been slow to start that process. You must have a great deal of influence, and we're not certain…And I've been consumed with my paintings…Robert with his work…Now…" She gazed into space, biting her lip.

"What if you do have to leave the country?" The kettle whistled, and Louise rose to pour hot water into a squat cast-iron pot.

"Where would I go, you mean?"

Louise nodded.

"Not to Tokyo, that's for sure. I would be seen as a traitor there."

"A traitor?" Louise frowned. This gentle artist was no Benedict Arnold.

"Japan is very different from America—you can scarcely imagine. My disobedience to my father. Marriage to a well-known American. Then there are interviews I've given, critical of some Japanese ways." She swallowed—hard. "I fear what might be done to me there."

"What could happen?"

Mrs. Oakley sat very still for a moment, then shuddered. "The emperor's government is particularly harsh where public disloyalty is concerned. The stories I've heard…Father would be unable to save me—even if he wished to." Her complexion paled. "I...would rather not speak of it—"

Louise wanted to reach out and take her hand, but it wouldn't be proper. This was her employer. Instead, "Do you and the professor still have friends in Paris?"

The other woman gave Louise an incredulous look. "The Nazis have taken over Paris."

"Oh, of course." Abashed, Louise sank back down in her seat; how many times had she seen newsreels of Nazis goose-stepping down some Paris boulevard?

"Robert does have friends in Peru. That's where he wants me to go. But how?" The Japanese woman gestured to her finely etched features. "Anywhere I go, I take this face with me—the face of the enemy. You think they will allow me on any ship or airplane?

"Besides." She raised her chin. "I will not leave Robert. He needs me now, more than ever. How could I go? If I lose him, I lose everything."

Louise stretched a hand across the table, propriety be damned, and the women's fingertips touched. "Mrs. Oakley, you're exhausted. Go on, take a bath, put on a fresh pair of pajamas, bed down in the guest room. I'll take care of everything."

◇◇◇

Once Louise heard the bath running—such a civilized sound— she took a deep breath. The apartment was quiet, her patient resting easy. She was beginning to get things under control at last.

The shards of the green porcelain vase still littered the hall-way. As she picked them up, Louise reflected on the sprawling, Upper West Side apartment. She'd never been in such an elegant home, unless she wanted to count that disastrous visit to meet Dr. Preston Atherton's mother at her imposing Fifth Avenue mansion. She didn't. This comfortable, book-strewn apartment filled with artifacts collected on the professor's many travels suited her just fine.

And, of course, Mrs. Oakley had put her own artistic stamp on the place. In the living room, a modern, black-lacquered mirror added elegance to a nook featuring two Arts and Crafts chairs with slatted wooden arms. Across the room, a carved mahogany chair with stylized peacock sides and teal upholstery sat beside a library table that could have come straight from a venerable British men's club. The scents of sandalwood and cinnamon permeated the air. And paintings hung everywhere.

As Louise placed the porcelain shards on the table next to a glass vase of bronze chrysanthemums, she gave one of the artist's own canvases a long look. The background had the quality of a rice-paper scroll. The foreground suggested a stand of bamboo blown by the wind. Louise could identify that much. But what about the pair of miniscule brush strokes of vivid green, almost like wings? And the wide, rough, green slash that thrust up and across the entire painting, until it bent back upon itself and ended in a tight spiral? Then there were the Japanese characters running down the right side. What could those spidery figures mean?

Mrs. Oakley had explained that her art blended the ancient, highly codified techniques of *Shodo*, or calligraphy, with abstract images that hit her, often with the force of a lightning bolt. Sometimes she would stand before her easel for hours, quietly, patiently waiting for the mental picture to form. When inspiration flickered, she wielded her brushes like a mad woman, completing the painting in a matter of minutes.

Feeling her artistic shortcomings keenly, Louise tilted her head to take in the curves and shapes from different angles. Then she spotted a line of words in English, white on white, almost transparent, near the bottom of the canvas: Cling new bird against / cold wind. Old branches blossom. / Cherry! Pink, then green.

Louise blinked. Suddenly the green slash made perfect sense. Brilliant! Mrs. Oakley was both poet and artist.

Time to check on her patient.

She found Professor Oakley breathing more easily, temperature only slightly elevated.

Good. She glanced at her watch. 11:48. All was quiet from the guest room as well. Louise eased into the red leather club chair by the patient's bed. With a sigh, she interlocked her fingers and stretched her arms above her head. It had been a calamitous day, but now it was over.

Chapter Five

As if in a trance, Helda Schroeder watched the last of the soap suds from the dinner dishes swirl around the drain. Breaking her gaze reluctantly, she dried her hands on a cotton dishtowel. Almost midnight. Surely everyone in the boarding house was asleep by now—even that night owl, Fraulein Sutherland. It was time to do what she'd been dreading. Yes, now was the time.

The oak door directly opposite Fraulein Rosen's room on the third floor groaned as Helda opened it. She crept up the attic stairs on tiptoe. The top stair creaked, causing her to jump and hold her breath for a full moment. But no one seemed to have heard. Her flashlight beam picked out brass-bound trunks, rope-tied crates, and a busty dressmaker's form wearing a half-finished cotton housedress—all covered with a layer of dust at least five years thick.

She stifled a sneeze. The room needed airing.

Then she shuffled past the great carved mahogany chairs and side tables, that huge oaken wardrobe, now on its side, taller than the ceilings in any room of this American house. What had they been thinking to bring all these old-world furnishings to a new-world home where they…where she…had been planning on building a brand-new life. The memory gave her a twinge. Her hand flew to her heart. She had learned not to cling to the past, to *der Vaterland*, but Ernest hadn't. Oh, how he clung—so hard there was no more room for work, for family—

Nein! Just get on with it! She began shifting hat boxes and the dress bags that hung from the rafters. Finally, from beneath a stack of men's shoe boxes, she retrieved a battered leather portfolio tied with cord. She clutched it to her chest.

Inadvertently she glanced out the double attic window: leafless branches lit by the street lamp, a neighborhood mutt sniffing a tree, an unfamiliar Studebaker parked across the street. She strained her eyes. Was someone behind the wheel?

Could it be…?

Dummkopf! What did it matter—someone parked on a public street? She was in her own attic—her home that she'd fought so hard to keep after Ernst had deserted them. Her husband hadn't shown his face in Brooklyn ever since. Why would he be nosing around now?

Helda untied the portfolio's brown cord. Letters postmarked in Berlin and Hamburg slid to the floor, revealing a battered passport and a folder holding a few photos.

She sank down on a nearby trunk. Tucking the flashlight under her arm, she shuffled through snapshots. Howie at Camp Siegfried—in his swimming trunks, at calisthenics with the other boys, marching in a parade. She tightened her lips. She should never have allowed Ernst to involve them in the Bund.

Good fellowship with other German-Americans—the homeland food, the songs, friends who spoke the old language—there was no shame in that. But that was never enough for Ernst Schroeder with his big dreams of returning *der Vaterland* to greatness. When the social evenings began to turn into Nazi rallies branding President Roosevelt as a communist and denouncing his "Jew Deal," she'd had enough of it.

With a deep sigh, she laid the snapshots aside. She hadn't climbed to the attic to relive memories of the Bund.

Ach! Here was she'd come for…the portrait.

Helda took a deep breath and trained the flashlight's cold beam on an image of her and Ernst in their wedding garb. How handsome he'd been, enough to bewitch a young girl's heart. And she…so innocent in her Bruxelles lace.

She allowed herself one long moment to contemplate their images. Then she removed the wedding portrait from its cardboard frame and ripped it directly down the middle.

Chapter Six

Monday, December 8, early morning

Relentless pounding rattled the front door of the Oakley apartment. Louise woke from a light doze. Who? What? Her watch read 2:14.

She glanced at the professor. Still sleeping.

Three additional blows. Louder, more insistent. She had to stop that racket before it woke him.

She ran to the foyer, threw the door open. "Silence!" she ordered. "I have a profoundly ill patient here." Then she saw them. Really saw them. Four men in fedoras and dark overcoats, silhouetted by the wall lights in the corridor. Large men. Men with faces hewn from granite. Louise drew a deep breath, stepped back to slam the door.

The lead man slapped a meaty palm on the thick oak, flashed a gold badge in her face. "Special Agent Cyrus Bagwell, FBI, ma'am. We have a warrant to search this residence." His face was long and sallow, with deep lines etched around the mouth.

Louise was stunned, but nonetheless she shot him the cobra glare she'd learned from Miss Willard, her nursing school supervisor. "I don't care who you are. My patient can't be disturbed."

The agent's eyes widened, but only for the space of a second. "We're not here for any sick man. We want the Japanese citizen Masako Fumi. Where is she?"

Louise was suddenly cold all over. Marion's gentleman friend had been right—the government was rounding up Japanese!

Without thinking of the consequences, Louise braced her rubber-soled nurse's shoes in the opening and propped spread hands between door and frame. Her heart was pounding—the FBI!—her government! Shuddering at her own defiance, she managed to snap, "Come back in the morning at a civilized hour."

Bagwell clamped both hands on her shoulders. Louise resisted, but she was no match for the man's superior strength. He twisted her out of the doorway and flung her against the foyer's oak paneling as if she were a rag doll. His voice was tense, but flat, as he and his men poured into the foyer. "We don't have time to waste, ma'am. Where's the Jap?"

Steadying herself with a hand on the wall, Louise kept her lips pressed shut. For a split second a sense of utter unreality paralyzed her.

The G-man strode into the living room, focused immediately on a vase of chrysanthemums that graced the lacquered table. His expression turned from grim to grimmer. One of the men had a camera, and Bagwell jerked his head toward the flowers.

"Get a shot of that, willya? Jap flowers."

Louise suddenly felt like a kettle on the boil. She shot forward. "Those are chrysanthemums—as American as you are. And Masako Oakley is an innocent woman who happens—"

His big hand was on her shoulder again, its mere weight a threat. "Lady, tonight there's no such thing as an innocent Jap." Louise had never seen such hard eyes—gunmetal gray. "You keep obstructing us, and I'm gonna arrest you. Impeding official government business."

"Arrest *me*?" For simply acting in her patient's best interests?

"Take us to her—pronto." The brute stench of power was in the air.

Louise gasped, but, undeterred, her mouth spoke the truth she felt. "I'm a nurse, not a cop. If you want her, find her yourself."

But Mrs. Oakley was already there, standing bewildered in the hallway. Louise knew she was a grown woman, thirty-eight years old. But in cotton pajamas, half asleep, with her straight black hair hanging down her back, she looked like a child, saying, "*Mon Dieu, qu'est-ce qui se passe?*"

"The suspect spoke Japanese," Bagwell snapped. "Get that down, Flanagan." A squat, rumpled man who looked like a police officer scribbled something in a notebook.

"Masako Fumi," Agent Bagwell intoned. "In the name of Franklin Delano Roosevelt, the President of the United States, you are under arrest as an enemy alien." His big hand clutched her arm. He towered over her. "You have ten minutes to get dressed and pack toiletries. Then you come with us."

"Go with you?" Masako whispered, her face pasty white.

"Get your toothbrush…a change of clothing…and, you know, whatever stuff you women need. Go on." He gave her a little shove, and she stumbled.

Louise caught the trembling woman in a protective embrace and stormed at Bagwell, "Do you have to be such a bully?"

"Listen, Nursie, I've about had it with you. You want to make yourself useful? Get the Jap into some street clothes. We've got work to do." He turned to his team. "Okay, guys. You know the drill—box up anything suspicious as evidence. Any question, it goes."

The men fanned out into the large room. A youngish red-head threw his hat on the credenza, then stripped off his coat and tossed it on top of the hat. He stood back, scrutinizing the comfortable furnishings. "Whew," he whistled through his teeth, "not doing too shabby for herself, is she, this little Nip?" He hefted an exquisite porcelain heron from a low table and tossed it in his hand.

"Nurse Louise—" Masako whispered weakly, and pointed.

Professor Oakley was reeling down the corridor. "What in the name of holy hell is going on out here?" Barefoot, barely able to stand, pajama top unbuttoned over his bony chest, the sick man snorted like a bull.

"Robert!" Masako pulled away from Louise and ran to her husband, almost knocking him over.

"You're going to kill this man!" Louise shrilled at Bagwell. "I'm calling his doctor, right now." She sprinted to the telephone, but scarcely did she have her finger in the dial when she felt the receiver ripped from her hand. The one called Flanagan picked her up bodily and sat her down on the telephone bench with a hard thump.

"Unhand her," Oakley croaked. Then another thump followed, louder. A shriek from Masako. Robert Oakley lay flat on the Persian carpet, wheezing as if he would never draw another full breath.

Louise struggled, and a nod from Bagwell ordered Flanagan to let her loose. She raced to Oakley, knelt beside him, her professional instincts taking over. Her patient was in trouble, out cold, pulse barely palpable in the notch under his jaw.

"I've got to get the doctor," Louise insisted.

Bagwell studied the unconscious professor, then motioned to a florid-faced, dark-haired man in his twenties. "Get him in bed, Tucker." He turned to Louise. "And you? Keep him, there. Ya hear me? Or you're goin' downtown with Madame Butterfly, and your patient will be carted off to Bellevue. Got it?"

Louise bit off her outraged protest.

The sturdy Tucker transported the professor to his bed, not without care. "Listen, lady," he said to Louise, as she settled a groaning Oakley on his pillows, "I'm City police, just along for the ride, so I can't really help you out. But lemme tell ya—ya can't fight this. Japs are being picked up all over the city tonight—by the Feds and police detectives. The orders come from the top—the very top."

"But, where—"

Tucker put his finger to his lips. When he left the room, he shut the door behind him. Louise heard the key turn.

Quickly, she reapplied the gauze swathe the professor had torn from his chest and repositioned his pillows to provide for maximum lung expansion. "Pain?" she asked, when his eyes fluttered open. He nodded, rubbing a flaccid hand over his right flank. Once she'd administered the pills Dr. Wright had left, she expected a hundred questions, but Professor Oakley simply closed his eyes and lay motionless.

He knows, Louise thought. He knows exactly what's going on. Like a wounded animal, he's retreating until he has the strength to fight.

Sinking down on the red leather club chair, Louise slowly became aware of sounds from elsewhere in the apartment. Thud after thud from the professor's study. Books falling to the floor? Then a crash as something shattered in the living room. She cringed. The key turned, the bedroom door opened, and Bagwell's bulk appeared against the brighter light of the hallway. "You," he barked, beckoning to Louise. "The Jap's got instructions for you…About her husband." His lips twisted, sour.

The living room was chaos, books and papers everywhere, dark rectangles on the walls where paintings had hung. In the foyer, wearing gray trousers and a blue cardigan, Masako stood handcuffed (handcuffed!) between two men—straight and proud. Louise's heart melted for her. She understood that in the short few days she had known Masako Oakley, the Japanese woman had become a friend.

"Nurse Hunter," Mrs. Oakley said. "I will be all right. Tell Robert that, and—take care of him. You know how that man is. Don't let him do anything stupid."

"Okay, lady," Bagwell said. "That's enough. You're going downstairs."

Between the two large officers, each with an arm hooked through hers, Mrs. Oakley was propelled to the door. A navy-blue coat from the hall rack was thrown over her shoulders. She looked at Louise, beseechingly. "Robert must get well. Tell him I said that. Tell him to do it for me. You will, won't you? I can trust you to care for him?"

"Yes. Yes," Louise vowed as the apartment door slammed shut.

Forgotten by Bagwell, who turned his attention to some photo albums his men had retrieved from Professor Oakley's study, Louise ran to the living room window. Idling under a streetlight in front of the building was a long black sedan. She watched until Mrs. Oakley crossed the sidewalk, the men still flanking her. She watched them put her in the back seat. She watched the car pull from the curb and head downtown, the only moving vehicle on the misty, sleeping street. She watched it until its tail lights disappeared in the darkness.

Then she stood and watched the darkness.

Chapter Seven

"An art show?" Cabby's just-one-of-the-guys grin evaporated. "We're at war, and you want me to write up an art show!" Her protest could be heard in every corner of the city room, even over the clattering typewriters and the insistent bells of the wire service tickers. The usual morning commotion had doubled. No, tripled.

Len Halper, the day-side editor, gave a short nod and dug in the mess of papers on his desk. Rearranging a sheaf of notes, he scanned the top page. "Take it down, Ward. Shelton Gallery of Contemporary Art, 24 West Fifty-seventh."

Cabby reluctantly put pencil to paper. An art show!

Buoyed by the pervading sense of resolve, Cabby had allowed herself to hope for a substantial reporting assignment. Until yesterday, the war had been Over There, bombs falling on strangers. Pearl Harbor had made things personal in a hurry. New Yorkers, even the fiercest isolationists, were mad, fighting mad. That morning on her way to work, she'd seen tight-lipped determination everywhere: on the packed BMT from Brooklyn, on the bustling sidewalks of Times Square, in the smoky elevator up to the third-floor newsroom of the Times building. The line of sober-faced young men at the Army recruiting center stretched around the block.

Cabby had just spent a long hour fuming as her male colleagues were sent to cover the real mobilization news. Bud

Smallwood was headed up to Kensico Dam; word was the city's water supply was threatened with sabotage. Bridge security was high on the defense list—the George Washington, Manhattan, and Brooklyn bridges particularly—and Fred Olson was sent to get the scoop. And that big power plant in Jersey? Joe Thatcher got that one.

Her assignment? A dainty little art show. Swell.

She narrowed her eyes at Halper and toughened her tone. "I wouldn't know a Picasso from a pisspot. What's wrong with James LaSalle? He's the art critic."

Len Halper had the stature of a college basketball star gone to seed and the face of a mournful basset hound. He shot Cabby a look from his stooped six-foot-two-inches. "You should watch your mouth, Ward—it's gonna land you in the homemaking section one of these days. Anyway, this is no highbrow art review. There's a real story brewing up there. Ever heard of Masako Fumi?"

The name rang a bell, but which bell? Masako Fumi. Was that the sukiyaki restaurant all the guys raved about? No, that didn't sound right. Cabby shook her head.

"Me neither. She's a Jap painter, just had a big show that LaSalle reviewed last week—one of those modern artists who paints like my five-year-old, all squiggles and splotches."

Cabby struggled to recall where she'd heard the name.

Halper went on, grinding out his cigarette stub in a filthy metal ashtray. "Her husband's an American named Oakley. Teaches at Columbia."

Oh, that bell. Sure. Fumi must be the artist married to Louise's current patient. She'd been talking about the couple for several days—so sophisticated, so well-traveled, the perfect match. Most of it had gone in one ear and out the other. But now, aha! Cabby had an inside source on the story. "What happened?"

"Vandalism."

"Vandalism? What kinda story is that?"

"Just wait. Bright and early this morning, someone tossed a brick through a window of the gallery exhibiting Fumi's stuff.

Apparently, there's a certain art-happy contingent that doesn't mind dropping a lot of loot on Jap squiggles. Anyhow, some bystanders got involved. Things got ugly. Well…ugly for West Fifty-seventh Street." Halper rolled his eyes, dragging the bags under them along for the ride.

"What makes it a story is that this Fumi was picked up last night with a bunch of other Japs suspected of being threats to the war effort. They ferried 'em all out to Ellis Island."

Cabby's pencil froze. Last night? Louise had been working last night—she'd left the boarding house around seven. She must've been right there when the Feds showed up. Great!

"So I want you to get up to Fifty-seventh Street. Interview the gallery owner. Find out what's so hot about this Jap artist and what's going to happen to her paintings now that her pals have smashed our Navy to smithereens."

Cabby slapped her notebook shut and stuck the pencil behind her right ear. "And," she added, "find out just exactly what makes her a threat to national security."

"You got two points with that one, Ward." Halper mimed an overhand shot. "Now get going."

Chapter Eight

Louise contemplated the wreck of the Oakleys' living room. The extent of the damage was revealed by a dim morning light that penetrated gray clouds scudding across the Hudson: paintings missing from the walls, sofa cushions thrown helter-skelter, the tubes of the big Magnavox radio strewn across the floor. While her patient was asleep, she should at least shelve the books, gather up the papers. She took a sip of the fresh coffee she'd made after Dr. Wright's whirlwind visit—thank god he'd pronounced the professor "better than he had a right to be" after the night's catastrophic events. But she couldn't summon the energy to get to work. Instead, she collapsed into an upholstered armchair, lowered her nose to her cup, and let the aroma carry her back to what seemed like saner times.

The mugs of sweet, milky coffee at Granny Hunter's kitchen table on Christmas Eve, when all the cousins were allowed a treat while their parents decorated the tree.

Her first sip of espresso on a date with a slick medical student. How he'd laughed when she sputtered the bitter brew all over the table.

The unending pots of black coffee that had fueled the probies' midnight cram sessions at Crandall House where the nursing students lived. And the exchange of heartfelt hopes and dreams. Where were all those girls now? How many of them would be enlisting in the nursing corps?

How many of them had had their hearts broken?

The telephone bell jerked Louise back to the appalling present. What now? She sped down the hallway to quiet the jangling phone, dreading whoever might be on the other end. What was the world coming to—when a simple object like a candlestick phone became a source of trepidation? Then, as the soles of her nursing shoes caught on a throw rug, she had a more hopeful thought: was it possible those hard-faced men had allowed Mrs. Oakley a call?

She stumbled the remaining steps and snatched up the receiver. "Yes?"

"Excuse me, Madam. Dedham, here."

The doorman's excruciatingly correct tones. From her first day on the Oakley case, Louise had suspected him of angling for a butler's job with one of the buildings' wealthier inhabitants. "Yes?"

"I have a Professor Lillian Bridges to see Professor and Mrs. Oakley."

Bridges? She knew that name. Louise hesitated. Then, "It's not a convenient time for callers."

A muffled conversation came through the receiver.

Dedham's voice returned, tones huffy. "The lady remains quite insistent."

Lillian Bridges was her patient's colleague at Columbia, and she most likely wanted to see first-hand how Professor Oakley was doing. Louise sighed. "Send her up."

She opened the door to admit a tall woman who looked nothing like Louise had expected. No old maid school-teacher, this, with sensible shoes and gray hair in a bun. Miss Bridges was an older woman—maybe as old as forty-five—and quite attractive, her dark hair cut in a stylish bob accentuating the silver streaks at her temples. She wore a well-cut wool coat the gray of this morning's blustery skies and a red hat that tilted over one eye. Entering the foyer, she nodded at Louise and strolled through into the living room. Then she stood there, incredulous, assessing the disorder. "The FBI…," she said, turning to Louise, "…they've come for Masako, haven't they?"

"As you can see. They took Mrs. Oakley away in the middle of the night."

"How positively dreadful." Professor Bridges' concern was palpable in her fine contralto. Her words were plumy, vaguely British in intonation—the same tones in which Preston's mother had spoken, Louise realized. A totally different accent than that of the girls in the boarding house.

Louise had long ago gotten over her debilitating girlhood shyness, but she felt intimidated by this lady's style and aplomb. She could never have imagined such sophistication. A professor!

Professor Bridges stared at Louise for a long moment, expression inscrutable, then she unexpectedly gave a warm smile, immediately setting the younger woman at ease. "Oh, my dear. I must apologize! I simply barge in here without even introducing myself. I'm Lillian Bridges, the Oakleys' good friend. You must be Masako's cherished Nurse Louise. She hasn't been able to stop talking about how wonderful you are with Robert."

Louise felt herself blushing. "I'm just doing my job," she said, and then wanted to kick herself. What a graceless way to receive a compliment.

"But, how is Robert?" A concerned expression suffused the woman's face. "This must have been such a shock for him." She peeled off a pair of red kidskin gloves that would have cost Louise a week's pay and jammed them in her coat pocket.

"He's as well as could be expected." As Louise spoke she could hear the inanity of the words.

"Well, my dear," the professor took Louise's hand and held it in both of hers. "I must see him—perhaps I can provide some comfort during this terrible time. And I can take in the flowers I brought yesterday." She dropped Louise's hand to point out the vase of chrysanthemums that had raised Agent Bagwell's suspicions. "I can't think why Masako hasn't placed them by Robert's bedside. My bright posies can hardly raise his spirits if they're out of sight."

Louise swallowed hard; Miss Bridges had such an air of authority that it wouldn't be easy to deny her wishes. "I'm sorry." She grimaced and hated herself for it. "He's sleeping. He can't be disturbed."

The wide gray eyes fixed her. "Then, dear, I'll sit quietly beside him until he wakes up." Professor Bridges was of the generation and class that could wield polite speech as adroitly as a fencing foil.

"I can't allow it. Really. No visitors. Doctor's orders." She tacked the last bit on impromptu, certain Dr. Wright would agree.

"Hmm." Lillian Bridges strolled to the window and looked out, apparently contemplating the Hudson's choppy waves.

Louise breathed more easily—maybe her visitor wasn't going to make a fuss.

The lady professor turned back from the window. "Well, if his doctor says…" She chewed her lower lip, and made the act appear pensive rather than crude. Then she spoke. "This is what I'm concerned about, Nurse. With Masako gone, someone must organize Robert's affairs, and I believe I'm the only one available to do it." She nodded her long chin. "The sooner I can talk to him the better, you see. I'll have to cancel what needs to be cancelled. Schedule his courses for next semester. Oversee his care. Call Rutherford."

"Rutherford?" Louise asked, feeling suddenly at sea.

Lillian Bridges waved an airy hand. "Robert's attorney, Rutherford Pierce. In Masako's interests, Robert must secure legal expertise at once. You see, my dear, Ruttie's father was at Harvard with us—well, I was at Radcliffe, but it's just across the street. We were all the best of friends."

A ray of hope seemed to emerge from behind the cloud. The Oakleys' lawyer! Perhaps this Rutherford really could help Mrs. Oakley—Louise would discuss it with her patient when he woke up.

Miss Bridges stepped toward Louise, rattling on, "Rutherford will get to work securing Masako's release right away. That dear girl cares nothing for politics—her art is her sole reason for being. She needs the best representation money can procure."

Louise caught a whiff of Chanel #5 and breathed in its subtle sweetness. She had never known a woman like this, one who was both attractive and feminine, yet seemingly so very much at home in the larger world of what Louise had always considered men's affairs—the university, medicine, the law. Certainly her mother was nothing like Professor Bridges; she dressed well, of course, but dithered constantly. What Louise wouldn't give for just half Miss Bridges' aplomb.

If Louise stayed on the case long enough, perhaps she could expand her knowledge of the world in which these two sophisticated woman—Lillian Bridges and Masako Oakley—dwelt. That world seemed to offer a far more engaging life than the stale, lady-like social rounds awaiting her at home.

But right now she had to summon the authority she did have, that imparted to her by a long line of plainer, sterner women—her nursing teachers and ward supervisors. Louise opened the front door. "I'll let the professor know about your offer. And if you'll leave your number, I'll call you as soon as Dr. Wright allows a visitor. Goodbye for now, Professor Bridges."

Chapter Nine

The air smelled metallic and thin, the way it always did when the streets were icy cold. Inside her heavy tweed coat, Cabby shivered as she dodged men in uniform hurrying urgently along Fifth Avenue. The buses and subways were full of them, too. Young faces—bewildered, excited, stoic—all intent on getting back to their camps and ships. Or those in street clothes on their way to the recruiting station. You could tell them by the look of serious purpose and far horizons in their eyes. For once she was glad she wasn't dating anyone steady.

Cabby turned her thoughts to work as she rounded the corner onto Fifty-seventh Street. Even though this art gallery deal wasn't in the same league as the men's assignments, it sounded like there might be some meat on the bone.

Especially if she could pry a few details out of Louise about this Masako Fumi dame.

The Shelton Gallery of Contemporary Art occupied one of four old row houses on the southwest side of Fifty-seventh. A tasteful dark-green canopy sheltered the entrance, but Cabby focused on the display window—or what was left of it.

The arched frame gaped with shards of glass. She shuddered; against the background of tightly drawn scarlet drapery, those shards looked like crystal fangs in an enormous bloody mouth. It would've made a great photo—too bad she didn't rate an assigned photographer.

Beneath the window, someone had printed in shaky block letters running with white drips, NO GO JAP SHOW.

Cabby stepped closer.

"Move along, sister."

Cabby jerked around. A beat cop stood wide-legged before the double entry doors.

"I'm a reporter," Cabby said, striding into the dimness created by the canopy. "Did you witness the vandalism?"

"Reporter, eh?" The flatfoot crossed his arms and rocked back and forth on his heels. "Getting a story for the high school newspaper, are ya?"

Cabby cursed her snub nose and petite frame. Pert. Elfin. Gamine—whatever that meant. Cabby had heard it all and wanted no part of it. Maybe if she were tall and lean with a fall of honey-colored hair she could comb into a pompadour, an elegant beauty like Louise, then people would take her seriously.

Mashing her peaked hat flatter to her crisp curls, she marched up to the cop, reached into her shoulder bag and flipped her notebook open to the press pass. "*New York Times*, officer."

His gaze roved up and down, not stopping at the card. "Well, now. I wouldn't mind lettin' ya in, sister. Looks like we're gonna be here for a while, and we could sure use the decorative value. But I got orders. No visitors, press or otherwise." His blue eyes turned icy. "So scram."

"But…" Cabby's gaze had been roving, too, searching for inspiration. It lit on a glass-encased placard to the right of the door: Arthur Shelton of the Shelton Gallery of Contemporary Art was pleased to represent the work of Masako Fumi and three other Asian artists whose names might be chop suey ingredients as far as Cabby could tell. Vintage decorative curios were also a specialty.

She cleared her throat. "I'm here to meet with Arthur Shelton. I have an appointment," she finished firmly.

"Yer here to see Shelton?" The cop chewed at his lower lip, blue eyes growing a degree warmer. "Don't go away." He reached for the doorknob behind him.

Whoopee, thought Cabby, he's actually going to let me in.

But the door opened to another blue uniform and a brief, whispered conference. It slammed shut with Cabby on the wrong side.

Chapter Ten

Lieutenant Michael McKenna cocked his head right. Then left. He tried tightening his eyes to slits, stepping closer, stepping back. No go. The four-by-six foot canvas on the wall of Shelton's main gallery remained a mishmash of bilious yellow, crimson, and fuzzy green. A line of Japanese characters ran up a whitish panel on the right side of the canvas, overlaid by a haphazard design of wine-colored drips and spatters. Like drifting clouds or damp tea leaves at the bottom of a cup, the painting could reveal everything or nothing. It told him nothing.

The body lying at the foot of the painting. Now, that said a lot.

A youngish man—once good looking. If you liked the weedy type. He'd been dead long enough to stink, several days at least, and his skull was smashed in at the base of the occipital bone where the head was propped against the wall. The sleeves of his dress shirt were rolled up to the elbows, his tie loosened, like he'd been attacked in the middle of some physical labor.

McKenna went down on his haunches, sweeping the tail of his overcoat well away from the smear of blood that trailed from corpse back to the archway leading to a smaller gallery. Ignoring the stench, he peered closer. Above the blood soaking the shirt collar, corn silk hair was combed back flat. A pointed chin dug into a concave chest, and the rest of the guy's slender frame flowed in a boneless curve on the terrazzo floor. No wrinkles around the eyes or mouth. Thirty, McKenna guessed, probably more under than over.

Deceased's identity? Arthur Shelton himself, owner of this ritzy art market. His errand boy who'd called in the murder three quarters of an hour ago—the twerp with the overdue haircut who was now cooling his heels in the vestibule—had confirmed that much.

McKenna hung his hands over his knees and exhaled through rubbery lips. Shelton's corpse would squawk even louder once the doc arrived—but already it was whispering that Shelton had been kind of young to own such a posh setup. At Fifty-seventh Street rents, yet. McKenna inched his overcoat sleeve back: 9:25. Doc Lefevers shouldn't be long—not much work for the medical examiner overnight; the shock of Pearl Harbor had put the kibosh on murder, for a while at least. McKenna was interested to see how long that would last.

"Hey, Lute."

McKenna swiveled his head to see Patsy Dolan shuffling alongside the blood trail. The slow-moving, wide-faced sergeant gestured like he was thumbing for a hitch. "Got somethin' in the next room. Looks like Shelton was crating up some paintings when he took the blow. Might not have known what hit him."

"I'd like to know what hit him. Have the boys found anything?"

"A hammer. No obvious blood on it, but they put it aside for the lab."

McKenna nodded and turned his attention back to the painting as he creaked to his feet. "Ya see a lion in that painting, Patsy?" Sometimes, his long-time sergeant had a way of framing up the obvious that led McKenna to unexpected insights.

The sergeant worked thick lips and tortured the spine of his slender notebook. "I see a lotta lines, boss. Curvy lines. Straight lines."

"Lion. I'm saying lion, Pats. The animal—king of beasts." McKenna gave a short laugh. "Look at the card beside it. 'Lion after the Kill,' 1941, oil on canvas by Masako Fumi. Just tell me, where's the god-damned lion."

"Oh. Well." Dolan pointed a husky finger. "That circle there—with the spot in it. It could be an eye. And that wavy outline. Maybe that's supposed to be its mane."

"And those grisly streaks and spatters?"

"Blood?"

"You're in the wrong profession, Patsy. You shoulda been an art critic." McKenna took the glossy show catalogue from a deep pocket and snapped it open to page one. "Picked this up on the way in. Listen"—he held the booklet at arms' length—"The collection's signature painting seems to address both a rampaging lion and its savaged prey lying just outside the boundaries of the canvas."

"Oh, yeah? Then Shelton's the gazelle that couldn't run fast enough."

"Yeah." McKenna gave the color photo on the brochure's cover another close look. Something was off.

In the photo, the Japanese letters stood out against a pale background. He raised his gaze to compare. On the painting, a transparent splash of reddish-brown hue veiled the characters. He reached toward the canvas, touched a fingertip to the radiating drips. Did artists change pictures like this at the last minute? But, jeez, with a scrambled-egg mess like this, what were a few colors more or less?

Dolan went on, "Shelton sure didn't get in here by running, though."

"Yeah." McKenna eyed the rusty-red trail across the terrazzo. Elongated smears punctuated with darker circles. Like a demented housewife mopping with blood, he thought with sudden clarity, and stopping to rest after every swipe. "Somebody went to a lot of trouble to drag Shelton in here and arrange him beneath that painting."

Dolan nodded. "A picture in itself."

"Huh?"

His sergeant surprised him by making an open square of his hands and extending them like a Hollywood director. "It's a different picture, now, with Shelton in the frame—posed all artistic like."

McKenna stepped back. He nodded slowly, taking in the sight with new eyes. "Yeah, a real beaut."

As he followed Dolan into the adjoining room, he gave the painting several backward glances.

"Here ya go, Lute."

Display cases holding sculpture and pottery dominated the floor space of this smaller gallery, but Dolan pointed toward the corner where a tipped-over packing crate rested against a mound of excelsior. Blood spatters stood out against the lighter-colored packing material. A brown tweed sport coat had been draped over a stack of already nailed-up crates leaning against the wall. Empty spaces in the parade of canvases showed which paintings had already been crated.

McKenna studied the title placards. "Hungry Ghost." "Teeth of the Dragon." "Awakening Demon." All by the same artist: Masako Fumi.

Who was this bloodthirsty guy, anyhow? He consulted the catalogue again. Found a thumbprint photo of the artist. Oh-ho. Not a guy. A woman—a very pretty woman. Her scanty biography merely told him that she was Japanese by birth but Western in education and culture.

"So what've we got, Lute?" Dolan broke the silence.

"Great timing, for one." McKenna fished a battered pack of Lucky Strikes out of an interior pocket. "Given what happened yesterday." He lit the cigarette and took a long drag. Exhaling smoke, he went on, "To put on a Jap art show, Shelton was either very brave or living in his own little dream world. Maybe the jackass that threw the brick out front had been here before. Maybe he couldn't stomach the idea of Jap paintings for sale in Manhattan."

Dolan jerked his chin back toward the larger gallery. "Stiff's been dead a couple of days. He was killed before the Japs took out Pearl Harbor."

"I know that. But hey—it's not like we didn't know war was coming."

"But nobody knew it would start yesterday."

"That's for sure." McKenna rubbed his forehead. While all New York was reeling from the horrifying news, he'd been out on Shinnecock as happy as a man could be. The weather was great, the fish were snapping, and he'd put one keeper cod and four nice blackfish in the box. Then he'd returned to the dock…

McKenna shook his head, took another draw of tobacco. "There's another thing about the timing."

"Yeah, boss?"

"This catalogue says Fumi's show was supposed to run until December 20. How come Shelton was taking her paintings down already?"

"Huh?"

"Just cogitate on that for a minute, will ya, Pats."

Dolan cogitated as another plainclothes man appeared in the archway that divided the two galleries. "Hey, Lute."

"Yeah?"

The cop balanced a packing case the size of a small bread box on his palm. No lid and one side had been busted in. He pointed to the excelsior inside. "A few rusty spatters in here, Lute. Looks just like the stuff in the corner."

"Where'd you find it?"

"Trash barrel in the basement furnace room—right on top."

Eyes glittering, McKenna nodded toward the packing crates. "Put it over there, it'll all go to the lab with that hammer."

"Another thing—Grady's got a reporter at the door."

McKenna's shoulders slumped a fraction of an inch. "Not already?"

"Ya might wanna see this one, Lute. The deal is—she says she's got an appointment with the stiff."

"She?" McKenna and Dolan said in unison.

"Yeah. I got a good look-see. She's one cute item."

Chapter Eleven

Without a word, a bald cop cracked the entry doors open, beckoned Cabby in from the cold, and led her through the gallery's stuffy, ill-smelling vestibule. A young man with a bowtie leaned against a reception desk and eyeballed Cabby as she dabbed a handkerchief to her dripping nose. His sandy hair swept the back of his collar, and, even though he looked sweaty and nauseous, he puffed on a cigarette for all he was worth.

The cop escorted Cabby into a roomy office furnished in spare modern decor, and she took the most inviting of the seats arranged around a kidney-shaped glass slab on tortured chrome legs. By the opposite wall, a similar glass slab functioned as a desk. Her reporter's eye noted a brand-new Dictaphone and a nameplate that read "Arthur Shelton" in angular Broadway-style lettering. Otherwise, the shining expanse was empty.

"Wait here." The cop held up a finger as if she were a dog.

"Sure thing, Pops." She took the opportunity to mull over the scene she had just encountered.

A broken window: yes. A nasty slur scrawled below the window: yes. But that wasn't all: not by a long-shot. Why the guard on the door? Why the secrecy? More of a story here than simple vandalism, that's for sure. Cabby felt her blood stir. Fanned out on the glass table among thick auction catalogues were some brochures on the current show. She reached for one, but, when a man entered the room, immediately dropped the little booklet. Showtime!

He was not a large man. Maybe five-ten. His eyes were as gray as his gray serge suit and the skin around them almost as wrinkled. He was, maybe, fifty. But, who was he?

She watched him lower himself with a faint groan onto a chartreuse S-shaped settee, take a deep, final draw on his cigarette and stub it out in a portable tin ashtray. Pressing the cap back on the tin, he replaced it in his pocket. After assessing her with a brief, professional glance, he said, "Show me credentials." Unstated was, if you've got 'em.

Cabby pulled out her notebook and flipped it open to the press card. He took it, positioned it for a good look, handed it back.

She could play it just as cool. "And you are?"

She thought she saw the corner of his mouth twitch, but the west-facing room was dim in the morning light, and the twitch could easily have been a cloud crossing the sun.

"McKenna," he said. It wasn't quite a bark. "Lieutenant Michael McKenna. Homicide."

She almost squeaked it: "Homicide! Ohmigod!" Then she remembered her professional demeanor, and frowned. But there really was a story here. And it was hers! Cabby's gaze darted around the office, as if she expected to find a bloody corpse hidden behind the chic geometrically patterned draperies. She took a hard gulp. "I mean, yes, of course—Lieutenant McKenna, Homicide. What can you tell me about the…murder?"

Just for a second, the wrinkles around his eyes became crevices. "Not a heck of a lot, girlie. So you had an appointment with Shelton, huh?" The door opened again and a younger detective, lean and blond, edged in and pulled out a notebook.

Holy cow! What a cutie! Cabby had to force her attention back to the older detective. A pencil appeared in her hand, almost of its own volition. "Victim's name?"

There was that twitch of the mouth again, that crinkle of the eyes, and McKenna asked, "When'd you make that appointment with Shelton?"

Cabby felt a flush crawl up her neck. Damn it—she was supposed to be an experienced reporter. "So, you're saying Shelton was the victim?" The pencil came into play.

"No, I'm asking you what your business with Shelton was." The gray eyes narrowed.

Belatedly she identified the putrid whiff she'd sensed in the vestibule. There was a corpse somewhere on these elegant premises! Then it struck her: she had just lied to a homicide detective about a man who was probably tucked away somewhere close by, cold, dead, and malodorous.

She let out a big sigh—she hadn't known her lungs could hold so much air—and took a closer look at the guy in charge. Cabby would have known McKenna was a cop anywhere. It was something about his eyes, as if he could perceive truth even if it came wrapped in tinsel and ribbons. No way she could manage to fool him.

She leaned forward. "I lied to the officer at the door." She said it factually, not confessionally—one professional to another. Implied: you know how it is, to get the job done, ya do what ya gotta do. She still hoped to come out of this with some dignity—and, if possible, with a story.

"You did, huh?"

"Yes. I didn't have an appointment. I was sent to cover the protest against…the Asian art show." She didn't want to bring in Masako Fumi Oakley specifically, not until she had a chance to talk to Louise. Truth-telling was all well and good: partial truth-telling was even better. "When I saw the cop guarding the door, I knew there was more going on here than a broken window, and I…I just followed my nose."

"A real newshound, huh?" His expression mellowed.

"Yes." She smiled. Here was an opportunity to form a working relationship with someone in law enforcement. She imagined herself telling Halper: "I'll get on to my police source about that."

She shrugged, charmingly, she hoped. "As a matter of fact, I never heard of Arthur Shelton until I saw his name beside the door."

"Is that so?"

She nodded. "And, now, Lieutenant, you say he's dead?"

"I didn't say any such thing. But I do have a few questions for you, girlie." Not so mellow, all of a sudden. "What's your paper's real interest in the Shelton Gallery? On a big news day like this, the august and venerable *New York Times* wouldn't send someone up here to cover an act of minor vandalism."

She sighed. This old cop just wasn't going to let her hold anything back. She swiveled her gaze toward the Cutie Pie, but he kept his eyes on the notebook. So, okay. Out rolled the story of Masako Fumi's arrest by the FBI.

McKenna replied with an expressionless, silent nod.

Why did he have to be so damn cagey? If she was going to get her scoop, she'd have to confirm the identity of the victim. Cabby tried one more tack. "So since Fumi is the star of this show, and the owner of the gallery turns up dead—"

"Don't trip over that nose of yours, Nancy Drew, Girl Detective. I haven't named any names."

Something told Cabby to remain silent and plaster on her most fetching smile. Louise's Southern ways must be rubbing off.

"Well." The word came out as a gravelly rumble. The detective snatched up one of the glossy booklets and waved it at Cabby. "Whaddaya think of this?" He tapped a finger on the full-color reproduction of "Lion After the Kill" printed on the cover.

Cabby studied the lurid image. "Hmm…" She scrambled to recall her one art-history course. What had Professor Zimbalist said about this type of painting? "Well, of course, it's deeply influenced by prevailing trends in the European art world. The modernist painter expresses his soul and personality by abstracting the essence of an object and presenting it in terms of mass, energy, and color rather than of mere figure."

McKenna glanced from the young woman's face down to the catalogue cover and back up again. "Is that so?"

She felt herself shrug. "I studied some art history at Hunter College."

"Di-i-i-d you?" He studied the catalogue's cover again. "Well, thanks for making it as plain as mud, girlie."

Cabby tilted her head and looked up at him with cat's eyes. "Look, I've cooperated—given you information about Fumi. Now, you can help me, right? Isn't that how it works? One hand washes the other."

"Oh, ri-i-ight." She noted a definite smile before he shot a question at Blondie. "Hey, Brenner, should we let her in on the story? Since the news is gonna be out in a coupla hours anyhow, a smart little girl like her might as well get the scoop. Don'cha think?"

Brenner shrugged.

McKenna held up a finger. "Listen good, 'cause this is all you're gonna get."

He gave her the name of the victim and the time of discovery.

"So it was Shelton! Who found him?"

"Desmond Cox, Shelton's assistant."

"That's the guy at the reception desk, the one with the eyeball?"

McKenna laughed. So, the old guy had a sense of humor. She'd have to remember that.

"When was Shelton killed?" Must be at least couple of days ago, by the odor.

"We're not releasing that until we're certain."

"How was he killed?"

"Ditto. But I'll tell you this—his body was found right underneath that painting I showed you in the catalogue."

Cabby looked up from her notebook. "Really? Now that's interesting."

"You think so, huh? What would you say if I told you Shelton had been killed while he was crating up the Fumi show—a couple of weeks before it was scheduled to end."

"I'd say that was interesting, too." The artist, she thought. Maybe the artist did it. Maybe she and Shelton had had a falling out."

McKenna only chuckled for a fleeting second.

Cabby chewed on the end of her pencil and sighed again. "I'm not gonna get anything more, am I?" Casually, she slipped one of the brochures into her bag.

"Nope. That's all she wrote."

Okay, so it was the end of the line with the homicide cop, but she had enough for a two-inch item, maybe more. She could call it in to the news desk now. That would shake up Halper and the boys!

"Well, thank you very much, Lieutenant." She held out her hand.

McKenna blinked, then took the hand and held it gently, as if it were made of porcelain. "Goodbye, Miss Drew."

"Ward. My name is Ward." She read the upturned mouth. "But, then, you knew that, didn't you? Very funny."

As she left the office, her attention had already skipped several paces ahead, to the young man in the vestibule. First she'd lure this Desmond Cox outside and interview him about finding the body. Then she'd call the news desk.

But a bellow from behind derailed her plans. McKenna's voice: "Dolan! Get Cox back here. Pronto."

Drat! Scratch the interview with Desmond Cox. Cabby went out and turned down Fifth Avenue, walking at a brisk pace. She checked her watch. Not quite noon. She might as well try to catch James LaSalle, the *Times'* art critic, before she got to her story. Just how important an artist was this Masako Fumi Oakley, anyhow?

Chapter Twelve

The window of Masako's prison framed it, the famous statue. But instead of the inspirational view every schoolchild knew by heart, she could see only the blank, draped back. Copper, weathered green. Heavy-folded robe. Head crowned with what looked like knives. Face averted. Lady Liberty had turned her back on freedom.

Masako had asked over and over. What had she done? What had any of them done?

"Enemy alien," the FBI agent said.

"A viper is a viper," the stern matron said.

"*Dio Mio*," the Italian woman on the next cot complained in horror, "they're making us sleep with Japs."

Chapter Thirteen

A peach-and-gray teacup lay shattered on the dark green counter beside the kitchen sink. *Satsuma*, Mrs. Oakley had called her treasured tea set, wiping each cup with a ceremonial cloth before she filled it to offer with both hands to her guest. In receiving the cup, Louise knew she was a guest rather than an employee.

Like its mates from a teakwood chest that had been carried off by the FBI, the delicate heirloom depicted geishas kneeling on bamboo mats with a background of misty mountains. The Federal agents had been particularly suspicious of any items that depicted kimonos, as well as pagodas or ceremonial masks.

Louise gathered up the remnants of the delicate cup and cradled them in one palm. What to do? Not throw them away, surely. She felt as if she were holding the Japanese woman's soul.

It was wrong—simply wrong—the way the bull-headed Agent Bagwell and his men had treated the Oakleys. Could the woman help where she'd been born? And, for goodness sake, what was suspicious about a professor of Asian history owning books and artifacts from Japan? The terrifying rampage of last night was not what America was supposed to be about, even an America under siege.

Louise's outrage grew as she bundled the porcelain shards into her pocket handkerchief, tied the ends and placed it on the shelf where the teak chest had stood. She couldn't let this pass. She had to do something—something to help right this wrong and return Masako Oakley to her home.

But she didn't know what that might be.

Chapter Fourteen

Unlike us cops, McKenna thought, still perched uncomfortably on the chartreuse settee in the dead man's office, this guy looks like he actually belongs here.

Desmond Cox, the long-haired gallery employee, sat facing McKenna and Dolan. He wore a gray V-necked sweater under his navy wool jacket and a bow-tie with colorful squiggles. His smoke was parked in an ashtray on the glass-topped table. "I'll help you as much as I can, officers. But I really don't know anything."

The young man's pinched nose and tight lips told a different tale. They were a dam, holding back a river. Once he got Desmond Cox talking, McKenna knew, those lips would be flooded with information.

He sat back, nonthreatening, easing the guy in. "Mr. Cox, when was the last time you saw Arthur Shelton?"

"I had Friday off, so it was Thursday—around closing time."

Dolan was fumbling with his notebook. McKenna made scribbling motions at him. The sergeant found the right page, licked his pencil and wrote.

"Why weren't you working Friday?"

A pause. Cox's expression became even more guarded. "Some friends rented a beach bungalow for a weekend party. Winter rates, you know. We left the city around nine o'clock that morning."

"Where was the party?" Still Mr. Nice Guy.

Another pause. "Fire Island."

"Okay." McKenna stood abruptly. His bad hip had had enough of the chartreuse settee.

Cox suddenly looked panicked. Had he interpreted McKenna's rise as some sort of accusation? "My friends can vouch for me."

The detective sighed. He didn't particularly like fruits, but he didn't arrest them for holding house parties. Rubbing his hip, he walked over to the narrow window and stood there looking out onto brick walls and a bare alley. A mangy gray cat slunk past a row of garbage cans.

McKenna swiveled on his good leg. "Tell me about Arthur Shelton."

"Arthur?" Cox blanched again. "I can't believe he's lying up there—dead! All that flash—that vitality. Where could it have gone?" Two distinct tears appeared, one in the corner of each eye.

McKenna eased onto the settee again. "I can't tell you where, Mr. Cox, but maybe I can eventually tell you why. That's how you can help us. Tell me about your boss. You were his assistant. Right?"

"Well—" Cox recrossed his long legs. "Associate is more like it. Arthur was grooming me to become his partner one day."

"Okay, got it. What else?"

"Well, Arthur came from the absolute, spot-on middle of nowhere—went to some cow college in Muncie, Indiana, before he moved to New York. But that doesn't really tell you what he was like. You want more than biography, I guess."

McKenna nodded. For starters, he thought.

Cox brooded a moment, then sat up straight. "Okay, besides flash and vitality, Arthur had courage—when it came to art, he had more courage than anyone I ever knew."

In McKenna's mind art and courage didn't go hand in hand. He screwed up his face. "How so?"

"Some people weren't happy about Arthur mounting work by a Japanese artist. There's a lot of bigotry floating around,

Lieutenant—even before yesterday's attacks. When you go through Arthur's files…" Cox made a vague gesture toward an old chest, the only piece of wooden furniture in the sleek, modern room. "That's Arthur's filing cabinet—a seventeenth century Tibetan blanket chest he had reconditioned. You'll find letters there from prominent collectors. Many protested his 'support for the enemy,' but a few praised him for mounting the Fumi show."

"Oh, yeah?" McKenna turned to Dolan. "Get Brenner in here—he can search the files."

"Sure thing, boss." Dolan went to the door, and returned after a brief conference with someone out of sight.

"We even had picketers," Cox continued, watching the unwieldy sergeant lower himself back onto the settee and find the right page in his notebook.

McKenna's right eyebrow shot up. "What d'ya mean—picketers?"

"Monday after the show's opening James LaSalle wrote a swell review. We had a lot of lookers wander in, so we thought everything was going to be okay. But first thing Tuesday morning, parading up and down the sidewalk in front of the gallery, there was this guy with a big sign."

"This would have been last week, right? What did the sign say?"

"It said No Go Jap Show—just like that damn scrawl out by the broken window. The son-of-a-bitch was there all day. Then the next morning, there were three of them. Again—all day."

"They interfere with customers?"

"What customers? By Thursday we were down to a big fat goose egg—the only people who walked through the door were Arthur's great friend…Lawrence Smoot" —Cox made a face— "and this lady professor he'd dragged down from Columbia. Shelton and Smoot were…well." He made a dismissive hand gesture. "And Lillian is a friend of the artist's husband." He laughed. "Nothing would keep those two away."

"So..." McKenna said, as he thumbed his jaw. "The toughs were scaring away trade. What'd your boss do?"

"Called the police. The desk sergeant at the Eighteenth Precinct said as long as the picketers weren't accosting people, they were within their rights—freedom of expression. By Thursday noon, there were six of them, chanting. 'No go Jap show, no go Jap show.' A couple of passers-by joined in and a crowd began to gather. Arthur took the situation in hand..."

"Hmm." McKenna turned his head. "Ya got all that, Dolan?"

"Yeah, Lute." He flipped a page.

Cox went on, "We decided the first lunkhead was the ringleader. I went outside, slipped the guy a fin and told him my boss had a proposition for him. He was game, so I brought him into the office." Cox looked around as if he could see the scene in his mind. Again McKenna detected a note of real grief in his expression.

"Then, Arthur comes in with a bottle of his best single malt and two glasses. He plied him with Glenfiddich. By the time he was done, the guy was mellow—plus a century richer."

"Whew!" It was Dolan. McKenna gave him the icy eye.

"Yeah. The mug went out, handed around some stray fives, and the picketers vanished."

"Only to come back this morning, paint his slogan and heave a brick through the window?"

"Yeah, I guess."

McKenna sat back, unconvinced. Once roaches scattered, they usually went in search of better pickings somewhere else. "So, what was this goon's name?"

"Arthur didn't ask."

Great. Just ducky. McKenna changed the subject. "So, that's the reason Shelton was closing the show?"

A hurt look danced across Cox's face. His features pinched in and it looked like he was building that dam again. "Arthur didn't discuss that with me. I thought he intended to keep Masako's paintings up."

A tap at the door and Dolan jumped up to let Brenner in.

Cox gave the blond, broad-shouldered cop an interested look that wasn't lost on McKenna.

"Hey, Brenner," he said. "Sit in on this, will ya? You been to college. You know about art. You'll be a big help interpreting Mr. Cox's information."

Brenner looked surprised, but he pulled up one of the tortured-looking chairs and sat, one ankle on the other knee.

Cox flipped his hair over his collar.

"Okay, Mr. Cox," McKenna continued. "This Masako Fumi—tell us about her. Brenner, you take this down."

"Sure, boss." He pulled out his notebook. It looked almost new.

Something that might have been a pout streaked across Dolan's features.

"Masako Fumi Oakley." Cox directed his nervous chatter at Brenner. "No matter what the great American unwashed thinks about the Japanese, Arthur knew Masako Fumi's paintings were simply earthshaking. Like the latest in Western modernism, her figures are nonrepresentational. But she also layers on calligraphic figures using the traditional mouse-hair brush. She makes her own Sumi ink from three-hundred-year-old slabs of vegetable soot and glue, the way Japanese calligraphers have done for centuries—"

"Wait." McKenna stopped the flow with a raised palm. "Old ink is a good thing?"

"Well, Lieutenant…" Cox swiveled his head. "Some people must think so. The opening reception was a smash—Arthur sold five paintings just that night. Five!"

"What's that add up to?"

"You mean—in money?"

McKenna nodded. No. In doughnuts, he thought. Who are these people?

"I'm not certain—Arthur keeps—kept—the books. But it must have been close to eighteen thousand dollars."

"A good haul, I'd say." McKenna reached for one of the glossy show brochures. "How come this painting looks different in the photo here than it does on the wall?"

"Huh?"

"This 'Lion After the Kill.' Up there in the gallery, the writing part is covered with some reddish gunk."

Cox winced. "Oh, that's wine. We had a nasty scene the night of the opening."

"What happened?"

"Tiffy De Forest happened. She used to be one of Arthur's most loyal patrons—had a good eye for a coming artist, and her stockbroker hubby didn't mind ponying up the funds." He paused for a moment's reflection. "He also didn't mind hovering in the background—whether Tiffy was displaying her latest canvas or her latest man." His wink was all-boys-together lewd.

"Oh, yeah?" McKenna took the bait. "Like that, huh?"

"Very much like that. But almost overnight, Tiffy-dear took a very vocal dislike to all things Asian. She sure wasn't invited to Masako's reception, but she showed up anyhow, high as a kite, itching to make trouble." Cox was getting into it now. McKenna had him pegged right—as an irrepressible gossip. "Tiffy made a beeline for Arthur. Lu-di-crous! She was spilling right out of that tight dress." He leaned forward. "Then the worst—she accused Arthur of being a traitor."

"What was Miss Fumi doing during this cute scene?" McKenna was becoming more and more interested in this lady artist. If that girl reporter had been right about Fumi being picked up last night by the FBI, it was going to be hard prying the artist loose from the Feds, but he intended to try; Shelton's body had been positioned right beneath her splashiest painting.

"Oh, well—we were all frozen in shock. Of course. Masako included. Then she began to scream—a wild mixture of French and English."

"French?"

"She grew up in Paris. Her father's some kind of Japanese big-wig."

"Really?"

"Yes, ambassador to France, I think he was. Anyway, Tiffy grabbed a glass of wine right out of James LaSalle's hand—red wine, of all things. I think she meant to hurl it at Masako, but it ended up hitting Arthur. And the painting."

"LaSalle?" Hadn't he just heard that name?

"Yes—the art critic. Imagine!"

"Sounds like a mess." McKenna kept his voice neutral. Couldn't these people find something better to do with their time—and, of course, their money?

Cox rattled on, "You bet. The doorman tossed Tiffy and her escort out. Then Masako wouldn't let Arthur clean up the painting. She said, 'That woman's hatred is part of the work, now. Let everyone see what she has done.'

"But, of course," he continued in an arch tone, "Tiffy only did it at Nigel Fairchild's urging."

"Nigel Fairchild?" McKenna repeated in surprise.

"Yeah. He was her escort." Cox's thin lips twisted in a sneer. "You know him?"

Know Fairchild? Hell, yes. The man was all over the papers and the airwaves, New York's answer to that ranting radio priest, Father Coughlin. Nigel Fairchild might come from an old Four-Hundred family, but he was a demagogue through and through—head of the local America First Committee.

Cox continued, "I never personally heard him talk about the Japs, but at a dinner party last summer, he railed on and on about how the Nazi takeover of Europe wasn't our concern. 'They got themselves into it,' he said, 'let them get themselves out.' European society he labeled effete and decrepit, doomed to perish. America was the hope of the world, young and robust, the 'coming nation.'

"'Besides, we're perfectly safe here,' he said that night. 'There's an ocean between us and Hitler.'"

Then Desmond Cox laughed and added, "Well, I wonder how safe he feels after yesterday's bombing attacks. Japan's a hell of a lot further away than Germany."

"Right," McKenna replied. "A lot of those isolationist chumps are eating their words right about now. You think Fairchild and the De Forest dame had anything to do with the broken window out front?"

Cox shrugged.

"Right. Okay." McKenna stood up abruptly and squinted at the young man. "Get your coat. You're going downtown with Detective Dolan."

Cox swallowed hard, his Adam's apple going up and down. He shot a wounded look toward the unheeding Brenner. "Am I under arrest? I didn't kill Arthur. My friends can vouch for me—we didn't get back to the city until late last night."

"Don't worry—we'll check with your pals, all right. But no, you're not under arrest. That picket ringleader sounds like someone who might have a few priors—so you're going to look at some photos down at Centre Street."

"Oh." Cox visibly relaxed.

"Yeah. Soon's you give me Miss Fumi's address and phone number."

No reason Cox needed to know that Masako Fumi currently was in residence at the federal detention center on Ellis Island.

Chapter Fifteen

In the time it took for Louise to answer the doorbell and let Dr. Wright in, Professor Oakley had forced himself into a sitting position and edged one foot to the floor. "Fetch my overcoat, Nurse," he ordered, as she followed the doctor back into the darkened bedroom. "I'm going down to Foley Square, talk to those imbeciles at the Federal courthouse."

Louise hurried toward her patient as a cold wind rattled the windows and seeped through cracks to lift the silk wall hangings.

"You want to kill yourself, Bob?" Dr. Wright eased the professor back on his pillows and hitched the bedclothes under his armpits. "Save it for later. I won't have you dying on my watch. You hear me?"

"I won't abandon Masako to those fools." The professor kicked the blankets away. Even that small exertion was too much. A series of coughs racked his barrel chest. Louise was alarmed to see his lips grow blue as he clutched his right side.

As she tucked the blankets tighter, Wright continued his lecture. "Listen, my friend, this lobar pneumonia isn't some undergraduate you can browbeat into behaving. If you don't rest and let your nurse keep the fever down...." He raised a forefinger and shook it in cadence with his words. "It will kill you. You hear me? It will kill you. And when you're gone." He paused. "When you're gone, Masako will be on her own. What will happen to her then?"

Professor Oakley sank into his pillows and, with a shuddering sigh, gave in.

The doorbell rang again.

◇◇◇

"Arthur? Dead? Murd—" Professor Oakley's chest heaved in a strained, painful cough. Louise winced. Lieutenant McKenna, the disheveled police detective at the bedside, his face tired and etched with wrinkles, paused only a split second. Then, "How long have you known Arthur Shelton?" he asked. "Where were you last Friday evening? Where was your wife?"

Louise tried to catch Dr. Wright's eye, but his gaze remained glued to his watch as he assessed the professor's pulse. Over the past few days, she'd been impressed by the dapper physician with his pencil-thin moustache and exhausted blue eyes. But she couldn't agree with his decision to allow this badge-flashing policeman to question their desperately ill patient.

Lieutenant McKenna lifted the hat he hadn't bothered to remove. He smoothed a hand over thinning hair and tugged the brim into place again. "Shelton was closing the gallery show," the detective prodded. "Was your wife angry about that?"

"Masako...?" Oakley gazed at the detective with disbelief. "Masako never hurt a soul in her life."

"Having her paintings taken down must have been a blow." McKenna's grey eyes held an unreadable expression. "Nobody would blame her for being mad."

"My god!" The professor's voice was strangled. "You're accusing my wife of murder!" He pushed up to one elbow and coughed convulsively.

Dr. Wright struggled to ease their agitated patient back into a semi-reclining position. Louise should have helped, but a sudden realization kept her rooted to a spot at the foot of the bed: she'd actually met this Arthur Shelton, the man who'd been killed.

On Thursday, her second night on the Oakley case, one of the professor's colleagues had dropped by to assure him that his classes were being covered in his absence. A younger man had accompanied Professor Smoot, and Mrs. Oakley had introduced him as the gallery owner who was showing her paintings. Arthur Shelton. Yes, that was the name. And now he was dead!

"Nurse!"

Louise gave a small gasp. Dr. Wright had both hands on the professor's shoulders and was attempting to keep him in bed by sheer force. Men! Her patient was behaving like a cantankerous old goat, and Dr. Wright not much better. She grabbed an empty basin and a damp cloth.

Both McKenna and the doctor stepped back while Louise wiped her patient's face. She put her mouth against his ear and whispered, "He's baiting you, Professor. Don't you see? The more upset you get, the more suspicious he will be. Just answer his questions calmly."

Oakley's nod was barely perceptible, but he stopped struggling and answered the detective in a weak, reedy voice, "Masako and I owe Arthur a good deal…" A panting breath. "Of course she was disappointed when he talked of closing the show, but she understood."

Louise's eyebrows shot up. That was not how she remembered it.

"Your five minutes are up, Lieutenant," Dr. Wright broke in with vehemence. "I can't be responsible for this man's condition if you persist."

"Just one more thing," the detective said. His gaze locked Oakley's. "Are you sure that neither you or your wife left this apartment on Friday evening?"

"Perfectly sure," the professor answered sharply. "Isn't that what I told you the first time you asked?"

"And that's it." Dr. Wright removed a stethoscope from his bag and snapped the ends around his neck. "Nurse, show the detective out."

◇ ◇ ◇

As they moved down the corridor toward the foyer, Louise registered a more detailed impression of the policeman. He had a slight limp and a trace of stiffness in the right leg as if he'd once been wounded, but his back was as straight as a ramrod and his face weathered from being outdoors. A self-assured man, obviously, not easily thrown. But where the G-men from last night had humiliated the Oakleys and treated them with outright contempt, McKenna seemed merely…dogged. A man doing his job without malice or unwarranted prejudice. And also without much pleasure, she'd bet.

At the door, he paused and asked her name. She gave it, trying to ignore the flash of anxiety that registered in her abdomen.

"All right, Nurse Hunter," he continued. "You tell me—were both the Oakleys here all night Friday?"

"On my shift, yes. From around seven thirty on. The professor's weak as a kitten, of course. And Mrs. Oakley never, ever, left him—even when I encouraged her to get a breath of fresh air."

The detective frowned wearily. "Well, that's all for now. You can go back to your patient."

Louise watched him plod down the fifth-floor hallway to the elevator, then she closed the door and sagged against the solid oak. Thank god he hadn't asked her any direct questions about Arthur Shelton. She'd nearly spoken out when the professor said his wife "understood" why Shelton had decided to cut her show short. Some instinct, however, had told her to wait.

The Thursday evening of Shelton's visit, Louise had been organizing her sickroom supplies when the art dealer mentioned his anxiety over the increasing opposition to the show. Masako Oakley had been offended, quietly but deeply. After some strained small talk, the Japanese woman had invited Mr. Shelton to speak with her in the den. Passing that room a few minutes later on her way to the kitchen, Louise overheard a heated argument. It was the only time Louise had known her patient's wife to lose her composure.

Perhaps Professor Oakley hadn't realized how strongly his wife felt. It would be just like that gentle artist to keep from worrying him. Even so, Louise thought, shouldn't she tell Lieutenant McKenna what she'd seen and heard?

She crossed her arms and took a deep inhalation. No, the first rule in nursing a pneumonia patient was to prevent any upset—emotional or otherwise—that might sap the patient's strength, and Professor Oakley had already had enough to fell a man half his age. From that perspective, it was actually her professional duty to keep quiet.

Troubled, Louise smoothed the skirt of her starched uniform. She started back down the hallway, meeting Dr. Wright near the telephone bench in the corner niche.

"I've administered a sedative. It should hold him until I make my evening rounds." The doctor continued with a rueful shake of his head, "I wouldn't have allowed McKenna in if I'd had any inkling Shelton had been murdered. I can hardly believe it. At Masako's reception, Arthur was as frisky and happy as a spring lamb rolling in clover."

Louise cleared her throat, deferentially, she hoped. She had something to say. Doctors didn't generally welcome a nurse's opinions, but she plowed ahead anyway. "Shouldn't Professor Oakley be in the hospital, Doctor? I've been concerned since my first night on the case. Like so many men his age, the professor measures his vigor by what he could accomplish ten or twenty years ago."

The doctor raised one eyebrow, and an ominous rumble came from his throat.

Louise hurried on. "Mrs. Oakley was always able to talk some sense into him, but now…" She spread her hands helplessly. "When he comes out of the sedative, I'm not sure I'll be able to keep him in bed."

Wright smoothed his moustache, first one side then the other. "Of course I want to hospitalize him, but the obstinate s.o.b. simply digs his heels in and refuses to go. And, now, with war looming, beds are suddenly in short supply. Half the old dears on the Upper West Side are having heart attacks. At least, they think they are." He sighed heavily. "You wouldn't believe the hysteria. Rumors of imminent invasion are running through entire buildings, and unlike Bob Oakley, some people see the hospital as the last safe place.

"So, no," he continued. "Hospitalization will have to be a last resort." He sighed. "But I do have an idea—Bob actually suggested it." His blue eyes quizzed her. "You're a clever girl, quite capable of serving as Bob's eyes and ears—even his legs if need be. I fear Shelton's murder will complicate things considerably. If this cop really considers Masako as a suspect, then she's in double jeopardy—from the government and from the police. Our patient will need a damn good lawyer, and you can help him find one.

"What if you take on a new role here, that of the professor's personal aide? I can find another nurse, but I don't have a clue where I could locate a personal assistant as competent as you would be. You could make phone calls, follow up on attorney references, write letters, run errands. As for nursing care, don't worry about that—I'll make arrangements with the agency."

Louise hesitated; these were the sort of thing the professor's friend, Lillian Bridges, had offered to do. She told the doctor about Miss Bridges' visit and her mention of Rutherford Pierce, the family lawyer.

He frowned. "Lillian has her own work, and you're right here on the spot. I'd rather have you in charge."

"I don't think I—"

"And as for young Rutherford, he wouldn't touch a civil liberties case with a ten-foot pole."

"But—"

The doctor touched her arm. "Listen, you know Bob's mind won't be at ease until he has some word that Masako is all right." He sank down on the phone bench and looked up at her. "I'm aware this is irregular, Nurse Hunter—believe me, I am. But I'm certain that if he knows everything possible is being done for Masako, he'll be much more manageable."

She considered this radical departure from nursing protocol. But then, why not? Masako's arrest was just plain…un-American. Even now Louise felt hot fury come over her at the recollection of last night's events. Where did her allegiances lie? With her patient and his wife, of course. Louise shouldn't let anything get in the way of the professor's recovery. And, it was more than that; it was a question of justice. Even if Masako's homeland had started a war, that innocent woman should be safe where she had chosen to live. "Okay, I'll do it. Just…tell the agency to send someone…" She thought of the nurses the professor had already tossed out. Capable girls, but not able to match wits with the learned Oakley. "Someone…"

"With a brain?" the doctor finished, as he picked up the telephone receiver.

Louise's face relaxed into a smile. "You understand."

"I'll call Sullivan's right now—for day and night coverage."

Louise nodded, anxious to get back to the professor. Not yet dialing, the doctor held her gaze for another moment. "I'll let myself out." Unbelievably, he winked. "I'm still capable of that—even though, like Bob Oakley, I'm no spring chicken."

She could hear the dial tone buzz as his expression grew serious again. "Just find the right attorney, Nurse Hunter, the very best you can get."

"But, who?"

"A man who knows how to fight racial prejudice. A radical—even a Bolshie, if you must. That will be the most salutary medicine you can provide for our patient."

A Bolshie. What was that? And where on earth would she find one? Louise chewed at a thumbnail. She'd bet anything Lillian Bridges would have been able to find a Bolshie.

Chapter Sixteen

Headed cross-town to Madison Avenue, McKenna pondered the scene at the Oakleys'. The sick man hadn't been much help, but he'd bet that pretty nurse knew something she wasn't telling. He'd have to keep her in mind. He was on his way now to question Nigel Fairchild at America First headquarters, but a radio call from Dolan suddenly changed his priorities. "Turn around," McKenna ordered the police driver. "We're going uptown. Columbia University."

On the way to look at mug shots, Desmond Cox had casually informed Sergeant Dolan that he'd already called Arthur Shelton's "special professor friend" to inform him of his loss, and that "Lawrence hadn't taken it well."

"Special friend?" Dolan questioned, a little slow on the uptake. "Lawrence? Do you mean that Professor Smoot you mentioned?"

"Yes. Arthur's dear, dear friend," Cox responded.

Dolan got it then and radioed the news to McKenna, who cursed himself for not picking up on the fat hint Cox had dropped earlier.

"Where can I find Professor Smoot?" McKenna asked.

Dolan's voice was muffled for a second, then: "If he's still at work, Cox says Smoot will be in the Arts-Humanities building up at Columbia."

Detour time. Fairchild could wait a while. If a homicide wasn't over money, it usually had a domestic or sexual twist, and if this Shelton-Smoot thing was as advertised, the professor might be more important than some rabble-rousing isolationist who objected to Jap art.

"Mind if I turn on the radio, Lute?" The driver already had his gloved hand on the knob. At McKenna's questioning look, he went on, "President Roosevelt is supposed to speak."

"Oh…sure." McKenna let out a deep sigh. Here he was fretting his brain over one dead art dealer while FDR had thousands of dead to worry about. And more to come.

Chapter Seventeen

Howie Schroeder was off his turf. He knew the blocks between school and home: every candy store, every news stand, every bully on the lookout for a kid he could strong arm into forking over pocket change. After he'd turned left on Bedford, into strange territory, he could be jumped any minute. His gut fluttered as he covered the unfamiliar blocks, but that was okay. He had to do this. Cheapy Hermann lived off Bedford up in Crown Heights, and Cheapy was the guy he needed to see.

Howie had questions Ma refused to answer. The more everybody talked about Hitler's stormtroopers, the more his scattered memories of that weird summer camp he and Cheapy had gone to bugged him. Even more since yesterday—"a date which will live in infamy" the president had called it. He would never in his life forget those words. When Mr. Klein, the principal, had trooped the whole school into the auditorium after lunch to hear FDR's speech on the big radio, Howie had felt like jumping up and cheering when he heard them—"A date which will live in infamy."

Everyone feared the next attack would come from Germany. Hitler. For a moment Howie felt himself sneering. At the movies, Charlie Chaplin and the Three Stooges played the little man with the toothbrush moustache mostly for laughs. Howie used to laugh, too, but then Miss Gilpin, his history teacher, said Hitler was no bumbling fool. She called him a lunatic determined to take over the world—no matter how many people got slaughtered.

And Ma wasn't amused either. There was something dark in her blue eyes whenever Hitler's name came up. It was as if the sun was swallowed up by one of those dark, towering storm clouds Mr. Levine in biology called nimbostratus. The kind that hung low and brooding and almost suffocated the earth. Ma wasn't talking, but Howie could read her moods like a book. He didn't know the details of what was happening over in Europe, but he was putting the pieces together and beginning to think that just maybe Adolph Hitler was evil incarnate.

Yeah—Hitler. Howie had to get that summer straight. But his memories of the camp on Long Island were fuzzy and out of sequence, like a movie with reels all mixed up. If he was lucky, Cheapy would remember all that junk. He was two years older than Howie, sixteen now, and a junior at a different high school.

Howie clenched his fingers around the silver dollar in his pocket. Cheapy Hermann had come by his nickname honest. Those years at Camp Siggy, he'd always been the biggest mooch. If your ma mailed you a box of cookies, watch out 'cause Cheapy was on you like fleas on a rat. If Cheapy wouldn't talk about Camp Siggy without incentive, Howie was prepared to sacrifice the birthday silver dollar he'd kept in a leather pouch since last February twelfth.

It was that important.

The weekend trips had started out as fun. He must've been eight or nine when all of a sudden summer Sundays were different. Instead of squeezing into his itchy suit and tight dress shoes and trudging over to Emmanuel Lutheran for some boring service, he'd been told to put on shorts. Ma wore a flowered dress with a straw hat and filled a picnic basket with sandwiches, potato salad, and thick slabs of chocolate cake. Papa, all spit-and-polish, in some sort of uniform, hustled them to the Flatbush station to catch the Long Island Railroad.

He was sure it had been a special train. While the parents yakked in the old language, he and Cheapy and the other kids ran up and down the aisles like they never would have got away with on a regular run.

His next memory involved some podunk town. Papa and the other men wore brown shirts and tall leather boots, and they marched down the burg's one main street to the campgrounds. He'd marched right next to Papa while trumpets blared and made you want to puff out your chest and pick up your knees. They sang German songs, and bright flags snapped in the breeze—the American flag, the German flag, and one other.... It was the image of that other flag that ate at Howie now. That and the townspeople's faces—half sneering, half afraid.

And then the next summer, Ma didn't want him to go to camp without them. She and Papa argued, but Howie went anyway—for two whole weeks. It wasn't fun anymore. Instead of swimming and hiking, they'd been made to work at clearing trees and underbrush from a hillside where the men were planning to build a clubhouse.

Howie slowed at the corner of Bedford and Pacific. This was Cheapy's street. He took a big gulp, then dodged a crowd gathering around a roast chestnut stand. Ignoring the smell that made his mouth water, he scanned the block for Cheapy's five-story walk-up. He hadn't been there for three or four years, but Howie recognized it right away—red-brick with a fire escape smack down the middle. He climbed to the third floor and found apartment 3-E.

Cheapy's mother answered his knock. She had dyed black hair, a pearl necklace that got lost in fleshy neck creases, and a growl in her vocal cords. She smelled like cigarettes.

Howie whipped off his cap. "Hello, Mrs. Hermann."

"Oh, my." She touched the pearls as she looked him up and down. "It's Howie Schroeder, isn't it?"

"Yes, ma'am."

"Well, well...so grown up. How is your mother, dear? I keep meaning to visit, but I know how busy she must be. Running that house...coping during this terrible time. And without Ernst..." Concern deepened in her brown eyes. She bent close, lowered her voice, placed a hand on his shoulder. "Helda's all right, isn't she? I mean, nothing has happened…"

Howie shuffled his feet. "Yes, ma'am. Ma's fine. I came to see Cheapy."

At her son's nickname, Mrs. Hermann frowned and straightened her back, thrusting the bosom of her nubby sweater within inches of Howie's nose. "Then you'll have to ask for him properly."

Howie ducked his chin. He'd just spied Cheapy coming through the French doors from the living room, but he'd never get past the mother if he didn't make like Little Lord Fauntleroy. He raised his head and spoke like he was reciting a poem in English class. "Of course, Mrs. Hermann. I'm sorry. What I meant to ask…well…Is Waldemar at home this afternoon?"

Two minutes later Howie watched as Waldemar opened his bedroom window, dug under his mattress for a pack of Camels, and lit up.

The lanky boy with the greased-back swoop of blond hair dangled his cigarette over the sill. "Want one? Ma'll never know if we keep the smoke outta the room."

Seated at the narrow student desk at the foot of the bed, Howie shook his head, then rubbed the thighs of his corduroy pants. He looked around the room highlighted with Dodgers pennants and balsa wood airplanes. Now that he was here, he was scared he might learn something he didn't want to know.

The older boy took a deep drag and blew a series of smoke rings that the breeze quickly tore to shreds. He turned to Howie with a grin. "So, what brings you all the way up here, squirt? Ain't seen you since your old man took a hike."

Ignoring the dig about Papa, Howie sat forward. Now or never. "It's about Camp Siggy."

"Camp Siegfried, shrimp. What about it?"

"Look, lay off the shrimp stuff. Okay?" He'd forgotten what a wiseass Cheapy could be. "I'm almost as tall as you, now. Just give me the dope—what went on out there?"

Cheapy shrugged. "Our parents hauled us out to Yaphank to learn how to be good little Krauts. You were there. We went on the train until your dad bought this big Packard and gave us all a ride. What else ya need to know?"

"I was just a little kid—I don't remember much. Calisthenics every morning, hauling branches and rocks all day, maybe some volleyball in the evening."

"You forgot the lectures?" Cheapy balanced his cigarette on the sill, hopped up, and crinkled his face into a stern mask. "Our rac-ce is bound by blood," he recited in Germanic tones. "Effry one of us is a countryman. No matter vhere the vind blows, ve must keep racial duties first and foremost in the heart."

"Racial duties?" Howie's stomach tightened.

"Yeah." Cheapy slumped back in the window and took another drag. "Old Fritzy was big on that. True Germans are all blood brothers, like when Indian braves cut their hands with knives and mix their blood. What a bunch of crap!"

"But we're Americans."

"You don't have to tell me." Cheapy shook his head. "But that didn't matter to Fritzy. In his book, we were all supposed to worship Hitler, no matter what. My dad used to say that a good German was a good American because we would keep America out of war. But not Fritzy. Ya know, now that I think about it, he was getting all of us good little *liebchen* ready to become soldiers for *der Fuhrer*."

"Fritzy—was he a fat little man with wire spectacles?" Things were beginning to drop into place.

"Yeah. Fritz Kuhn. Your dad was tight with him. My dad, too. Them and Mister Mueller and Billy Krueger's dad. They kinda ran the show at Camp Siegfried—ran the whole god-damned German-American Bund. Until the big fight, that is. That's when my dad stepped down. He said the organization was getting out of hand."

Another memory worked its way to the surface.

One night, after lights out, he'd been curled up in his bunk when he heard screaming and yelling. All the boys from his tent ran out onto the path. Howie clenched his toes—he could feel his bare feet on the sharp gravel like it was happening right now.

Men and older boys from the camp were fighting the townspeople, fists flying, bottles breaking. Ax handles and clubs pounding flesh. Mr. Schultz, the hardware store guy, had run right past them, his eye blackened, blood streaming down his face. Then their counselor hustled them back in the tent and closed the flap. He'd even tied it shut so they couldn't get out. Howie had covered his head with a pillow and lay stiff as a poker, trying to pretend he was home in his own, safe bed.

"What was that fight about?" Howie asked Cheapy in a whisper.

"Local guys taking info to pass along to the government, writing down the license plate numbers of cars in the parking lot. G-men don't like Nazi stuff going on right under their noses."

Nazi stuff. That's what he didn't want to remember! The flags bearing swastikas flying right up there next to the Stars and Stripes and the banners of George Washington. Marigolds planted in the shape of the swastika. And…worst of all—Papa cheering at a Bund rally, joining the other men in the enemy salute. The Kraut salute.

The Nazi salute.

How could Howie have forgotten that? Spit filled his mouth—his jaws ached—he felt like he was going to be sick. Right there. All over Cheapy's bed.

"Course we stopped going out to Yaphank then." Cheapy flicked his butt away and closed the window. "All that Nazi stuff turned out to be a bunch of crap, and old Fritzy got in trouble for stealing money off the Bund. I'm supposed to keep my trap shut about it, but I guess it's okay to talk to you. You were there. Plus, wherever he's got to, your dad's still in it up to his armpits."

"What?" Cheapy's words slammed Howie like a tomahawk. "Papa went to California."

"Your…papa. He's as big a Nazi as Fritz Kuhn ever was."

Something exploded behind Howie's eyes. He threw himself at Cheapy and shoved hard. The other boy's skull hit the bed's maple headboard with a sharp crack.

"Boys!" Mrs. Hermann's voice from the other side of the door stopped Howie from piling on. Her tone was shrill as she rattled the knob. "What's going on in there? Open up."

Cheapy pushed up on his elbows while Howie glared at him, breathing hard. Their eyes tangled for a long moment. Was Howie gonna be tossed out? But then Cheapy looked away.

"Nothing, Ma," he called out. "Just wrestling."

"Well, tone it down. You're not out on the street." Her heels clattered away.

Cheapy sat up and rubbed his head. His whisper was fierce. "Shit, Howie. What'd ya wanna go and do that for?"

Howie fought to keep his voice from cracking. "My dad's not a Nazi. He quit the Bund."

Cheapy snorted through his nose. "That's what you think."

"He did. Papa went out west to find a better job, but then he got sick. He's going to start sending us money real soon and someday we'll go out there, too. Pasadena. Ma says!"

"Stupid kid. Don't you know nothin'?" Cheapy jack-knifed off the mattress and stuck his mug in Howie's face. "I hear the grownups. Your dad didn't head west. In '38 he and a bunch of other guys went to Germany. They went to meet with Hitler himself—and your dad never came back."

Chapter Eighteen

"Tell me about your relations with Arthur Shelton," McKenna asked the distraught professor behind the desk. Based on nothing more than his photo in the department corridor, McKenna had pegged Lawrence Smoot as a pretentious, condescending know-it-all and decided to take a hard line.

Smoot choked on an inhalation of cigarette smoke. "Well— really, Lieutenant." He opened both eyes wide and flapped his hands as he coughed.

Lillian Bridges, the elegant English professor who'd been drying Smoot's tears when the detective arrived, hovered over the man like a mother lioness with her cub, casting McKenna a look of reproach.

"Business relations," McKenna clarified and waited.

"Business. Ah, yes. Well…" Stabbing out his unfinished cigarette, Smoot lowered his eyelids. "I taught Arthur everything he knew."

"Did you now?" McKenna asked dubiously.

"About the art business—yes." Smoot wiped red eyes with a monogrammed linen handkerchief and cleared his throat. "You've got to understand about Arthur. He was the most charming man—magnetic."

"Everyone felt it," the lady professor added. "Women as well as men. Arthur was truly one of a kind." She laid a hand on Smoot's shoulder.

Smoot patted her long fingers. "Well said, Lillian. One of a kind. But when we first met, the dear boy had more gall than knowledge."

"Shelton's associate seemed to think he was topnotch where art was concerned."

"What associate?" Smoot asked, frowning.

McKenna raised an eyebrow. "That's how Desmond Cox described himself."

Smoot gave McKenna a reproving look. "Well, if you're going to listen to young Desmond…"

Bridges gave a delicate snort. "Desmond Cox was Arthur's errand boy. Nothing more."

"That so?" In the hallway outside the office, McKenna heard the sudden tromp of feet and the subdued voices of young men.

Smoot followed McKenna's gaze. "Our students—God bless them—changing classes." His voice fell into the deeper register McKenna associated with recitation: "What passing-bells for those who die as cattle?"

"Huh?"

"Only the monstrous anger of the guns. / Only the stuttering rifles' rapid rattle / Can patter out their hasty orisons. Do you know Wilfred Owen, Lieutenant? One of the greats of our generation—ours, meaning yours and mine, of course. Did you fight in the last war?"

"Oh, poetry." McKenna, refusing to be distracted, pulled a notebook from his jacket. "Let's get to it. Tell me, Professor—when did you meet Arthur Shelton?"

Smoot made an effort to gather himself. "Three years ago, at an auction of Asian art. Robert and Masako Oakley were with me." Smoot turned to the dark-haired woman. "I seem to recall that you tagged along, too, Lillian?"

"Yes, I did." An ambiguous look crossed her face. Was it because of the "tagged along?" McKenna doubted that this striking woman would enjoy the role of fifth wheel. "Arthur and Lawrence," she continued, "we go…went almost everywhere together. Often with Robert and Masako. I've known Robert

Oakley for years and years, since I was at Radcliffe and he at Harvard."

McKenna glanced at the diplomas hung among the Japanese prints that decorated Smoot's walls. "You went to Harvard, too."

"Yes. Robert and I shared an interest in the Far East. We were also in Drama Club together. He was Tybalt to my Romeo. Claudius to my Hamlet."

Bridges added, now smiling, "And there was the *Macbeth* where we three donned black robes and fright wigs to play the witches." She snorted a giggle. "A bit of Shakespearean drag for you and Robert."

"Sounds like one, big happy family." McKenna tried to keep any hint of revulsion out of his voice. He'd never cared for women who hung around with fruits and didn't understand why any regular guy would make a friend of one. He turned back to Smoot. "But, tell me about you and Arthur Shelton."

"Arthur and I…we hit it off right from the start." Smoot paused and looked up at the ceiling. Then he cleared his throat again. "And he fit right into the group. After that auction we all went to dinner and ended up at Masako's studio. Arthur was terribly impressed with her work."

Smoot rummaged under the piles of blue exam books covering his desk and came up with a silver cigarette case. He tapped a cigarette on its shiny surface, stretched a hand toward a jade tabletop lighter, then paused and extended the open case. "Lieutenant?" he offered with a hint of jauntiness. "Lillian doesn't partake."

McKenna shook his head. Shelton's body had been discovered only this morning, but Smoot was trying to appear as if he'd already conquered his grief. Pansies! McKenna willed himself not to squirm. Maybe that's the way those guys operated—here today, gone tomorrow—he wouldn't get it if he lived to be a hundred.

"But," he said, "I understand not everybody is so hot on Mrs. Oakley's paintings."

"Those protesters at the gallery, you mean?" Lillian Bridges shuddered. "Lawrence and I were forced to run their gauntlet last week."

Smoot broke in. "It's war fervor. Arthur got calls and letters from malcontents charging him with disloyalty. Even before the bombing attacks, it had gotten so anything connected to Japan or its culture was suspect. I imagine that now things will only get worse—you see the trouble the attacks have caused for Masako."

"You know about her arrest, huh?"

Miss Bridges answered, "The morning papers said the FBI had raided Japanese homes and businesses. Of course, I went over to the Oakleys' immediately."

Smoot sighed. "Poor Robert."

"Why 'Poor Robert?'" McKenna asked, recalling Oakley's almost hysterical concern over his wife's detention. He'd bet Oakley would rather his friends worry about Masako than about him.

"Well, Robert has had more than his share of tragedy." Smoot took a quick draw on his cigarette. "Virginia, his first wife, died—close to eight years ago. What a nightmare—and in such a backward country, too."

"Really? Where was that?" McKenna was naturally curious when it came to death.

"Algeria. She died in agony. Food poisoning most likely— underdone goat, rancid oil. Who knows? The food in North Africa always keeps one guessing."

"Algeria?" That was a hell of a note. McKenna had a vague image of dusty robes and camels with bells on their harnesses. Geography had never been his strong point, but, then, he hadn't had the luxury of a fancy education like these two.

"Yes. We were on a tour of Egypt and North Africa for Arts and Science faculty. Robert just about collapsed. Thank god Lillian and I were there to prop him up."

Smoot glanced at Bridges, and she took the cue. "I organized a ferry over to Marseilles and we took a steamship home, the three of us in saloon and poor Virginia's coffin in the cargo hold. We expected Robert to wallow in despair forever. He surprised us, though." She crossed her arms. "Within the year, he'd gone to Paris, met Masako, and married again."

"I see." These two had yakked long enough to get all relaxed and confidential. He'd just keep that mood going for another minute. He rose and ambled over to the framed prints—landscapes of rolling hills, misty waterfalls, and blossoming cherry trees. "These are really pretty." They sure as hell didn't look anything like the bizarre paintings in Shelton's gallery.

"Pretty, Lieutenant?" Smoot waved a hand at the collection. "Surely you can do better than that. Those are antique prints of even older *Yamato-e*." He tented long, finely boned hands. "Notice the striking compositions that feature natural landscape and the four seasons." He nodded into his ascot, the consummate professional educating one of the *hoi polloi*. "Masako Fumi borrows a great deal from the *Yamato-e* style, especially the poetry that follows the theme of the painting itself. You see—there on your right—the complementary text appears at the very edge."

"Oh, yeah?" McKenna waved a lazy hand and wandered back to his seat. "Did you buy those babies from Arthur Shelton?"

Smoot took a haughty tone. "Those babies, as you call them, predate Arthur considerably."

"Yeah?" Another slow nod, inviting disclosure.

"I'm the one with the expertise, Lieutenant. I took Arthur under my wing, taught him all about Asian art and introduced him to Asian artists working in the West." Smoot shifted in his leather chair. "As well as to patrons who happen to have deep pockets."

Lillian Bridges chimed in. "Lawrence is right. Arthur did well for himself because he had a great eye and was a natural salesman, but his initial success sat squarely on Lawrence's shoulders."

The monogrammed handkerchief came into play again as Smoot dipped his chin toward Lillian Bridges.

"So—" McKenna leaned forward. "Will the gallery close now that Shelton's gone?"

Smoot took a longer draw on his cigarette. "I suppose that's a question for the lawyers."

"Had Shelton made a will?"

"Who makes a will at thirty-one?" Smoot shook his head.

"Okay." McKenna scribbled a last note, stood, and reached for his hat. But he kept notebook and pencil in hand. "That should do it for now." Over the years, he'd noticed that the mugs sometimes came up with the straight dope when they thought he had one foot out the door. He made his good byes mild and casual. With his hand on the doorknob he turned back. "Just to round out the case, where were you on the evening of Friday the fifth, Professor Bridges?"

"Me?" The lady's hand fluttered to her throat. "That was last Friday? Hmm. Oh, yes. I thought I was coming down with a cold, so I skipped office hours and went home around four. I stopped at a delicatessen for some chicken soup, and then—straight to bed."

"Can anyone confirm that?"

"Well, no. I live alone." She gave a dry laugh. "How odd—I do believe that's the first time I've ever been asked for an alibi."

McKenna scribbled again, then rounded on his heel to address Smoot. "And you?"

Smoot was suddenly very still. "I can't stop thinking about that, Lieutenant. Arthur and I had theater tickets, and I dropped by the gallery around 7:45 to pick him up. I knocked and knocked at the front door, but he didn't answer. Finally, I got miffed and went to the play on my own."

"Hmm. Any sign of movement in the gallery? Noise? Lights?"

Smoot shook his head, cigarette forgotten, gathering ash in his hand. "It was totally dark and quiet. I thought Arthur had forgotten and gone somewhere else."

"What time did you leave?"

Smoot appeared to think. He dunked his cigarette in a cup that held an inch of cold tea. It extinguished with a hiss. "Just before eight. I had to step lively to make the curtain."

"What was the play?"

When Smoot hesitated and creased his forehead, Bridges bustled in. "*Junior Miss*, wasn't it? At the Lyceum. You told me about it."

That's one place you didn't accompany the boys, McKenna thought.

"Yes, of course." Smoot's tone rallied a fraction. "I ended up sitting next to an empty seat in a packed house. Perhaps the usher would remember—Arthur and I are frequent patrons."

McKenna nodded. "When the doc sets a margin on the time of death, we'll check that out. It's possible Shelton was killed well before the play began."

"I se-e-ee." Smoot stretched the word to three syllables. He rubbed his chin and took a moment or two to respond. "Well, I was grading exams here from mid-afternoon on."

"Anyone see you?"

"I doubt it. The department empties out fast on a Friday afternoon."

"You take a cab down to the gallery?"

A slight head shake. "Subway."

"Hmm." McKenna clamped his hat on and asked, "Did Shelton often stand you up?"

Professor Lawrence Smoot looked a little green around the gills. A wet, thick noise sounded from his throat, then, "No, Lieutenant. Never."

What's this? McKenna questioned silently. The guy's actually getting teary again. Maybe Smoot was feeling Shelton's death more than he'd given him credit for.

◇◇◇

Outside, McKenna noted the young men strolling across the muted winter grass in groups of two or three. Their expressions were unnaturally serious, their tweeds and flannels dark. His eye was drawn to a Barnard coed whose red skirt flapped in the stiff breeze. Even this pretty young woman wore a frown.

He took a deep, icy breath. The campus mood was grim for good reason. He'd tried to brush off Smoot's poeticizing, but the words had struck him nonetheless: "What passing-bells for these who die as cattle?"

McKenna had never been led to think a college education was for someone like him. Well, maybe City College, or, at a real stretch, Fordham. But he'd have been as likely to walk on the moon as attend the Ivy League Columbia. He didn't even know if this university admitted Irish Catholics.

War was much more democratic. Everyone was admitted— even these boys born to privilege.

McKenna stopped at the ornate iron gates that divided the well-tended campus from busy Broadway. He glanced back toward the students.

How many of these kids'll end up on battleships in the Pacific? Flying bombers over Germany?

How many will never come home?

What passing-bells for those who die as cattle?

Chapter Nineteen

To Masako Fumi Oakley, Agent Bagwell looked like a man who had been put together by machine—the proper number of eyes and limbs, but no personality, no heart. Functional, but lacking a soul.

Marched from her cell to a cramped, stale-smelling office by the sullen matron, Masako struggled to gather her wits. She had not slept since her arrest. All had been chaos, the ride to the Federal Building on Foley Square, where she had been marched into a holding cell with other frightened Japanese women. Then, later, the crowded van to the Battery and the cold ferry ride to this island prison. Everyone snatched from home, bewildered, lost, terrified.

"Where are you taking me?" she had asked, as the FBI agents forced her from her apartment.

"You don't need to know," was the response.

"What have I done?"

"That's what we intend to find out."

Now, here was Agent Bagwell again, in this windowless room.

"How is my husband?" She had to ask.

He raised his gaze from a sheaf of papers. "What is your name?" he asked.

"Masako Fumi Oakley. You already know that. How is Robert?"

He stared at her with cold gray eyes. "Your husband is not my concern. Just answer the questions." Smoke wafted straight up from a cigar in a flat metal ashtray. At a smaller desk, the stenographer's pen went scritch, scritch.

"Where were you born?"

"Tokyo."

"Japan?"

"Yes. Of course."

"Just answer the questions. Where were you educated?"

"Moscow. Paris."

"In Japanese schools?"

"Yes. Russian schools and French schools, also. Then I studied philosophy at the Sorbonne—before I went to art school."

The agent's face was utterly blank. "When did you come to the United States?"

"In 1934."

"Do you have any relatives in the Japanese government?"

Masako sighed. "My father was ambassador to Russia, then to France. I don't know what post he holds now."

"I do." Bagwell sank back against the wooden chair. He reached out to tap the ash from his cigar but set it down without taking it to his mouth. "When was the last time you were in contact with him?"

A lump in her throat thickened her response. "What does my father do?"

"Miss Fumi, answer the question."

Oto-san. Oto-san. Even now you injure me. "We have not spoken for fifteen years. I was very young."

"Why not since then?"

"He…he…my family disowned me."

"They disinherited you?"

"That's not strong enough for what disown means in Japanese culture. The word is *engiri*. I am no longer their daughter."

Scritch, scritch.

"Why not?"

I wanted to live my own life. I wanted to think my own thoughts. I wanted to study Western art. I wanted—

"Answer the question."

"I wanted to be free."

Chapter Twenty

"Last I heard, you were on your way to Foley Square, Lute."
Brenner peered through the windshield, navigating the black
sedan through the maze of dim, narrow streets that led to the
Bowery. "What did you get from the Feds?"

"Nuts is what I got." In the back seat, a sour taste rose in
McKenna's throat. "Some blowhard from Washington read me
the rules and regulations. Those G-men won't back down as long
as Masako Fumi Oakley is in federal custody—where they're
concerned, national security trumps a local homicide any day.
Now they intend to confiscate her paintings from the gallery,
and I'll be lucky if I get to interview the lady anytime before
1950. God, those guys piss me off."

He glanced forward just as the car's headlights picked out a
shuffling figure crossing against the light. "Brenner—look out!"

The young detective smashed on the brakes. They were all
thrown back, then slung forward.

"Watch it, buddy—almost bought yourself a plot on Hart
Island, there," Brenner grumbled.

"Skunked." Patsy Dolan reset the toothpick dangling from
one side of his mouth.

Good guess, Pats, McKenna thought. You oughta go on
Double or Nothing. With that brain you'd clean up. He didn't
say it, of course. Dolan did the best he could with what he had
between his ears. Besides, the play of neon and shadow on the
car's windows didn't encourage levity. With the Third Avenue

El forming a rackety roof, and seedy hotels and dives crowding street level, the Bowery was the ultimate refuge for the destitute and derelict. Thank the Blessed Virgin he'd never had to pound a beat down here.

McKenna turned his attention back to the matter at hand: the ringleader of the art gallery picketers. Desmond Cox had picked him out of the mug book without hesitation. A low life named Herman Rupp who called the Bowery home.

"This is it, Lute." Brenner slid the car to the curb and turned off the ignition. Gold and black lettering backlit by a smoky interior announced Breslin's Pool Hall—2 1/2 cents a cue. "From what I hear, Rupp's so regular, he oughta be punching a time card." Brenner twisted around and stretched a long arm along the seat back. "The pool hall from seven-thirty to eleven, Clancy's Bar for a nightcap, then back to the Sunshine Hotel by midnight."

Dolan exposed his radium watch dial. "Eight o'clock on the nose, Lute."

"Okay." McKenna unbuttoned his overcoat, touched two fingers to the pistol in its shoulder holster, a ritual gesture. "Take it easy, boys. Don't wanna lose him out the back door."

The door's recess stank of stale urine and cheap wine. They entered without announcing themselves. Breslin's was just big enough for three tables, each flooded with light from a green-shaded ceiling fixture that harked back to the gaslight era. A battered bar held down one wall, along with a glass counter displaying boxes of cheap cigars. Slatted benches finished off the perimeter, sagging beneath flyspecked boxing posters.

McKenna spotted Herman Rupp right away. The man lining up a shot on the middle table was no sap. More like a lug who preyed on the saps. He was fat but powerfully built, with a thick neck and short arms. Thin hair combed down with water made a manful effort to cover his shiny scalp, but the mottled dome was winning. His beard was tougher. There'd always be a blue shadow on that jaw, no matter how close the big guy shaved.

Rupp, ignoring the three cops who'd fanned out like wolves surrounding a spring lamb, took his shot and sank it in a corner pocket. Then he reclaimed a long black cigar from the table railing and took a juicy suck. Meanwhile, his buddies blended into the shadows. From the corner of his eye, McKenna caught sight of the proprietor in a white apron slipping through a door to a back room.

"Herman Rupp?" McKenna approached the table.

"Who wants to know?" The pool cue clunked onto the felt-covered slate. Rupp crossed his arms over a corduroy jacket with the elbows poking through. Between the fingers of his right hand, the cigar stood up like a rigid dog turd.

"McKenna. Homicide Squad."

Almost imperceptibly the yegg's shoulders relaxed. Guilty of something, McKenna thought. But not murder.

"Now, what could McKenna of Homicide want with a law-abidin' citizen such as myself?"

McKenna rattled off the dates and times of the picketing outside the art gallery.

"So?" Rupp asked warily, applying the cigar to rubbery lips. "You here to run me in for not having a parade permit?"

McKenna took his time, smiling all the while. "Swanky joint, that Shelton Gallery."

"Yeah. I guess." His eyes narrowed, almost lost in cheek fat.

"Somehow you don't strike me as the kind of art lover who'd give a damn what Shelton hung on his walls."

"Maybe it's Japs I don't like—whether they're droppin' bombs or paintin' posies." Cigar ash rained on the floor.

"Maybe someone who doesn't like one particular Jap hired you to picket."

"Could be." Rupp shrugged. "My memory ain't what it used to be."

As if he had Rupp's entire life history committed to three-by-five note cards, McKenna added the details of the payoff Cox had described. "Shelton's dead," he finished. "Murdered." He took note of Rupp's complexion—suddenly pale.

"So, maybe you read about it in the papers," McKenna pursued.

Dolan and Brenner moved closer, crowding out what light there was.

"That arty-pants fairy and me did business. That's all. I ain't got nothin' to do with no murder." Rupp reached for his cue again. Brenner got there first, stowed it in the wall rack.

McKenna hitched one hip up on the table, the one that wasn't aching like a bad tooth. "I see it like this." He nodded, speaking slowly. "Shelton coughed up a wad and you called off your boys. You'd also had a nice look around his office, figured the guy was rolling in dough. Yeah…So, one night after he'd closed, you came back to shake him down for another coupla c-notes. Shelton said no. You fought. He ended up hitting his head on something." McKenna swung his leg. "Probably something you brought along for the occasion."

Rupp's dark eyes darted right and left, showing a lot of white. "I didn't go to no gallery. I was right here bangin' the balls around."

"I didn't say which night Shelton was killed."

"It don't matter. I ain't missed a night here since I was laid up with flu last winter."

At a flick of McKenna's left index finger, Dolan headed for the back room. Rupp's gaze followed him.

"You can remember all the way back to last winter?" McKenna drew his eyebrows toward his hat brim.

"Yeah." Rupp curled his lip.

"Then you shouldn't have any trouble recalling who paid you to picket in the first place. Somebody musta."

Rupp looked like a man who'd suddenly had ice water poured down his collar. "Like, maybe, somebody who had it in for Shelton, ya mean?"

McKenna nodded. "Now you're getting it." He swept an arm toward the nearest bench. "Why don't we step over here and talk about it? Nice and friendly like, from the very beginning."

Chapter Twenty-one

Cabby paused in the butler's pantry, carefully shifting the armful of cups she was trying to smuggle back into the kitchen without Helda's notice.

Damn. Soft sounds met her ears. The landlady must still be stirring around, wiping the counter or flipping through recipes. She'd blow a gasket if she saw all these cups—evidence of late night cocoas prepared on a forbidden hot plate.

"Hey, who's there?" A cracking voice called.

Cabby relaxed with a shallow sigh—it was only the kid. Howie wouldn't care if she and Louise were hiding an elephant in their room.

"Just me," she said, as she ferried the illicit cups to the sink and shook soap flakes out of the blue Lux box. "Where's your mom?"

Howie barely glanced up from the thick books spread out on the table. "Prayer service at church. Pastor called it special. You know—"

"Oh, sure. I get it." At Helda's Lutheran church, the congregation would be mostly Germans. Cabby turned the taps, adjusting until the water was good and warm. Her thoughts ranged free while she scrubbed the cups under the rich white suds. The Reich hadn't declared war yet, but everyone knew they would. Would the Lutheran flock be praying for a last-minute change of Hitler's Nazi heart? Or simply asking God for the courage to withstand the inevitable?

Howie was being unnaturally quiet. He must be worried, too. When war came, it wouldn't be easy for a German kid in any American neighborhood.

Cabby turned to see the boy's nose buried in a book. "Doing your homework?"

"Naw. I finished it."

"What's so interesting, then?"

Howie looked up, head tilted. His lips were tightened in a hard line, but his rounded jaw, still soft with baby fat, made him look young and vulnerable. Cabby could feel his distress from across the room.

"Wanna talk about it?" She went over to him, dish towel in hand.

"It's Ma's photo albums." Howie flipped a page of snapshots with an impatient finger. "I'm trying to find somebody."

Cabby eased into a chair. Sepia-toned rectangles with pinked edges stared up from the dark page. A picnic by a lake, an elderly woman waving from a porch, a young woman holding a chubby baby. Cabby took a closer look. The woman's light hair framed her bunched cheeks as she gazed lovingly at the baby dressed in an old-fashioned christening gown.

"That's your mom," Cabby cried, surprised at how young Helda had been. If that baby was Howie, the photo was taken only fourteen years ago, and Helda looked as if she might still be in her teens. "Is that you on her lap?"

"Yeah." Howie turned to another page. The pages were rough where photos and their adhesive brackets had been torn away. Tracing the outline of a missing snapshot, he said, "That one was Papa. After he took off, Ma practically shredded all his pictures."

Oh, so that explained the absence of husband and father. Poor Helda—leaving home and family for a new country, then her marriage gone bad. Cabby's imagination flooded with images of a drunken Mr. Schroeder slapping Helda around, maybe even hitting Howie. But whatever had happened, the boy still missed his dad. His eyes were shiny with unshed tears.

Howie gulped and said, "I thought I might spot Papa in a group photo, one Ma might've missed. But I'm running out of time. She'll be home soon, and she'll throw a fit if she sees I've drug these out."

"Let me help you." Cabby reached for one of the leather-bound albums. "If you can describe him…what does your dad look like?"

"Tall and skinny. Blond, curly hair that sticks up in the front."

Cabby grinned. "Kinda like yours. You must be a lot like him, huh?"

"No," Howie snapped, flipping sullenly through pages.

Oh. "Okay." Cabby opened her album. They worked in silence, studying the shots that contained several people. Memories of her own father's outbursts and rants played in her head. If her mother'd had Helda's backbone—the gumption to tell the big oaf to hit the road, the character to work hard and make a living for herself and her children—Cabby's life would have been a lot different. She glanced at Howie's bent head. The kid wanted to make a connection with his dad. Sure, she could understand that, but Howie might not know when he was well off.

She continued paging through the album, but no tall, skinny man stood out. Howie hadn't found anything, either. Eventually, footsteps sounded in the butler's pantry, then paused. Not Helda. The landlady always let herself in through the back door.

"Ethel?" Cabby called the Mouse's real name. Well, she could hardly call her Mousie to her face, could she?

But it was Marion who stepped into the kitchen, looking impossibly slim in black satin lounging pajamas and high-heeled mules. "Really, darling. I've been mistaken for many things, but not little Miss Ethel Furnish." She turned up her nose. "Please!"

"Oh—Marion." Cabby shook her head. Why had she assumed it was Mousie? "What do you want?"

"Well, if you must know, I wondered if Helda could spare a couple of tea bags."

"Won't tea keep you awake?"

"No, silly, the bags are for my eyes. A tea compress will make them sparkle at tomorrow's audition." Marion drifted over to the table. "Ooh, you're looking at photos. I just love photos."

Just as Marion's red nails grazed the thick, black page, Howie slammed his album shut. "The tea bags are over in the canister." As the tall woman regarded him with pursed lips, he hastily gathered the albums into a pile. "Ah, thanks, Miss Ward," he mumbled before disappearing through the butler's pantry.

"Somebody needs to teach that boy some manners." Marion sneered, hands on hips.

"Leave Howie alone," Cabby retorted. "The kid's all right." She threw her dishtowel at her housemate's head. "As long as you're here, you might as well help me dry."

Chapter Twenty-two

"She was a classy dame, Lieutenant. No spring chicken, but a looker." Herman Rupp shrugged. "At least what I could see."

"How old?" McKenna had established that on Monday, the first, Rupp responded to a classified ad in the *New York Post*. A union agent, dependable and experienced with picket lines, was invited to call a certain number between noon and half past for more information. Rupp didn't remember the number, but, no problem—Brenner could look it up in last week's paper. The main thing, Rupp was having trouble describing the anonymous lady who'd arranged to meet him in front of the Oyster Bar at Grand Central.

"Forty?" McKenna persisted.

Rupp continued to shake his head. "Who can tell with broads these days—the stuff they do to themselves. She had wavy hair sticking out of this hat-veil contraption—covered one eye like Veronica Lake's—blond, but that coulda come out of a bottle."

McKenna shifted on the hard bench, to ease his hip. "What else? Give me more."

"Okay." Rupp squeezed his eyes shut for a second. "Nice bod. Tall. Had on heels, but barefoot she woulda been five seven, at least…And she had this way of talking. Uptown. I figured maybe she lived in a hotel or had a buncha maids."

"Why?"

"She seemed used to giving orders."

"What'd she want you to do?"

Rupp glanced down at the stogy that had gone out in his hand, tossed it at the nearby smoke stand. "Hey, ya see that? Bulls-eye."

McKenna sighed. "We ain't got all night."

"Yeah...Well, she wanted some guys to picket that art gallery. Carry placards, hassle people going in. Make as much noise as we could."

"Right up your alley, huh?"

"Yeah." A smile stretched his blue-black jaws. "I could do that."

"Was the anti-Jap thing her idea?"

"You bet. NO GO JAP SHOW—she came up with that. It was part of the deal."

"And what was the deal?"

"She started off with twenty-five for three days' work. But I jewed her up to fifty. I got expenses, see?"

"Tuesday, Wednesday, Thursday." McKenna held up a finger for each day. "So, by the time Shelton called you inside, your work was almost done."

"The guy was waving dough in my face. You think I was gonna turn it down?"

"No, of course not." McKenna stood up, seemingly ready to go. "But I wonder—why'd you come back on Monday morning?"

"Huh?" Rupp made a face like a puzzled chimpanzee.

"Somebody threw a brick through Shelton's front window and painted No Go Jap Show underneath."

"Wasn't me," Rupp shot back. "Or my boys."

McKenna nodded slowly. He believed him. "If we find the lady, we'll have to get you over to Centre Street for a line-up."

Rupp nodded uncomfortably.

McKenna buttoned his overcoat. "By the way, how'd she know you were on the job? You could've taken the fifty and run."

"She was no dummy. Came walking down Fifty-seventh that first day, swinging her purse, cool as a cucumber. But she got hot when she saw it was only me hauling the placard around. Told me I'd better get some more guys."

"Or what? What was she gonna do?"

Rupp shook his head. "I don't know. But, I'll tell ya, boss. I didn't think it would be healthy to cross her."

Chapter Twenty-three

When Louise dragged herself into the boarding house around 9:30, the girls were gathered around the console radio listening to *The Inner Sanctum*. Just what she needed—spooky organ music and creaking doors. But the place was warm and well-lighted, and the aroma of dinner still hung in the air. Sanctuary, that's what the house felt like.

All afternoon, as soon as Professor Oakley had come out of his sedative, he'd run her off her feet. She'd phoned his attorney, Rutherford Pierce, only to be informed, as Dr. Wright had predicted, that his firm did not have "the requisite expertise in civil and immigrant rights."

"That little shit!" Oakley burst out. "His father was my roommate at Harvard."

None of the attorneys Louise found in the phone book would touch what they called "an enemy alien case." When she tried to reach Agent Bagwell, the idiot girl on the switchboard droned, "Federal agents are not accepting calls."

Each time Louise returned to the sickroom with bad news, the professor grew more obstreperous. Finally the nursing agency sent a suitable RN. Thank god—Louise didn't think she could have lasted another second.

To top it all off, exhausted and frazzled on her way home from the subway, she'd been dragging her feet down Flatbush when she tripped on a broken sidewalk in front of Kramer's Cat's Paw

Shoe Repair and fell to her knees. By the time she staggered into the boarding house parlor and threw herself into an overstuffed armchair, she was fighting back tears.

"Lou-lou!" Cabby cried, jumping up from the green parlor sofa. "Where have you been? What have you done to your knees."

Marion gave a shriek. "You look terrible! Just terrible!"

Ruthie gasped. "What happened to your stockings?"

Louise waved away their concern about her scrapes, swallowed a sob and dabbed at her eyes. "You won't believe it. Mrs. Oakley, my patient's wife…she was arrested, dragged down to Ellis Island last night and charged with being an enemy alien."

Cabby's eyes took on a sudden gleam. "And you were there?"

Louise was too distressed to notice her roommate's avid interest. "Yes. I tried to keep the FBI out of the apartment, but they came crashing in. They just took her! It's not right. It's not American."

"*Ach du lieber*!" Helda, wearing her shapeless tweed coat and exuding an outdoor chill, stood in the archway that led to the butler's pantry, flanked by a wide-eyed Howie.

Every eye was fixed on Louise, the radio chatter forgotten in the background. "Mrs. Oakley's just a little wisp of a thing, and we haven't heard a word from her. The professor is deathly ill with pneumonia, and I wouldn't be surprised if the worry kills him."

"*Mein Gott*! His wife is German?" Helda cast a frightened glance toward Howie.

"No—not German. Japanese."

"A Jap," Ruthie squealed. "Well, no wonder!" Her lips twisted in disdain. "I can't believe you'd work for one of those Japs, Louise. Don't you care about our country?"

"Shut up, Ruthie!" Alicia barked.

Mousie examined Louise with a new interest.

Louise blinked back more tears. "Um, Alicia. Could I talk to you—privately?"

Cabby followed them out of the room

At the bottom of the staircase, her hand on the rounded oak newel cap, Louise pivoted. "I said privately, Cabby." There was so much at stake that for once Louise ignored the rules of Southern politeness.

◇◇◇

Alicia rented a single room on the third floor, a large chamber near the attic stairs, with a high peaked ceiling and two tall windows. An old divan covered with a pink chenille bedspread looked comfortable, and Louise sat down. This was the first time she'd been in Alicia's room. Everything was shabby—a sagging bed, a badly worn carpet, a bare bulb hanging from a frayed cord. Books were everywhere, and a big oak desk between the windows was covered with notebooks and papers.

Alicia plopped down on her mattress. "Don't pay any attention to Ruthie—she's so dumb she can't see past the end of her nose. We have a saying in Yiddish, *a shtik fleish mit tsvei oygn.*"

Louise looked at her, puzzled.

"A piece of meat with two eyes."

Louise started laughing, and then she couldn't stop. She howled with laughter until tears flowed. When she wiped her eyes with the bedspread, she saw that Alicia was grinning.

"I guess that is funny," the Jewish girl said. "I've been hearing it all my life—never thought how hilarious it is." She bounced up. "Take your stockings off, Louise. Those scrapes look bad. I'll get my first aid kit."

Louise pulled her skirt up and unsnapped the suspenders on her garter belt. She peeled off the ravaged hose. "Just give me the kit. I'll take care of it."

"Good." Alicia handed over the red-cross stenciled tin box. "The sight of blood makes me wanna puke."

Dabbing at her knees with gauze and Mercurochrome, Louise winced, but told Alicia about her frustrating search for a lawyer. "I couldn't believe it. They all absolutely, categorically refused to represent Mrs. Oakley."

"Cowards!" Alicia snorted.

"You're studying law, Alicia. Would it help if I went down to the Federal Building and talked to someone at the FBI? Attested to Mrs. Oakley's good character. That's what the professor would do if he could."

Alicia shook her head. "Now, listen, Louise, you're smart as hell, and you've got a good heart, but going to Foley Square is a waste of time. You can't fight this on your own." She nodded once, emphatically. "And, as it happens, I know someone who might be able to help your patient's wife."

Louise looked up. "Oh, yes?"

"The perfect person—one of my professors at Brooklyn Law. He specializes in Constitutional Law."

Louise clutched the bottle of antiseptic. Excitement tensed her muscles. This might be the first good news she'd heard all day. "Is your teacher…a Bolshie?"

Alicia laughed. "Abe Pritzker would probably call himself progressive. He's also been called a radical and a dirty fighter. The man might not be everyone's cup of matzo-ball soup, but at least he's never been afraid to fight abuse of power. He's famous for it, actually. Sometimes he even wins."

"Oh, Alicia, do you think he'd defend Mrs. Oakley?"

Alicia laughed. "I think a detained enemy alien would be catnip to this guy. Listen, I've got an early class with the Great Man himself. I'll ask him—then I'll call you. Where will you be?"

"At the Oakleys'. I'll give you the number. Call me there."

She rose from the divan, stretched her arms over her head. Maybe she could sleep tonight.

Chapter Twenty-four

Tuesday, December 9, early morning

Even though the mattress reeked of ancient urine, Masako burrowed deeply so the other women in the cell would not hear her sobs.

Robert? No word. Not one word. That awful Bagwell man wouldn't give her even one scrap of news.

Her husband was dead—she knew it. Her arrest must have killed him. Otherwise he would have come here for her—pneumonia be damned—storming past the guards, thrusting aside that nasty matron, growling like the bear he was. But so many hours. Hour after hour. No word from Robert. He was dead—she knew it.

If only she could pour her grief out on canvas. She'd tried to slip a small case of oil paints and brushes into the bag with her toiletries, but the guard had snatched them away. Not essential, he'd snarled.

Not essential? Cadmium Red? Yellow Ochre? Chromatic Black? Not essential? Permanent Green Light?

How else to capture this dull winter sunrise? The gray-green harbor waves. The jagged concrete skyline. That rusted tugboat passing, gray gulls in its wake. The tumult raging within.

She stifled a sob, tried not to breath—Robert was dead. He had died alone, without her. And what had she done to be kept from him? Nothing.

Robert was dead, and all that was left—this dull pain in her heart. This weight of utter weariness. This blood-dark behind her eyes.

How to express it? Should she open her veins for the color?

Chapter Twenty-five

The fifth-floor corridor of the Oakleys' building was richly carpeted and lit by widely spaced brass wall sconces. The *New York Times* lay in neat rectangles in front of apartment doors. This morning's dose of gloom and doom, thought Louise. No, that wasn't fair. War news would dominate, but the *Times* would also contain birth announcements, weddings, news of local doings. Life went on, no matter what devastation tyrants caused.

As Louise bent to collect the Oakleys' paper, a door clicked open across the way. A brunette swathed in a satin negligee, hair bobby-pinned in flat spirals, was retrieving her own paper. She rewarded Louise's "good morning" with a slammed door.

Whew! Had the neighbor seen Masako being taken away by the Feds? Had she decided the professor and the artist were dangerous fifth columnists? Louise tucked the paper under her arm and rang the Oakleys' bell. With luck, any hostile response to the couple wouldn't go farther than the building.

Kitty, the relief nurse, opened the door. Louise had taken an instant liking to the brisk, compact woman in her fifties. Last night, she'd settled in with a minimum of fuss and quelled the professor's anxious questions with a skilful mix of firmness and sympathy.

Now Kitty reported their patient had slept well after a moderate dose of codeine administered per Dr. Wright's orders. "His fever is down, and I'm going to start his bath," she continued.

"He has a hundred questions waiting for you, so if you're smart, you'll take advantage of the lull. Make yourself some coffee. Read that paper."

Good advice, but it felt odd remaining in her blue wool jacket and Glen-plaid skirt instead of changing into a uniform. Odd to leave the intimate details of nursing care to someone else. To delay facing the newspaper's inevitable bad news, Louise squeezed orange juice for the professor and brewed coffee for herself. Once she'd sat down at the scrubbed wood table, the urgent headlines screaming up from the front page threatened to knock her hard-won calm completely off balance.

"1,500 Dead in Hawaii"

"Hostile Planes Sighted at San Francisco"

"Philippines Pounded"

Louise took a sip of coffee. She closed her eyes and let the warm liquid bathe her throat. *Later, I'll read every word. Later.* Right now, all she could handle was news of the city. She turned to the second section, then gave a strangled cry.

There was Mrs. Oakley's photograph! And: "Japanese Artist Tied to Fifty-seventh Street Murder—Miss Fumi Detained as Threat to National Security." It got worse. Louise sat bolt upright, scanning the article furiously.

The FBI sweep of Sunday night…Police sources confirm… The body of Arthur Shelton, dead several days…Avant-garde artist, who had taken the city by storm…

The unnamed reporter noted that Shelton's body had been propped beneath Masako's signature painting. His clever phrasing made that into proof positive that the Japanese woman had killed the gallery owner. Who was this wrong-headed jerk, anyway? She'd have to ask Cabby. Her feisty roommate could set the guy straight.

Kitty's voice drifted down the hall. "No you don't, Professor Oakley. You get back in bed, and I'll get Nurse Hunter."

Louise pressed a fist to her mouth. *Oh, no!* The professor mustn't see this article—not in his fragile state. He'd barely survived the arrest and not fared much better under questioning by that policeman yesterday. To see it all rehashed in the *Times* could kill him.

She ran to the doorway and called, "I'll be right there—just give me a minute."

Moving quickly, Louise spread the paper in the sink and emptied coffee grounds over it. She pulled the trash can out of the utility closet and buried the sodden bundle under orange rinds and other malodorous debris. Then she pressed the button to call up the dumbwaiter and sent it all down for the janitor to deal with. After flicking bits of orange off the cuffs of her white blouse, she scrubbed her hands.

A moment later, Louise entered the sickroom with a tray bearing juice and a couple of hothouse roses in a crystal bud vase, apparently another floral offering from Professor Bridges. Kitty sent her a private smile as she slipped out to await the day nurse.

"About time," the professor harrumphed.

Undeterred, Louise deposited the tray with a pleasant—she hoped—smile. "And good morning to you, too, Professor. How do you feel?"

Oakley plucked at his bedcovers. "How do you think I feel? My wife is a prisoner, and for as much good as I can do her, I might as well be de—" He finished with a deep cough.

Louise bolstered pillows and tidied blankets, murmuring words of encouragement all the while. Masako's situation was bound to turn out well—Louise's housemate had a professor at Brooklyn Law who might jump at the case. And didn't Professor Oakley have influential friends on his side? And the force of moral authority? No sense taking a pessimist's view.

The sick man twisted his face. "You're just trotting out some of your applied psychology. Keep the old man's spirits up so he won't die on you."

"Can you blame me?" Another nervous smile.

Oakley's quivering hands sought hers. He squeezed with more strength than she could have predicted. "Only one thing could raise my spirits this morning. A good lawyer for Masako—cost be damned. Who is this Brooklyn Law fellow? One of those rabble-rousers?"

"His name is Abe Pritzker."

"Humph." He cocked his head. "Pritzker? Wasn't he involved in that Boss Hague case in Jersey City? He won on First Amendment grounds?"

Louise shrugged. "Could be. Alicia calls him a champion of the people."

"A Bolshie, you mean."

"I mean a rebel who isn't afraid to challenge powerful institutions." Louise thought of the newspaper buried in the garbage. Surely Abe Pritzker would be more courageous than the lawyers who'd already turned down the case.

"I never thought I'd hear myself saying something like this." Her patient's eyes burned above his grey beard like black coals in a fiery grate. "But maybe that's just exactly what we need—a good, old-fashioned, left-leaning rabble-rouser. They took that Hague case all the way to the Supreme Court."

He nodded decisively. "Hire him then, if you believe he's the right man. I'm depending on you, Louise. Trusting your good sense. Stick with that lawyer, find out what's happened to Masako and bring me word that she hasn't been harmed."

She nodded slowly. The professor called me Louise, she thought, fully aware that she was moving farther and farther from her role as private-duty nurse.

◇◇◇

"Abe Pritzker agreed? Oh, thank god." Louise's knees suddenly felt weak and she sank down on the telephone bench in the hall. She couldn't wait to get back to the professor with the news, but questions came first. "When can I meet him?"

Alicia's excited voice came over the wire. "Be at his office at four p.m. He's already working on permission to visit Mrs. Oakley—"

"Today?" Louise could hear her voice rise an octave.

"He's going to try. Before that, he wants you to sit down with Professor Oakley and make notes about Mrs. Oakley's arrest.

What the agents said and did. What questions they asked. What items they took. Is Oakley well enough for that?"

"He'll do what he must." Louise twisted a strand of hair around her finger. "But exactly what should we try to remember?"

"Every little thing. Pritzker will have to dig for the elements of the case. In Enemy Alien hearings, the Feds aren't obliged to reveal either the accusations or the evidence. Backtracking over their movements Sunday night may the only way to figure out why they targeted Mrs. Oakley."

"I'll get right to work," Louise responded, ransacking the bench's one drawer for a notepad and pencil. "And Alicia, I really don't know how to thank you."

"I didn't have to do much. Honest Abe was just waiting for a case like this." The law student's nasal laugh filled Louise's ear. "Another crack at the Supreme Court, maybe? Wait until you've met Abe Pritzker, Louise. You may want to strangle me for ever mentioning his name."

Chapter Twenty-six

"Ya want coffee, McKenna?" Captain Joseph Dwyer had his finger on a buzzer that would alert Bernice, his secretary, to gear the percolator up for a second round.

McKenna shifted his weight in the wooden chair. He wanted this meeting to be as brief as possible. The upshot was a foregone conclusion and he had a case to work. "No, thanks, Cap."

"It's not squad-room swill. Bernice has a dab hand. She might even be able to rustle up a Danish or two." Dwyer leaned forward, hands folded over the unmarred blotter centered on the desk. A leather cup of pencils sharpened to lethal points sat at his right hand; on his left, a hefty marble P.B.A. paperweight held down an official-looking document.

"Nah." McKenna recognized the document and the handwritten answers to its printed questions—his retirement application. It didn't worry him. The folded *New York Times* beside it—now that was making him sweat under his collar. Frowning, he ran a finger between damp flesh and stiff cotton. Gayle had never strangled him like this. Now that he was doing for himself, he'd have to tell the Chink at the laundry to go lighter on the starch.

Dwyer regarded him with narrowed blue eyes. The homicide chief, who'd been a skinny runt a year behind McKenna at the police academy, had matured into a broad-shouldered, silver-haired officer with a chiseled profile. Jawline sagged a bit, though, McKenna couldn't help but notice.

His hand unconsciously went to his own jaw, then, quickly, back to his right knee. The sound of typing clattered through the frosted-glass door panel. "Let's get on with it."

"Sure thing." Dwyer slid the retirement application from under the green-swirled marble and waved it like a pennant. "In other circumstances, I'd pass this on to the pension board with my blessing." He positioned the document at arm's length and read, "Michael Francis McKenna—joined the force in '21, appointed detective four years out of the academy, lieutenant since '37. Two commendations for meritorious conduct." Dwyer raised his gaze and his eyebrows. "One of 'em got you that lead in your hip…"

McKenna shrugged. "Doesn't slow me down much."

Dwyer eased back in his leather chair. "You've put in your time, Mike. Served with dedication. Earned your pension twice over, but—"

McKenna threw up a hand, palm out. "I got it. Lousy timing all around. The force will lose a shitload of recruits to the Army, and the rumor mill has it the mayor won't be requesting exemptions for any cops who're called up."

"Well." Dwyer arranged his features carefully. "That's bound to happen, even though Fiorello hasn't…Well…But, no—right now the department can't afford to lose any of its old hands."

"So, just give me that back, will ya?" McKenna leaned across the desk, plucked the paper from Dwyer's hand and, with one swift tear, destroyed his hard-won retirement.

The fishing shack on Shinnecock—gone. Hours reliving old times with Gayle, on those rare occasions when she managed to recognize him, gone. Gone, all gone. Only wartime duty remained, and who knew how long that might last? Six months? Ten years? The rest of his life?

Truth to tell, he'd been holding his breath the last few weeks. What if he caught another bullet just before he left the force? Who'd take care of Gayle then? Who'd go up to Harrison twice a week to wheel her around that pricey rest home's garden paths, trying to spark a few memories from her addled brain?

Memories of their first kiss at the Democratic Club dance.

Memories of the apartment on Vestry Street. Their twenty-odd years together.

Memories of him.

McKenna stood, breathing slowly and deeply. "That it, Cap?"

"One more thing." Dwyer's fingers curled around the folded *Times*.

McKenna sank back down. When was he going to learn to keep his trap shut? He'd read the paper on his way over to headquarters and wanted to kick himself. Behind that cute figure and those dark curls, Miss Cabby Ward was the same as all the crime-beat reporters he'd ever tangled with. To them, facts were just something to whip up into a scandal that would sell papers.

"What got into you, anyhow?" Dwyer unfolded the paper with a snap. "Blabbing to a reporter like that? Now that the Shelton case is in the public eye, you can bet the yellow press will jump in with both feet. Bernice has fielded over fifty calls this morning. Joe Schmoo wants to see this Jap dame charged, and the DA wants to know why you're letting grass grow under your feet."

Jesus, Mary, and Joseph—he'd been afraid of this. "Good police work takes time, Cap. You know that. And I'm not convinced—"

Dwyer made a chopping motion with the side of his hand. "What've ya got, so far?"

"Not a lot. No surprises in the autopsy—Shelton was hit with a heavy, blunt object. Crushed his skull and the brain tissue underneath. Blood stains on the floor and packing boxes show only his blood type—AB, one of the rare ones. And fingerprints are a wash—too many people have passed through that gallery to yield anything useful."

"Any candidates for the heavy, blunt object?"

McKenna shook his head. "We had a hammer—Doc says it doesn't match the wound. Odds are the killer took the weapon with him and gave it the toss. The boys are still looking."

"Him? This Masako Fumi's no him." Dwyer flicked the newspaper photo with his fingers, the one from the gallery brochure.

"Gotta say, she sounds like one dangerous dame—Lucrezia Borgia and Mata Hari rolled into one. Jap version, that is."

McKenna rubbed his chin. He saw where the captain was headed and didn't much care for it. He just wasn't convinced that the Jap artist had clonked Shelton. The careful arrangement of the corpse under Fumi's painting meant something. Sure. But he'd never seen a Japanese woman big and strong enough to bust a guy's skull, then heft his dead weight fifteen to twenty yards. Fumi was in this somehow. But not as the killer, he'd bet his bottom dollar.

"So, what's Fumi have to say for herself?" Dwyer's face was set in an expression that meant no good.

McKenna leaned forward, resting hands on knees. "Nothin'. The Feds won't let me at her, and her husband is stonewalling. Oakley swears his wife wasn't upset about Shelton closing her show and that she never left their apartment on Friday evening."

"You know the ropes. Lean on him a little."

"No dice, Cap. Oakley's got pneumonia, and his doctor's giving me a red light."

"And the FBI won't let you talk to Fumi?"

McKenna was glad he hadn't accepted a Danish. His breakfast cornflakes suddenly felt like iron filings grinding around in his stomach. "Jurisdiction." He almost spat the word. "The Feds aren't playing give and take with their charges out on Ellis Island. I took the ferry over and was denied entry at the gate. The brass at Foley Square aren't about to cooperate."

Dwyer selected a pencil from the leather cup and grinned. His hand hovered over a notepad. "Name of the agent in charge?"

"Bagwell. He's not returning calls."

"He will." The pencil scratched. Dwyer tore off the top page of the notepad and crossed to the frosted-glass door. A short conversation with Bernice ensued. Once he'd returned, Dwyer stood over McKenna and announced, "Give it twenty minutes and try again. I think you'll find Agent Bagwell more cooperative."

Not for the first time, McKenna was reminded that the homicide chief was a personal friend of Commissioner Valentine. On the wall over Dwyer's desk, there was a photo of the two together, shaking hands at some podium. There were other photos, too, nicely framed in gilt-trimmed black. McKenna's gaze landed on an eight-by-ten of Dwyer and party at a plush night club, the Stork maybe, or El Morocco. That little squirt next to him was the mayor—Fiorello, the Little Flower. While McKenna had worked his way through the ranks the old-fashioned way, clever Joe Dwyer had been playing the game: trading favors with powerful protectors and getting his name in Walter Winchell's column.

That's why Dwyer could run interference with the FBI and McKenna would retire—if he lived 'til the end of this god-damned war—at the rank of lieutenant. But there was no time for grousing, the captain was ushering him out of his office and into the secretary's.

The motherly Bernice looked on, beaming, while Dwyer pumped his hand. "Glad you decided to stay on, McKenna. I know I can count on you to get enough dirt on that slant-eye Fumi for the DA to run with."

"No guarantee it was her." McKenna cleared his throat.

"Look, Lieutenant" —Dwyer blinked and jutted his chin— "you got a case with an obvious suspect whose countrymen just catapulted us into war. Thanks to your running your mouth to some damned reporter, the whole city's watching. Grab a police launch, lights and sirens, the whole shootin' match, take a coupla uniforms and get back out to Ellis."

Boy, that little Jap makes one convenient suspect, McKenna thought, as he nodded noncommittally. He had a different take. His agenda was headed by finding the dame who'd hired Hermann Rupp to picket the Fumi show. And he still had to corner Nigel Fairchild for a chat. If the girlfriend who'd tossed the wine at Fumi's painting turned out to be Rupp's blonde, so much the better. By then, Brenner would have finished going through Shelton's papers, and some of the other boys would've checked on Lawrence Smoot and Desmond Cox's stories.

Little by little the case would come together. Cases almost always did, given enough patience. But how far would Dwyer's patience stretch?

◇◇◇

McKenna managed to get out of the chief's office without making any promises. He took the elevator up to Homicide only to be greeted with a stack of messages from the squad secretary.

Doris stared at him over the tops of her glasses, crimsoned lips in a disapproving curve. "The one on top is a reporter. From the *Times*, she claims. She's called three times."

Without giving it a glance, McKenna crumpled the message into a ball and banked it off the rim of the trash basket. It was the first thing he'd done that day that actually felt good.

"So what should I tell her when she calls again, Lute?"

He smiled grimly. "You tell Miss Ward I'm not taking calls."

The rest of the memos held no surprises. Three young detectives announced they were joining up, the newly-minted air raid warden ordered all lights out in unused offices, and the assistant chief had called a meeting to discuss a wartime shift roster. McKenna shoved the folded memos into a pocket, wondering how much actual police work could be accomplished in the midst of frantic war mobilization. He was no stonewalling isolationist, but, by god, he'd have been a lot happier if Roosevelt had been allowed to keep us out of the war.

These kids lining up at the recruiting center had no idea what hell they were in for. He did. He'd been in the last one.

"Lute?"

Doris was looking at him with raised eyebrows. There was no time for dwelling in the past. McKenna took a deep breath, tapped a finger on the secretary's desk. "Call down for a driver, would ya, hon. I gotta get moving."

Chapter Twenty-seven

"Won't take my calls?" Cabby wanted to throw the heavy telephone receiver through the nearest window, but the cord was too short, and Halper would probably dock her pay.

Clutching the phone so hard her knuckles ached, she made her voice as sweet as Louise's. "Then could I leave a message for Lieutenant McKenna?

"No? No calls or messages?" Cabby banged down the receiver. Fuming over a desk crowded with a typewriter and half-empty cups of coffee, she muttered, "Just who does this washed up flatfoot think he is—standing in the way of the public's right to know?"

And smack dab in the way of a second Cabby Ward triumph.

Her story had run that morning, center column of city news. Above the fold. Halper had actually come over to her desk and said, "Good job, Ward," in front of all the guys. Her article must have also caught the publisher's attention; as she'd crossed the lobby early that morning, Sulzberger had given her a nod. Arthur Sulzberger lifting his hat to Cabby Ward! Nothing had ever felt so exhilarating, not even that wild night in Joey Gaetano's Buick coupe. Until the last minute, that is, when he got religion, and pulled back—

Damn that McKenna! She'd assured Halper she had the detective eating out of her hand, and now he wouldn't even talk to her. She needed more dope to keep the story rolling.

Cabby grabbed her sweater from the back of her chair, jerking it so hard a button went flying. In five minutes, she was in the elevator. Another five and she was on the platform waiting for the IRT that would take her down to Worth Street and the medical examiner's office. She had a contact there—Ralphie Stolfo, a skinny clerk with a toothbrush moustache. She'd let him take her out for spaghetti a couple of times. Good ol' Ralphie would come through with some dope on the autopsy. Enough to squeeze out a second story, she hoped.

But when Cabby pushed through the door announcing NYC Office of Chief Medical Examiner, her heart dropped to her stomach. A middle-aged woman with a square, no-nonsense face sat unsmiling behind Ralphie's desk, watching Cabby cross the empty waiting area. The collar on her navy blue suit jacket was buttoned so tight it was a wonder she could breathe.

"Good morning," Cabby announced with more confidence than she felt. "I'm here to see Ralphie."

"Mr. Stolfo joined up," the woman replied in nasal tones.

Cabby folded her arms tightly, surprised at her sudden rush of emotion. Skinny Ralphie who was afraid to steal a kiss? Ralphie in the Army? Then she had another think. Of course, you didn't have to be Superman to tote a rifle. Lots of Ralphies—guys from the block, guys she went to grammar school with—would be going. If not now, soon.

"May I help you?" The receptionist glanced sideways, toward the blank sheets of paper and carbon waiting in her Remington Standard.

"Uh…I need some information on the Shelton case."

"Case number? Date and borough of death?"

Case number? Shit! "Arthur Shelton, the West Fifty-seventh Street art gallery murder. Maybe you read my article in this morning's *Times*." Cabby couldn't resist a proud smile.

The woman sat back and patted her springy, salt-and-pepper curls. "Reporter, huh?"

"Guilty as charged." Cabby flashed her press card. "But, really, all I need is a quick look at the doc's report. Ralphie always lets me take a peek."

The receptionist drew herself up. "Autopsy reports can only be requested by next of kin—in writing."

Silence reigned for several anxious seconds. Cabby could hear her heart beating against her eardrums.

Then an inner door opened, and a balding man in a gray flannel suit came to loom over the receptionist's desk. "Have you finished my letters, Mrs. Harding?"

The iron maiden suddenly turned to mush. The wheels of her desk chair squeaked as she swiveled to the typewriter stand. "Two of them, sir." Her eyes sought his approval as she handed over a manila folder. "I'll get to the last one just as soon as I finish with this…lady."

After a brief glance at the letters, boss man slammed the folder on the desk top. "I said in triplicate, not duplicate." He tore the neatly typed pages in half. "Do them again and, for god's sake, get it right this time."

Mrs. Harding paled.

Cabby waited until the man disappeared behind his door, then leaned over the desk. "Look, we're both working girls, right? I got a boss just like that one, and he's gonna kill me if I don't get the story." She smiled appealingly. "Help a girl out, whadda ya say?"

Mrs. Harding looked her right in the eye. She stood up, smoothed her skirt, and crossed to a metal file cabinet. She returned with a single stapled document, which she placed on the desktop within Cabby's reach. "I'm going to the ladies room for five minutes. I expect you'll have to leave before I get back." Then she retrieved a leather bag from her bottom drawer and walked out with head held high.

Cabby didn't bother with her notebook. The important stuff would glue itself to her brain. She started with the last page of the report. Manner of death: homicide. No surprise there. Cause of death: depressed skull fracture…intra-something hemorrhage…ugh! She flipped to the front page. Where was the time of death? She quickly digested a wad of medical jargon. Apparently, because Shelton's remains had been lying on a cool terrazzo floor, his internal temperature reading may have been skewed. The best Dr. Lefevers could do was to set a span. Friday evening, which she already knew—six p.m. to ten p.m.

Hmm, Cabby thought, as she hurried from the office, wonder if Louise can tell me where Masako Fumi was last Friday evening between six and ten.

Chapter Twenty-eight

She was in the windowless room with Agent Bagwell again. Cigar smoke again wafted straight up, like the smoke from a factory chimney on a windless day. Behind the battered wooden desk, the man shuffled through a sheaf of papers and pulled out something Masako recognized—the brochure from her show.

Oh, had the opening been only a week or so ago? Another life ago. Another world ago.

"Masako Fumi, these paintings of yours—they are very… modernistical, aren't they?" He thrust the brochure toward her.

"I suppose you might call them that." In the harsh fluorescent light, the colors had lost their vitality.

"Why do they contain Japanese writing?"

"It's tradition. The words and the image are one. Together they give the painting its soul."

"Soul? Do you mean they're part of your Shinto religion?"

She sighed. "Everything is part of my religion. Even you, Agent Bagwell."

He blinked and sat back. His wooden desk chair creaked. "I don't come into this, Miss Fumi. This is about you." He pulled out a piece of cheap five-and-dime paper and smoothed the wrinkles. He read it silently, then looked up at Masako. "Where you live, Miss Fumi, can you see the Hudson River from your windows?"

"Well, yes, but—"

"You see ships?"

"Yes, but—"

"Do you keep a record of them?"

"A record?"

"I know you know what I mean. Battleships. Troop ships. Military convoys." He retrieved the Shelton Gallery brochure and narrowed his eyes. Tapping the reproduction of "Lion After the Kill" with a heavy finger, he looked back up at Masako.

"It's code, isn't it? These Jap characters are perfect for encrypting information, aren't they?" He sat way back and the chair creaked again. "Miss Fumi, you don't have to tell me you've been spying for your father, Hisashi Fumi, Minister of Whatever—I already know."

Chapter Twenty-nine

Fifty-seventh Street, with its galleries, jewelers, and swanky restaurants, was a far cry from the Bowery, but McKenna's talk with Herman Rupp had led him right back to the Shelton Gallery. Desmond Cox's alibi had checked out—an all-male house party complete with amateur theatricals and drag revue—a lavender hell McKenna didn't even want to try to imagine. But it made Mr. Cox more valuable as an informant than a suspect.

McKenna handed him a list of names Brenner had made from the complaint letters in Shelton's file cabinet. "You familiar with any of these ladies?"

The gallery assistant scanned it and gave a knowing smile. "Sure. They all objected to showcasing Japanese art. Arthur showed me the letters as they came in."

"Oh, yeah? You know any of the gals personally?"

"I've met them all—here and at Arthur's social dos. Listen, you want some coffee? I just made it. French roast."

"Sure. Thanks. That would go down good." It was blustery out, and the wind howled west to east on the midtown cross streets, straight off the Hudson. This kind of day McKenna never could get warm, despite heavy overcoat and knitted scarf. Coffee would be just the ticket, though he wasn't quite certain what "French roast" meant. He settled onto one of the skinny chairs, trusting it would hold him.

Cox's coffee was hot and black and strong, and it came in a chartreuse cup that matched the settee. McKenna finished half the cup before he set it down next to his hat on the glass-topped table and leaned forward.

"This is gonna sound like a strange question, Mr. Cox, but could any of those dames possibly remind you of Veronica Lake? Blond hair and all?"

Desmond Cox snorted. "If you want to compare any of them to an actress, you'd do better to think along more ample lines, Marie Dressler, say." He held up an index finger. "Except for one. Mrs. Gregory De Forest has quite a lot of style—I'm told she worked at *Vogue* before she married her stodgy stockbroker hubby. Tiffy is actually the one who made the nasty scene at Masako's opening reception—along with Nigel Fairchild."

"Yeah." McKenna made a note. "You told me about that. Apparently she wrote a letter to the *Times*, too. Complaining about Jap exhibits at the Brooklyn Museum."

"That's Tiffy. But, Lieutenant…" The gallery assistant cocked his head. "You can't possibly believe Tiffy De Forest dispatched Arthur because of Masako's canvases. Now—someone who stole a march on her with a Paris gown, maybe…" He smiled at his own joke.

"What about hiring the lugs who picketed the Fumi show— would Mrs. De Forest be up to that?"

Cox thought a moment. "Hard to picture Tiffy crossing paths with men like that, but I suppose she could've gone slumming. Since she's been in Fairchild's thrall, her behavior has been erratic."

"Like?"

Cox waved an airy hand. "One hears rumors—a friend of mine spotted Tiffy up in Harlem one night, staggering out of a blues club with her evening gown ripped down the bodice."

"Drink taken?"

"Something taken."

"In Fairchild's company?"

"You bet."

McKenna made another note. He'd gone earlier to the America First headquarters on Madison Avenue for a brief word with Nigel Fairchild, but that silver-haired gentleman had stone-walled him.

"Time of national crisis. Crucial decisions to be made. Yes, yes, he knew Mrs. De Forest. A thoughtful and generous supporter of the cause. Friday night? Speaking date at the Metropolis Club. Sorry. Sorry. Phone's ringing. Long distance call. National headquarters. Sorry."

And an inner door closed behind him.

On a bulletin board in the reception area, a flyer bearing Fairchild's smiling mug backed up the dinner-speaker claim. McKenna would get back to him later, anyhow. Make him sweat.

Now he picked up the chartreuse cup, but held off drinking. "Okay, Mr. Cox. New topic. You notice any cracks in your boss' relationship with Lawrence Smoot?"

The gallery assistant's cup rattled against the saucer, sloshing coffee on the table-top. After some furious mopping with a brilliantly white handkerchief, Cox answered, "They seemed the same as ever. Lawrence besotted with Arthur, and Arthur using him for all he could get."

McKenna nodded. "That's how it was, huh?"

Cox shrugged. "That's the view from here. Lawrence had a multitude of contacts in the Asian art community. Of course, Lawrence did more for Arthur than make a few introductions."

"Go on." McKenna sipped at his coffee, watching Cox closely.

"How do you think a middle-class boy from Indiana managed to afford all this?" Cox made one of his dramatic gestures. "Lawrence came up with a loan. Seed money, he called it."

"How many seeds we talking about?"

"Twenty grand."

McKenna plunked his cup down. "I haven't seen any paperwork on that deal."

"You wouldn't have—it was purely a gentleman's agreement. I only heard about it in snips and snatches." Cox crossed one leg over the other and settled more deeply into the settee. "I find it pays to keep my ears open."

"You coulda told me about this yesterday." And so could Professor Smoot, McKenna thought to himself.

"Ah. But, Lieutenant, you didn't ask."

McKenna stood up, reached for his hat. "Okay, one more thing. Brenner says you two inventoried the gallery stock and found one missing item?"

"You mean, besides the Fumi paintings the G-men hauled away?" Cox followed the question with a snide grin.

McKenna gritted his teeth. He didn't like to be reminded that the damn Feds had gotten their way. Again. "Yeah, that's what I mean."

Desmond Cox rolled his skinny shoulders, amused.

This guy needs a good haircut and maybe a slap in the puss, McKenna thought. The coffee that had gone down smoothly now left a bitter taste in his throat.

"There's only one thing I can't account for—an antique Japanese brush pot. Jade. Arthur was about to send it to a collector in San Francisco, so he probably mailed it off. But, funny thing, the postage isn't noted in the expense roster. Arthur was meticulous about that sort of detail."

Jade. Brush. Pot. McKenna wrote, then looked up from his notebook. "Would it have gone in a box about so big?" He spread his hands to indicate the small wooden packing crate they'd found in the gallery trash. The one with traces of blood.

"Yeah," the gallery assistant said. "That's it."

Bingo.

Chapter Thirty

It was lunch hour, and the crowded elevator stopped at each floor of the Times building. Cabby barely noticed that she was squeezed between a cigar-puffing sports editor in a checked jacket and a scrawny copy boy with bad teeth whose hands wouldn't stay where they belonged. She was strategizing.

Her scrap of information about the time of death was something, but not near enough to wow Halper. To top her article in this morning's edition, she needed more.

She needed Louise.

Her roommate had found herself right in the middle of Masako Fumi Oakley's arrest Sunday night. She probably even had inside dope on the Shelton murder; after all, the gallery owner had been killed while dismantling Mrs. Oakley's art show. But Louise had avoided her last night and this morning, suddenly becoming chummy with Alicia. How could she get Louise to tell all? Really spill it? That girl could be so maddening, using the Southern drawl everyone found so charming to gush on and on, hiding more than she revealed.

Cabby inched away from copy boy's roving hands and waved Cuban smoke from in front of her face. Besides, could she use her roommate like that? Should she? Oh, she wanted another feature story so bad she could almost taste it—like a Coney Island hot dog with sauerkraut and mustard dangling just out of reach… But Louise was so…exasperating—she probably wouldn't tell Cabby anything.

When the doors popped opened on the great Gothic lobby, Cabby made sure to step on checked sportcoat's toes and gave the creep with the hands her well-practiced elbow jab, taking keen pleasure in his anguish. Then she launched herself into the stream of hungry workers heading toward the brass-framed revolving doors that would deposit them on Forty-third Street.

She'd almost reached those doors when she saw, from the back, a slender figure in a fashionable camel-hair swing coat with padded shoulders. Cabby stopped short. She knew that coat. Surely that was…

She rushed up, grabbed the woman by the arm, and spun her around.

"What the—" All big blue eyes and outrage. Then, "Cabby?"

"Louise! I was just thinking about you!" Cabby grabbed her roommate's hand and frowned. "What on earth are you doing here?" She took a second look—what on earth had happened to Louise? Despite the swanky coat, she looked bad—blotchy cheeks, lusterless pompadour sagging over her forehead, her lipstick—well, how on earth could a girl go out with no lipstick?

But Louise clearly had a set purpose in seeking her out. "Listen, Cabby, the reporter who wrote that article about the murder of Masako Oakley's art dealer? I've got to set him straight. He makes Mrs. Oakley look like a killer. Why did he have to put in that bit about the body being found beneath her painting?" She shuddered. "Who is this guy? I'm gonna give him the what-for. Can you put me in touch with him?"

Oh, shit! Cabby swallowed hard and patted her roommate's arm. "You look like you could use a good, hot lunch, Lou-lou. How about we talk at the Automat?"

"But—"

Cabby inserted her arm into Louise's and urged her toward the huge revolving doors. "Shh, shh, let's get some food first. You look like you're at your wits' end."

Chapter Thirty-one

The cold air hit Louise with the force of a Mack truck. This was the New York winter she'd been warned about. She shivered and pulled her coat tighter, but when she turned onto Broadway with Cabby, the bustling scene momentarily made her forget she was freezing.

Times Square had mobilized for war. Flags flew from every lamppost and window, the red, white, and blue a patriotic counterpart to the Christmas decorations and the garish signs. Some plate-glass windows had already been crisscrossed with tape to withstand damage from possible air attacks. On the corner, a Salvation Army band played "Silent Night." Louise could barely hear the gentle carol above the din of idling motors, blaring taxi horns, and vendors shouting their wares: "Chestnuts! Roasted chestnuts!"

For two cents, Louise would head for the subway and Brooklyn. She was suddenly too tired to contend with the pushy pedestrians gazing up to check the war news on the electric zipper or shoving through the crowds to Christmas shop while the stores still had goods to sell. But she had to talk to Cabby, and then Professor Oakley was counting on her to meet Alicia's law professor at four o'clock. She forced her heavy feet to keep up with the younger woman's strides.

The large red sign just ahead on Broadway announced: HORN & HARDART. Cabby elbowed past a lady in a fox stole and pushed into the Automat. Louise followed more slowly, gaping at the opulently decorated restaurant with its glass-fronted revolving food dispensers. A far cry from the friendly hash slingers behind the steam tables at the Blue Boar Cafeteria back home. And what was that wonderful aroma? Coffee, yes, but also baked beans and chicken and beef stew and…Suddenly starving, she took out her change purse and got busy. Soon Louise and Cabby each had a chicken pot-pie on a tray, and Cabby had added a slice of pumpkin pie. Louise held her ceramic mug under a shiny dolphin's-mouth spout. A nickel dropped in the slot produced a flow of steaming coffee.

Cabby slapped her tray on the first empty table and sat down. "Good," she said, "we don't have to share with some stranger."

Louise spread the paper napkin on her lap and got right to the point. "So what's the name of the reporter who wrote that horrible article?" She broke the crust of the pot-pie with her fork. Steam poured out and sauce oozed through the break in the pastry. Suddenly she was eating as if it were her first meal in a week. "You've got to write a story, to set the record straight—"

"Whoa, sister. One thing at a time." Cabby had started with her pumpkin pie. Her fork paused. "I've got some questions for you."

Louise drew a protesting breath, but Cabby mouthed on, "I've been dying to hear more about Mrs. Oakley's arrest. You fell asleep so fast last night, I didn't get a chance to ask you."

"Well, it was terrible. The G-men were brutes. My shoulder's still bruised from when they shoved me into the wall."

Cabby's fingers itched to get out her pad and pencil, but she knew nothing would shut Louise up faster than if she started taking notes. She'd just have to remember. "Did the agents find anything particularly interesting?"

Louise spoke between bites. "Hard to tell. It all happened so fast, and my patient went into shock. I was afraid I was going to lose him then and there. But this morning, I spent over an hour making notes on what we could both recall about the arrest." Louise hefted her purse from the empty chair beside her, pulled out a white, string-tied envelope, and tapped it with her finger.

"It's all right here. Every question the agents asked. Every journal they took. Every item and photograph."

"Is that so?" Cabby glued her eyes to the envelope. Louise obviously considered the professor a great scholar and his wife a living doll, but what did she really know about them? She'd only been on the case a few days, and this soft-hearted southern belle was surely naïve in the extreme. Cabby, on the other hand, knew that smoke signaled fire. With what she'd learned from McKenna and Halper, she suspected a four-alarmer. She forced her gaze away from the tantalizing envelope. "What are you going to do with that?"

"Well, I talked to Alicia. She's arranged for one of her law professors to help the Oakleys and he'll need this information. He's up on everything about civil liberties Did you know that for the past year or so the FBI's been keeping dossiers on a lot of people, not just Japanese but Germans and Italians, too?"

"Uh-oh. Germans, too?" For a few seconds, Cabby forgot the notes. "You think they'll come after Helda?"

"Who knows? Alicia says they're looking at anyone they think will constitute a threat to the nation's peace and safety."

"Nah. Not Helda," Cabby said, twisting her paper napkin into a bow. "Now, a Jap I can see. This may sound cynical, but, hey, it's easier for the government to nab someone who looks like an alien than someone who looks like your neighbor."

Louise slapped the envelope on the table. "Masako Oakley is no security threat. She's an artist, for crying out loud."

"Well, they must think they have something on her. They've detained about four-hundred Japanese from Manhattan alone, but I can't imagine they'd bother over nothing."

Shredding the napkin, Cabby thought about Helda. Would G-men actually arrest the landlady because she'd been born in Germany? What would happen to that cute kid, Howie? As a matter of fact, what would happen to the boarding house? Would it have to close? Oh, no! She couldn't move back home—where would she live? Cabby coughed to dislodge a lump that had suddenly blocked her throat.

Louise picked up her fork and trailed it through congealing gravy. "Mrs. Oakley told me her father was a diplomat for the Japanese government."

Abruptly, Cabby glanced up. "That would certainly be a reason to monitor her."

Louise frowned. "Masako has had nothing to do with her family for…years."

"Hmm." What a story! If only Cabby could get a peek inside that envelope.

Louise slid the notes into her purse, which she set back on the empty chair between the two women. She felt her neck muscles relax, then her tight shoulders. Cabby might be brash to the point of being annoying, but she was trying to help. Louise considered a second cup of coffee. A slice of pie might hit the spot, too. She glanced toward the dessert dispensers.

But, first, "Cabby, I want that reporter's name."

"Uh—so." Cabby leaned forward, eager to squeeze something more out of her roommate before Louise caught onto her. "That painting they found the corpse beneath? 'Lion After the Kill'? A pretty vicious title for a piece of artwork. What's the dirt on that?"

"The dirt?" Louise froze, appetite gone. She didn't like the avid look on her roommate's face.

Then it struck her.

"You wrote that story! That's why you don't want to give me the name of the reporter! You…you…You don't care about helping Mrs. Oakley. You think she killed that man!"

Cabby glanced around. They were drawing curious stares. A sailor in dress whites stopped at their table, grinning. She scowled at him, and he moved on. "Louise, don't you realize what great material this is? There's obviously a link between Masako Fumi and Arthur Shelton's murder. Could she have been upset about—"

As angry as she'd ever been in her life, Louise jumped up and grabbed her bag. "Cabby, I can't believe I trusted you." She turned on her heel and hurried toward the exit.

Cabby followed, pulling on her tweed coat. At the revolving doors they stared at each other for a frosty moment as the Automat's patrons pushed in around them. Then Louise spun her way out onto the now-snowy sidewalk.

Cabby was right on her heels.

Louise jerked her gloves on, and yanked the straps of her unwieldy purse over her shoulder. Then she pivoted and stared Cabby straight in the eye. "I'm simply furious with you. I've never known a girl so determined to make it in a man's world—whatever the cost. To tell you the truth, I find that kind of ambition highly unattractive."

Cabby went rigid with anger. Just as Louise turned to walk away, the string-bound envelope fell from her purse to the pavement. Automatically Cabby swooped it up and held it out, but her roommate was already ten paces ahead.

"If you don't watch out," Louise threw over her shoulder. "You're going to turn into one of these horrid career girls no man will ever want to marry."

Stung, Cabby stuffed the envelope into her own bag. Her heart hammering in her chest, she caught up with Louise.

Businessmen hurried past them in wool topcoats and dark fedoras. Secretaries who'd forgotten their rubber overshoes skidded on the slushy pavement. Someone jostled Louise so hard she staggered and almost fell. She looked around, expecting an apology, but everyone just hustled on by. That's right—she was in New York now.

Suddenly sirens wailed from every direction.

"Oh, no," she said, "not a fire. Not in this terrible cold."

"This is no fire," Cabby responded, wide-eyed. The blasts repeated themselves. One long, one short. Pedestrians halted, some confused, some terrified. Then the sirens' wail was joined by the whooo-whooo of fire trucks and the oooga-oooga of police cars. Cacophony. For an endless few seconds the Times Square crowd was absolutely paralyzed.

A man in a helmet and a khaki trench coat shouted, "Air Raid! Everybody seek shelter!" But very few people moved.

They just stood there, en masse, faces shocked, looking up at the overcast sky.

It sounds like the end of the world, Louise thought. Although newsreels had shown horrific scenes of bombing raids in London and Paris, she hadn't realized the sheer panicked terror the warnings would bring. The immediacy of it in her body. Her heart was cold in her chest. She could hardly breathe. Was she going to die right here on Broadway?

But Cabby just stood there listening, staring up at the sky. She shrugged. "Looks okay to me. Must be a drill." She started walking again, keeping her bag tucked under her arm.

Then the continuous blast of the all-clear sounded, and everyone snapped back to normal.

New Yorkers! Louise thought, and raised her arm to hail a taxi.

Chapter Thirty-two

Sun Rose lipstick, Tangee compact, wrinkled handkerchief, roll of wintergreen Lifesavers, bank passbook, three keys, change purse, notebook, address book, black knitted gloves, ticket stub from "Unfaithfully Yours" at the Paramount, two unused bus transfers.

As Louise's cab sped down Broadway toward the Brooklyn Bridge, she had the entire contents of her bag spread out on the back seat. But she couldn't find the envelope with the notes she'd made about the FBI raid. Darnation! She remembered stuffing it in her bag as she'd walked out of the Automat with Cabby. After that, nothing. She groaned—she'd probably lost it in the air raid drill.

Oh, wait! Just before the alarms sounded, someone had jostled her—hard. She remembered stumbling—almost falling. Could that have been a deliberate shove rather than just some random bump?

Then she had a wild thought—could an FBI agent have been following her? Could he have overheard her tell Cabby about the notes? Did the FBI not want any details of Masako Oakley's arrest recorded?

No. She was being paranoid. She'd been clumsy, that's all, and the notes had fallen to the pavement. They'd probably been kicked into the gutter by now.

But, damn. She'd need them when she met with Abe Pritzker. If all went well, Louise would accompany him to Ellis Island to "monitor Mrs. Oakley's emotional wellbeing," as Mr. Pritzker had told Alicia he intended to phrase the need for the nurse's presence. "Don't worry," Alicia had soothed her on the phone, "the Great Man will get you in. He knows the ropes." She laughed. "Let's just hope he doesn't find himself hung with one of them someday."

The "Great Man" wouldn't be very impressed if Louise had failed to follow his instructions. They passed City Hall. She rubbed her stomach, absolutely sick. Professor Oakley was too ill to relive that night again—she'd simply have to reconstruct the notes from memory. Thank god she'd perfected her recall in anatomy drills in nursing school. If she could still name the twenty-seven bones of the human foot, she ought to be able to at least summarize notes she'd written only that morning.

Louise plucked the pen and notebook from the heap of items, then tumbled everything else back into her handbag. Fortunately, she had a silent taxi driver for a change. She sat back against the cushioned seat and began to write.

Chapter Thirty-three

Helda was annoyed. It was already dark, and Howie hadn't come home from school. The cake had been iced, the meat loaf was in the oven, the cans of peas open, and where was that boy? She paid her son fifty cents a week to stoke the furnace, serve the boarders, peel the dinner potatoes, and complete other chores. He usually did as he was told. But here it was a quarter to five, and no potatoes peeled.

Ach! Every day she worked her fingers to the bone to support them both. If that boy thought he was going to run the sidewalks with his school friends he'd have to think again.

She snatched up a large bowl and pushed out of the door onto the small kitchen porch. The potatoes were low in the barrel, beginning to sprout. Enough for dinner, though. She heaped the bowl high, reentered the kitchen, clicked on the radio, and began to scrub the spuds with a stiff brush.

She was halfway through the pile when the newscast came on. Both potato and brush splashed into the sink. "Government officials today announced the detention of German residents nationwide. In New York, the arrests ranged from Yorkville pretzel makers to an engineer and his family living at the Waldorf Astoria."

Ach du lieber! Howie! Was that why he was late? He was arrested? Panicked, Helda rushed from the kitchen. Miss Rosen was in the parlor reading a thick textbook. "Have you seen my

Howie? He does not come home from school today, and now I hear the police pick up Germans all over the city."

Alicia jumped up, thumb buried in the book to hold her place. "I've been sitting here for at least an hour, and he hasn't come in." Her tone was sober. "What would Howie do if he was stopped on the street? He's a hot-headed young man—"

"He is not a young man—he's a boy—fourteen years old, *mein Gott*!" Helda's hands fluttered, and she twisted the skirt of her apron. "It must be his…he can't be punished for his… for his father's…" She suddenly felt lightheaded and choked on her words.

Miss Furnish, the girl the others called *die Maus*, poked her head around the entrance to the parlor and stood there, staring round-eyed.

Alicia said, "If the G-men have Howie, they'll be here after you—"

A sudden heavy pounding at the door and the three women gasped.

"Run, Helda," Alicia whispered, giving her a little push with her free hand. If they found the landlady gone, maybe they'd just move on to the next poor soul on their list. She'd tell them Helda was out. She didn't mind lying. Her parents had told her time and again—in bad times, do what you must to survive.

But Helda wasn't moving.

"We'll cover for you. Out the back—quick." Alicia nodded toward the kitchen, but Mousie stumbled into the parlor and blocked the landlady's way. What a dope!

The fierce banging came again. Helda felt as if her feet were buried in concrete. This must be just like the Gestapo raids back home! She took a deep breath and pulled away from *die Maus*. Resolve straightened her spine. "No, Miss Rosen. Running is no good. That's coward's way. Whatever it is, I must face it."

She pulled off her apron, flung it on the sofa, crossed the floor in determined strides, and yanked the door open.

Patrolman Drury, the local beat cop, held an agitated Howie by the arm. "Is this little hero yours?"

"*Jah!*" Helda exclaimed, flabbergasted. She grabbed the boy in a fierce embrace. "This is why you come? Where was he?"

"Get off, Ma!" Howie struggled in her arms, but she held him tight.

Alicia drew close to Mousie. She whispered, "What the hell were you doing? Trying to get Helda arrested?"

"It's only a Brooklyn cop," Mousie replied.

"But we didn't know that."

Mousie tugged at her baggy sweater. "Guess I'm just clumsy. I wasn't trying to cause trouble."

The friendly cop was rubbing a meaty thumb over Howie's hairless jaw. "He was trying to enlist over at the Bushwick recruiting center. Good try, lad, but you can't pass for eighteen."

"Enlist?" Helda looked horrified. "You're just a boy."

Howie glared at her. "You lied, Ma." He shoved her away.

She stumbled. His words were a knife in her heart.

Drury grabbed the boy's arm, serious now. "Now, see here, son..."

Howie shook him off and jumped back. Helda couldn't believe it. This child—her son—defying a police, facing down his mother, holding back tears, shouting, "You've been lying ever since Papa left."

"What you say?" Helda's hand drifted to her fevered cheek.

Howie balled his hands into fists, breathing hard. "You told me Papa went to California—but he didn't! He went with the Bund—"

"*Halt die Schnauze!*" she barked. Then she slapped him.

Howie went dead white and silent.

A nightstick appeared in Drury's hand. He beat it into his palm and nailed both Helda and Howie with an icy stare. It was as if, with those three words of German, they had both become the enemy.

Alicia spoke up. Somebody had to calm this crisis down. "Officer, this is a family matter. Helda can take care of it, I'm sure."

Helda swallowed hard, then stepped between Howie and the patrol cop. "Yes, I take care...Please."

"Well…" Drury said, slowly lowering his stick. He fixed Howie with a withering gaze. "You mind your mother, son. I don't want to find you at any Brooklyn recruiting center again." He slapped the stick in his hand and transferred his gaze to Helda. "And don't forget I'm keeping my eye on…both of you."

"Howie will do right. I promise no trouble here." Helda nodded vigorously. Then she jerked her chin at the boy. "Go to your room. Now."

"But, Ma, I gotta do the potatoes."

"*Raus mit du!*"

Howie started toward the stairs, head down, dragging his feet. "I don't care," he muttered under his breath. Only his mother was close enough to hear. "Nobody's gonna keep me from joining up. Krauts, Japs—I'll kill 'em all."

Helda's heart turned to lead.

Chapter Thirty-four

The Coast Guard ferry bounced off the choppy harbor waves. Across the strip of dark water, the lights of Ellis Island came on one at a time. Louise knew that several hundred "enemy aliens" had been transported there. So far, the word "imprisoned" was not being used. The official term was "detained," as if the inmates were merely inconvenienced, something akin to being slowed by slushy streets in rush-hour traffic.

Louise braced her feet and shrank back against the ferry's wooden bench, grateful that she wasn't prone to seasickness; the godawful New York cold gave her enough to contend with. The blustery wind cut right through her coat and threatened to send her pork-pie hat flying at any moment.

Her companion didn't seem at all fazed by the rough crossing. Abe Pritzker was a tall, rangy man who looked nothing like the sort of miracle worker he'd proven to be so far. Louise associated miracles with the flawless, floating-on-clouds Jesus pictured in the family bible back home, but the only thing Mr. Pritzker had in common with Jesus was that he, too, was a Jew. Though hatless, he leaned over the ferry's railing with harbor spray freezing on the tips of his shaggy hair, grinning like a lunatic as he gazed at the rapidly approaching brick walls and pepper-pot domes of the detention center. His only concession to the raw wind was the overcoat collar turned up around his ears.

Abruptly, Louise snatched her hat off and stuck her icy hands inside. Then her hair caught the wind and beat against her cheeks like frozen twigs.

She sighed. She'd never been so cold in her life. The temperature had plummeted with the sun. Tomorrow—for certain—she'd make time to buy herself some real Yankee winter clothes.

Abe Pritzker wasn't a type of man Louise knew anything about. His broad features, leathery skin, and unkempt dark locks wouldn't have inspired confidence if she didn't know he'd bullied Agent Bagwell into allowing him an interview with Masako Oakley. She'd been amazed when he'd followed that trick with screwing an immediate meeting time out of the notoriously unaccommodating immigration authorities who were in charge of the internees' confinement.

Now the attorney joined her on the bench. Above the combined din of the boat's engine and the rhythmic crashing of its hull on the waves, he yelled, "Where are you from, Nurse Hunter?"

Surprised by the question, Louise gulped in a blast of frigid air. "Louisville," she stammered. "That's in Kentucky."

He laughed. "'Mistah Pree-it-zkeh,' you said when you knocked on my office door. I could tell right off you were a Southerner. But I mean your family. Everyone in this country has roots somewhere else, and last time I checked, Kentucky was still part of the U. S. of A." He waved a large, reddened hand. "We came from Lithuania. My parents first stepped on American soil right there on Ellis Island, in 1909."

Louise didn't think she'd ever met anyone from Lithuania before. She didn't even know where it was. "Were you born here, Mr. Pritzker?"

"Just barely." He laughed again. "When they got off the boat, Ma was big-as-a-house pregnant with me. She says she squeezed her legs together until they reached Manhattan—just to make sure I'd be born an American." He cuffed her shoulder. "But say, can the Mr. Pritzker stuff. Okay? I'm Abe, just Abe."

Louise winced from both the cold and his playful blow, but managed to raise a smile anyway. Abe was different, for sure—so blunt, so outspoken. So in need of a barber's shears. But if Abe Pritzker could do something for Mrs. Oakley when everyone else had refused to even try, she'd just have to get used to his brash ways. "Okay," she replied. "Abe."

"So, where is your family from, Louise?"

"Oh, we're just Americans. I've heard my grandmother mention England. Scotland, too. But that would have been a good two hundred years ago. Maybe more."

Abe held her gaze as if he expected further revelations. His big frame blocked the worst of the wind, making her feel small and protected, but not loosening her tongue. Finally he said, "So, not Jewish, then. Didn't think so. Too bad." He winked. "Well, maybe someday you'll tell me what brings a Southern beauty north to nurse cantankerous New Yorkers." He finished on a wide smile that caused Louise's heart to give an unanticipated thud.

She felt a flush climb her neck. This wasn't the way it was supposed to go. After Pres' defection she'd sworn off men, at least until she had a steady job and more security. Until a time when her life wouldn't feel so…out of control. Even then, Abe Pritzker would hardly be the kind of man she'd want to…keep company…with. No, not at all. Her breath was smoother now. She cleared her throat. "We're almost across. Perhaps you could tell me what you plan to do for Mrs. Oakley."

"All right." He sank back, hands dangling between his legs. If he was miffed, he didn't show it. "This won't be an easy case. The notes you made for me will be a help, but I saw that piece in this morning's *Times*…"

Louise twisted her fingers inside her hat. A scurrilous piece, thanks to her conniving little roommate.

But Abe was continuing, "Taking everything into consideration, Masako Fumi Oakley has at least three strikes against her. Number one—she's a civilian enemy national, the daughter, actually, of a minister in Tojo's government. Over the past several years, Hisashi Fumi has been a strident voice for Japan's mauling of Chinese territory."

"But Masako's husband is a respected professor at a prominent university," Louise burst out. "Shouldn't that count for something?"

"He's a professor who's lived in Japan." Abe gave her a straight, serious look.

"As a boy, yes. His parents were missionaries."

"And as an adult he's traveled frequently in the region and devotes the bulk of his scholarly work to Japanese history. Before Hitler turned Europe upside down and Japan jumped on *der Fuhrer's* coattails, Dr. Oakley was pursuing plans to set up an independent Institute for Asian Studies, drawing experts from around the world."

Louise scraped a strand of wind-blown hair from her mouth. That hadn't been in the notes she'd transcribed—and then rewritten. "How did you find that out so quickly?"

Abe shrugged. "I have cadre of eager student volunteers who love poking their noses into injustice. They're great little researchers."

"Students like Alicia Rosen?"

He nodded with gusto. "Miss Rosen is one of the best." Then after a lop-sided smile, he added half under his breath, "I'll have to be sure to thank her for bringing Louise Hunter to my attention."

Louise was glad to feel the ferry bump the deck. Or was that little thump her heart again? Why did she always have to be so susceptible to unsuitable men?

She and the attorney lined up to disembark with a few other bundled-up stalwarts. "What about the other two strikes against Mrs. Oakley?"

"Oh, number two is her artwork adorned with Japanese calligraphy."

Louise opened her mouth to protest, but Abe held up a finger. "Try to see this from the FBI's viewpoint. The calligraphy could contain sensitive information. Perhaps, along with the abstract

shapes in the artwork and maybe even the choice and arrangement of the colors, it could contain coded material."

"That's nonsense!"

"I think so, too." He raised bushy eyebrows. "But Special
Agent Bagwell has ordered all the paintings that were shown
at the Shelton Gallery taken away for thorough study. He
also thinks it's possible the text could be propaganda aimed at
encouraging enemy aliens living in America."

"Oh, come on," Louise responded in a withering tone.

A seaman unhooked a chain, and everyone in line shuffled
forward. Bumped by an angry looking man in a long overcoat,
Louise caught her toe on the gangplank and lost her footing.
Abe reacted quickly, clasping her around the waist and setting
her back on balance. Through her embarrassment, her nostrils
picked up the subtle sweetness of cherry tobacco. Ah, Abe was
a pipe smoker, like her father.

She murmured her thanks, then continued, "I just don't
see how Mrs. Oakley's paintings could do a spy or concealed
partisans any good."

"It really doesn't matter if her paintings actually help the
enemy or not. It's her intent that matters. One man's paean to the
beauties of the countryside is another man's propaganda. See?"

"Yes," Louise agreed with a sinking heart. She recalled Agent
Bagwell's suspicions based on a perfectly innocent vase of chrysanthemums. How much more could he make of Masako's
enigmatic art work?

"Strike three," Abe said, striding along with a grave look, "is
the murder of Shelton, the gallery owner."

She turned to look into the attorney's deep-set brown eyes.
"But, Abe, she didn't—"

He interrupted with a hand on her shoulder. "So you told
me on the phone. And again in my office. And again in the car
on the way down to the Battery. And I'm willing to accept your
assessment of her character unless I learn otherwise, but you'll
never persuade Agent Bagwell. He's decided that the Japanese
are an inherently greedy, evil, underhanded race, and nothing's

going to change his mind. Unfortunately, recent events haven't proven him wrong."

"Has he questioned Mrs. Oakley about the murder?"

"I doubt it. I got the impression it would suit Bagwell's purposes to leave the accusation hanging until after she's had to face the Enemy Alien Board. That taint of suspicion could tip the scale toward the government's side. If the cops fingered somebody else for that murder, it would sure pull the rug out from under Bagwell."

"Then we'll just have to make sure they find the real killer," Louise said with a sharp nod.

Abe heaved a deep sigh.

Chapter Thirty-five

Lieutenant McKenna was in his office writing reports for the Captain. Or, rather, with a leaky fountain pen, he was scrawling notes that Doris would type up into a meticulous, grammatical, beautifully spelled report to send to Captain Dwyer's secretary. Bernice would make certain the Captain read it and acted on it, and then would file it somewhere at the tip of her fingers where she could find it instantly upon request. McKenna knew that nothing at Headquarters would ever get done if it weren't for the secretaries. He had a sneaking suspicion that a good percentage of those girls were smarter than he was. Doris, for sure.

Not that he'd ever let her know it—or anyone else, either.

But Doris had gone home early, and darkness was gathering at winter speed when his phone rang. He picked up the bulky black receiver. "Yeah? McKenna here."

It was Doris' counterpart from the Feds. Agent Bagwell had authorized a permit for Lieutenant Michael McKenna to interview Masako Oakley at the Immigration Detention Center on Ellis Island. She'd appreciate it if he would come pick it up at Foley Square before the FBI office closed at five.

McKenna slammed the receiver down and glanced at the wall clock. Holy shit! 4:48!

He grabbed his hat and took off, cursing the federal pencil pushers every limping step of the way.

Chapter Thirty-six

"Fifteen minutes," said a broad-shouldered, deep-voiced matron. "No physical contact. No passing of material without prior permission." Her thin lips fired the regulations with crisp precision.

The matron's rubber-soled shoes squeaked as she ushered Louise and Abe into a large, high-ceilinged room with a wooden counter running across it; a foot-high barrier on that counter separated internees from visitors. Abe Pritzker pulled out one of the chairs for Louise, then sat next to her.

They waited. And waited. An odor of boiled cabbage began to permeate the air. Louise wrinkled her nose. From the corner of her eye, she caught a streak of movement in the corner of the vast room. She clutched the attorney's arm. "Was that a rat?"

He didn't bother to look. "Probably."

Then an armed guard materialized and took a wide-legged stance behind them.

"Now we're getting somewhere," Abe whispered out of the side of his mouth.

Through a far door, the matron led Masako Oakley into the room.

Louise gasped—the Japanese woman was so pale. She wore the same gray trousers and blue sweater she'd left the apartment in two days earlier. Her hair was dull and scraped back in a ponytail. Slumping onto her chair, she seemed to take no notice of her visitors. She merely bowed her head and directed her gaze downward.

"Mrs. Oakley?" Louise said.

Masako started, and her eyes suddenly came to life, gleaming black.

"Nurse Louise." Her hands fluttered. She drew herself up, ignoring Abe Pritzker. "Oh, no! My Robert. He is dead?"

"No, no." Damn these people! Even if some detainees did present a danger, they at least deserved news of their families. Even a convicted murderer was entitled to that small comfort. "Professor Oakley is holding his own. Please don't worry. He has round-the-clock care, and Dr. Wright stops by twice a day."

"It's true?"

Louise nodded. "I wouldn't lie to you."

"Thank god for that," Masako whispered. She hung her head again and covered her face with her hands. Her thin shoulders began to shudder.

Louise continued, the words rolling out, "He'll be better once he knows you're all right. You're not ill, are you? Are you eating? Sleeping? How are they treating you?"

The Japanese woman went very still. "They ask me questions, over and over. I do not have…answers that please them."

Abe leaned forward, focusing on Masako as if she were the most important client he would ever have. "Mrs. Oakley, I'm Abe Pritzker, an attorney here to help you at your husband's request. Do you understand?"

She furrowed her brow. "Can you arrange my release? I must get back to Robert."

"I hope so, eventually. But it may take some time." An apologetic shrug seemed to be an effective part of his physical vocabulary. "I'll be brief. The government has set up Hearing Boards consisting of prominent citizens. These boards will try the cases of aliens who've come under suspicion. That's you. However, they haven't announced when the hearings will begin, we don't know what the charges will be, and you're not allowed the presence of an attorney when you face them."

Masako went even paler. Louise wanted to take her hand over the partition, but was stopped by the guard's gimlet gaze.

Abe continued, "Your own testimony will be crucial in over-riding the FBI's accusations. You will need to convince them you're no threat to America. All I'm allowed to do is assemble supporting documents for your file. Is there anyone besides your husband who could vouch for your loyalty?"

"Surely this Board would respect the word of Robert's colleagues—Lawrence Smoot and Lillian Bridges. And of George Wright, our family doctor." Her voice cracked as Abe noted the names in slanted printing. "Agent Bagwell thinks I'm a spy—"

"Okay, I have to ask"—Abe drummed impatient fingers on the countertop—"in the papers they took away from your apartment, the FBI won't find anything to support that theory, will they? Personal letters to or from Japan? Japanese newspapers or magazines you've subscribed to? Memberships in Japanese organizations?"

Her eyes grew round. "Nothing. I was three years old when I left Japan. And I—" She frowned. "The government men took things from the apartment?"

Abe nodded. "Quite a few things. Books, photos, maps."

"Those are Robert's. He must be furious." Masako threw Louise a despairing look.

"His concern for you overshadows everything else," the nurse answered. "That's why you must answer Mr. Pritzker's questions. So we can get you home."

But Masako had something else on her mind. Her hands fluttered to her face—dry leaves stirring in a breeze. "They didn't touch my paintings, did they?"

Abe loosened his tie and sighed audibly. His hair, uncombed after the windy crossing, hung ragged around his bony face. "Your paintings…" Abe stared at her for a few seconds, then said flatly, "The G-men took your paintings away. They think the captions might be an attempt to communicate with Japanese nationals."

"Yes. I've tried to explain that the texts are short poems inspired by the themes of the paintings."

"Give me a for instance."

Masako shut her eyes, sighed helplessly. "I can't think."

"Try. If the poems are absolutely innocuous, translations might convince the board that they have no propaganda or security value."

Masako didn't answer. She looked like a drowning woman.

Scarcely knowing where the words came from, Louise blurted out, "Cling new bird against cold wind. Old branches blossom. Cherry! Pink, then green."

A smile altered Masako's expression. "That's from the painting in our living room. I didn't realize you'd paid such close attention."

"It's beautiful. I was trying to understand," Louise replied, feeling she'd thrown the Japanese woman a lifeline.

As Masako nodded deeply, Abe raised his eyebrows at Louise. "You read Japanese?"

Masako answered instead, "That particular series of paintings included English translations, but the works Arthur chose to display were from a later series in my studio embellished with *Shodo* only. Please"—her folded hands hit the counter with a dull thud—"tell me my studio is not invaded. My paintings—they are as precious to me as children." She tapped the place over her heart.

"Studio?"

"Yes. On Bleecker Street."

"This is the first I've heard of a studio. Bagwell didn't mention it." Abe crossed one long leg over the other, lassoed his knee with his arms. "But then, like every other government facility, Foley Square has been in chaos…Hmm. It's possible they've overlooked it."

Masako glanced over at the guard, then lowered her voice. "Please. Someone must secure my paintings right away." Her eyes brimming with tears, she turned toward Louise.

So did Abe. He said, "If we can get that poetry translated, it would help a great deal."

Louise dithered. "I…Well…" Yes, she was working as Professor Oakley's assistant now, but she didn't know anything about how to transport art work.

"I can help. I'll hire a van," Abe encouraged.

"Robert will give you the key," Masako whispered.

"But what would I do with the paintings? I can't take them back to the apartment. They wouldn't be safe there."

Masako thought for a moment. "Have you met our friend, Lillian Bridges? She has plenty of room, and the authorities would never bother her—*her* ancestors came to America three centuries ago."

As if from a far distance Louise heard her voice agreeing. "Yes...all right...I know Professor Bridges wants to help. If your paintings are still at Bleecker Street, I'll see that she gets them safely."

"Bless you." Masako's face lit up for an instant, then darkened as she stared past Louise and the lawyer. "Who is that? Does he come for me?"

Louise and Abe turned at the same time. A man in a well-worn, dark overcoat was striding across the waiting room. His gait rolled like that of an old ship's captain, and his unbuttoned coat flapped with each step.

"A black crow." Masako's words were thick and slow. "Another carrion bird come to pick my bones." She ducked her forehead to her hands.

The guard hurried to intercept the newcomer, who paused to show his badge and identification card.

"Oh, no." Louise gripped the attorney's arm.

"You know that man?" His eyes were mere slits.

"He's Lieutenant Michael McKenna," she whispered. "He came to the Oakleys' apartment on Monday."

"McKenna? Homicide, right?"

"Yes."

"Mrs. Oakley, say nothing—" Abe whirled toward Masako, but the Japanese woman wasn't there. Head down, shoulders slumped, she was gliding back the way the matron had brought her.

Chapter Thirty-seven

Cabby looked across the bedroom to where her carefully arranged tweed coat hung on the coat rack. Beneath the coat was her handbag, and in the bag was the large envelope containing Louise's notes on the Oakley arrest. She watched as Louise fell into bed without even cold-creaming her face.

She and her roommate had barely spoken since the air raid drill in Times Square. Was it only because of their argument that the nurse was giving her the deep freeze? Could she suspect… No—Cabby thought not. If she was any judge of character, Louise had weightier problems on her mind than lost notes. First, she'd missed dinner, and it was Tuesday, German chocolate cake night. Now, it seemed, Louise had fallen into an exhausted sleep within seconds.

Cabby had qualms about what she planned to do, but, dammit, she was a journalist. It was wartime and the public deserved to know about enemies in their midst. Cabby had a feeling this story was going to be a doozy, well worth a boat load of sacrifice. Even friendly relations with her roommate.

Down in the parlor the other girls were listening to the radio and talking. When the Kay Kyser Orchestra came on with "Praise the Lord and Pass the Ammunition," the idle chatter stopped and Cabby's housemates sang along. Nonetheless, Cabby waited until they'd all gone to bed and the house was silent before she tiptoed across the room.

Slipping down the back staircase into the kitchen, Cabby laid her supplies out on the table: notepad, bottle of ink, fountain pen, and her roommate's notes. She couldn't do much with the murder angle until she talked to McKenna again, so she focused on Masako Fumi Oakley's arrest and detention. She detailed the G-men's questions that Louise had transcribed, also the exhaustive search of the Oakley apartment. She concluded with the agents' apparent interest in the Japanese characters scattered through the artist's sketchbooks and paintings.

There. Finished. Cabby would go into the office early, type the piece up, and get it to Halper by nine.

She crept up the backstairs of the now silent house, donned her green-plaid flannel pajamas, and went to bed across from a steadily snoring Louise.

Nothing was more important than getting the story. Right?

Chapter Thirty-eight

Wednesday, December 10, before dawn

It got worse and worse every time they brought her to this windowless place of cigar smoke and florescent lights and scritch, scritch. The matron had awakened her and led her down darkened corridors. She was exhausted and numb, as though moving through an anesthetic haze.

"Miss Fumi, do you know that Arthur Shelton is dead?" Agent Bagwell eyed her, as a cobra watches a mouse.

"Dead? Arthur?" Not Robert? "Last time I saw Arthur, he was in perfect health."

The FBI man moved around the desk. He hung over her. His body smelled of meat. Sickening.

"Did you kill him?" He poked a stubby finger in her face.

Kill him? She couldn't be hearing him right. First she was some sort of spy? Now a killer?

"Look at me, Miss Fumi." Bagwell straightened as she mechanically complied. "The New York City Police think you had a very good reason to kill Arthur Shelton."

Masako's hand went to her forehead. "I don't understand."

"He was closing down your gallery show. You saw that as a betrayal." Bagwell pronounced the word with relish.

She tried to gather her thoughts. Her show—her solo show—she'd been thrilled, but now it held little meaning. "Not a betrayal. I was upset—over everything. Just upset."

"Upset? Enraged is more like it." But, then, suddenly, Agent Bagwell went back to sit behind the desk. The deep lines etched by his mouth squared as he attempted a smile. If she were to paint that smile, she would compose it in right angles. "I could be your friend, you know."

You are lying. She didn't think she said it aloud. "My... friend?"

"You bet. The New York City police are convinced that you murdered Arthur Shelton. They intend to arrest you for homicide, but you're safe as long as you're in our custody. Don't you see?"

Masako touched slim fingers to her eyes. She yearned suddenly to be invisible.

"Don't you see?" he repeated. "The police will convict you and send you to the electric chair. You'll fry like bacon on a griddle."

See? She saw nothing. She tried not to see him. She imagined a thick pane of frosted glass before her eyes.

"But I could arrange it so that you can go home."

"Home!" The frosted glass melted. To see Robert. To care for him. She would do anything this man wanted. "Home!"

"Yes," he said. "Home. If you tell us what we need to know, we can see that you get safely back to Tokyo. I'm sure your father would be thrilled to have you home, safe and sound." He attempted another bracketed smile.

Not home, then. The man knew nothing about home. She would slit her wrists rather than return to Japan—even in peaceful times. Her father...

Bagwell watched her, his gray eyes reflecting nothing. Especially not her image. He did not need to see her, she thought. The man without a soul already knew what she looked like. She looked like the enemy.

Chapter Thirty-nine

"Where's Cabby?" Alicia asked, pulling out a chair at the boarding-house table and glancing around. "She's never been one to miss a meal."

Louise shrugged. "When I woke up she was already gone." All the other girls were present, even Marion, who seldom graced them with her presence at breakfast. The house smelled deliciously of sausages, but everyone seemed slightly out-of-sorts. Even Ruthie was scowling as if she had weighty matters on her mind.

"Cabby musta left real early," she said. "For once I didn't have to fight her for the bathroom." She craned her neck to stare toward the kitchen. "But what I want to know is—where's breakfast?"

It was ten minutes after eight, late for the ever-punctual Helda. Bleary-eyed, Louise—who'd slept almost twelve straight hours but still didn't feel rested—stared across the dining room at three grim etchings over the cold fireplace. A brace of dead rabbits, mountain crags with wispy-bearded goats, a stag at bay. Great—truly appetizing. Helda's taste in home décor was Germanic, to say the least, heavy with oak and crewel and outdoor grotesquerie.

And this morning Helda's décor matched Louise's mood. Her mother had phoned last night—Ben and Ted had gone down to the Navy office. They'd soon be in the thick of it.

Louise had been raised with the belief that her country was always in the right, and that every citizen should rally to its defense. But, her baby brothers in uniform, toting rifles!

Shooting at people! Louise could hardly bear to think about it. And how could America be right when its own agents were mistreating a woman who had absolutely nothing to do with the attack on Hawaii?

Cabby was another concern. Was her roommate sore over being described as—what had Louise called her? "An unpleasant career girl." Louise rubbed her forehead, stung by the memory of her own words. Just because she was in New York now didn't mean she should forget she was a lady. She'd have to apologize for that remark. Definitely.

Then maybe she could persuade Cabby to write a story more partial to Masako.

But could her roommate persuade that crotchety editor she always griped about to publish it?

Louise sipped from the glass of juice on the plate in front of her. Her lips puckered. Her whole mouth puckered. Pineapple, canned and acidic. Well, what did she expect? Fresh pineapple in New York in December? She set the glass down. Later she'd pour the juice into the big spider plant by the upright piano. Maybe it would kill the ugly thing.

She had just reached for one of the crusty little rolls Helda called *brotchen*, when the butler's pantry door flew open and Howie hefted in a platter of pale German sausages. He slapped it down on the long table with a dissonant clunk. The boy's face was like a storm cloud, and he slouched back into the kitchen without a word.

"What's the matter with our little Hansel?" Ruthie asked, reaching for the serving fork and spearing two plump sausages. She smiled for the first time that morning. "Oh, yummy! But I'll have to live on black coffee and cigarettes for the rest of the week—this is gonna go right to my boombassadie!"

Howie was back with a bowl of scrambled eggs, which he plunked down on the table before stomping out again.

Marion studied the sausages and chose the smallest one. "I've never seen that kid in such a foul mood. What's going on with him?"

It was quiet Mousie who ventured an opinion. "Boys that age," she said vaguely. "You know…" Her beady black eyes were fixed on the closed pantry door.

A loud clang came from outside. Something shook the dining-room wall. Everyone startled, and Ruthie gave a little shriek.

Alicia ran to the window. "The coal truck, ladies, only the coal truck." Coal clunked down the chute to the basement bin.

Whew! Louise thought, as her heart rate slowed, everyone's so jumpy.

Helda entered through the butler's pantry with a pot of coffee. "I hope that boy was not rude." She filled their cups. "I don't know what is wrong with him. He snap and snarl ever since that police bring him home!" She left the room, muttering to herself in German.

Loading their plates, the boarders seemed to forget all about Howie. Ruthie was wearing a new blouse, sheer white nylon over a black slip. Louise thought it made her look cheap. But the stenographer got right to the point of what was on everyone's mind. "This war is gonna be so hard on all of us." She paused to reach for another sausage.

Alicia glanced at her with surprise. It wasn't like Ruthie to be so astute. "You're right," she said. "Like everyone else, Howie's already feeling the strain. Once Hitler finally declares war on us, things could get even worse."

"Cabby and I got a taste of it yesterday," Louise said. "We were coming out of the Automat, and suddenly the world went crazy. Sirens. Horns. Men yelling. It was deafening. I couldn't breathe. It went on and on. I thought it was a real air raid, bombs and all."

"I'm not talking about that kind of stuff, silly!" Ruthie shook her head, annoyed. "What I mean," she clarified, "is—at Gimbels they already limited stockings to three pairs per customer. You shoulda seen the ladies lined up five deep at the counters yesterday. I spent half my lunch hour waiting!"

Alicia leaned over toward Louise. *Sotto voce*, she said, "That girl has the IQ of a bagel."

Surprisingly, Mousie spoke up again, looking directly at Ruthie. "Yesterday at Macy's women were storming my counter for brassieres, too. It's really not right, you know. That's hoarding and the government has asked us not to do it."

Ruthie's mouth fell open. "Do you mean to tell me that you work in ladies undergarments and you're not putting brassieres and girdles aside for the duration?"

"Of course not! Rubber goes into gas masks and lifeboats—planes and tanks, too. The troops need rubber worse than we do—that's why it's going to be rationed soon." No one at the table had ever heard so many words from Mousie at one time. Miss Goody-Two-Shoes.

Helda, entering with a fresh pot of coffee, sank down into Cabby's empty chair. "*Ach du lieber*—no rubber! That means no corsets. It's just not healthy, no corset—our wombs will fall." The landlady cast a sideways look at Howie, who'd come in behind her and was emptying the waste baskets.

"That's not true," Louise said, trying to hide her growing irritation. "Girdles aren't good for you. They displace your internal organs. And then, your abdominal muscles—"

"Oh, Louise, you think you know everything," Ruthie interrupted. "In home-ec they told us—"

As she buttered a crusty roll, Alicia rolled her eyes at Louise. "She should have paid closer attention in home-ec," she muttered. "Those sausages are sheer fat—they're going to stay on her boombasadie forever."

"But what are we going to do about stockings!" Ruthie moaned. "Men go crazy for my legs. I need those stockings. I figure I've only got two or three years left to snag a rich husband, and my gams are my best feature."

"Don't worry, Ruthie," Marion was saying as she glanced through a newspaper. "My friend at Foley Square says there'll always be stockings for girls who know how to get them."

Louise stopped eating and shifted in her chair. What was wrong with these women? Didn't they have brothers? Sweethearts? Wasn't the war real to them? The young nurse shuddered.

Alicia noticed her discomfort and placed a hand on her arm.

Louise scooted her chair back, pulling away from Alicia. That was it! "Goddammit all to hell!" She snatched a surprised breath—unlike these New Yorkers, she wasn't used to using curse words—then she jumped up and slammed the palm of her hand flat against the table.

The women jerked in their seats. Even Howie stared at her wide-eyed.

"That's enough about stockings!" Louise snapped. "You want to talk about wartime sacrifice? My twin brothers just joined the Navy—they could have their ship blown out from under them. That's sacrifice."

Marion lowered her paper and pursed her lips. "Well, re-e-e-e-ly, you don't have to throw such a hizzy. We're perfectly capable of worrying about our boys and our stockings at the same time. How old are your brothers, anyway?" She smirked. "I do hope they're older than twelve."

"What do you mean?" Louise's anger turned to puzzlement.

Marion stabbed a red fingernail at her tabloid newspaper, the *Daily Mirror*. "I just read this little article. Seems they not only have child brides in the wilds of Kentucky, but child soldiers, too."

"You're kidding, right?" Ruthie said.

"Not at all. Some yokel recruiter's been signing up boys just out of grammar school."

Louise's shoulders dropped. She'd had to endure so much ribbing about being from Kentucky. "Are you a hillbilly? Did you wear shoes to school?" She sank down in her chair. "That must be in the mountains—they're still pretty backward in those isolated small towns."

Jane Willis, one of the older boarders, rose with the *Times* tucked under her arm. In her quiet way, she took the floor. "Don't let our Marion needle you, Louise. You must be strong for your parents' sake. It's not easy, having a boy overseas, much less twins."

Helda agreed with an emphatic nod and drifted over to squeeze her son's shoulders.

Howie scowled.

Chapter Forty

"Who's your source for this piece?" Halper barked, grinding out his smoke in a half-filled ashtray. He peered at Cabby over the tops of wire-rimmed glasses. In spite of the splotch of dried egg on his chin, the editor had the daunting authority of a hanging judge in a one-horse Western town.

She handed him the pages of Louise's neat penmanship. "Someone who was there at the time and took notes."

Halper didn't smile. This wasn't going the way Cabby had anticipated. She felt her stomach tighten. The nickel doughnut she'd had for breakfast wasn't sitting well. Usually she thrilled in the noisy ebullience of the newsroom, typewriters clacking, phones ringing, teletypes clattering, men shouting "Copy!" But a fierce headache had crept up on her, and, between the morning tumult and the thickening fog of cigarette smoke, she felt as if she might throw up.

The editor ran his eyes over the notes with the speed of a brand-new Pontiac roadster, and then handed the papers back to her. "Where'd you get this?"

"Confidential source." She slipped the folded bundle into her purse. So confidential she doesn't even know about it.

"Confidential, huh?" His blubbery lips went in and then out. "Look, Ward, nothing is confidential from me—I'm the guy the shit's gonna fall on if anything's phony about this story. Who's your source?" He held her typed article up with a thumb and forefinger on each corner and twisted it as if he were about to tear the page in two right down the middle. Cabby could almost hear the ripping sound.

Her hands flew up to her face. "No. Don't! It was Professor Oakley's private-duty nurse." He tossed the page down, tapped another Camel out of its packet, and lit it with a tarnished silver lighter. "His nurse, huh? She was there when Fumi was arrested?"

"Oh, yes." Cabby nodded like a wobbly headed carnival doll. "This is a totally accurate account. Straight from the horse's mouth."

"And this nurse?" Halper looked up as nosy Bud Smallwood slouched in and sat at the desk adjacent to him in the U-formation that made up the City-room hierarchy. "What's her name?"

The editor had lowered his voice, but Cabby could sense Bud's ears flapping. She swallowed, then whispered, "Louise. Louise Hunter. My roommate."

"I see. And why did Nurse Hunter give you these notes?"

"Oh, she didn't." It was out of her mouth before she knew it.

"She didn't, huh." He scowled. "Does she know you have them?"

She hung her head. "No." It was another whisper.

"You're off the Fumi story, Ward."

She choked out a hoarse "Yes, sir."

Swiveling around in his oak desk chair, her editor exhaled a steady stream of smoke and stared out the soot-coated window. Cabby stared, too. Gray, heavy skies. Looked like snow. Halper swiveled back and tore her article into tiny pieces.

He shook his head slowly. "Didn't they teach ethics in your journalism class, Miss Ward?"

She opened her mouth, but he didn't wait for a response. Leaning forward, he said, "You're a good little hustler, sweetie, and I like your work, so I'm not gonna fire you. Yet. But you're skating on thin ice here. I don't want to see this kind of shoddy reporting again. You understand?"

Shoddy? The word was like a knife in the heart, but she nodded. "Thank you, Mr. Halper."

She began to rise from her chair, but he waved her down. "Wait a minute, here's your next assignment—try not to botch this one. Ya know the America First Committee?"

"The…isolationist group?" Oh, yes. She knew it. Her father had joined last spring, ranting about Winston Churchill and those damn Jews.

"Yeah. Them. Nigel Fairchild, their local chairman, is giving a talk tonight at the headquarters on Madison Avenue. I'd be interested to find out what that bunch is up to now that war's been declared."

"Uh, me, too. The Pearl Harbor attacks rendered them irrelevant in one fell swoop."

"I'd like to think so, but I'm sure there's a few of those goose-steppers who'd be more than happy to see Britain fall to Hitler along with the rest of Europe." Twisting his expression into something reminiscent of a wizened apple, Halper mimicked, "Why risk American peace and prosperity to save Britain's ass?

"So, go cover the meeting. Five-hundred words. Got that?" Halper pulled the cover off his typewriter and rolled a sheet of paper into the carriage.

Cabby jumped up from her seat, grateful to still have a job. "Yes, sir. Mr. Halper, sir." She'd get right on Nigel Fairchild. A high-society holdover from the Old Guard who saw Roosevelt as a traitor to both class and country. Liked to shoot his mouth off.

Halfway out the door, she pivoted around. "And, sir? I won't disappoint you." She tried to follow that with something more eloquent, but Bud Smallwood was sneering from behind his desk, and shame silenced her.

Chapter Forty-one

If it had been a tweedy, mannish man with horn-rimmed glasses sitting behind a neatly ordered reception desk in Columbia's Art Humanities department, McKenna wouldn't have felt a qualm, but his mental file-box didn't contain a heading for a woman who seemed quite so brusque and in command. Well, maybe it did—the nuns who'd tormented him for years at Holy Cross Parish School on West Forty-third Street.

His stomach did the customary little lurch when he thought of the good Sisters, so he flipped his wallet open to the police ID and summoned his most official voice. "Where can I find Professor Lawrence Smoot?" Smoot's office had been dark and deserted when McKenna approached it that morning. Perhaps the man was teaching a class somewhere in the vast, ivy-covered building, in which case McKenna would never find him without help.

The secretary twined her fingers inside the palms of her hands and pressed thumbs to her lips. "You're too late," she stated in a voice resonating with doom.

"Too late?" Good god, the man's croaked himself, McKenna thought. Could that be it? Smoot and Shelton have a falling out over the loan of twenty grand. One queer kills another. In a fit of delayed remorse, Smoot commits suicide. Neat.

But, no. The secretary's grim voice went on. "Professor Smoot isn't in. After his eight a.m. class, he sprinted out of here like Jesse

Owens. Now, he's missed his ten o'clock, and I haven't the slightest idea why." Her lips stretched. She stabbed a finger toward a desk calendar. "You were here on Monday, I know. That was the day he barricaded himself in his office. Since then he's been slinking around looking like an undergraduate pulling all-night cram sessions. I don't like it. I have a department to run, and we can't have professors leaving classes unattended and neglecting office hours. This is Columbia—it's simply not done."

"You have Smoot's address on file?"

"Of course," she replied without making a move.

Jesus, Mary, and Joseph. "I'd like it, please."

The Dragon Nun flipped through a small box of index cards, used a blank one to write down an address, and handed it to him. "Whatever Professor Smoot's situation is, arrangements must be made. When you find him, officer, tell him to call Thelma."

McKenna felt something akin to pity for Professor Smoot.

◇◇◇

The address wasn't far. McKenna's driver let him out on one of the quieter Upper West Side streets lined with three-story brownstones. While he waited on the stoop to be admitted to the professor's parlor-floor apartment, McKenna tried to put together a series of Smoot's actions that would fit the evidence.

First, Smoot attends the Fumi opening, so he knows that, despite Mrs. De Forest's little tantrum, the show is raking in the cash.

And what cash! McKenna shook his head. Brenner's search of the files had nailed the exact figures: twenty-two thousand five hundred. Quadruple his yearly salary—for those messes! Even after Shelton had split fifty-fifty with the artist, printed up that brochure, and put on a swanky soiree, the dealer was over ten grand to the good.

Okay, so Smoot begins to wonder how long the lucky streak will last in the face of mounting opposition to the show. On Friday, he visits the gallery and asks Shelton for all or part of the twenty grand he's owed. Shelton refuses and Smoot goes wild, swinging the first object that comes to hand. Maybe that heavy brush pot? Then he stages the scene with the body under that lurid painting—makes it look like one of the crazier Jap art protesters argued with Shelton—and he hurries to the theater in the hope of establishing an alibi.

Nix on the alibi, though. The boys had found an usher who remembered Smoot sitting alone, but Doc Lefevers' generous estimate on time of death meant that Smoot's presence at the play wasn't going to save him. And the professor hadn't come up with any corroboration on his earlier whereabouts.

Yeah, well, it might've just worked that way.

The buzzer admitted McKenna into a cramped foyer. Smoot frowned when he saw his visitor, but bowed him toward a corridor that entered a living room painted in restful tones of blue and peach. As he'd expected, an Asian influence predominated on walls and in display cabinets, but the furniture was unadulterated modernism—tubular steel, glass cubes, and woven leather straps that struck McKenna as remnants off a construction site. He sank into one of the tilted lounge chairs but kept his feet firmly planted and his back straight.

Smoot closed the book that lay on the glass side table, reclaimed a smoldering cigarette from a kidney-shaped ashtray, and asked, "Drink, Lieutenant?"

"Ya kidding? It's not even noon." That clearly hadn't stopped Smoot. A glass with an inch of rye sat on the table between an ivory cigarette box and an ashtray full of butts. The room reeked of smoke and booze, the stench of despair.

Smoot shrugged. "Sometimes a man needs a little liquid courage—whatever the hour."

McKenna got that. The day he'd left Gayle at the rest home up in Harrison, he'd burned rubber all the way back to Manhattan, garaged the car, then stopped at the first bar to get well and truly pissed. And that had been eleven a.m. But what was biting Smoot? Grief? Or guilt?

"Have you come to tell me you've found Arthur's killer?" Smoot clutched the highball glass.

"Early days yet. Still following up leads." McKenna pointed to a mirrored cabinet that held some odd little metal objects, but kept his gaze on Smoot. "Got any brush pots in your collection, Professor?"

"Brush pots?" Smoot's expression was puzzled.

"Yeah." Thanks to Desmond Cox, McKenna had the lowdown on brush pots. "Learned men all over the Orient kept these pots on their desks to hold the brushes they wrote their squiggly letters with. A lot of 'em were made of precious materials. Heavy stuff—like jade. Proof of the scholar's high status. Kinda like a guy wants to show off an expensive car."

"I'm well aware of what a brush pot is." Smoot crossed one leg. "I just don't happen to collect them. I prefer more exotic items. These cricket cages, for instance." He nodded toward the mirrored cabinet.

McKenna sat up even straighter. "That's what those things are? Cages for bugs?"

Smoot smiled easily. "The cult of the cricket was peculiar to Chinese gentlemen of leisure. They kept them as pets and found their chirping melodic."

"Ya don't say?"

"Oh, yes. To encourage their songs, they tickled the crickets with tiny brushes. Collectors can specialize in different areas of cricket paraphernalia—brushes, tweezers, cage cleaners, ceramic feeding trays. I happen to prefer the cages." He stubbed out his cigarette. "Why the interest in brush pots, Lieutenant?"

"There's one missing from the gallery."

"Really? Arthur never mentioned it." Smoot stretched a hand toward the cigarette box.

McKenna realized Smoot had gotten more of a rise out of him with the cricket cages than he had with the mention of brush pots. Smoot would have to be one cool character to be able to discuss the murder weapon so casually. Or maybe it wasn't the jade pot that had smashed Shelton's skull after all. McKenna wasn't about to drop the possibility of Smoot's guilt. Time to bring out the big guns.

"You lied to me the other day," he stated flatly.

"I beg to differ." Smoot froze as he creaked the box lid open. "I gave an honest answer to every question you put to me."

"It was a lie of omission. I asked you about your business relations with Shelton, and you managed to sidestep the issue of twenty thousand simoleons."

"So, Miss Desmond has been blabbing, has he?" Smoot pursed his lips. "Is it relevant? A loan between friends?"

McKenna swore in his head. "That kind of dough is always relevant."

"Well—" Smoot thought for a second or two, rose, and patted the pockets of his soft smoking jacket. "Out of nicotine, Lieutenant. You'll have to excuse me for a moment."

"Yeah, sure."

McKenna waited until Smoot had passed into the hallway, then heaved himself up from the leather basket chair. It was like struggling out of a hammock. When he reached the door the professor had vanished through, he stopped and cocked an ear. Smoot's voice came from somewhere deep in the apartment.

Words McKenna couldn't make out, pause, more muffled words.

A phone call, then, in response to his question about the gallery seed money. He whirled and swept his gaze around the room. No phone extension. When the professor returned, brandishing a pack of Pall Malls, McKenna was back across the living room admiring the cricket cages.

During the rest of the interview, McKenna felt like one of those old Chinese guys tickling their crickets through the bars of those tiny cages. He poked and prodded, but Smoot wouldn't sing any tune he wanted to hear. Yes, he'd helped Arthur with some start-up cash, but it had been an open-handed, pay-whenever-you can sort of gesture. No, he wasn't hounding the dear boy. Certainly not. He believed in plowing profit back into the business until it was well on its way.

Only one question drew blood. Did Desmond Cox and Arthur Shelton socialize outside of work? Smoot bristled at that and gave McKenna an earful about snakes in the grass and foxes guarding henhouses.

McKenna was about to pack it in when the buzzer sounded. Smoot sashayed out, almost gleefully. A far cry from his earlier demeanor.

When the professor returned, it was in the company of a distinguished man in a cashmere overcoat and homburg. Mr. Overcoat shifted his briefcase so he could shake McKenna's hand. He then withdrew a card from a silver case.

"Caspar Mandlebaum, Lieutenant. I'm Lawrence Smoot's attorney. From here on out, any questions for the professor will have to go through me."

Chapter Forty-two

Cabby loved the New York Public Library. When she was a kid in the Bronx, it had been her salvation. Her father would come home smashed and start throwing furniture around, and she'd sneak out of the apartment. She'd skulk up to the Kingsbridge branch and hunker down with a book until Mrs. Katz touched her on the shoulder to let her know it was closing time. It was always the same book, *Little Women* by Louisa May Alcott.

She'd pull out a chair at the table in the A-B section of the fiction stacks, open the book just anywhere, and cry into its pages until the tears dried up and she was in Jo March's world again. Jo was more of a sister to her than her real sister, Eileen. It wouldn't be wrong to say that Jo March had shown Cabby writing could lift her out of a dead-end life.

So, for comfort, once she'd left the building after Halper's dressing down, Cabby headed directly down Fifth Avenue to the majestic main building of the New York Public Library. It had been snowing all morning, and, except for a shoveled path in the very center, the wide flight of library steps was covered with snow. Standing on the wet sidewalk, looking up, she was flanked by Patience and Fortitude, the identical stone lions guarding those steps. Nonetheless she was more conscious of those other twin monsters, Shame and Disgrace. Her face was hot—her entire body was hot—with humiliation. Even with snowflakes falling on her cheeks, she was burning.

And the worst of it? Halper was right. Stealing Louise's notes had been a shoddy act. How could she have done that to her roommate? Blinded by her success with the Shelton homicide piece, she'd resorted to shortcuts and unethical practices. Shoddy. That's what Halper had said, "shoddy."

Cabby swiped at a tear that was beginning to freeze beneath her left eye. If she was such a bad reporter, maybe she should just quit. She envisioned herself marching back up to the newsroom, typing the letter of resignation with an efficient clatter of keys, and shoving it in Halper's face before she stalked out.

And then what?

No, Cabby Ward wasn't a quitter. And she wasn't a bad reporter, either. Patience and Fortitude, that's what she needed. And a good-size dose of Integrity. She placed one booted foot on the first marble step. Up she climbed, step by step. Patience. Fortitude. Integrity.

She'd meant to begin by researching Nigel Fairchild and America First in preparation for tonight's assignment, but, somehow, she ended up in one of the palazzo-like third-floor reading rooms with *Little Women* open in front of her. Next to her at the long oak table a scrawny gray-haired man was reading a Yiddish newspaper. On the other side of the bronze reading lamp a plump girl with her brown hair in a loose chignon was writing on a thick pad of lined paper. A guy who looked like a professor, youngish, with a dark goatee, got up to retrieve yet another tome to add to his pile of shabby books.

A woman lugging a heavy baby in a blue snowsuit passed Cabby's desk, capturing her attention. Her nose was red with cold and her coat far too light for the season. She didn't look as if she belonged here. Cabby wouldn't have been surprised if the young woman had come into the library just to get out of the cold. She reminded her of Eileen, her sister, pregnant at sixteen and now, at twenty-four, the mother of three with another on the way and no end in sight.

Do you want to end up like Eileen? Cabby asked herself, rifling the pages of the book through her fingers. *You've worked* so damn hard and taken so many risks to get where you are. Do you want to jeopardize all that? What the hell are you doing? Halper gave you an assignment. Get your butt moving.

Nigel Fairchild? Where could she find out what he'd been up to? Let's see, she'd look in the New York Social Register—that should be next door in the reference room. Then she'd go down to the periodicals room on the first floor and read through some of Walter Winchell's gossip columns. Someone like Winchell would surely be keeping an eye on a goddamn socialite isolationist s.o.b. like Fairchild. And then she'd scoot on down to the *Times* morgue and read through the back files on America First.

She picked up *Little Women* and took it to the returns window.

Chapter Forty-three

Helda had never liked Anna Frommer. She was certain the tight braids coiled around the top of Anna's small head strained at a multitude of unchristian thoughts. One snip with a pair of sharp shears, and revenge, envy, and pettiness would come rushing out, like the evils escaping Pandora's box.

So she felt a chill tremor of anxiety when she looked up and saw who was knocking on her kitchen door. Once Helda had stopped attending Bund meetings with Ernst, the only contact between her and Frau Frommer had been the occasional exchange of frigid nods at church. Now here was the *gute frau* knocking on the door as if she was a friend stopping by for morning coffee. Puzzled, Helda moved to admit her fellow congregant and relieve her of the heavy cast-iron pot she carried; it was necessary to be hospitable to other Lutherans—but she didn't have to hurry.

"Frau Frommer, what a surprise to see you," Helda said in German. Then, begrudgingly, she added, "Come in. I will put the coffee on. What is it you bring me?"

"Just a little *hasenpfeffer*. I know you like the homeland food." Frau Frommer was short and thin, with a bosom shaped like a stale jelly roll. "I also know you could not make this for your boarders to eat—they would not like it. Americans…*ach*!"

"*Danke, danke.*" Helda switched to English. "So thoughtful." It was no longer safe to converse in German, even at home.

Anyone might be listening. They were only talking about rabbit stew, but American ears could hear sinister meanings. She remembered the suspicious look on the policeman's face yesterday when she had yelled at Howie, *Halt die Schnauze!* What had the officer thought? That Helda was commanding her son to join the stormtroopers?

"Come. Sit. The coffee will be just a minute."

"*Nein. Danke.* I will be going. The bake sale for the Ladies' Relief Society is Saturday, you know, and I must set the yeast for my *apfelkuchen.*" Standing in the doorway in her second-best navy faille, Frau Frommer continued, "In these perilous times, we must all do what we can." She slipped off the quilted oven mitts with which she had carried the iron pot, and whispered, "As is, of course, your dear Ernst."

Helda ceased breathing.

From inside one of the mitts, the churchwoman retrieved a small white envelope and, with a knowing look, slipped it into Helda's hand.

Helda stared at the little envelope, unable to force a word past her paralyzed tongue. It was marked PRIVATE, and it was addressed to Mrs. Ernst Schroeder.

In her husband's handwriting.

Chapter Forty-four

When Abe Pritzker phoned on Wednesday morning, Louise was hoping he would take her back to Ellis Island for a second talk with Mrs. Oakley. The lawyer had other plans. He needed her to smooth the way at his initial meeting with Professor Oakley. But first he wanted an introduction to Lawrence Smoot, one of the friends he hoped would provide Masako with an affidavit to bring before the Alien Enemy Hearing Board.

So, now they sat in Smoot's large office. When the Columbia professor and Arthur Shelton had visited the Oakley apartment the previous week, the fastidious Smoot might have stepped out of a Macy's display window. But today silvery beard stubble covered the lower part of his face, his eyes were bloodshot, and his skin seemed too large for his bones. Something more than the attacks on Pearl Harbor must be eating at Lawrence Smoot, Louise thought.

Then, it hit her: Oh, it had been like *that* between him and Arthur Shelton. Of course, Professor Smoot was grieving over the art dealer's death. Louise shook her head at her own naiveté. She should have tumbled to that relationship right off.

Despite his obvious distress, Professor Smoot readily agreed to vouch for Masako. Abe explained the procedure. The Board would need to be assured of Masako's lack of interest in Japanese militarism, of her plans to remain in the United States, as well as of her favorable reputation as artist and teacher. While Smoot jotted notes, Louise poked around his art-filled office. On one of the bookcases, among dusty textbooks and oversize art books, she came upon a five-by-seven snapshot in a mosaicked frame.

It was a holiday snap, a happy group posed in front of…was that a camel? Professor Oakley, the tallest person, dominated the photo, wearing camp shorts and shirt. Louise almost chuckled. The professor Louise knew was a distinguished gentleman; but, in his younger days, with that black beard and those muscular legs, he'd qualify as what the girls called "a dreamboat." He had his arm around a plump, pleasant-looking lady wearing a flowered skirt and large sun hat.

That must be his first wife, Virginia, Louise thought. It seemed odd to see the professor with any woman other than Masako. If she didn't have the evidence right in front of her, she wouldn't even have been able to imagine it. A thinner Lawrence Smoot and another lady, who was squinting into the sun, flanked Oakley and his wife.

Oh—she recognized that other woman: Lillian Bridges, younger, more beautiful, stylish even in her sand-colored safari suit.

"Happier times, my dear." Smoot's mellifluous voice sounded right in her ear.

Louise jumped. She hadn't realized he and Abe were finished. The professor took up the photo and sighed. "If only we could make time stand still," he said. "Just for a bit." Then he turned the photo toward Abe and pointed. "Here's the person you were asking about—Lillian Bridges. You can catch her at Robert's this evening—she mentioned she'd drop by with some flowers. I'm sure she'll be more than happy to write up a statement for Masako."

Louise had called Professor Bridges yesterday evening to ask her about keeping Masako's paintings from the studio on Bleecker Street. There'd been no answer, and she had to admit she'd let it slip her mind. Next to that soignée, self-assured lady, she felt like some little bumpkin who just rode the hay wagon into the big city. Shame on you, Louise chastized herself. She'd secured the studio key from Professor Oakley, but she couldn't organize moving the paintings until she had Miss Bridges' agreement to house them. She'd just have to remember to call her this evening. Masako would be desolated if the FBI got their hands on those paintings, too.

◇◇◇

When Louise and Abe left the humanities building, the temperature had plummeted and an icy mist that wasn't quite rain fuzzed Columbia's lofty evergreens and columned buildings. Everything appeared slightly out of focus, and the cold sliced right through Louise's nylon stockings. She added boots to her mental list of things she needed if she stayed in New York.

Hatless, as usual, Abe noticed her shoulders shivering and her teeth chattering. He slung an arm across her back. "We've got to get you warm, sweetie-pie."

Louise wiped her damp cheeks with gloved fingers. Sweetie-pie?

He bundled her into the gray Ford sedan he'd parked on Morningside Drive and, heading downtown, navigated the slick streets of the West Side, parking with a flourish in front of a delicatessen restaurant across Seventh Avenue from Carnegie Hall. What Abe insisted would be a life-saving elixir turned out to be a bowl of the best chicken soup Louise had ever tasted, and it warmed her up just fine. She swallowed every drop of that soup, and all the little round dumplings, too. Abe called them matzoh balls.

"Delicious. Just what I needed. Thanks." She sat back, smiling a little as a waiter delivered steaming mugs of coffee. How nice it would be to have nothing on her mind except having lunch, maybe taking in a piano concert across the street. With Abe.

"I know a couple of East Side delis that do it better. But this is closer to the Oakleys'." The lawyer's mind had obviously returned to the case. "Is the professor well enough to understand the recommendations available to the Board? His wife's immediate release is probably too much to hope for. I'll be jockeying for parole under the sponsorship of an upstanding citizen, so he should be thinking about who might be appropriate. Unfortunately, internment for the war's duration is also a possibility."

"He can understand." Louise nodded tersely. Back to business.

"Of course," Abe continued as he spooned sugar into his mug, "given who her father is, there is a more unsettling possibility—repatriation."

Repatriation? Louise bit her lip. "Surely they wouldn't pack Mrs. Oakley off to Japan." She recalled their conversations at the kitchen table. Suddenly her nerves were on the alert. What had the Japanese woman said about going back to Japan?—she feared what might be done to her there.

Abe shrugged. "I hate to say it, but she's valuable property to the Feds."

"Property? What a thing to say!"

"That's how they think of her—human collateral. Prime material for a high-ranking prisoner exchange, probably for some embassy muckety-muck stranded in Tokyo when war broke out." Abe took a slurp of coffee. "I have the feeling Bagwell is going to play Mrs. Oakley's situation for all he can get—it could make his career."

"But that's outrageous!" Louise heard her voice grow shrill. The small restaurant was beginning to fill up; several people turned to stare in her direction. She lowered her tone and reached across the table to grab Abe's wrist. "You can't tell Professor Oakley about this."

Abe raised a skeptical eyebrow. "From what you've told me about your boss, it sounds like Oakley's a man who won't settle for a sugar coating."

"Generally not." Louise sipped at her coffee, thinking furiously. Abe was right about the professor; he had listened with great attention to everything she said. Professor Oakley would be angry if he found they'd withheld information. "At least let me explain that part. I'll know just how far to push him."

Abe stood, reached for his coat on a wall hook. "You got a deal on that one, honey."

Chapter Forty-five

"Where's Perroni? And Brenner?" McKenna looked around the squad office. Patsy Dolan was holding down his usual place, the broad chair at the head of the conference table that had also seen its share of card games and deli sandwiches. Two of the younger guys, Dawson and O'Connell, balanced their butts on the wide window sill, jawing over the Giants' chances in the playoffs. That left almost half of McKenna's inner circle missing.

"Dunno where Brenner is, Lute, but, Perroni, he joined up." Dolan made a half-ass salute that would never have been tolerated in McKenna's old unit.

"Shit!" There went one of his best men.

"Yeah—him and his cousin went in together. Doris told ya this morning—don'cha remember? And when she brought the coffee, she dumped his notes in your box there."

McKenna rubbed his midsection, trying to remember back. That fatty pastrami on rye wasn't sitting well. Neither was Masako Fumi Oakley's second refusal to come to the detention center visitor's room that morning to talk to him. What a cockamamie situation! Just when the FBI gives the go-ahead, the subject digs in her heels.

And, she's in Federal custody, so there's not a damn thing he could do about it.

Oh, yeah. Back to this morning. While Doris had been yakking, he'd been flipping through some tabloids he'd picked up at the newsstand on Grand. Just like the Cap had warned, the yellow press had jumped on the Fumi story. Miss Ward's *Times* piece had stuck to the basic facts, but these scandal rags had spun their juicy stories out of thin air. One had the lady using her art studio as a sake-soaked academy for Jap assassins. Another featured a headline that read "Pansy Murder Laid to Hot-blooded Nip." Readers—and there were a lot of 'em—would be calling for Mrs. Oakley's head on a stick. He wondered if Bagwell knew about those stories.

Then he wondered if maybe the G-man had planted them.

"Notes, notes." McKenna grabbed a fistful of papers from the in-box on his desk, checking for Perroni's blocky handwriting; the young detective had been investigating several loose ends.

Okay, here was something. The number Hermann Rupp had called about the picketing job was a pay phone—no real surprise there. Telephone company was tracking down the exact location.

And this on Smoot: in good standing at his university, tenured, generally well-liked by students and colleagues, recently published a paper in a journal of Asian Art.

Yeah, yeah, yeah. As nothing else leapt out of the stack, McKenna pushed away from his desk and called Dawson and O'Connell to the table. "I wanna go back to the victim, see if we've missed anything. How about Shelton's rooming house on West Fifty-first? Anything interesting turn up there?"

"Nothing, Lute." Dawson shook his narrow head. He was a small man with a shock of chestnut hair and the look of an over-grown schoolboy, especially when he grinned. His current expression was more of a rubber-lipped frown. "Everybody we could get to talk agreed they hardly ever saw Shelton—course, it's mainly theater and restaurant workers who keep odd hours themselves."

McKenna nodded, not surprised. On first inspection, he'd decided Shelton only used the cheap room to store his extensive wardrobe, clean up, and sleep whenever he wasn't spending the night in Lawrence Smoot's bed. He wasn't the only transient who patronized the rooming houses, bars, and cafés west of Seventh Avenue and Broadway. The district had earned the nickname of the "Faggy Fifties" because it was full of young pansies kicked out of the house, secret homosexuals eager to mingle with their own kind, and refugees from America's heartland who saw this part of the city as the only place where they could let their hair down and be themselves.

Shelton's mother had said it best, when McKenna had made the sad call to inform the art dealer's parents of his death. In sorrowful tones, she told him, "Arthur was too sensitive for Muncie. He just never fit in here."

I'll bet he didn't, McKenna had thought at the time. That conversation, as well as the shabby, lonely room, had convinced him that Arthur Shelton's real life centered on his gallery. The solution to his murder would, too, McKenna bet. He rubbed his hands and addressed his team. "Okay, what about the murder weapon? Who's on that? Dolan?"

"Nothing going there." The sergeant looked like a frog who'd just lost his best friend. "I got twelve men on it. We extended the search out another four blocks in all directions. Shrubbery, trash cans, sewers, you name it. Nothing. We sure it's one of them paint pots?"

"Brush pot. Or something similar in shape"—McKenna cupped his hands like they were encircling a quart milk bottle, moved them up and down about nine inches— "A jade brush pot is unaccounted for. Doc Lefevers found a particular pattern of bruising on Shelton's forearms. Looks like he tried to fend off an attack with a heavy, rounded, blunt object. He might've turned to grab the hammer he was using on the packing crates and that's when the killer clonked him a good one."

McKenna turned his gaze toward O'Connell. He'd assigned the big redhead the task of questioning all the letter writers who'd been at Shelton about the Jap show—all except Tiffy De Forest. McKenna wanted to save that little lady for himself. "Anything?"

"No, Lute. These are society types and it was Friday night. They all have alibis from about a hundred people at dinner parties and charity balls. Even the opera."

McKenna belched, immediately felt better, then nodded. He hadn't really thought this line of investigation would turn up anything, either, but you had to be thorough. That was police work. Gayle used to say it was like searching for lice with a fine-tooth comb.

All that didn't explain Brenner's absence, but he'd probably be here soon. The sergeant often rushed into a meeting a few minutes late. To convince everyone how busy he was, McKenna sometimes thought.

Speak of the devil…Sergeant Brenner came through the door, out of breath, clutching his side. Sweat beaded on his forehead. "Sorry I'm late, Lute. Finally took the stairs—that goddamn elevator is so slow."

Brenner didn't quite hide his smirk. Busting to tell something, McKenna figured. The sergeant was an ex-beat cop with a good eye for detail. He was also ambitious. McKenna couldn't blame him. Brenner had a young wife and a couple of kids that would keep him out of the war for a while. He'd take advantage of the opportunities provided by the many detectives caught in the draft and go as far as he could. No sin in that, as long as he did good police work.

"Whadda ya got?" McKenna reared back and crossed his arms.

"The door-to-door boys just dredged up a guy on Fifty-seventh Street—apartment across from the Shelton Gallery—reported seeing someone arrive by taxi around seven p.m."

"Got an ID on this someone?"

Brenner grinned. Took his time answering. "It was an Asian woman."

"Is that a fact?" McKenna heard his own voice as a deep echo, like they were in a cave instead of the squad office. This was the last development he would have predicted. He glanced around. Dolan and the two younger detectives were looking from him to Brenner with barely concealed excitement.

Not so fast, McKenna thought, this case just doesn't have the feel of…done. "Did the witness see the Asian woman go into the gallery?"

Brenner just couldn't lose the smirk. "He saw her disappear under that green canopy and head toward the entrance. She caught his interest 'cause she wasn't dressed for the street. She was wearing some kind of silky loose pants with a trench coat over. Seemed upset."

"And then…" McKenna sat forward, all ears.

Brenner shrugged. "The guy was frying fish. He went back to the kitchen to have his dinner and doesn't remember looking out front again."

"Okay." McKenna got to his feet, tapped a pencil on the tabletop. "We'll get to the bottom of this. Brenner, you take Mrs. Oakley's photo back to your witness—see if you can get a positive ID Dolan, you're on the cab companies. Find that trip sheet." McKenna spread his hands and asked the air. "Is there a doorman in the Oakley's building?" He answered himself, "Yeah. Sure there is. Dawson, you're on him."

Chapter Forty-six

A middle-aged woman with pinched cheeks and graying hair arranged in small, precise curls bustled into the overheated meeting room of the America First headquarters. In the gloomy illumination provided by a frosted-glass ceiling light, Cabby immediately pegged her as a timid old maid, probably a society-family discard who'd been forced to eke out a living on a small inheritance. What other type would wear such heavy horn-rimmed glasses or that ancient blue serge dress, probably very nice in 1930, now with shiny seat and elbows? When the woman crowded in next to her, ignoring the many other vacant chairs, Cabby changed her assessment.

"You haven't been to one of our meetings before, have you, dear?" Innocuous words in a cultivated accent, but the underlying tone, and the look that accompanied them, could have come from a longshoreman on the Brooklyn docks. Whoever she was, this woman was no lightweight.

"This is my first." Cabby chose her words with an uncharacteristic degree of care. She lifted her wrist to glance at her Timex, as if she didn't already know it was exactly 7:43. "I'm interested in hearing Mr. Fairchild, but he seems to be late for his own lecture. Does this happen often?"

The gray-haired woman settled several bags on the floor and then rifled her purse for a sac of pink mints. "Not often, but I am beginning to have my doubts about our leader's dedication to the cause."

"Oh? Really?" Cabby responded, breathing in a powerful mix of peppermint and mothballs.

"Well, yes." Her neighbor raised surprised eyebrows. "You haven't heard about the kerfluffle last Friday evening?"

"No-o-o." Cabby mentally filed away the word "kerfluffle" for future use. "Tell me." Her fingers had that familiar reporter's itch. If Fairchild failed to show, his absence could make for a more interesting story than the one she'd expected.

From the depths of her purse, Cabby's neighbor plucked a folded green paper, opened it, and waved it as prelude to answering, "Well, this past Friday evening a hundred of us gathered at the Metropolis Club for a dinner meeting. Mr. Fairchild was to speak on 'The Yellow Peril and the Danger to Civilized Mankind.'"

"The Yellow Peril. Oh, my, yes," Cabby replied, when it became clear that a response was expected. A hundred, huh? There couldn't be more than thirty in the hall tonight.

The woman raised a finger. "I'll have you know we waited all the way through Waldorf salad, chicken cordon bleu, then coconut cake and coffee, and he never came! Do you call that dedication?"

Cabby shook her head vigorously, as she reached for the green flier and gave it the once-over. Instead of handing it back, however, she folded it between two fingers and tucked it under her arm. After a moment, it found a new home in her jacket pocket.

The woman sat back, oblivious. "And, then, only two days later, the Japanese attacked Hawaii..." Abruptly, she bowed her head, her expression stricken. "Followed by Mr. Roosevelt's war declaration—horribly misguided."

Horribly misguided? Cabby swallowed a gasp.

"I am simply terrified," her neighbor went on, "that Roosevelt will next declare war on Germany. As dear Mr. Lindbergh has reminded us, we have only a one-ocean navy and cannot win a two-ocean war. Joining the hostilities against Germany would be a sorry overreaction."

The hostilities against Germany? Cabby blinked. "But, what if Hitler declares war on us first?—"

"Then it will be all that Mr. Churchill's fault!" Miss Peppermint whispered. "He and President *Roosenberg* are thick as thieves—oh, here's our speaker. Finally!"

Following her neighbor's lead, Cabby rose to her feet and applauded as Nigel Fairchild paraded down the center aisle. The silver-haired man waved as if his audience filled the room and hung over nonexistent balcony railings. Cabby had a close view of his face as he stopped to wring Miss Peppermint's hand. Though his lips smiled, the rest of his features were set in an expression of bitter disappointment.

Fairchild may have arrived, Cabby thought, but he sure ain't a happy man.

Chapter Forty-seven

In the hushed, fifth-floor corridor of the apartment building, Louise inserted her key in the Oakleys' lock and jiggled it when it stuck. "After insertion, you must pull back a fraction of an inch," Professor Oakley had instructed. She'd had no problem earlier in the day. Was it Abe Pritzker standing so close behind that made her fingers shake?

As Louise finally convinced the key to turn the lock, the door flew open from inside.

"What the—" She jumped back, smack into Abe, who caught her around the waist. He seemed to be making a habit of that.

Lillian Bridges' cheeks were flushed, gray eyes bright with anger. Instantly, however, her expression changed to relief. "Oh, Nurse. I'm glad you're here. Robert has been waiting. Then she turned toward Abe. "You must be the lawyer. Sorry for the reception—I thought you would be more police."

Abe hustled Louise into the apartment foyer. "Police?"

"Yes! Some damned detective is harassing Robert about Arthur's murder. You must do something."

Louise made an abrupt move toward the sickroom, but Abe held her back. "What detective?"

"Lieutenant McKenna—a real…hardnose."

"Oh, yeah?" Abe frowned, then sucked his teeth. "And who are you?"

Louise jumped in. "This is Professor Bridges. I should have introduced—"

"Don't be silly." Lillian clutched Abe's overcoat sleeve with both hands. "The police rang the bell not five minutes ago, insisting on seeing Robert. Three officers. I begged them to wait until I could summon George Wright, but" —she drew herself up and smoothed her silver-threaded dark bob—"my words went unheeded. Now Mr. McKenna has tossed me out of Robert's room and that nurse in there is next to useless. Do hurry."

She started down the hall. After trading glances, Abe and Louise followed. "What's McKenna questioning the professor about?" the lawyer asked.

"Masako," Professor Bridges threw over her shoulder. "He wants to know where she was the night Arthur was killed."

At the door to the sickroom, a uniformed nurse in a drooping cap slipped out with a half-full glass of juice on a kitchen tray and closed the door behind her. Her expression revealed neither concern about the police confronting her patient, nor any interest in who these new strangers might be. Louise glared at the woman's retreating back. Obviously not a nurse in Kitty's league.

Or her own.

Lillian Bridges attempted to push through the door, but something prevented her. When Abe added his shoulder, they popped into the dimly-lit bedroom only to be stopped by a young man in a double-breasted gray pinstripe suit. He held up his palm like a traffic cop. "Didn't I tell you to stay out, ma'am?" Then he registered the newcomers. "Who are these people?"

"Who are you?" Abe countered.

"Sergeant Brenner. Answer my question."

Louise left Abe to deal with the sergeant and did a slow burn as she looked around. The room smelled of fever, dying roses, and human waste. Bedpans and vases both needed to be emptied. She'd have a talk with the Registry.

Then she caught sight of Robert Oakley, who looked even sicker than yesterday. Nonetheless, Lieutenant McKenna had drawn the red leather club chair right up to the bedside and was firing questions one after the other. Behind him, a dumpy older detective applied a pencil to a small notebook. At an exclamation from Abe, McKenna sent the group at the door a sharp glance.

Oakley saw them, too. He struggled to sit up.

"I'm here, Robert," Lillian Bridges called, but Oakley trained his gaze on Louise. "Is that you, my dear? Have you seen my Masako?"

Evading Brenner and the disgruntled lady professor, Louise darted across the room to take the professor's hot, clammy hand. "Not since yesterday. But she's all right. Abe…Mr. Pritzker here…has been calling to check on her." Louise dipped a washcloth in a basin of tepid water on the nightstand. Wringing out the wet cloth she mopped her patient's face and forehead. Taking a deep breath, she turned to McKenna."Is this really necessary? I can't emphasize enough how dangerous it is for him to be distressed."

McKenna turned his sober gaze on her and raised a big hand. "We'll be out of here sooner if you don't interrupt."

Brenner had gone out of the room for a moment. He came back to deliver a few words in his boss' ear. With a pained grimace, his expression impassive, McKenna shifted his weight in the chair. He addressed Abe. "Okay, Mr. Pritzker. Since you're here, ya might as well stay. But keep it quiet, okay?" He aimed a finger jab at Professor Bridges. "And that goes for you, too, lady. Any more outbursts and it's twenty-three skidoo. You got that?"

Lillian Bridges pressed her hands to her mouth, eyes wide with an emotion Louise couldn't identify. Anger? Alarm? She and Abe drew closer to the bed. Louise had to wonder just how long the lawyer could keep his own mouth shut.

McKenna renewed his questions. "Admit it, Professor Oakley," he prodded. "Your wife was angry at Shelton for shutting down her show."

Oakley plucked at the sheets with agitated fingers. "You still suspect her of murder?" With mammoth effort, he rose to one elbow. "Have you seen Masako's paintings? They celebrate life, not death. Just take a look in the living room."

McKenna opened his mouth, but Oakley wheezed on, "Oh, no, you can't look at her paintings, can you?—your men ripped them off the wall." Tears flooded his eyes as he fell back. "Who knows what you've done with them."

Louise whispered, "Settle down, professor." Then she glared at McKenna in frustration. If she had MD instead of RN after her name, she'd give all three policemen the heave-ho.

McKenna paid her no attention. "Don't go making any assumptions about what we did or didn't do. I understand the FBI confiscated some art, but my guys didn't touch a thing. In fact, we pulled every string possible trying to keep the Feds from getting the paintings at the gallery."

He fell silent for a moment, looking over a small notebook, and the strains of a swing tune filtered through the open doorway. The agency nurse must have turned on the kitchen radio—way too loud. Louise shook her head. When they got the police out of here, she'd chase that lazy cow from the apartment. She threw Abe a pleading glance, but all the lawyer offered was a shrug. Professor Bridges still had her hand to her mouth. Her knuckles were white.

McKenna slapped his notebook against his palm. "Let's quit pussyfootin' around, Oakley. Do you still claim your wife was here last Friday evening?"

"*Claim*? I said so, didn't I? Where else do you think she'd be?"

"The whole evening?" McKenna sat forward.

Wheezing breath. "Of course, the whole evening!"

"You wouldn't maybe have been asleep—at least part of the time?"

Louise didn't like the sound of this. Of course the sick man drifted in and out of sleep.

Oakley turned his head restlessly on the pillows. "This is ridiculous," he muttered feebly, barely moving his lips.

McKenna levered himself out of the chair. He traded glances with the older detective. Louise could read his expression: Why do they always think they can get away with this stuff?

Now looking down on her patient, McKenna asked, "If your wife was here the whole evening, how come we have a witness who swears he saw an Asian woman get out of a cab in front of the Shelton Gallery at 7:15 the night Shelton was murdered?"

Robert Oakley bolted upright. "She was here. I told you she was here, and she was!" He coughed, hard, and began to wheeze.

Louise watched his face turn from porcelain white to beef-steak red and was horrified to see a glob of rust colored sputum hit the white sheet.

"That's it," she ordered. "Everybody out." When McKenna didn't move, Louise stepped nose to nose with the detective. "What are you trying to do—kill this man? Get out. Get out all of you!"

The lady professor gave a moan and wrung her hands.

Abe edged in and began backing McKenna and his men toward the door. "Surely, Lieutenant, you don't want to be liable for Professor Oakley's death?"

Even as she turned her attention back to Oakley, Louise recognized the threat of potential litigation.

"And, remember…" Abe continued his slow advance as the cops retreated. "Mrs. Oakley is not the only Asian woman in Manhattan."

"Yeah, counselor." McKenna halted, an overcoated mountain of determination. "But—not only do we have that witness, Sergeant Brenner here tells me we've just located the cab driver who picked her up in front of this very building and drove her to the gallery. The doorman downstairs confirms that he hailed the cab for Mrs. Oakley around seven o'clock."

Lillian Bridges sucked in a deep breath, and Louise's heart sank as McKenna drove his point home.

"So you see, counselor, there's no doubt about the identity of the woman at the Shelton Gallery at the time Arthur Shelton was murdered. It wasn't just any Asian woman. It was Masako Fumi Oakley. No doubt at all—it was her."

Chapter Forty-eight

Wednesday night, several hours later

Louise shivered in the darkness and moved closer to Abe, hoping his lanky height would block the raw, salt-tinged wind that blustered off New York Bay. Damn this thin Kentucky coat, anyway.

It was a chilly, starry night on the Battery. Gulls cried. Flags flapped. Mooring lines creaked in the choppy black waves. Across the Bay, the massive buildings of the immigration center hunkered on Ellis Island, yellow window lights shining in regimented rows. To the left, the great Statue dwarfed the buildings.

When they'd left the Oakley's apartment on their way back to Brooklyn, Louise had impulsively asked Abe to take her to the Battery. She didn't know exactly what she wanted there. Another look at Ellis Island, she told him.

But it was more than that. It had something to do with freedom and justice. Trust and friendship.

Detective McKenna's eyewitness evidence against Masako Oakley replayed in her head. Over and over. Slow, fast, then slow again. It was like watching the newsreel of that dreadful Hindenburg crash. Her faith in the Japanese woman's goodness, and in her own judgment, threatened to collapse in flames, just like the doomed airship. She couldn't forget now that she'd dismissed Masako's argument with Arthur Shelton as a minor tiff. She'd kept it from McKenna, hadn't even told Abe. Now this…

Louise squeezed her arm under Abe's, staring at the distant walls that confined Masako and the other foreigners who'd been picked up. She'd always prided herself on understanding what made people tick, and, despite all, she just couldn't believe Masako Oakley had killed Arthur Shelton. It went against every ounce of intuition she possessed. Did the police have the same agenda as the FBI?

"Penny for your thoughts," Abe's deep voice rumbled.

"I was just thinking…" she answered slowly, "well…it's the easy way out, isn't it?"

"What is?" He gave her one of his disconcerting smiles, and she swallowed hard.

"For the authorities, I mean—framing Mrs. Oakley as a killer."

"Framing? That's a pretty strong accusation. And, you've got to admit that McKenna's evidence could make for a powerful case against her."

"She's Japanese. With no family here except her seriously ill husband. Nobody will care if they just ram—"

"Listen here, Louise." He placed his hands on her shoulders, turned her toward him. "You can't let emotion blind you to the necessity for a thorough police investigation and whatever results it turns up. And…let me remind you, please, it's not my job to defend Masako Oakley against a murder charge. I don't want there to be any confusion about that. I'm not a criminal lawyer. My job is to guarantee her equal protection under the law. The Fourteenth Amendment applies to every person, citizen or not."

"Equal protection won't matter a damn if she's sent to the electric chair," Louise shot back.

Abe squinted down at her and smiled again. "Well, well. Aren't you the little spitfire?"

Louise drew herself up to full height and squared her shoulders. Her eyes were level with his loosened necktie knot. She stepped back. "Don't patronize me, Abe Pritzker." Turning away, she gazed out at the onion-domed fortress. Tears sprang to her eyes.

This was a far cry from her first visit to the Battery on a sunny afternoon last September. Preston's strong arm had encircled her shoulders as she took her first-ever look at Lady Liberty. Under the clear blue sky, the bay had spread out like an undulating green lawn plowed by luxury liners and squat tugs that reminded her of the toy boats her brothers had sailed on the lake at Cherokee Park. She and Preston had slathered hot, salty New York pretzels with mustard and made plans for the future.

No ocean-going liners tonight. That sort of luxury travel was over for the duration.

So was Preston. For the long, long duration.

She should have known it wouldn't work. The tall, dark-haired cardiology fellow she'd first met at the Kentucky Baptist Hospital had seemed like a fairy-tale prince. Intelligent and self-assured, but funny, too, and always ready to head downtown with a group of nurses and interns for a show or a hamburger. Then, later, whiling away the summer evenings on her porch swing, meeting her parents. She could never have imagined that Dr. Preston VanDyke Atherton would crumble under his mother's disapproval like an earthen dam in a raging river flood.

Her fiancé's mother had turned up her patrician nose after one meeting over luncheon at the Atherton mansion: no son of hers was going to marry a nobody nurse—from Kentucky of all places. Not even if her son had lured that nobody to Manhattan with a one-carat tiffany-cut diamond and the promise of happy ever after.

Louise suspected that Pres had been forcefully reminded of the possibility of disinheritance. Within days of his hasty, strained apology, he had taken off to London to volunteer in the British Army Medical Corps, and Louise had found herself alone in this strange, overwhelming metropolis. She could never go home now, not without a wedding ring.

She lowered the hankie from her dripping eyes. It was simply the chill wind that made them tear, she told herself.

Abe had moved away, to purchase a sack of roast chestnuts from a vendor at a charcoal brazier. Their delectable aroma mixed with cigarette smoke and permeated the crisp air. Farther along the railing, a thin sailor in a navy peacoat stared out to sea, smoking one cigarette after another. Several yards beyond, an Italian family crowded around a middle-aged woman, who keened as she held out pleading arms toward Ellis Island. The woman's eerie lament sounded in one endless, wordless vowel. Was it her husband who'd been detained? Her son? Perhaps her father?

Louise stared for a short moment. Then she pulled her gaze away, feeling like an interloper. Abe was back. He held out the chestnuts. "Peace offering?"

She nodded, sliding her hand into the warm sack, burning her fingers.

"Don't misunderstand me, Louise," he said. "I have no desire to 'patronize' you. It's just that, you know, that magnolia skin, Georgia-peach beauty of yours is so at odds with what turns out to be a truck load of intelligence and determination—"

"Oh, Abe, stop it! This is no time for flattery. I just want to make certain Mrs. Oakley gets a fair shake. And I won't rest until—"

"Okay! Okay!" He stepped back. "All business, huh? So, hear me, now. I've asked around about that cop, McKenna. He has a reputation as a straight-shooter. I can't see him framing anyone. The Federals, on the other hand…they've pulled some pretty smelly deals, especially where organized crime is concerned. Over the years, Hoover has proven himself more interested in results than in above-board procedures. Now that we're at war, his goons will feel even more justified in cutting corners."

Louise pressed a couple of hot chestnuts into her palm. "I wouldn't trust that Agent Bagwell as far as I could throw him."

"Me, either."

"So what can we do?"

"Number one, I'm going to have to bend over backwards to keep the homicide case separate from the enemy alien case. Two, we need to do whatever we can to assist McKenna in finding Shelton's killer. Unfortunately, Mrs. Oakley's presence at the art gallery the evening of the murder..." He paused, and then went on, "complicates that...considerably..."

Louise was watching him intently, listening hard to every word. When he trailed off, she stared up at him and smiled. "Fourteenth Amendment aside, you don't think she's guilty, either."

"Don't look at me like that." He frowned. "I'm having a hard time keeping my hands off you."

"Oh," she said, and dropped the chestnuts.

When he kissed her, it was all she could do to keep from melting into his arms. Instead, she pulled away, breathless, uncertain, emotions roiling. His hands on her shoulders, he gazed questioningly at her for a long moment. Then his expression altered as he seemed to answer his own question. He dropped his hands. She saw his Adam's apple bob up, then down.

"Sorry," he said, swallowing again. "I was out of order there. You're just not that..." He fumbled with the chestnut bag, shoved it into his overcoat pocket and retrieved a pair of ratty leather gloves, pulling them on with great attention to each long finger. He took a deep breath. "You don't have to worry, Louise. I won't do that again."

Unaccountably, she felt bereft.

Chapter Forty-nine

Researching America First back at the *Times* morgue, Cabby had found a series of articles covering Charles Lindbergh's massive rally in Madison Square Garden last April. Nigel Fairchild himself had introduced "Lucky Lindy," who'd proceeded to caution a flag-waving, cheering crowd against supporting Roosevelt.

The European war, the famous pilot insisted, was not America's war. It lay squarely in the laps of Franklin and Eleanor—warmongers the pair of them. Ten thousand people in the Garden, and an additional fifteen thousand listening to amplifiers in the rain-soaked streets, roared approval. Britain was doomed, Lindy opined. If we joined her in the fight against Hitler, she would drag us down with her, heralding the demise of global democracy. Thus it was America's moral obligation to isolate our great nation from Europe's problems and preserve the last staunch bastion of freedom and equalitarianism on earth.

A mere eight months ago, Cabby thought, the masses had lapped up Lindy's stew of isolationist rhetoric with a spoon. Thousands of America First membership applications had been filed during the days following that speech. But who'd shown for tonight's meeting? Only a handful of misfits. How quickly things change.

Now Nigel Fairchild's baritone resonated through the tinny microphone of the America First meeting room. "My friends, the news is not good...."

Cabby's neighbor, the peppermint lady, retrieved a small paper flag from somewhere in her bags and waved it half-heartedly as the speaker continued. "While our cause of nonintervention in this unfortunate global strife is wise and just, and we have backed it with a full measure of devotion…" He paused again for an owlish stare, then breathed out heavily. "We must face facts. We. Are. At. War."

A man of middle height, deep into his fifties, Fairchild wore a well-tailored Norfolk jacket in brown tweed. His broad shoulders were set in a posture of resolution, and his silver hair was folded into a natty pompadour. A burly man in grey broadcloth had followed him to the dais and now sat to one side, observing the rapt audience with eagle eyes. Cabby didn't get it, but Fairchild obviously possessed some forceful personal magnetism.

Who were these people?

A large-bosomed woman in the row across the aisle, sporting a button that read, BUNDLE FROM BRITAIN: YOUR SON?

A number of Germanic-looking working men, middle-aged and older—likely fellow-travelers with the Bund.

A few plainly dressed young men who might be pacifists by religious conviction—Quakers and such.

But who was that woman with the expensive plumed hat sitting alone down front? Twisting to get a glimpse of her face, Cabby noted curtains of elegant blond waves framing a portrait of adoration: a true believer whose gaze never left the speaker.

Cabby nudged her neighbor. "Do you know that lady?" she whispered with finger discretely extended.

"What?" Miss Peppermint scowled. "Oh, that's Tiffy De Forest. One of Nigel's staunchest supporters. Rather empty-headed, I suspect, but she's generous with donations for the cause." As she followed this with a growled order to hush, Cabby directed her attention back to Nigel Fairchild.

"No one could have done more for American peace and self-sufficiency than our organization." Fairchild made a fist and pounded his chest. "But I am devastated to inform you, my dear friends, that, in the interests of national unity, the America

First Committee has voted to immediately cease all activities and disband."

"Huh?" Bewildered looks flew around the audience. "What?"

Cabby could feel her neighbor's cold, stunned horror, and, after a moment, the heat of her outrage. Miss Peppermint hissed. A handful of the others followed suit. She jumped up from her seat. "Traitor!" she yelled. "Turncoat!" Then, rising in pitch, "Warmonger!"

The man in gray stood, tense and ready at the edge of the dais. A bodyguard, Cabby thought, here to protect Fairchild from hecklers.

From the front row, Tiffy De Forest sent back a piercing look.

"Miss Garrison, please." The woman with the Bundles from Britain button had also jumped up. She came over to pat Miss Garrison's back as if she were calming a colicky baby.

"Esther, my dear," Fairchild pleaded into the microphone.

But Miss Esther Garrison wasn't mollified. Her chunky club heels beat out a protesting rat-a-tat-tat as she stormed out of the room. A seedy man with overlong hair followed her. The rest sank to their seats again, trading uneasy looks. The man in gray sat down, too.

Wow! Cabby retrieved her notebook from her bag and began to write, recording Fairchild's announcement word for word. She looked up when a shadow blocked her light. The large-bosomed woman hovered. "Who are you? I haven't seen you here before."

"Oh," Cabby said, flipping the notebook shut to reveal her *Times* press pass clipped to its cover, "I'm here to cover the meeting."

The woman instantly adopted a mask of caution. "The *Times* is no friend to our cause." She appropriated Miss Garrison's seat, crowding close to peer over Cabby's shoulder. "I'd better make certain you get it right."

Not missing a beat, Cabby scooted over one seat and rendered her shorthand even more illegible than usual.

"I apologize for the unfortunate interruption." Nigel Fairchild returned to his prepared agenda. "When I say that the time has come to disband, I speak for the national Committee. It is now, of course, the duty of our members to remain loyal to the government of the United States, to support our military and our president."

Fairchild took a handkerchief from his breast pocket. He lowered his voice and his tone altered. "Now I go beyond the decision of the national Committee and speak for myself—and perhaps for many of you." He mopped his face. "My friends, it is a great pity that our president has not seen fit to come to a negotiated peace with Mr. Hitler. The Germans are a Christian people and a white race. If they declare war on us, we can trust the struggle will be civilized."

Cabby narrowed her eyes. Civilized? What was civilized about the Nazi invasion of Poland? Or of Holland?

"On the other hand," Fairchild continued. "Japan is a vile yellow snake that has revealed its capacity to strike at our very shores. Our energies must now be directed toward defeating Japan." He paused, this time to mop his brow. "We fight to preserve our race."

A deep murmur of agreement ran through the sparse audience, like the sound of some ancient beast arising from the mud. It sounded to Cabby like the primal hatred she might expect to hear at a Klan meeting somewhere in the depths of a Mississippi swamp. Her veins chilled. This pompous man was appealing to the very worst in the American character.

Fairchild was thundering now, following each sentence with the whip-like snap of an arm. "We must take our unsullied American ideals to the streets of our cities. Every man must do his utmost to rid us of the Japanese still in our nation. And every woman, too."

Fairchild paused for a smile at Tiffy De Forest. Cabby heard a jealous hiss from her large-bosomed neighbor.

His voice resumed, silky with assurance. "My friends, we must all take responsibility—personal responsibility—to remove the Japanese race from our shops, our eating places, our universities." He leaned over the lectern. "Every influence of the rapacious yellow horde must be wiped out. Even our cultural ideals have been tainted. Why, I myself witnessed a display of Japanese art only a week or so ago right on Fifty-seventh Street—in one of our most prestigious galleries. Shameful!"

Cabby sat up very straight. He must be talking about Masako Fumi Oakley's show.

"Now, my friends…" Fairchild touched the handkerchief to his upper lip. "I stand ready to address the questions I know you must have." As clothing rustled and chairs scraped throughout the meeting room, Cabby made a lightning connection. She pulled Miss Garrison's announcement of Fairchild's long-scheduled lecture out of her pocket. Friday night—December the fifth, the very night Arthur Shelton had been killed—Fairchild had missed his dinner speech. One hundred acolytes waiting, and he had stood them up. Why? Had he been taking "personal responsibility"—to shut down an art dealer who'd championed a Japanese artist?

Ignoring a tiny internal voice that advised caution, Cabby jumped to her feet. "I have a question, Mr. Fairchild."

"Yes, my dear." The silver-haired speaker favored her with an avuncular smile.

"Given your zeal for the cause, how come you skipped last Friday night's speaking engagement at the Metropolis Club?"

Every head in the place swiveled in Cabby's direction. Fairchild's smile dwindled, became an angry frown. He signaled his burly henchman with pointed look. The man in gray broadcloth stepped off the dais.

Oh no, Cabby thought, bad move. Alley Oop's gonna toss me out on my can. I'll be lucky to get home with my skin intact.

Chapter Fifty

Howie stretched the plaid blanket over the rolled pillows and sheets, then backed to the doorway to admire his work. Yeah, this was the way they always did it in books. If Ma peeked in his bedroom door, she'd think he was fast asleep. If she came in to lay a hand on his shoulder and listen for his breathing like she sometimes did, then the jig was up. She'd scream and yell—and bawl—but too bad.

He'd be long gone, and it was all her fault—for lying to him in the first place. All that shit about California, making him think Papa would send for them any day.

After Patrolman Drury had dragged him back from the recruiting center, Howie had finally gotten Ma to spill the beans. It was like Cheapy said. Papa was on Hitler's side. Ma didn't know where he was or what he was doing, but he'd gone over to the enemy.

"Ma…" he'd asked, "if Papa is a Nazi, does that make us Nazis, too?"

For an instant, there'd been fear in her eyes. Then, "*Nein*. Never. Don't ever say that. Don't even think it."

His throat was raw and he knew he should shut up, but he went on, anyway, "If Hitler is so bad, why does Papa like him?"

Ma had pressed her lips together then, so hard her mouth creases looked an inch deep. She said, "You're too young to understand. When the time is right, explanations will come."

"When will that be, Ma?"

"When I say." Hands on hips. Glare. Conversation closed.

That had been two days ago. It had taken him that long to decide what he had to do.

◇◇◇

Hopping a train wasn't the piece of cake he'd imagined. While exploring the huge yard, he stumbled across a pair of bulls, railroad detectives. One carried a club that made Patrolman Drury's nightstick look like a Tinker Toy. The other toted a rifle. They chased him forever, until he fell through a gap in the fence and slid down an embankment, landing him in this hobo camp. Now Howie was warming his hands at a fire in a rusty oil drum, beneath a cold, black sky, now streaked with ragged clouds. After the tangled maze of criss-cross tracks and hulking boxcars, the hobo camp outside the Jersey City rail yard seemed like a refuge. He had a hundred questions for these tramps. How did you know where the trains were going? Did anyone ever get locked in one of those boxcars and starve to death?

Above the dancing flames, a grizzled man's face looked like Ming the Merciless in the Flash Gordon serials. But his voice was kind. "You oughta go home, kid. Ridin' the rails ain't what it used to be. Now it's just a bunch of bums up to no good. Back when I started, decent people caught the train to find work. Had to—we had no money and no food."

Howie couldn't stay home. He knew what he had to do—his papa was a Nazi, and his duty was clear. "I gotta catch a train, Mister. I just need you to tell me how to do it."

The other men around the fire shook their heads. A colored man with a ragged eye patch told a story about a kid who'd had his legs cut off by the train wheels. "His momma had to bury him in three pieces," he finished in a hushed whisper.

Howie tried to ignore the sick feeling in his stomach. "You don't understand—I can't go home. I'm gonna hop a train, with you or without you. The sooner, the better."

A rough-looking kid with a cap pulled low spoke up. "Ya wait outside the fence or the bulls'll get ya. When the train's barely moving, ya pick out an open car and run alongside…"

"Yeah?" Howie's breath stuck in his throat. This kid was only a couple of years older than him, and he had the deadest eyes the Brooklyn boy had ever seen. "And then?"

"Then throw your bag up, grab onta the edge and swing yourself through the door. But ya can't let your legs go under the car, see?"

Howie nodded slowly. He felt like he had to crap, but he said, "Okay. I can do that."

"Then now's the time, kid. Hear that?" The grizzled man held up gloved fingers like a priest giving a blessing. A locomotive whistle tooted on the wind. "The one-twenty. Pennsylvania Railroad, southbound."

Howie gave the hobos several backward glances as he left the warmth of the fire and scrambled up the bank. In the dim glow from the rail yard's pole lights, he found the tracks and stationed himself behind a bush. Soon he saw the glare of a locomotive headlight, heard the massive engine chuffing toward him. Howie hunched over like the hurdlers on his high school track team before the starting pistol popped. Every muscle tensed; his knees shook.

The engine rumbled past. Pretty slow, just like the kid with the dead eyes had told him. You can do this, Howie told himself. After six or seven cars went by, he burst from his hiding place and ran alongside the train. Soot and cinders stung his cheeks, forced his eyes to narrow slits. Legs pumping, he picked out an empty boxcar and focused on its open door.

Faster—the train was picking up speed—he had to run faster. The clatter from the wheels filled his ears. Nothing else existed except the deafening noise and the empty black rectangle of the boxcar door. His chest hurt. Was he losing ground? It was now or never. Howie heaved his pillowcase bag through the opening.

With a mammoth effort, he made a grab for the edge, missed. Tried again and made contact. The train's momentum jerked his feet out from under him. Oh, fuck! He was holding on for dear life, legs dangling free. He could feel the wind from the big wheels.

"We got cha, kid. Hang on." Voices from above. Strong hands gripped his jacket collar and the seat of his pants. For a few seconds, he hung in space like he was flying.

It would've been glorious, if he hadn't been so goddamn scared.

Then two men pulled him into the boxcar. He rolled a couple of times, and, when he pushed up on weak knees, he saw five or six others crouching in the corner of the car. Uh oh. Were these ragged people bums or decent folk? He didn't have a clue.

Chapter Fifty-one

Thursday, December 11, after midnight

Helda didn't wait for the one a.m. knock on the door. The red Bakelite clock over the stove said 12:50. Ernst, according to his note, would be here any minute. Donning her winter coat and pulling on wool gloves, she stepped off the kitchen porch into the backyard. The cold embraced her in its deadly clasp. Frozen grass crunched beneath her feet.

That rattling? What...? Oh, next door. Mr. Bidwell's whirligigs. He made the little wind machines in his basement woodshop and attached them to the fence—a man sawing wood, a kicking mule, a woman hoeing. Silly to be so jumpy over toys.

She had not turned any lights on, but still she moved deeper into the shadow of the porch, to the ell corner where the wood frame joined the brownstone exterior of the main house. She would hide herself there so she could see him coming. So she could see Ernst before he saw her. It was the darkest kind of night. Clouds scudded across the sky. Smelled like rain. But she wouldn't let that stop her from waiting outside. She would not invite Ernst in. *Nein*—no more *Liebchen*, smiling, baking sweet things, apologizing. Groveling.

Mein Gott! That *gespentisch* wail? Something slithered around her ankles. She shrieked. It meowed. That pest of a tom cat! No matter what she told Howie, he kept feeding that beat-up, mangy, stinking beast. She gave the cat a little kick, and he yowled off down the street.

She had too much at stake now to allow Ernst Schroeder access to her home. The boarding house, finally paying its way. Her papers filed to become a citizen one day. An American! She wouldn't let him ruin any of that.

And, of course, she must keep Ernst away from Howie. He must never know his father had returned. Four years now since her husband had put the interests of *der Vaterland* above those of his son. Well, then, he'd made his choice. Let him live with it.

She straightened her shoulders, resolute.

He must have been waiting in the bushes, for he grabbed her from behind and spun her toward him, his hand over her mouth to prevent a scream. "Not a word, Helda." Ernst spoke in German. "Not the slightest sound. If I am caught, it is over for me. You understand?"

She nodded, her heart thudding like the engine on the train that used to carry them out to Camp Siegfried.

Slowly he released his hand, allowed her to breathe. His expression, as he stared into her eyes, was intense and ambiguous, at once aloof and needy.

Mein Gott, Helda thought, he wants me still to love him.

The years back in Germany had not been unkind to Herr Ernst Schroeder, true believer in the *Reich*. Still tall and straight, and more fit than ever, he had retained his Teutonic good looks, the blond hair unsprinkled with white, the blue eyes still deep and compelling.

After months of arguments, he had deserted her without a word, left his son to worry and grieve. He had not provided for them. For all he knew, they could now be destitute. And he dared to come to her with that look in his eyes!

She pulled away, crossing her arms over her chest, and waited.

He sighed and stepped back. "You hate me."

"What do you want?"

His stance stiffened. "I want to see my son."

"*Nein.*" She glared at him. "*Nein. Nein. Nein. Nein.*"

"He is my son. I have the right." Ernst towered over her. Even in the dimness, she could see he was dressed like any American—tan trench coat, creased trousers, good shoes.

"He is tucked up in bed, safe and sound, like a boy his age should be. You will not disturb him."

"He is mine!" Ernst moved to brush past her.

She shoved him with all her strength, and, caught off guard, he stumbled into a leafless lilac bush. "You," she said, "a lot you cared for him when you and your Bund friends sailed back to Germany with who knows what wicked purpose in mind!"

"*Der Vaterland!*" he cried. As if that one word made his priorities self-evident.

"*Der Vaterland,*" she spit out. "What is that compared to your son? Your family? That you should throw us over to enlist in service to its cause? Hitler's cause!"

"No more talking! It is my destiny." He threw his shoulders back. "And I will have my son."

She glared at him, feeling only contempt. "You think I don't see your game? Now that Howie is getting big, you want to recruit him for *der Fuhrer—nein?*" This was no longer the man she'd married. "Howie is an American. He stays here, where he belongs."

Ernst grabbed her arms. "He is a German—"

"You take one step toward the house," she said, "and I will call the police."

His grip tightened.

"I will scream."

He stood there, staring at her, as if in calculation. Then he spun her away from him, turned on his heel and stalked off. She followed him with her eyes until he passed under the corner streetlight and vanished down the sidewalk. She continued standing in the dark night, watching the spot where he no longer was.

If you make one move to recruit my son, she thought, I will kill you.

Chapter Fifty-two

Ri-i-i-ing! Strident, off-pitch, unstopping.

Head emerging from a pillow sandwich, Cabby moaned. It couldn't be morning already! But her alarm wasn't lying; the bedside clock's glow-in-the-dark hands spanned a wide angle between seven and twelve. Cabby silenced the noisy beast, rubbed her eyes and yawned. A headache made itself known, a dull pounding behind her brow. No wonder. She'd spent half the night dreaming about the burly man in the gray suit chasing her down nightmare alleys. She couldn't imagine what had gotten into her, challenging Fairchild as she had. It wasn't until she was on the subway, feet planted wide as she hung onto the porcelain handle and swayed back and forth, that she began looking over her shoulder. The stations roared past the windows one after the other like lighted rooms in a world of darkness, and she had far too much time to think about the possible consequences of her rash question. After they crossed over into Brooklyn and the crowd thinned, she began to relax. No burly henchman in gray to be seen anywhere.

Now, without switching on the lamp, Cabby eased her toes toward the cold floor to search for her flannel slippers. There, one foot warm, at least. Now, the other…

Light flooded the room, and she squealed. "Lou-lou! Good god, what are you doing here?"

Her roommate, whose honey-colored hair was wound around metal curlers, pushed up on one elbow. "I live here, remember."

Louise's flannel nightgown reminded Cabby of something her mother might wear. Strike that—something her mother might wear if she were a cloistered nun in an Arctic climate.

Cabby said, "You weren't here when I went to bed."

"I got in late." Louise swung her feet to the floor, grabbed a pink chenille robe, and lumbered over to her dresser. "You were snoring to beat the band."

She had been lying awake since five, replaying yesterday's double whammy: McKenna's revelation, and, even more shocking...Abe's kiss.

Louise turned her back on Cabby and gave her reflection in the dresser mirror a long look. More shocking, and, yes, to be honest, quite thrilling. What had he said? Intelligence and determination. Sure, sure. But...what else? Her...magnolia... beauty? She chastised herself—she shouldn't be so vain! But what else? He felt...what? He...couldn't keep his hands off her? Louise shivered with unholy delight.

Cabby shivered, too, as she watched her roommate rummage around for soap and washcloth. Helda was generous with their meals, but the landlady sure was a miser when it came to coal. Was it only the bedroom's chill that had turned Louise's expression as opaque as the East River at midnight?

Cabby hadn't seen her roommate since their argument at the Automat. She didn't like the way they'd left things. Apparently Louise didn't, either, because she wasn't snapping at her. Maybe the girl wasn't so bad. She hadn't caved in to her mother's demands that she scoot on home like a frightened rabbit—and she sure was showing a lot of gumption defending a Japanese woman when most New Yorkers would just as soon throw that dragon lady off the Brooklyn Bridge.

Cabby realized she didn't want Louise mad at her.

"Ah, Lou...er, Louise." She pulled on her own robe. "I was just surprised to see you because I thought you'd still be at work. Your patient didn't...die, did he?"

"No—thank god. He's holding his own, but barely. Dr. Wright arranged for a relief nurse to cover my shifts. He thinks I can be of more use to Professor Oakley by helping free his wife."

"Real-l-ly? That's swell, but can your pocketbook take the punch?"

"I'm actually still getting paid, working with…the lawyer and all." Louise flushed.

Cabby's sharp eye caught the sudden rosiness of her room-mate's cheeks.

"Not that I intend to share any details with you," Louise said with a straight look, "not unless I want to read all about it in the *New York Times*." She tossed a hairbrush in her bag and headed for the bathroom down the hall.

Whew! Cabby scampered to the door and watched as her roommate's pink-flowered back passed Marion's room and disappeared around the corner. Okay, Louise was still mad as hell. Maybe, just maybe, she did suspect Cabby of lifting the Oakley notes. She stared at the ceiling, rubbing her sleep-crushed curls. A soap opera heroine from one of her mother's radio shows would come clean and beg forgiveness on bended knee. Should she?

"Nah!" Cabby blurted out loud. Halper'd already given her enough grief to last a lifetime. No need to invite a tongue lashing from Louise. She'd just sneak the notes back into her roommate's purse.

No, into her coat pocket.

After one more glance down the empty corridor, Cabby closed the door, dug the envelope out of her bag and fetched Louise's swing coat from the tall stand in the corner. She'd tear the pocket lining and stuff the envelope in as if it had dropped through. Genius!

When the door burst open, Cabby had Louise's coat spread out on her bed. "Lou-lou!" she cried, making a frantic bid to stash the envelope under her robe.

Louise recognized the thick envelope with its dog-eared corners. Abandoning her forgotten shampoo bottle, she crossed the worn carpet between them. "Oh," she breathed. "You! I should have known."

Cabby braced herself for the inevitable: anger, outrage, even hysteria. Surely Louise would demand a new roommate. She was amazed to see only a look of reproach on the nurse's face.

Louise spoke slowly. "Do you realize how hard it was to reconstruct those notes?"

Cabby shook her head, "I'm sorry," she stammered, "really sorry. I...borrowed...them to write a follow-up article. But when my editor found out I'd...taken...the notes without your permission, he almost canned me." Cabby thrust the envelope into Louise's hand. "It was...shoddy. Just a shoddy, rotten thing to do..." A decisive nod. "Believe me, you don't have to worry about anything like this happening again. That's a promise."

Okay, she thought, it's all out in the open now.

Louise tossed the envelope on her rumpled bed. These notes had been so important only a day ago. Now...

Suddenly she was aware of Cabby's pleading eyes. Louise had no idea what big city newspaper editors looked like, but an image from the movies streaked across her brain—the overambitious reporter catching hell from a gruff man in suspenders and a green eyeshade. Well, maybe Cabby's repentance over the theft of the notes would make her think twice before trying another stunt like that.

"Forget it, roommate." Louise managed a tight smile. "Water under the bridge."

Cabby felt an invisible weight lift off her shoulders. She decided another olive branch was in order. "Listen, last night I found out something that might get your Jap lady...er...Mrs. Oakley...off the hook." She told Louise about Nigel Fairchild's absence from his scheduled speaking date the night of the Shelton murder. "And that in itself wouldn't mean anything except that he hates Japs. Also, he mentioned having been at Mrs. Oakley's gallery opening, and how 'shameful' he thought it was for Shelton to mount that show."

"Is that so?" Louise immediately latched onto the implications of Cabby's news. Her instincts were right after all. Masako may have been on the scene, but someone else killed Shelton.

She grabbed her roommate by the shoulders. "Cabby, have you told Lieutenant McKenna?"

Cabby shrank back. "Well, no. I haven't had a—"

Louise let go. "You better—after that dirty trick you pulled, you owe me. Call him right now. If you don't, I will—"

"Hold your horses, girlie. I just woke up." She was torn—Halper had ordered her away from Shelton's murder, but Fairchild was a different matter. What the hell! She'd tell McKenna. She didn't have to write anything up unless her information actually led to Fairchild's arrest. Halper couldn't fault her for keeping an eye on the old America Firster—he'd handed her the Fairchild assignment, for cripe's sake.

"Cabby…" Louise's gaze threatened to burn a hole in the air between them.

"Okay. Okay. I'll call police headquarters right after breakfast." Cabby's insides squirmed as she recalled the number of times McKenna's secretary had refused to put her through. "Better yet, I'll track the man down and tell him in person."

"Girls!" Alicia Rosen appeared at their open door, breathless and wide-eyed. She was only half-dressed, cardigan sweater smashed under her arm and black hair straggling down her back. "Howie's disappeared! He's gone!"

Louise and Cabby traded shocked looks. "What do you mean, gone?" Cabby asked.

"He just disappeared—sometime in the middle of the night. Helda's a wreck. Cabby, he talks to you. You know anything about this?"

Before Cabby could respond, Louise interrupted. "I'll bet he's trying to enlist again, somewhere farther afield. Maybe Manhattan. But Helda shouldn't worry. No recruiter in his right mind would believe Howie's eighteen. They'll send him right home—just like last time."

Cabby had sunk to the edge of Louise's bed, face buried in her hands.

"What's with you?" Alicia's question took on a suspicious tone.

Cabby swallowed hard. Those photograph albums! Howie's preoccupation with his father. "I don't know if it means anything…"

She paused. Howie hadn't sworn her to secrecy…A cold fist tightened around her heart. But he was only a kid, damn it, and there was a war on. Could he have lit out to track down his German dad? Sheesh, she wouldn't put it past him! Boy, oh, boy! He could end up in big trouble. Up in Yorkville, where the German immigrants lived, beer hall windows had been smashed and strudel bakery signs had been scrawled over with swastikas. In these flammable days, violence could crop up anywhere. And, then, of course, there were the Feds…

Yes, Cabby realized she had to tell Helda what little she knew, and that prospect made her feel sick at heart, sicker than anything else had since the dreadful day of Pearl Harbor.

Chapter Fifty-three

Abe Pritzker's big voice came over the telephone wire louder than life. "You got ten minutes to get ready, Louise. We're going back to Ellis Island."

"We are?" Louise stood at the phone in the upstairs hall, still unbathed and in her pink chenille robe.

Her caller slammed down the receiver. Right ear ringing, Louise hurried to throw on a wool skirt and a cashmere sweater set. She was dabbing on some lipstick just as a car horn began to blare. Damn that man! It would only take two minutes for him to come to the door like a proper gentleman. She grabbed her coat and a thick red wool scarf that belonged to Cabby—who'd gone to the kitchen to console a distraught Helda—and ran downstairs and outside.

Abe's gray sedan was at the curb, passenger door swinging open. Louise jumped in. As Abe pulled away, shifting through clanky gears, a pair of schoolgirls sent them a curious stare and a man in a tan raincoat regarded the car with an intense frown.

"Well?" Louise gave Abe a sidelong look, only to find him skewing his gaze at her. Each snapped eyes forward. So that was it? The only acknowledgement of last night's kiss? She sighed.

"We gotta catch McKenna, sweetie. Before he sets out for Ellis. He doesn't know it yet, but we're going with him. Hang on—gotta get across the bridge."

Louise caught her breath. And hung on. They zipped up busy Flatbush Avenue, veering around a rag collector in his horse-drawn wagon and almost plowing into a double-parked milk-delivery truck. When Louise could breathe again, she brought up Cabby's suspicions about Nigel Fairchild.

"Man oh man." Abe sucked air in through his teeth. As Louise ticked off each of Cabby's points, his grin widened. "Wouldn't—that—be—just ducky."

◇◇◇

"What the hell you two doing here?" McKenna had been watching the police launch approach while eating a hot buttered yam from a street cart. The excursion across the harbor would be cold and damp, so he'd wrapped a heavy knitted muffler up to his chin and stuck wool gloves in his pocket. Now, with a scowl, he tossed the rest of the yam into a barrel, wiped his hands on a handkerchief and strode toward the unwelcome visitors.

The lawyer was yanking Professor Oakley's nurse along the paving stones, hand on her coat sleeve. Man, that nurse had been a bulldog yesterday, but this morning she was all big-eyed and docile, more like a cocker spaniel. Hmm. Did that mean she'd finally realized how much trouble her employer's wife was in?

Abe Pritzker spoke first. "I called your office, Lieutenant. Doris told me you'd be here."

"Doris?" How the hell did this Jew lawyer know the name of McKenna's secretary? How the hell had he gotten even an iota of information out of her? Pritzker was slick all right. McKenna'd been asking around. Everybody agreed—the civil-liberties attorney worked angles nobody else had even thought of.

Abe Pritzker barreled on. "There's no way you're going over to harass that little Japanese lady without her attorney present. She has a right—"

"Look, Masako Fumi lost any rights she had when Tojo bombed Hawaii—or so the Feds tell me." McKenna wasn't quite certain of that—this enemy alien jazz was new territory—but he wasn't about to let this shyster get away with bamboozling him into anything.

The lawyer's eyes narrowed. "Not true, Lieutenant. In arresting Mrs. Oakley the Federal Bureau of Investigation violated at least four constitutional rights, beginning with the Fourth Amendment's guarantee against unreasonable search and seizure. I'll fight them on that, but *you*, Lieutenant, you are not the federal government. You are a city homicide detective investigating a criminal case, and, in said criminal case, my client has a right to legal representation."

Louise cast Abe a surprised glance—he'd changed his mind about handling the murder case? He went on without acknowledging her. "Is there room on that police launch for us? Or do I hire a water taxi and charge it to the city?"

Louise was grateful when, after some wrangling, McKenna capitulated. Only Masako herself could explain the mysterious gallery visit, and Louise wanted to see McKenna's face when the Japanese woman came up with a perfectly innocent explanation. Now was also an excellent time, Louise judged, to let McKenna know about Fairchild.

If he didn't already know.

"Lieutenant McKenna?" she asked, "Have you heard from my roommate, Cabby Ward?"

"That sneaky little newshound? Miss Ward is your roommate?" McKenna rubbed his forehead, amazed as always at what a small world New York could be. This pretty Southern girl, landed with a Bronx big-mouth like Ward, and both of them involved with his case. Whadaya know? He went on, "I haven't talked to Miss Ward since she skewed the stuff I gave her about the Shelton murder into a story more fit for the tabloids than the *Times*."

Louise repressed a smile. McKenna had Cabby's number all right, but that wasn't important now. She said, "Then I guess I should let you know what she found out last night." As Abe listened intently, she once again recounted Cabby's tale about her America First assignment and Fairchild's missed speaking date.

McKenna let Nurse Hunter's words sink in. So the girl reporter was still working the Shelton story like a dog with a bone, was she? And damn it! Miss Ward might even be on to something. In the short interview Nigel Fairchild had granted

McKenna, he'd been very definite about his speech at the Metropolis Club on the evening Shelton was killed. A bold-faced lie apparently.

The more McKenna thought, the better he liked it. When witnesses had confirmed Mrs. Oakley's taxi ride to the gallery, he'd thought the case was over. He had his perpetrator, and the Cap would climb off his back. But, no. His gut had never been happy with it. No. no, no. No way could the tiny, frail woman have ever been strong enough to whack a tall, healthy, young American man over the head.

He was still interested in why Masako Oakley had left her husband home in bed in the throes of pneumonia, but at least he had an additional strong lead to follow. Fairchild. Ha! Now *he* would make a satisfying collar.

McKenna found himself grinning at the pretty nurse in the red scarf as the police launch bumped the dock.

◇◇◇

Even from the doorway of the large visitation hall, Louise could tell that Masako had somehow shrunken into herself. Maybe it was the mustard-colored dress far too large for her. Or the armed guard, shoulders squared, rifle at the ready. It was almost as if, overwhelmed by this massive facility and the power behind it, Masako Oakley had decided to be…not quite there.

The nurse shoved past Abe and McKenna.

Masako raised her pale face on the other side of the partition. "Robert? Is he still alive?" Her question was as insubstantial as a wisp of smoke.

Louise was dimly aware of Abe following close behind, getting her a chair while he and McKenna remained standing. "Yes, yes, Dr. Wright is attending him closely. The professor sends his love and absolutely forbids you to worry on his account." Louise wanted to continue her assurances, comfort the Japanese woman any way she could. But the forces of law were literally breathing down her neck. "It's time to focus now. To answer these men's questions as fully as you possibly can."

Abe waded right in without waiting for a response. "Mrs. Oakley," he said, with a sideways jerk of his thumb, "you saw this man day before yesterday. He's Lieutenant McKenna of the New York City homicide squad, here about the murder of Arthur Shelton. You don't have to answer his questions if you don't want to. In any case, I'm here to advise you."

Masako Oakley turned her gaze slowly, slowly, toward the police lieutenant. Yes, she remembered. The carrion crow. Another one to pick her bones. Not enough to be questioned for hour after hour by Agent Bagwell. Blistered by accusations of treason and murder, threatened with repatriation to Japan, pressed into mute submission by his unrelenting demands.

And finally, when Agent Bagwell let her be, she was crammed into a room just large enough for two, but with ten women sharing crowded bunks. Women jabbering all day in Italian, German, and what she thought must be Romanian.

Now the police! She swallowed painfully. Her throat was no longer a tube for speaking, just a pouch to store aching, unshed tears. Maybe if she didn't look at the wrinkled policeman he would go away. She shut her eyes, but his questions drilled into her ears. What was he asking about? Arthur's death. Her painting of the hungry lion, the one that had grown out of memories of her father. Arthur? The gallery. Her paintings. Her studio.

Something clicked, and Masako's eyes flew open to seek Nurse Louise. "Did you get my paintings?"

"What paintings?" That was the policeman, tone puzzled. The lawyer looked as if he might speak but didn't.

Louise put a subtle forefinger to her lips. Later, she mouthed. Since Lieutenant McKenna stood behind her chair, he wouldn't see her response to Mrs. Oakley's question. He seemed like a...decent man, but who knew what bureaucratic hell the Bleecker Street studio would get caught up in if the authorities learned about it.

Masako understood. Nurse Louise was trying to protect her. She must co-operate. The artist shook her head, as if in a daze. "What paintings?" She turned a vacant face toward McKenna. "My paintings are all gone. I don't understand."

As he stared for a long, contemplative moment, she resisted the compulsion to let her eyelids sink closed. Finally he asked, "Mrs. Oakley, why were you at the Shelton Art Gallery at 7:15 the night of Arthur Shelton's murder?"

Oh, no! Was that when Arthur had been killed? How could this world be so cruel? "I...I..."

Her three listeners leaned forward, lips parted, each intent on the words that must be crowding the delicate woman's mouth.

But Masako fell silent and bowed her head. The world—and time—turned to lead, barely moving. Maybe if she didn't listen to the policeman, didn't speak, took her soul into a hiding place, she could become invisible. Just like with Agent Bagwell. She summoned the pane of frosted glass, thicker, more opaque. And disappeared.

Chapter Fifty-four

Cabby hoped Halper had been too busy jawing with the guys to notice her sneak into the news room a good twenty minutes late. But no. Here he was now, slack jowls still pink from a vigorous morning shave, hairy knuckles curled on her desktop.

"Glad you decided to grace us with your presence, Ward."

Cabby raised her gaze from her typewriter, but kept her fingers on the keys. "Sorry, Boss. Had to see a man about a dog." She resorted to the male euphemism to keep his questions at bay until she had a chance to lay out the whole story she'd begun looking into.

"Yeah? Well, Ward. I got something right up your alley." Halper's grin was unreadable.

"Oh, yeah?"

"Get out that fancy hat of yours."

Cabby rolled her eyes. She had a formerly chic peacock-blue hat with a tipsy high crown, a narrow brim and a feather. She'd bought it for fifty cents at a lah-di-dah Fifth Avenue church rummage sale, and the only time it ever graced her unruly curls, tilted at a jaunty angle, was at the society-ladies luncheons Halper sent her to cover. But why did her editor have to come up with one of his lightweight assignment today?

"You're going to the Waldorf," he continued. "Buncha downtown business women are celebrating the first anniversary of their charity organization."

She sighed.

"What's your problem?" The editor straightened, crossed his arms.

"I've covered a hundred of these dos—Park Avenue matrons picking at shrimp cocktail while some snooty dame with a lorgnette sanctifies them for their good works. Why don't you send Bud for a change—or any of these guys?" Cabby swung an arm in a half-circle that took in the entire news room. "I've got an important story on the burner."

Halper slapped a hand to the back of his neck and rubbed hard. "That's your trouble, Ward, you're always flapping your mouth. Listen a god-damned minute, will ya?" The harsh overhead light gleamed dully on his green eyeshade. "A good reporter has to learn to listen."

"All right." Cabby abandoned her trusty Underwood and clenched her hands on her lap. "I'm all ears," she replied with a forced smile, but she wasn't about to drop her line of inquiry. She'd struck a nerve with Nigel Fairchild last night. A guilty nerve? Maybe. And she'd already started following it up.

"This Waldorf deal isn't for society types, Ward. It's for working women—like you. Editors, doctors, entrepreneurs—top-level gals." The editor shot her a glare. "They give up their lunch hours and evenings to help out on the blocks where they work. They've been providing warm clothing, meals and recreation for kids who roam the streets while their parents clean office buildings at night. Now they plan to take Mrs. Roosevelt's advice and turn their attention to war work. Is that important enough for you?"

"Yes, sir. It is." Cabby twisted uncomfortably in her seat. Just yesterday, the First Lady had praised the woman of England who'd rushed to fill jobs vacated by their fighting men. Mrs. Roosevelt's message had been crystal clear: except in work that required brute strength, a woman could perform as well as a man. Oh, yes—Cabby could get on board with that!

"Good." The editor consulted a slip of paper jotted with the particulars. "The chairwoman, a Mrs. Howard McClellan, expects you at a quarter to twelve. Ask her about the classes they're setting up."

"Classes?"

"Map reading, telegraphy, martial arts, fingerprinting, anything that might become useful as the war heats up."

"Fingerprinting? Like the cops do?"

"Civil Defense wants as many civilians' prints on file as possible."

"Why on earth?"

He twisted his blubbery lips. "It might end up being the only way to identify bombing victims."

"Oh." Swallowing past a lump in her throat, Cabby took the paper from Halper. "Okay, I'll get the story and have it written up by four." The editor continued to hover by her desk, so she added, "Sorry…about the attitude, I mean."

Halper nodded, but still didn't move. Finally he asked, "So—what's this hot story you were blathering on about?"

Oh, good. "Well…you know how you assigned me to cover the America First meeting last night?"

"The group is dissolving, right? Hard to call for staying out of war when war lands right on your doorstep."

"Yeah. I'm writing a piece about Fairchild's announcement now, but listen to this—that ranting old fart could be smack in the middle of the Arthur Shelton murder."

Halper pressed his lips together. "Didn't I tell you to leave that alone?"

Cabby sprang from her seat and tipped her chin back. At five-foot-two, she'd never be able to look Halper in the eye, but she could try. "I did leave it alone—until it got thrown back in my face. Just listen"—she held up her palm—"Fairchild and Tiffy De Forest, this society gal who's been decorating his arm, made a huge scene at the opening of the Masako Fumi Oakley show. Tiffy actually tossed a drink at the featured painting. Accused Shelton of being a traitor to his country."

"Your nurse buddy tell you this?"

"No, I got it from James LaSalle. Yeah." Cabby nodded triumphantly. "The *Times*' very own art critic—I looked him up this morning to ask if he remembered Fairchild from the opening. LaSalle witnessed the whole drink incident—it was his wine she tossed. And I got a good look at Tiffy De Forest at the meeting last night. She was in the front row, hanging on Fairchild's every word."

Halper shrugged. "Okay, so Fairchild and his honey had political differences with Shelton. That doesn't automatically translate into murder."

"Keep listening. On Friday evening, when Shelton was killed, Fairchild was slated to be the dinner speaker at the Metropolis Club. He failed to show—no reason given."

"Still…" Halper raised his shoulders skeptically, but Cabby could read the gleam in his eye. He was interested, by damn, the old crustacean. She went on quickly, "And, last night, you should have heard Fairchild. He urged his supporters to rid the city of all things Japanese. Shops, restaurants—art galleries! He actually said 'art galleries!'"

Halper thought a moment, then rapped out, "The cops consider Fairchild a suspect?"

"I don't know," Cabby admitted.

"Has he been questioned?"

She could only shrug.

With a sigh, he sank into the battered wooden chair beside her desk, pulled the pencil from above his ear, and tapped her hand with it. "Look, Ward, so far you only have half a story. You gotta work the cop angle. Get onto the lead detective. You know him, right?"

"Yeah, I know him. Lieutenant Michael McKenna." Who treats me like a case of influenza.

"So go to your police source and lay out all the Fairchild info. Get the investigator's confirmation or denial on the record. Then—and only then—you'll have something we can publish." Halper stuck his forefinger out like the muzzle of a gun. "But the Waldorf ladies first, right?" He pointed in her direction and clicked his tongue before rising—with an even more-prolonged sigh—and moving on to Bud Smallwood's desk. "And don't forget the hat," he shot back over his shoulder.

Cabby sat down and propped her chin on her hand. She felt like the fairy-tale princess who'd been ordered to spin straw into gold. First it was Louise who assumed she had the lieutenant's ear, then her boss. Damn that McKenna! She'd tried another call that morning—and his secretary wouldn't even take a message!

She started tapping the typewriter keys, slowly at first, and then picking up speed. A plan was forming. By the time she'd yelled "copy," and handed her America First piece to a freckled copy boy, Cabby's plan was nearly complete and she was smiling broadly. She snatched the blue hat from where it was smushed into her bottom drawer, licked her thumb and forefinger to straighten the feather, and grabbed her coat. She'd make just one little stop on her way to the Waldorf-Astoria. Right here in the Times building.

Chapter Fifty-five

Retired *Times* reporter Mervyn Uhl had made a career of parking his skinny frame at precinct houses and milking desk sergeants and detectives for information. Whether it was his perpetual grin or liberal sharing of the half pint of Four Roses in his pocket, Merv was a legend on the police beat. Although his gold watch had been bestowed in '38, the tomatoes he then tried to raise in his Queens backyard withered on the vine, stamp collecting was boring as hell, and what was it with these old guys who ran model trains around their attics, anyway? Second childhood or something? So every day, Merv climbed into the same dirty suit he'd worn for decades, caught the Flushing Line to Times Square, and made his rounds, dispensing Lucky Strikes instead of cheap booze.

Today the schmoozer had parked his elbow on the marble and brass-trimmed shoe shine stand on the ground floor. Cabby found him jawing at Jimmy, the shoeshine boy, whose actual boyhood went back before the turn of the century. Jimmy was applying himself to his work, and the owner of a pair of scuffed brown wing tips, bored senseless by Merv's spiel, had buried his face in that morning's edition.

"Merv Uhl," Cabby said, as she skidded to a halt. "Just the man I want to see."

Uhl swiveled his head, blew a smoke ring, and grinned. "Hey, girlie, what'cha still doing in the newspaper life? Thought a cutie-pie like you would have a ring on your finger by now."

He finished with a look that landed somewhere between a wink and a leer.

Trying not to flinch, Cabby shook her head. Merv meant well. No sense in getting worked up over an old man's failure to sniff the winds of change. Girls like Ruthie Boyle might think the sun rose and set in dragging some guy to the altar. But not Cabby Ward. No screaming brats and shitty diapers for her.

She lowered her voice and leaned in close. "Know any of the guys on the Homicide Squad down at Headquarters?" Whew, the old guy could use a shave, a shower, and a bottle of Listerine.

Merv worked his lips in and out before replying, "I know all of 'em—at least the ones who been around for a while. Who ya want the dope on?" He dropped his cigarette butt and ground it out under the sole of his shoe.

"McKenna. Michael. Lieutenant."

Merv nodded. "McKenna's a good cop, started off in the Tenth Precinct. He's honest—and a lot sharper than all his joking around would make you think."

It took Cabby a moment to respond. "Joking? We talking about the same McKenna?"

"Yeah. There's only one. Quick with a comeback. Keeps the boys in stitches."

Cabby thought back to the detective she'd met at the Shelton Gallery, the guy with the look of a graveyard-bound elephant. Baggy, slow-moving, his cop brusqueness barely covering a heavy load of sorrow. "Are you sure? My McKenna cracks a smile about as often as the Dodgers win the pennant."

Merv stared at the floor, forehead creased. To give him time, Cabby stifled the questions crowding her tongue. The thwap-thwap of Jimmy's buffing rag filled the silence and the tannic smell of the polish tickled her nose. People passed in dribs and drabs, heading for the Forty-third Street exit, but a dark-suited man smoking a pipe was the only one to give the odd group a curious glance.

The old newspaperman finally spoke. "I guess the thing with his wife hit McKenna pretty hard."

"His wife died?" That would explain the wrinkled clothing, the other signs of a man on his own.

"Worse."

Cabby raised her eyebrows.

"McKenna had to put her away—in a rest home. She has... something. You know, it starts with forgetting your wallet— pretty soon you'd forget your head if it wasn't stuck onto the top of your neck."

"Senile dementia." A mellow baritone chimed in. Cabby and Merv both turned toward Jimmy the Shine. He'd collected his dime and settled on a wire stool to have a smoke. His thick mahogany hands shook a coffin nail from a pack of Camels. "My Aunt Cleo had that. Senile dementia caused by hardenin' of the arteries. She forgot how to eat. Just wasted away to nuthin'." He shook his head. "That's one bad business." A long satisfied draw on his cigarette followed.

I'll say, thought Cabby. And then, lightning quick, her thoughts barreled on. In her estimation, most men were creatures of habit, especially where food was concerned. With no wife to come home to, McKenna must eat his meals out. It was a long shot, but— "Hey, Merv, any idea where Lieutenant McKenna has his supper?"

"Why?" An admonishing look came into Merv's faded blue eyes. "If you're willing to cool your heels a while, you can always catch him at Homicide."

"Well, ah...that's just it. Halper has me on another assign- ment, and I don't have much time—plus my little talk with McKenna has to be on the strict QT."

"Halper, huh. That guy still the hardest of hard asses?" His hand flew almost instantly to his mouth. "Uh, oh. Ladies pres- ent. Shoulda watched my mouth."

Cabby broke out in a laugh. "I work in the newsroom, remember. Even you couldn't come up with any language I haven't heard."

From his stool, Jimmy rumbled out a deep chuckle.

Cabby glanced at her watch. "Spill it, will ya, Merv. McK-
enna? Supper?"

"Okay." The old reporter shrugged. "The Centre Street brass
favor a pricey restaurant on Grand Street called...Headquarters.
Get it?" His shoulders shook at the wit of it all.

"And guys farther down the line—like McKenna?"

"Well, you might run him down at a chop house, also on
Grand. Louie's. A lot of the detectives eat there."

Finally, Cabby thought, as she fumbled in her bag. "Thanks,
Merv, thanks a lot. Have a shine on me." She flipped a coin
toward Jimmy. At least she could make sure the old guy's shoes
were clean. For once.

Chapter Fifty-six

"What is *wrong* with that woman? Why won't she talk?" Abe Pritzker fulminated over a fried flounder sandwich. Abe and Louise were eating lunch at a sawdust-floor restaurant on Beekman Street near the Fulton Fish Market. "Doesn't she realize we're on her side?"

"Masako is in shock, Abe."

"Oh, yeah?" He ripped off another bite.

"And in a deeply depressive state. Her ego is retreating, protecting her from the stresses of the outside world." Louise spooned in a gulp of creamy fish chowder. "It's an unconscious defense mechanism."

He returned the remains of his sandwich to the plate and leaned back in the rickety chair. "Say, you really know this psychiatry stuff."

She shrugged. "We got a bit in nursing school. I was interested, so I just kept reading."

"You just kept reading, huh?" He appeared deep in thought as he took out a pipe and fingered its smooth wood. "Well, tell me, Dr. Hunter, what treatment would you prescribe to snap her out of it?"

Stung, she let the heavy spoon splash into her bowl. "Don't mock me!"

"I'm not. I take you very seriously." He reached over and touched the back of her hand.

She pushed the bowl away and crossed her arms. "You called me *Doctor* Hunter!"

"Yeah, and why not? Why couldn't you become a physician? So brainy you read psychoanalytic theory on the side." His expression grew even more sober. The unlit pipe went back in his pocket. "What I'm asking is—assuming we ever get ourselves back into that fortress they call an immigration center—what can we do to get Mrs. Oakley to talk?"

Louise thought about the long, free-flowing conversations she and Masako had enjoyed while the professor had been sleeping. She sighed and wiped her fingers on a coarse paper napkin. "I know just exactly what would do it."

"What?" The lawyer sat forward eagerly.

"A cup of jasmine tea, her own kitchen table, and a sympathetic ear."

◇◇◇

Later, leaving the Ninety-sixth Street subway station, Louise heard the wail of an ambulance in the distance. Her breath tightened, and she immediately thought of Professor Oakley. She gave a wry inward laugh as she turned north on Broadway. Seven million people in this city, and she immediately assumed the siren wailed for her patient.

It was an uneventful winter afternoon on the wide sidewalks of the upper West Side: a pair of tightly corseted ladies coming out of a Childs restaurant; a colored housekeeper strolling along, red wool coat open over a neat black uniform; a policeman twirling his nightstick and winking at her. But something was happening on Ninety-eighth. A revolving light pulsated in plate-glass windows next door to—

That was the Oakleys' building! She burst into a run and reached the white-and-red ambulance just as orderlies were preparing to load a stretcher. At first all she saw were blankets. Then the fabric shifted and the professor's face came into view, beard bristling, lips and skin dangerously blue.

He opened one eye. His lips moved, but no sound issued.

Does he recognize me? Louise wondered. Dr. Wright was there, too, expression grave under his brown fedora.

"What happened" Louise asked, panting.

"The nurse called me around eleven—temperature spiking one hundred and five. Sliding into delirium from lack of oxygen." Dr. Wright shifted his leather bag, motioned the orderlies to proceed.

Someone stepped in between them—Lillian Bridges in her red hat and elegant gray coat. "Is that Robert? Oh, no! I was just coming to see him." She let her gladiolas drop to the sidewalk and bent over the stretcher. "Robert—you must hang on."

"Step back, Lillian, please," the doctor said. "The sooner we get Bob into an oxygen tent the better."

Louise shuffled back as well. Watched the heavy doors close with a sick feeling. "The crisis can't be far off," she whispered bleakly.

Dr. Wright nodded. "He'll have a better chance of surviving it in the hospital, though. The old fool." He shook his head. "If I hadn't been so besieged with all this war hysteria, I would have insisted on hospitalizing him days ago." His voice trailed off as the ambulance sped uptown with a wordless wail.

Louise and the doctor watched it go. Like Professor Bridges, gathering up her bruised flowers, they shivered in the raw wind.

Chapter Fifty-seven

Twenty minutes later, Louise added a plate of sandwiches to her order of tea and wondered if she'd made a mistake in accepting Lillian Bridges' invitation.

As the ambulance had roared away, Louise planned to make her own way to the hospital. But Professor Bridges twined her arm around Louise's and said, "They won't let us see Robert until the nurses have him settled. Meanwhile, I've had no lunch. Come to Schrafft's with me—my treat. We can keep each other company."

Louise, still a bit dazed, permitted herself to be led down the street. At the corner, the older woman had tossed her armload of imported flowers in a trash can.

"Yes, waiter," Lillian Bridges now said, "I'll have a cup of tea, thank you. Nothing else."

Nothing else? But she said she'd had no lunch.

At the next table, two uptown ladies in small feathered hats were being served chocolate sundaes smothered with whipped cream and nuts. Louise's mouth watered. She'd finished the bowl of chowder in the fish market restaurant, but with all the meals she'd had to skip lately…

"I understand you saw dear Masako at Ellis Island. How is she?" Professor Bridges shrugged off her coat to reveal a beautifully cut ice-blue suit in fine wool and a white blouse with a ruffle falling from the collar.

Louise sighed in something that might have been envy; she'd dressed so hastily when Abe called this morning that she knew she didn't fit in at this sophisticated tearoom. Lillian Bridges outclassed her, hands down.

Now the professor regarded her with a serious expression. "My dear? I asked about Masako. How is she?"

"How is she?" Louise took a sip from her iced water as she repeated the question. "I wanted to talk to you about that. Abe Pritzker and I went back to the detention center this morning. We couldn't get a word out of her. Mas— er, Mrs. Oakley is too depressed to cooperate."

"Appalling, isn't it? The situation she's got herself in—" The remainder of Lillian Bridges' statement was drowned out by a busboy collecting dirty china at a nearby table.

Huh? What was she talking about? Mrs. Oakley hadn't gotten herself into anything. Her arrest was a direct result of misguided governmental policies. "She's done nothing wrong," Louise said. "And, actually, she's more worried about her husband than about herself."

Lillian Bridges sat back and folded her slim, white hands. "Well, it's killing Robert."

"Oh!" Louise decided a change of subject might be a good idea. "I need to ask you—Mrs. Oakley doesn't want the FBI to get their hands on her remaining paintings, those at her studio on Bleecker Street. She thought you might volunteer to keep them at your apartment. Would you? They'd never think to look there. Mr. Pritzker plans to have the Japanese captions translated by someone we can trust, so the Feds can't claim they contain coded secret information."

The professor pondered, twisting her fingers. Where most women of her age would wear a wedding band, Miss Bridges displayed a deep blue sapphire set in heavily carved gold. A museum piece, thought Louise, a jewel fit for the hand of a Renaissance queen. She had to admit the ring looked perfectly at home on her companion's graceful hand.

"Well, well," Lillian Bridges finally replied. "I hadn't given Masako's studio a thought. But you're right—Arthur would have chosen to take only the works he thought would make the biggest splash. There must be a number left."

"Right. And I have the studio key. Professor Oakley gave it to me yesterday."

"Did he, now?" Miss Bridges dropped her gaze and refolded the napkin in her lap.

The aproned waiter delivered Louise's plate of sandwiches. They were cut into finger-sized rectangles and topped with watercress. While he fussed with the tea, her companion made an abrupt brushing motion with her hand, knocking over an empty cup. "Take my tea away." Her tone was brusque. "Bring me a martini instead." She turned to Louise. "Do you want one, dear?" Without waiting for a response, she continued, "of course you do. Waiter, make that two martinis. Dry."

Louise objected. "But I don't—"

"Nonsense! This is my treat." Lillian Bridges regarded Louise carefully. "You were saying about Masako…?"

"Oh…well, of course, if keeping her paintings would put you in danger…"

She gave a confident laugh. "I'll like to see the Federal Bureau fence with me. Maybe they can get away with threatening these recent immigrants, but Mother and I are members of the DAR."

Louise nodded silently. Masako had said Lillian Bridges was inordinately proud of her ancestry. "Everybody's from some- where else," Abe had said. But did it really matter when? Aren't we all Americans?

She didn't think she'd pass that philosophy on to Professor Lillian Bridges.

The martinis were delivered post-haste and set on scalloped paper coasters by the expressionless waiter. Louise's companion took a long sip and nodded at him. "So," she continued, turning her attention back to Louise, "Of course I'll take the paintings. How about moving them tomorrow morning? I have a seminar in the afternoon."

"Yes, fine."

Another gulp from the delicately stemmed glass. "You must call Desmond Cox at the gallery for the name of a bonded art mover. I'll meet you at the studio. Perhaps that lawyer fellow would like to tag along."

Louise had formed the vague image of Abe renting a panel truck, but, yes, of course, those art works were valuable. They should be transported correctly. Deep in thought, she picked up a chicken salad sandwich and ate it in two bites. It was on thin, crustless bread, and there were chopped grapes and walnuts in the filling.

Lillian drained her martini. Between nibbles of olive, she said, "Masako is not doing well, you say? Robert's hospitalization won't help any, I fear."

"No," Louise responded. "Not at all. That's why I'm not planning to tell her. No one should." She gave Lillian Bridges a long, cautionary look and took a sip of her tea.

"Very proper, I'm sure." Lillian was eying Louise's martini. "Not imbibing, dear?"

Louise shook her head.

"Well, then…" Her hostess commandeered the glass.

Yes, Louise thought, lunch with the intelligent and fashionable Lillian Bridges had probably been a mistake. Also, a revelation. Louise wouldn't be asking this erratic woman for any further help or advice.

Chapter Fifty-eight

Jesus' robe was the same blood-red as the fear coursing through Helda's heart, the sky behind him Virgin Mary blue. Usually the sanctuary of Emmanuel German Lutheran Church was a place of refuge for Helda. Today, try as she might, even on her knees she could not pray. Her gaze remained fixed on the stained-glass window that loomed behind the pulpit. If only she could take some comfort from it—an ecstatic Christ kneeling in Gethsemane, wrapped in flowing crimson.

Where was her son? Had Ernst taken him? Had her husband come back during the night? Had he entered the house, perhaps through that window in the dining room, the one he knew had a broken latch? The one he had never gotten around to fixing? Had Howie welcomed his father with open arms?

Even before Helda had found Howie's bed empty, she'd lain awake, tortured by her own fears. She knew Ernst hadn't come back to New York on his own—he must have been sent back. A chemical engineer by training, he would be of most value to Hitler back here in the USA. Ernst and those other members of the Bund who had returned to Germany—for training, that was all Ernst would say at the time. Yes, she feared she knew all too well why he had come back. Was her son, her Howie, perhaps even today, being trained as a Nazi saboteur?

Dear Jesus, what should I do? Help me, oh, help me, Good Shepherd. I've never felt so lost, she prayed.

She could not call the police. If her fears were true, they would send the FBI after Howie. Perhaps they would come for her, too, take her to Ellis Island as they had taken Herr Roeber from the butcher shop. The young ladies in the house had been comforting, but she could not tell them about Ernst. She had gone to Frau Frommer, who had brought Ernst's letter, thinking Ernst and Howie might be hiding at the Frommer house. The curtains were drawn. No smoke came from the chimney. No smell of cooking at the kitchen door. She knocked and knocked, but no one came.

So here she was sobbing in the front pew of Emmanuel Lutheran, enveloped in the familiar odor of beeswax and lemon polish, the scent of prayer.

A hand on her shoulder and she jumped. "Oh, Pastor, you startled me," she said in German to the middle-aged clergyman with his white hair all fly-away and spider-web veins on his dumpling cheeks.

He answered in English, "My dear Helda. Whatever is wrong?"

She shook her head—she would say nothing—but he pressed on.

"I know you have had your troubles over the past years." He paused. Significance deepened his brief silence. "But never have I seen you so distraught."

"It's Howie, Pastor." She burst into tears.

Pastor Ulrich let out his breath, as if in relief.

"Helda, my dear." He sat next to her and took her hand. "Howie is a good boy—you know that. He will cause you no grief. Come, come, Liebchen. This is your church home, and I am your brother in Christ. Tell me, what has he done? Is he smoking? Has he taken a drink?"

"Oh, Pastor, no." She grasped his comforting hand. "I cannot tell you. No one can know."

Now both his plump hands were on hers. "I insist, Liebchen," he said. "There is nothing you cannot say to me. And, who knows, perhaps I can help you."

The sanctuary darkened as a cloud crossed the sun. Helda shivered. "Howie…has run away. I'm looking everywhere. I can't find him, and no one knows where he has gone." She choked on a sob.

He patted her. "All boys run away at times. It's just natural. Why, Jesus himself…He will come home."

She couldn't hold it in. "Oh, Pastor Ulrich," she burst out. "It is worse than you think. Ernst is back. I don't know how or why, but he came to me last night. I fear Howie has gone to join him and the others."

The clergyman dropped her hands as if they were on fire. He pulled away from her on the hard oak pew.

"Do you…" Her hands reached out to him. "Do you… perhaps know where Ernst is?"

"Ernst? *Nein!*" His expression was horrified. "I am a loyal American. I know nothing about those—"

"Hans! Hans!" It was Frau Ulrich's reedy soprano. She pushed through the carved oak doors from the narthex and came huffing down the aisle. "It has come. Oh, *mein Gott*, it has come."

The pastor pushed himself further away from Helda. "What, *mein frau*? What is it?"

"On the radio. I just heard. Roosevelt—the president. It has finally happened. He has just this moment declared war on Germany!"

"*Mein Gott*," the pastor said. "Where will this end?"

As Helda shuffled back down the aisle, Jesus' robe appeared blood red as before, but the blue, blue sky behind him had clouded over into gun-metal gray.

Chapter Fifty-nine

When the two cops came out of Louie's Chophouse, Cabby shrank back into the recessed entrance of a nearby Western Union office. She'd been waiting outside Louie's big front window for the best part of an hour, legs freezing in her last good pair of nylons. Now she clapped her gloved hands together; only the nervous bustle on the Grand Street sidewalk kept her from jumping up and down. McKenna, at last!

The block-long wedding cake that housed Police Headquarters was right across the street, and Blondie, er, Detective Brenner, strode toward it as if he were on a mission. Cabby sighed—get a load of those shoulders! McKenna stayed put in front of Louie's. Just for a moment, he crossed his hands in back under his over-coat, giving him the appearance of an old-fashioned lady wearing a bustle. He looked right, then left, rocked back on his heels and looked up, his eyes locked on an enormous shiny pistol advertising one of the neighborhood's many gunsmiths. It struck Cabby that the man didn't have anywhere in particular to go.

The thought made her feel sad—but just for a second. Then she darted out from her hiding place: it was now or never. "Lieutenant, could you spare a minute?"

McKenna dropped his hands and sighed. "Aw, not you, girlie. Not you—not on top of Louie's Hungarian pork chops."

She ignored the unwelcoming frown. "I'm asking for one minute of your time—just one. There's something urgent you oughta know—it concerns the Shelton case."

He huffed out a huge beer-fumed breath. "About Fairchild? Yeah. Yeah. I already know."

Cabby stepped back, jostling the flow of pedestrians heading over to Chink-town for some cheap chop-suey, or to the uptown bus and home. "You can't possibly know!"

McKenna chuckled. "Your friend, the nurse, got to me first."

Why, that…"Well," she continued, "don't you think Fairchild deserves a look-see? Could be he's gone vigilante—killing anyone associated with the Japanese."

The left side of McKenna's mouth crooked up. He dodged a delivery man with a basket of fish on his shoulder and looked at her with skewed eyes. "So you attended an isolationist meeting?"

"On assignment, yes. America First has shut its doors." She let a note of pride color her tone. "Read about it in tomorrow's *Times*."

McKenna didn't respond right away. His eyes, smudged with dark circles, seemed to view something gloomier than the cheery light spilling through Louie's window. "Hmm," he finally said.

Cabby felt a sinking sense of disappointment. "You're not one of those guys ready to swallow Fairchild's anti-Jap paranoia, are you?"

He gave his head a solemn shake. "Pearl Harbor sent a lot of folks scrambling onto that bandwagon—no surprise. But, no, it's not that. There's good and bad in every race—no one knows that better than a guy who's been on the force twenty-odd years." He paused to shake a cigarette from his pack, then tipped it toward Cabby. "Miss…Drew?"

"No." Her shoulders relaxed. At least he was mellowing a bit, getting back to the banter he'd briefly thrown her way at the art gallery.

"Don't smoke?"

"Tried. Never could inhale."

"Good for you." He lit the cigarette and exhaled into the wintry air. "They'll kill me one of these days."

The crowd of workers from the surrounding shops and office buildings had thinned, nonetheless Cabby sensed that McKenna felt confined, hemmed in. "Let's walk," she proposed.

Nodding, he took her arm. And after a few steps, he took up where she'd left off. "Your roommate said you had a flier for that America First dinner Fairchild was supposed to speak at. The one he didn't show up for."

"Yes."

"Got it on ya?"

She opened her purse and produced the folded paper. She didn't hand it right over, though—no siree. "You telling me you'll look into Nigel Fairchild?"

McKenna's eyes crinkled in that smile that wasn't quite a smile. "What makes you think I haven't already been doing just that, Miss Ward? Maybe I also have cause to be interested in the blonde who seems to keep popping up. Mrs. De Forest attended that meeting last night, didn't she?"

"She sure did." Wow, I'm finally getting somewhere, Cabby thought as they passed a salumeria with clusters of salami and bologna hanging in the window. "Look, Lieutenant, can you confirm all that for me—on the record?"

But before McKenna could respond, a black-and-white squad car pulled up to the curb. "Hey, Lute!" Dolan leaned out the passenger window. "We got it all set up for tonight."

The driver of a panel truck behind the black-and-white blocking the lane laid on his horn, starting a chain reaction of honking vehicles. Cabby could barely hear McKenna's response over the hubbub, but her eyes began to sparkle. As McKenna waved the squadie back into traffic, she burst out, "Tonight? What's going on tonight?"

He took off his hat and ran a hand over his thinning hair. "I'll make ya a deal, okay? Hand that paper over and, tomorrow morning, you'll get an exclusive on whatever goes down tonight." He replaced his hat and glanced around. Though the trio of passing secretaries in cheap, pretty hats appeared oblivious, he lowered his voice still further. Cabby, still not committing herself, tilted her head to hear every word.

"Ever since we got the word on that dust-up the night of the Fumi gala, we've had Fairchild in our sights. So far, he's one cool customer—every time I run him down, he finds urgent business somewhere else. But, now, if I have him cornered and can throw this in his face—" McKenna grasped the paper and gave a tug.

"Uh, uh." Cabby held on tight. "Only if I can go with you."

"Not on your life, girlie." McKenna dropped his hold to shake a finger in her face. "You're going nowhere but straight home."

Cabby flared, cheeks suddenly hot in the cold breeze. "I'm a reporter. You can't tell me what to do."

"Maybe not." McKenna's shoulders broadened; he seemed to grow two inches. "But if you set one foot in the Stork Club tonight, I *can* have you arrested for interference. Last thing I need is an eager beaver like you in my way."

The Stork! Of course, that's where all those Fifth Avenue types hung out. Cabby felt fizzy and excited, as if her veins were pumping with Nehi soda. "Is there going to be a raid?"

"A raid? At that swanky joint? Just try it!" McKenna shook his head. "No. We're having a little talk with the gentleman is all."

He reached for the paper again. This time Cabby let go. What was it they said about losing the battle to win the war? She would plan a flank attack.

"Well…" She crossed her arms, ducked her head, and said meekly, "I guess you need to go on, then. I'll just stop by head-quarters tomorrow morning."

At her sudden docility, McKenna narrowed his eyes. "Where do you live, Miss Ward?"

"Brooklyn. Near Prospect Park."

"You take the BMT?"

"That's right."

"The station's right over there." He took her arm again and began weaving between the oncoming pedestrians. "I'll walk ya."

"There's really no need." She tried not to speak too sharply.

"Yeah. There is. I won't rest easy until I see the doors close behind you on that train heading straight out of town."

Chapter Sixty

"You're with me, Pats." McKenna kept his eyes on the manila folder he'd been reviewing by the dim glow of the unmarked car's ceiling light.

A grainy copy of a full-length *Life* magazine photo stared up at him: Helen "Tiffy" De Forest at some bash that required a slinky gown. Tall. Blonde. This could be the lady who'd hired Herman Rupp to picket the Shelton Gallery.

Under Nigel Fairchild's direction?

They were driving up Fifth Avenue now, just passing the brightly lit Christmas windows of B. Altman's. "Brenner, you'll stay out front. Keep the motor running in case someone decides to take a powder."

Patsy Dolan had been shifting back and forth on the slick backseat, fidgeting. "How's this gonna play out, Lute?"

"Do I look like I got a crystal ball? It's gonna play out by ear, of course." McKenna turned the photo over and rifled through the rest of the folder's contents one last time. Newspaper clippings and typed notes described Tiffy's student days at Miss Porter's, debut at the Ritz-Carlton, and a short stint at *Vogue* as an editorial assistant. That was before marriage to Gregory De Forest, investment broker at Daddy's firm and well-known drunken sot.

Dolan shrugged shoulders that were already up around his ears. "Naw, it's just…well…the Stork ain't our beat. And on the phone, Hannigan from the local precinct was razzing me.

Braggin' about the favors he's gonna call in for this one. How'd you get us in there, anyhow?"

The big sedan turned the corner and slid to the curb in front of the famous nightspot. Though Dolan didn't push the question, and Brenner kept his eyes on the approaching doorman, their curiosity hung in the air like a rancid fart. Okay. McKenna slapped the folder shut. He'd clue them in. Since the favors to Hannigan would surely involve them, his boys deserved to know.

"We're just lucky the owner has union troubles. Sherman Billingsley has been fighting to keep the organizers out of his kitchen for years. It's not a pretty scene. He has three daughters who've been targeted by the union's goon squad. Hannigan and his boys keep a good watch on 'em"

Dolan cleared his throat. "I get it, boss. Billingsley's appreciative, so Hannigan touched him for a favor…"

"And now I get to kiss Hannigan's butt. It's the way of the world." McKenna levered the door open just as the doorman reached the car. Though it was obviously killing him to cater to cops, the short Italian in the gold-trimmed livery escorted McKenna and Dolan the length of the green canopy. He couldn't resist a subtle sneer as he passed them in to the Greek maitre d', who lifted the Stork Club's golden chain with a rakish twinkle in his eye.

At least this guy's having a ball, McKenna thought, then wondered why. Maybe Fairchild stiffs on tips.

"Your party is already seated, gentlemen. Right this way." He grinned.

"The camera girl know the drill?" McKenna asked in a whispery growl.

"Like the back of her lily-white hand," the square-jawed maitre d' also whispered, then asked in a louder tone, "Will you check your coats?"

McKenna shook his head; they had to be ready for anything. He and Dolan followed the Greek past the barroom entrance and through a thick glass door into the main dining area. Mirrored panels reflected soft light that played over the closely spaced tables. On the crowded dance floor, women in ankle-length gowns and men in evening dress or service uniforms dipped and swayed to a rumba beat. The actual melody could barely be heard over laughter, conversation, and the tinkling sound of cash registers at the bar. Several famous faces stood out as the two cops dodged waiters to wend their way toward the far end of the room. Was that Orson Welles smoking the long cigar? And that woman in black sequins—Claudette Colbert?

McKenna swiveled his head to see if Dolan was suitably impressed, but his sergeant was staring past him, eyes bulging like a toad's. McKenna followed his gaze. Mother of god! It was Rita Hayworth—just ahead, holding court at a big round table with boys from the Army, Navy, Coast Guard and Marines. Her red curls cascaded over white shoulders bared by a gown cut low in both back and front. As they went past, she threw her head back in a raucous laugh, and McKenna got an eyeful. Whew!

As they reached the Fairchild table in a shadowy corner, a crooner launched into an old tune and the room quieted. Cigarette smoke swirled in the spotlight. McKenna paused, ambushed by a sudden memory. Bing Crosby's "June in January" had been one of Gayle's favorites. They'd danced to it many a time—but never again. Never again. Damn he missed—

The maitre d' bumped McKenna's shoulder, breaking the moment. Nightclub noise engulfed him once more. And angry words. Nigel Fairchild had jumped to his feet and was berating the retreating Greek in tones of stalwart indignation. "How dare you? Come back and remove these…persons. They are not my guests."

Uh-uh, McKenna thought as he removed his hat, so Pats and I are "persons." Fairchild doesn't want to announce that we're cops. Behind all that bluster, he must be scared shitless.

Mrs. Fairchild, a deep-bosomed matron whose doughy cheeks were pinked with rouge, appeared puzzled by the newcomers. Her lips couldn't decide on a haughty smile or a censuring frown. Beside her a fair man with narrow shoulders and a premature paunch sagging over his cummerbund also rose to his feet. His expression mirrored Fairchild's, but he swayed ever so slightly. McKenna had him pegged immediately—Gregory De Forest, under the influence of one too many of the martinis whose empty glasses were strewn across the table top.

And Tiffy herself? Where McKenna expected to see wariness or bewilderment was only an unfocused stare, tiny pupils surrounded by cornflower blue. Ohhh, boy!

McKenna turned to Gregory De Forest. "I'm glad to see you're on your feet, Mr. D. Mrs. Fairchild looks like she could use a spin around the dance floor."

The broker bridled, in the manner of a man more accustomed to giving orders than taking them. But at Fairchild's stern nod, he escorted the lady away, meek as a lamb. McKenna pulled out a vacant chair for Dolan, then one for himself. Fairchild smiled a shade too brightly as he, too, sank into a seat.

So far, so good, McKenna thought. Their corner was attracting curious glances, and the Stork's camera girl hovered a few yards away. A froth of petticoats flashed under a tap-dancer's skirt that barely covered silky thighs. She sent McKenna a wink.

Fairchild caught it, too. "Okay, Officer, you've made your point. I'll be glad to stop by headquarters tomorrow. We can discuss whatever you like then."

"Too late then, Fairchild." McKenna shook his head. "You and your girlfriend will answer questions right now—or Toots over there will get some nice shots of you being grilled by homicide. I'm sure Winchell would love them for his column."

Fairchild ground his teeth, nostrils splayed. "I don't know how you got to Sherm, Lieutenant. But goddamn—he's going to pay hell for this."

His infuriated tone finally pierced Tiffy's haze. A fall of golden hair rippled as she shook her head and touched Fairchild's sleeve. Her words were slightly slurred. "Whas going on, Nigel? Where'd Marge and Gregory go?"

The older man clasped a hand over hers. "It's nothing, darling. Don't worry your pretty little head. We're just going to chat with these nice policemen for a minute."

Some light came into the woman's eyes then, letting McKenna know his presence struck a nerve. He shook his head. How had a classy dame come to this—sleeping with this political blowhard under both their spouses' noses, doping to the point she hardly knew where she was? What made a gal like this tick?

Checking that Dolan had his notebook at the ready, he asked, "Mrs. De Forest, do you know a man by the name of Herman Rupp?"

"I don't believe so." She spoke softly, but carefully, puzzled gaze peeking out from under her swooping hair. "Why?"

"A woman of your description hired him to picket the Masako Fumi show at the Shelton Gallery."

She frowned, and Nigel Fairchild drew his eyebrows up. "Picket? Like union strikers?"

"Yeah. Signs and chants—'No Go Jap Show.'" McKenna looked back and forth between the two. "Sound familiar?"

Fairchild shook his head and looked puzzled.

"How very amusing." Tiffy's tone displayed marginally more energy.

"You saying you didn't arrange the demonstration?" McKenna made it sound just a little skeptical.

She looked bemused. "I actually wish I'd thought of it."

"You didn't hire him?" He reached for Dolan's notebook, turned back a few pages, pretended to read, scowled, and handed the notebook back to his partner.

"No, I didn't," the socialite said, staring at the girl singer who had just taken the microphone, "but I have to hand it to whoever did. That jerk Shelton deserved to be picketed." She pushed a strand of hair off her cheek and sat up straighter. "He had some gall—mounting a Jap show at the very moment those Nips were plotting to blow our ships out of the water. Little monkey bastards." Her face contorted—vapidly pretty to frankly ugly in one second flat.

"Did he also deserve to be murdered?" McKenna shot back.

Dolan's pencil hovered in mid air. The girl at the microphone was singing "Take the A Train." Her sultry voice cut through the cigarette haze and drunken babble. McKenna briefly thrilled at the sound. He wished he could really listen.

Before Tiffy could speak, Fairchild tightened his hold on her fingers. He answered, "Of course not, Lieutenant. It wouldn't be civilized to kill people because they don't agree with you. But we do have the right to express our opinions."

Tiffy nodded, clutching a gold-beaded evening bag with her free hand. "Why are you bothering us, anyway? All the papers say the Jap killed Shelton because he was taking her paintings down." Her bright-red lips were set in a prim pout. "She ought to be behind bars."

Fairchild locked eyes with McKenna for a moment, then smiled like the cat at the cream. "But you can't lock her up, can you? The federal government beat you to her. She's on Ellis Island with the other Nips—beyond your jurisdiction."

Jeez, McKenna thought, pressing his lips together. How did this asshole know anything about jurisdiction?

Fairchild continued, "You just want to find someone you can pin the murder on. Well, scratch us off your list. America First may be a thing of the past, but I have highly placed friends who won't take kindly to Tiffy and me being harassed over nothing."

McKenna leaned across the white tablecloth. "Over nothing?" His voice dipped a threatening octave. "Mr. Fairchild, I have a ton of witnesses to your little stunt at the opening of the Fumi show—Mrs. De Forest threatening Shelton and tossing wine all over one of his priciest canvasses."

Fairchild dropped Tiffy's hand and laid both of his on the table. "My friend is very emotional, but she realizes she was out of line at the art gallery. Don't you, Tiffy? Tiffy?"

Tiffy had retreated behind those empty eyes again. Now her head sank over her folded arms until smooth curls dusted the table.

"You've upset her." Fairchild sniffed. "I really think it's time for you to leave."

Oh, no, it wasn't. McKenna had one more card up his sleeve. "Dolan," he said, holding up a finger in a prearranged signal.

The sergeant moved an ash tray and a couple of the empty martini glasses. Then he rummaged in his coat pocket and withdrew a folded, light green paper, slapping it down and spreading it out on the tablecloth.

"Read," McKenna ordered Fairchild.

The isolationist made a show of donning gold-rimmed glasses and took his time perusing the flier. Tiffy kept her head lowered. The gold beads on her clutch bag flashed in the light as she turned it over and over. McKenna kept an eye on her, and let her know it. If he could just figure out what made this broad tick, he'd know how to play her.

"So"—Fairchild sneered, looking up—"an announcement for one of my many speaking engagements. What about it?"

"That dinner meeting covers the time of Arthur Shelton's murder."

"Ah, well." He sat back and spread his hands as if that ended the matter.

"But you weren't there." McKenna kept his voice flat.

"Wasn't I?" He waved away a shapely cigarette girl proffering her loaded tray.

"Nah. You never showed—your supporters were very disappointed."

Fairchild's hands played among the silverware, a twisted napkin, the eyeglasses he'd removed. "Well, I give so many speeches. It's hard to remember each individual one. I suppose something must have prevented me."

"What?"

"What?"

"Yeah. What prevented you?"

Fairchild's fingers were practically dancing now. A bead of sweat formed where silver hair met forehead. "Well…perhaps you'd do better to ask my wife. She keeps tabs on our calendar better than I do."

Sure, thought McKenna. "I'd like to hear your take on it. Now."

"Ah, well—what night was it again?"

"December fifth. The Friday before Pearl Harbor."

While Nigel Fairchild wrinkled his brow like a kid reciting his times tables, Tiffy sprang to life once more. She raised her head, smoothed her hands over her cheeks and stared at the sheet of green paper.

"What are you asking? The Friday before Pearl Harbor?" Her voice was brittle, and she turned to Fairchild. "That was last week. Don't you remember, darling? I wanted to hear Duke Ellington at the Cotton Club. You were angry. You had some boring old dinner to go to, but I made you take me up to Harlem instead. Remember what I promised you…?" She whispered in Fairchild's ear, and his face went dark red.

"Remember, darling?" she went slurring on, seemingly oblivious to his embarrassment. "We met Muffy and Rodger there, and we all got so stinking pissed? We didn't get home until noon, and Marge was so fucking mad. Don't you remember, darling?" She whipped her head around and stared challengingly at McKenna. "Muffy and Rodger certainly will."

Shit! McKenna thought. Sounded like Fairchild might have an alibi for the night of Shelton's murder. But the operation at the Stork Club didn't have to be a complete loss. With an ambiguous smile, McKenna returned Tiffy De Forest's stare. He had her pegged now. This babe ran on thrills—men and drugs and breaking all the rules. And money, but that went without saying.

Her pinpoint pupils were beginning to widen in those cornflower blue eyes—she'd soon need another fix. Very soon. So—she liked older men, did she? He reached across the small table top and ran his fingers along her bare arm. "You are so lovely, aren't you?"

With a flutter of eyelids, she set her beaded bag on the table and placed her carmine-tipped fingers on his wrist.

McKenna smiled appreciatively.

"Grab it, Patsy," he said, and Dolan made a snatch for the beaded bag.

Chapter Sixty-one

Alicia sat cross-legged on the bed beneath a poster of anarchist labor leader Emma Goldman, her unbound hair forming a dark mane around her pale face. Louise sprawled on the divan. "Has Professor Pritzker been able to help your friend?" Alicia asked, biting into an apple.

"Oh, yes," Louise replied. "I don't know how he did it, but we've been to Ellis Island twice." She was leafing through the pages of a book that lay open beside her. "The man's a steam hammer. Nothing stops him," she continued. "He just doesn't seem to care about…" She spread her hands wide in bafflement.

"He's not afraid of anything—is that what you're trying to say?" The tart scent of fresh apple suffused the air.

"Well, yes. I mean…he's going up against the United States government! In wartime!"

Alicia laughed. "And *mano a mano* as my Puerto Rican friend says. He's got a reputation for fighting tyranny in any form—and thriving on the battle."

"Tyranny?" Louise felt the word awkward on her tongue, as if she'd never before had to pronounce it aloud. "I never thought of the US government in that light…"

"Really?" Alicia, brow furrowed, looked at her as if she were some sort of alien species. "Why not?" She shook her wiry curls in disbelief. "Slavery? The Indian wars? Didn't you ever take a history class?"

Louise felt as if she were getting in over her head. "Well, no. Not since high school—except for the history of nursing, of course. But—" she said, clearing her throat, "back to Mr. Pritzker. I've never met anyone like him before."

Eyes narrowed, Alicia cautioned, "Watch it, Louise. Pritzker's a *mensch*, but...he is a man. And you," she continued, "are a very attractive woman."

Louise sat up abruptly and arranged her face. "I didn't think you'd be such an old granny, Alicia," she replied. "I know how to take care of myself around men."

"Okay, but...this particular man marches to his own drummer..." Alicia looked as if she had something more to say.

"No," Louise responded, a little too forcefully, "enough about that. I came up here to ask you what we can do for Helda."

"Oh, the poor woman! She's beside herself with worry...too jumpy to cook even...That meal!" Alicia made a gagging sound.

Louise laughed. "Some of those leftovers must have been a week old! As soon as I smelled that big chunk of sauerbraten, I snatched the bowl off the table, ran out back and threw the stinking stuff in the garbage can. She didn't even notice."

"Louise!" Marion called up from the second floor hallway, her drama-school voice projecting through the thick door. "You up there?"

Louise jumped up from the divan and opened the door. "What is it?"

"You've got a phone call. Says her name is 'Professor Lillian Bridges.'" Marion captured the professor's patrician tones exactly.

Oh, dear. Louise should have called the woman right away after Abe had let her know about the moving van arrangements. It was just...well, Louise realized she didn't relish talking to her again. Miss Bridges was a complicated lady, and Louise didn't quite know how to take her. But she was an old friend of the Oakleys. And willing to risk harboring Masako's paintings from the authorities. That was the important thing.

"Be right down," Louise called.

Chapter Sixty-two

Cat piss! Cabby tried not to breath. Cat piss, sour milk, and rotten eggs. Jeez! The crap she had to deal with for a story!

Okay, so, even in this pricey neighborhood, it stank. Get over it!

Checking around to make sure no one was watching, Cabby squeezed between a bread delivery truck and the corner of a building and started down a second narrow alley. If she had her bearings right, the kitchen entrance to the Stork Club ought to be right in the middle of the block.

Before she'd crossed Fifty-third and turned east, she passed the lighted show windows of Saks Fifth Avenue. On the other side of Fifth, the illuminated towers of Saint Thomas' Episcopal Church shone reassuringly monumental.

Yeah, quite a neighborhood indeed. Everything wealth could buy: God, Couture, and Sin all jammed into one square acre of city real estate.

A few yards ahead, a cone of yellow light swept the dark alley. She pulled up short. A guy wearing a work jacket over a white bib apron stepped out of a door. He carried a wire delivery basket, the kind fitted out for loaves of bread. Of course—the truck at the head of the alley had said Heitzman's Blue Ribbon Bakery. Here was her chance.

She hailed him as he passed by. "Hey, buddy. Ain't that the Stork Club?"

He looked her over. "Who wants to know?"

Hand on one hip, she pasted on her perkiest smile. "Just a girl who wants to surprise her boyfriend." The guy would've been halfway good looking if it hadn't been for his acne-pitted cheeks. "He's one of the waiters, and it's his birthday."

He shrugged. "Yeah, that's the Stork, but don't expect to get past the goon on the kitchen door. They've been having union trouble, so he's really on the ball."

Oops, she hadn't prepared for that. But this guy had been admitted, hadn't he? Sure he had, because he looked like he belonged. "Hey, I got a deal for you, buddy. A dollar for your apron and basket."

"Huh?"

"You heard me." She fished a dollar bill out of her purse and held it up. Lunch would be bologna and mustard sandwiches for the next week.

"A buck, huh?" He hustled out of his jacket and reached behind to untie the apron strings. "Look, sure I'll sell you the apron, but I've gotta hang onto the basket. It'd come out of my pay."

"Okay, fifty cents then."

"Uh-uh, sister. You want my apron, it's a buck." With a shit-eating grin, he dangled the stained length of fabric just out of her reach.

The big jerk! If she wasn't in such a hurry, she'd show him how to bargain. But, who knew how far McKenna had gotten with Fairchild? So, a buck it was. Trotting down the alley, Cabby cinched her tweed coat in tight and pulled the apron over her head.

What now? Searching her bag for more inspiration, she turned up a plaid scarf, slicked her curls down with spit, and tied the scarf peasant-style behind her neck. Her eyes had adjusted to the dim light, so it was easy to make out a wooden fruit crate on top of an ashcan across the way. Moving quickly, she lined it with old newspaper, mashed the lid down and approached the Stork's back entrance.

Okay, just grab a few deep breaths and march right in. Easy to say, but her knees were shaking. Her first outside assignment in journalism class had been to interview some minor government functionary about a new park. Even when Cabby had produced her Hunter College identification card, his witch of a secretary hadn't believed a girl could be a student reporter. It wasn't until the old bat had called the college that Cabby got in.

She had learned something that day: she had to have twice the brass and double the hustle of her male colleagues. Now, she took in a lungful of oxygen and pulled the door handle.

The muscle-bound guy in the black turtleneck didn't give her a second glance. Toting her fruit crate, she proceeded down a long corridor and turned a corner. Noise and heat told her the working kitchen was on her right, so she ditched her crate and apron in an empty storage room on the left. The dining room was up a flight of stairs so narrow that waiters slipped past each other sideways. Whoever planned this joint, it hadn't been anyone who'd ever served food for a living.

A bald-headed waiter on the stairs was too harassed to challenge her, but, as she entered the smoke-hazed dining room, a captain made a beeline in her direction. She'd fluffed up her hair, loosened her coat, and pulled down her neckline, but she was still one of the few women in the huge dining room not wearing evening attire. "The ladies' lounge, if you please," she intoned in her poshest Upper East Side voice. After an uncomfortable pause, he directed her and then retreated to soothe a red-faced man complaining about an overdone filet.

What with the smoke and the lights and the music, Cabby couldn't see anyone she knew. Where was McKenna? Surely he hadn't concluded his business with Fairchild. That silver-haired old buzzard wasn't likely to roll over like a lap dog, and the homicide detective was as stubborn as they come. Time to get moving.

Slowly, and with her most jaded expression, she circled the room. Was that Rita Hayworth? Oh, my god!

Then, from a nearby corner, sounded a woman's shrill complaint. A blonde in a sleek white dress jumped to her feet, drawing all eyes, including Cabby's. Tiffy De Forest! Flushed, hysterical, waving her arms. Gotcha! Cabby started in her direction.

But what was going on? Tiffy swung at Nigel Fairchild with a beringed fist. "Get out of my way," she screeched in a voice that could shatter glass.

McKenna jumped up and stretched his bulk across the table, making a grab for the screaming woman. She easily twisted away. Then the other cop was on his feet. Cabby could see a dainty gold bag in his meaty hand.

Tiffy's purse? Why?

Her view was suddenly cut off by a man's broad shoulders. Many of the Stork's patrons were out of their seats, babbling, gesturing wildly, responding to the domestic drama at the Fairchild table as if a bomb had hit the nightclub. In that one moment, the recent tensions—the gut-wrenching attack in Hawaii, the day's war declarations—broke out in a panicky communal fever.

Cabby braced herself and started toward Fairchild's corner. But the crowd resisted her efforts, pushing her back.

The captain burst through—"Ladies and gentlemen! Please!" The Greek maitre d' and a trio of waiters followed hard on his heels.

Cabby dove in behind them. Then—ooof!—a drip in a tuxedo entangled his arm with hers. He yelled out, "Tiffy, darling, I'm coming! I'm coming!" But Tiffy's hero was so plastered he spun himself and Cabby both smack into a tray of éclairs and pastries.

Cabby hit the floor, and a sharp pain sliced through her wrist. Oh, shit! It hurt like hell. But, by god, she wouldn't let it stop her. What a story: "Fairchild in Brouhaha at Stork Club."

Spattered with sticky cream filling, she crawled one-armed through a sea of fancy skirts until she found an empty chair to push up on. Above the hubbub, she heard McKenna's voice booming, "Stop, Madam. Not another step. That's a police order!"

On her feet again, hand dangling uselessly, Cabby saw Tiffy. Twisting like a pale eel, the woman clambered over several chairs and pushed past scandalized diners. Gold glinted from her right hand. She'd regained her purse and was making for the passage to the kitchen stairs.

"Stop that woman!" McKenna yelled.

Cabby popped onto tiptoe. McKenna and the other cop were hemmed in behind a wall of bodies. They'd never reach Tiffy before she escaped down those stairs. But she—Cabby's heart beat faster—she was only a few steps away!

Having played plenty of vacant-lot football with the neighborhood boys, she knew exactly what to do. With a mammoth lunge, she tackled Tiffy by the legs.

The aging debutante fell like a sack of potatoes, arms and legs sprawling. The beaded bag she'd clutched so tightly bounced over the carpet and popped open in front of Cabby's nose. A rainbow of bright yellow, red, and blue pills spilled across the floor, followed by a syringe and a half-filled glass vial.

Cabby grabbed for the bag, clutched it, Tiffy shrieked obscenities and yanked. The pain in the younger woman's right wrist flared white hot. Over the crowd's intoxicated giggles and McKenna's barked orders, the orchestra launched into "Somewhere Over the Rainbow." Or was that simply Cabby's imagination as she lapsed into a brief, pain-free unconsciousness?

Chapter Sixty-three

Masako stood by the barred window looking out. Behind her she heard the women readying themselves for their narrow cots: tears, wailing, the quiet sharing of confidences in an alien language. Harsh, unprovoked laughter from an Italian girl in a magenta sweater. In broken English, a recipe for Jell-o salad.

Before her she saw the silent statue with its heavy arms, its legs immobile beneath the copper robes.

She stared and stared, willing her arms, her legs inflexible, insensible like those of Lady Liberty. Her heart, anesthetized.

Chapter Sixty-four

Friday, December 12, after midnight

On the sidewalk outside Mount Sinai Hospital, Cabby stamped her feet and knocked her knees together, trying to coax some circulation into her frozen extremities. The blue-black sky was too cold to be hazy, and streetlights threw out sharp-edged electric halos. An ambulance swung in behind her, red lights ablaze and siren wailing. Two orderlies wrestled a stretcher out of the back hatch, but Cabby didn't give them more than a glance. She'd had enough excitement for one night and wanted nothing more than to curl up in her own warm bed.

Thank god! Here was McKenna pulling up under the canopy in the unmarked police sedan.

The old guy had been real nice. He hadn't fussed anything like what she'd expected, and he'd allowed her to cover Tiffy De Forest's arrest and subsequent transfer to the tender care of the vice squad. Nigel Fairchild had escaped arrest for now, but, as Tiffy's suspected conduit to drug suppliers, he was sure to come in for some tough questioning. Cabby would love to see that pompous ass get the third degree.

It wasn't until after the Stork had returned to its elegant orgy of dining, drinking, and dancing that McKenna had noticed Cabby rubbing her swollen wrist. He'd immediately sent his sergeant home and had driven her up to Mt. Sinai, where an x-ray revealed what a dog-tired intern called "a moderate ligamentary sprain." With her right arm in a sling, she'd be typing left-handed, hunt-and-peck style, for a week or so.

Cabby, now at the curb, reached for the door handle and was surprised when McKenna loped around the sedan to help her into the car. Oddly touched at his concern, she let him settle her aching wrist on a folded blanket retrieved from the trunk. With few vehicles on the street at that hour, they sped unimpeded down Broadway, past tall buildings scattered with lights, and slowed only as they passed the still-illuminated theaters of Times Square. The occasional chatter from McKenna's police radio did nothing to disrupt an air of quiet intimacy fostered by the solitude and darkness. Thanks to the intern's pain tablet, Cabby soon slipped into a waking daze, half planning, half dreaming her story for the next issue: "Prominent Club Woman Seized in Drug Case."

"What you asked me earlier?" McKenna spoke unexpectedly.

"Huh?" Cabby startled, coming out of her fog.

"You know—outside Louie's? About whether I was against the war, like Fairchild." Steering with his knees, he peeled the cellophane from a pack of Lucky Strikes and, with the tips of his thumb and forefinger, tweezed out a cigarette from the full package.

"Oh, well..." That wasn't exactly what she'd asked, but it was interesting he'd taken it that way.

The car wobbled a bit as he lit the smoke and took his first drag. "I was there, you know, for the last one."

"Were you?" She was alert now, the dark ambiguity of his tone catching her attention. "Was it hell?"

"Yeah. And hell is too mild a word for what we went through." He seemed to be in a ruminative mood. "One thing I learned, though—ya make assumptions about people without any basis, it'll come back to bite you." He waved the cigarette for emphasis, and its glowing tip made a fiery arc in the darkness.

Okay, back to the discussion about Jap-hatred they'd had on Grand Street. Cabby forced herself to remain silent. Halper would have called this a "listening time."

"In '17 the draft was breathing down my neck, just like it is for the boys now. I volunteered for the Army Tank Corps—being surrounded by thick metal plates seemed a lot safer than dodging across battlefields with a rifle."

"Was it?" They'd reached the Brooklyn Bridge, and mist was rising off the East River, smudging the dark hulks of steamers and cargo ships. Blocks away, lights glared in the Navy Yard. A blackout—like the one in London—was coming, she knew, but it sure hadn't started yet. The Yard was one huge, bright sitting duck.

"Hell, no. Nothing was safe over there." He took another long drag on the cigarette as they bumped over the bridge. "Does the Argonne Forest mean anything to you?"

"I've heard of it..."

"Well..." The light was red at Tillary Street. McKenna pulled the car to a halt. The imposing Borough Hall was just ahead.

"Picture this—mud and smoke—noise that would bust your eardrums. Thousands of men fighting over a couple acres of scabby ground. I was driving a light tank with my commander taking the shots. Made decent headway until I hit a tank trap—trenches dug by Kraut engineers, then flooded. Diabolical. Flipped our tank. Water was coming in fast. 'You first,' I told the lieutenant, but he was already halfway through the hatch. Got stuck and I had to push him out. By that time I couldn't see a damn thing. Muddy water up to my chin. I aimed my head where I thought the hatch was—and hit steel." He turned his head and looked Cabby in the eye. "I was seeing stars then. The mud and the water and the steel roof—thought I was a goner."

She was wide awake now and listening hard. "What happened?"

"Guy pulled me out and set me on my pins."

She thought of heroic American soldiers. "Your lieutenant!"

He snorted. "Hardly. He woulda been heading for the hills like his backside was on fire. That chicken sh...ah..." McKenna took a last lungful of smoke, rolled the window down and flipped the butt out. "No, it was a Kraut. By then they were using kids—he was sixteen if he was a day. I'll never forget his face—scared wide-eyed. He pointed back to our lines and said something I didn't understand, then, '*Schnell.*' That I knew, so I took off and never looked back."

"I got it," Cabby said, as the light changed to green and McKenna threw the car into gear. "You've been to hell and back, so you agree with Nigel Fairchild about staying out of this war."

"That's probably the only thing I agree with him on." McKenna nodded. "But what the hay, it's too late now. The President signed the declarations this…ah…yesterday…afternoon. Now we've got the whole pack of 'em to fight."

Cabby nodded, recalling how she'd felt when the formal declaration of war had come through on the wire. She'd been in the City room, with the December darkness beginning to fall outside the large windows, writing up the story of the women volunteers' luncheon. Suddenly the news made the rounds, buzzing from National desk, to City and then to Foreign like a grim version of that kid's "telephone" game. For the first time, she realized that she was afraid, truly afraid. Not just for herself, but for everyone. If this war was anything like the last one, more people would die from starvation and disease than from the fighting itself. Women, children—millions of them.

And what made Americans think we'd be spared?

"So, no," McKenna concluded, turning onto Flatbush. "I'm no isolationist like Fairchild. But believe me, if I were eighteen again, with this war coming on, I sure as hell would think about serving in some noncombatant position as a pacifist rather than going around killing sixteen-year-old German boys. Or Japanese boys, for that matter." He craned his neck, reading street signs. "Then…in the last war, I mean…that would have earned me a white feather. But, ya know, if I were the man I am now, I wouldn't give a damn."

"No, I don't think you would," Cabby said, pensively, as she pointed ahead to her street. If only her father had been anything like this man, her life would have been a different story. She wondered if McKenna had any children.

She wondered if he had any sons.

Chapter Sixty-five

Helda looks so young, Cabby thought, as the landlady ran down the porch steps with unbound hair streaming in waves and sprigged flannel nightgown billowing behind. All dignity forgotten, she was calling, "Howie? Do you haff Howie?"

"No," Cabby replied, bumping the car door closed with her hip. Good god, that boy hasn't come home yet?

McKenna had insisted on walking Cabby to the door. As Helda reached them, Cabby noticed a sudden gleam of interest before he slipped on his cop mask. He was looking at Helda in that certain way—exactly like Joey Gaetano used to look at her. Hmmm.

Louise followed Helda out onto the cold pavement. She carried an orange-and-yellow crocheted afghan that she threw around the landlady's shoulders. Cabby acknowledged her with a nod. Trust Louise to take care of someone in distress.

In tears, Helda collapsed on Cabby's shoulder. "I don't know what to do. Nobody knows where he is."

Cabby started to check her watch. With a wince, she remembered she'd put it in her purse when the intern had wrapped up her wrist. "What time is it?"

"1:30," said McKenna, gaze still on Helda.

"Oh, you poor thing." Cabby patted Helda's back with her good hand and the landlady began to wail in earnest.

Louise gave a big sigh and spread her hands helplessly.

Cabby threw McKenna a desperate look. Since he seemed so taken with Helda, maybe he would help. "Her fourteen-year-old son's disappeared," Cabby told him. "Help us get her into the house, will ya?"

McKenna hesitated, so Cabby threw her good arm around Helda's waist. The detective then supported the landlady gingerly by the elbow. The rumpus had awakened a next-door neighbor, a fat woman in a woolly robe, who came running out on her porch, pulling curlers out of her hair. With an authority born of long practice, McKenna waved her away. Together he and Cabby fumbled Helda up the steps and into the front parlor. Louise directed them to the large horsehair sofa.

"What should I do?" Helda sobbed, clutching a satin Niagara Falls souvenir pillow to her chest. She curled up in an agonized ball and continued sobbing.

"She's been like this since midnight," Louise said. "It may be time for a sedative. I don't know what else I can do."

McKenna reached out, impulsively it seemed, to brush a tendril of hair from Helda's eyes. "Aw, come on, lady."

"Helda," Cabby said, "this is Lieutenant McKenna of the police. Maybe he can give you some advice about finding Howie."

Helda looked up, desperate blue eyes wide. "You can get my Howie back?"

McKenna stood speechless.

Cabby watched the detective quizzically. His reaction to Helda both amused and enlightened her. Even at his age—he must be close to fifty!—he was vulnerable to women? Well. Well. So, it went on that long between the sexes? Whaddaya know?

Finally the detective reached into an inside pocket and pulled out his notebook. After clearing his throat, he asked Helda, "What does the boy look like, Ma'am, and how long has he been gone?"

"Wass goin' on?" A groggy Ruthie, wearing red flannels, slouched down the stairs and through the parlor archway. "All this noise this hour of the night?" She registered McKenna's presence with a start. "And who the hell is he?" She paraded over and peered into his face. "You the guy who's been hanging around outside?"

Someone's been hanging around? Louise thought as her hand flew to her heart. Oh, no! Was the FBI following her?

Oh, god! Cabby thought with a shudder. It's the guy in the gray suit—Fairchild's goon!—if he finds out what happened at the Stork, I'm a goner for sure.

Ernst! Helda cried and covered her face with her hands.

Chapter Sixty-six

Friday, morning

When Abe turned the Ford onto Bleecker Street, the ball of tension between Louise's shoulders began to ease. Finally they would secure Masako's studio paintings and have the captions translated before the Feds could use them to further their own agenda. Last night, a heart-to-heart talk with Cabby had freighted this errand with even more weight. During the nightclub adventure with Lieutenant McKenna, Louise's roommate had learned that Fairchild might very well have an alibi for the night of Shelton's murder. Masako Oakley was back in double jeopardy. The screws were tightening on her enemy alien case, and she was once again the prime suspect in Arthur Shelton's murder.

All the way from Brooklyn, Louise and Abe had planned what he only half jokingly referred to as "the heist." Professor Bridges would meet them at the studio. So would the art movers recommended by Desmond Cox. They'd swath the canvases in padded moving quilts and transport them in a van up the West Side elevated highway to Lillian Bridge's apartment. A legacy from a deceased great-uncle, Lillian would inform any nosy neighbors.

To Louise, Greenwich Village felt almost like home. Unlike the dizzying vertical lines and breakneck speed of the rest of Manhattan, these quaint blocks struck her as a real neighborhood. She could easily envision Masako painting here, gaining inspiration from the interlacing branches of the winter-bare trees that lined most every street, the wrought iron gates offering glimpses of brickwork courtyards, the shabby mixed facades of nineteenth-century townhouses—wood-frame, brownstone, brick.

Now, Abe positioned the Ford parallel to a beat-up green Nash in front of a four-story row house on Bleecker Street and began backing into a cramped parking space. Even though they were early, Lillian Bridges already paced the sidewalk in front of the old building, elegant in a soft, green, Irish tweed jacket and brown trousers. As Abe jockeyed the sedan to the curb, she flipped her cigarette at the gutter, strode toward them, and yanked open the passenger-side door before Louise had even grasped the handle.

"Come on, you two. What are we waiting for?" Lillian briskly led the way inside the building and toward the stairs at the rear of the hall.

"You've been here before?" Abe asked her, following at his own pace.

"It's been a while, but, yes. Masako was shy about showing her work. Robert, however, enjoyed giving friends what he called a 'sneak peek.'"

They rounded the second floor landing and Abe went on, "Was? You make it sound like the little lady won't be doing any more painting."

Lillian stopped on the stairs and, with a twist, turned to face Abe. "I suppose that's in your hands, Counselor, but I tremble for her. I truly do. Family ties to Emperor Hirohito's government. Prime suspect in a murder case…."

Abe gave the woman an enigmatic smile. "Don't sell me short, Professor. I still have a few tricks up my sleeve."

Louise gulped. Abe radiated confidence. But unless the Japanese woman was willing to come up with a rational explanation, how was he planning to deal with her presence at the gallery on the night of the murder?

"But first," he continued, "I have to confront the loyalty question."

"In these times," Lillian murmured darkly, "loyalty is hardly a minor matter."

"Listen, lady," Abe shot back, "even G-men have to produce evidence. So far all Bagwell and his boys have thrown at us is racially biased speculation."

The professor gazed at him soberly, then began climbing the stairs again. Her words floated back over her shoulder. "I suppose my agreeing to harbor the paintings will be of some help."

"I expect so." Abe's voice carried over the hollow clumping of their footsteps. "Would you be willing to help me with something else?"

Lillian stopped at the third-floor landing. Wan light from the wire-enforced window lit one side of her face. "What's that?" She looked genuinely curious.

"I assume you know that the Immigration Act of 1924 excluded Mrs. Oakley from obtaining American citizenship—along with just about anyone from the Far East."

"Ye-e-ss?" In the half-light, her patrician features reflected the strain of the past few days.

"But Mrs. Oakley always intended to go through the process of at least obtaining permanent resident status, right?"

"Yes. She and Robert were both keen, but I understand it's quite a shockingly involved process for a Jap." Without further remark, Lillian began climbing again.

Abe coughed. "Well, if you could swear out an affidavit as to her intention…"

"Of course." The words drifted back. "Anything to help poor Masako." They'd reached the fourth floor. "Louise, dear," Lillian Bridges said, turning to her, "I believe Robert entrusted you with the key."

The old-fashioned iron key creaked in the lock but turned without a hitch, admitting them into a large, dusty room that smelled faintly of oil paint and turpentine. The light in the studio was so dim that Louise thought her vision had gone hazy. Heavy clouds had threatened rain all morning, and the slanting skylight didn't provide much illumination. She felt the wall inside the door for a light switch, found one, and flicked it on—only to reveal that their mission at Masako Fumi Oakley's studio was nothing but a fool's errand.

Louise stood stunned with disbelief. The riot of color, of texture, of shapes she'd anticipated was nowhere to be seen. The dingy stucco walls were bare; the large, paint-spattered easel was empty. There wasn't a water color, an oil painting, a picture scroll or a rudimentary sketch to be seen. Nothing.

Lillian Bridges gasped, obviously staggered by the absence of the paintings.

Abe pushed past the two women, whipped off his hat and ranged around the dusty room like a wolf in search of prey. He shook a faded blue smock hanging from a hook, pawed through a neat array of paint boxes, ink bottles and brushes stacked on some rough shelving, and then moved to a work table to examine a roll of virgin canvas and some stretcher boards.

"Damn." Abe whirled from the table. "Is there another room?" he asked Lillian.

The professor had been turning slowly on the thick heel of her sensible club shoe. "No. This is it." She stared at the paint-spattered easel as if, by sheer force of will, she might conjure up a canvas. "There should be thirty paintings—at least. Last time I was here they were all over the place, hanging on those hooks, on the floor leaning against the wall four or five deep. Arthur took—maybe—twenty for the show."

She plopped down, in a most inelegant manner, on an ancient blue plush settee, and an explosion of dust motes momentarily hovered in the air. "Obviously, they've been stolen." She rubbed a slender, long-fingered hand across her face. "Robert will be so upset."

"I'll call the police." Louise reached for the telephone on a small table by the door and dialed O for Operator.

Abe slammed his hand over hers, disconnecting the call. "Slow down a minute. Just think about it—there's no sign of a break-in. Also, there's a far more likely possibility."

Louise was quick to understand. "The FBI, right? Someone must have told them about the studio. And—"

Abe jumped in. "And in that case, there's no sense in making an official report. That would just complicate things for Mrs. Oakley. Now, we've got to get out of here and head off those movers."

"Right!" Lillian nodded emphatically.

Louise, with a self-conscious glance at the other two, retrieved the flag-embroidered handkerchief from her purse and began to wipe off the heavy black telephone receiver.

Never before in her life had she considered it necessary to worry about fingerprints.

Chapter Sixty-seven

So, McKenna thought, that's what an antique Japanese brush pot looks like. Kind of like a vase, but instead of flowers, it held a scholar's writing brushes. He licked his finger and turned another page of the slick auction catalogue Desmond Cox had sent over. Here was another pot, this one carved out of a thick segment of bamboo, and another made of jade. He pulled the chain of his desk lamp and bent to study the last photo, more to gauge mass and heft than to admire the scowling samurai warrior incised on the front.

Over a foot tall with a rim as thick as his little finger—that pot could have busted Shelton's head for sure, and kept on holding brushes for another five-hundred years. Too bad his boys hadn't been able to run down anything even remotely like it.

Shaking his head, McKenna closed the catalogue and creaked his desk chair back. Funny what people would pay big bucks for. Personally, he wouldn't give a dime for a curio that just sat around on a shelf, and this one wasn't even pretty. Now, that new Penn reel he'd had his eye on—that sweet little spinner—he'd be willing to drop some coin on that. Sighing, he laced his fingers over his midsection. How long before he'd be able to get out to Long Island again? Spend a day with the fish? Forget this crazy, suicidal world for a few hours?

For exactly one blessed minute, McKenna was transported to that shining expanse of water on Shinnecock Bay. Then the intercom crackled to life and he reached to press a button. "Yeah?"

"Lute, I know you told me not to bother you...but Bernice just called up...and ah..."

Doris was too cool a customer to dither, but she was coming close.

"Just spit it out, hon." McKenna's tone was weary. He was already ahead of the squad secretary.

"Captain Dwyer wants you down in his office—pronto."

Chapter Sixty-eight

"Proud of yourself, McKenna?" The speaker was Captain Joseph Dwyer, his subject the arrest of Helen "Tiffy" De Forest, his attitude…Well, the less said about his attitude, the better.

"Whadda you want me to do, Cap? There were blue birds, reds—even schmeck—right under my nose. You want me to ignore that crap? In public?"

McKenna would be damned if he'd hang his head over a perfectly good collar. He ground his back teeth together. He'd handed the narcotics boys a sure thing. If they followed the trail through Nigel Fairchild and a couple of dirty doctors, they'd end up bagging half the morphine and barbiturate tablets that kept café society so damn mellow. If rumors were correct, the importers worked out of a Mexican freighter somewhere in the harbor. Of course, it was always possible the narcotics squad was going to cool their heels on this one and let the war take its natural toll on the drug trade.

Too bad that wouldn't work with homicide.

Dwyer ran a hand over his close-cropped silver hair. "What I want is for you to leave vice to Vice. Now get busy preparing your case against Fumi for the DA. What's your holdup?" His lips twisted into a condescending smile. "And don't blame the Feds—I got you access to the goddamn detention center three days ago."

McKenna was beginning to steam. "The holdup is that Mrs. Oakley is still a ninety-pound china doll that couldn't have moved Shelton's corpse two feet, much less dragged him clear across that gallery."

Dwyer rolled his eyes. "Maybe she had some help. The way I hear it, she was definitely on the scene."

"So you heard that, did you?" Shit. Then somebody must've had their mouth to your ear, McKenna thought, because I haven't finished writing up that report yet. He took a slow breath. "Yeah, we have an eye witness for her getting out of a cab and entering the gallery, but I'm thinking Shelton was still alive when she left."

"Why?"

"Masako Fumi Oakley isn't the one who heaved a brick through Shelton's window. And she sure as hell didn't hire a lowlife goon to picket her own show." He bit his lip to reign in his temper. "If I've learned one thing about this gal, it's that her paintings mean more to her than anything in the world—after her husband, that is. She fought to go to art school, fought to be a painter. Christ, she broke with her family over it. Even renounced her native country. Look, Cap," McKenna said slowly and clearly, "somebody has it in for this lady. I don't know why, but I'd bet ten dollars to a doughnut Shelton's murder is tied right into it."

Dwyer leaned back in his desk chair and tented his fingers. "And, at first, you thought that somebody might be Nigel Fairchild."

"Yeah."

"And you were wrong about that."

"Yeah. But Fairchild's not the only possibility."

Captain Dwyer eased forward. His blue eyes were piercing, but his voice took on the quality of maple syrup—sweet, thin, and smooth. "Let me lay it out for you, Lieutenant, the DA isn't the only one breathing down my neck. There's Washington, too. Turns out certain influential people think Mrs. Oakley could be very valuable right about now."

McKenna was momentarily thrown. "Valuable? What the hell does that mean?"

"Look, Pearl Harbor caught us all by surprise. A lot of Americans were trapped behind enemy lines."

"What, like businessmen, diplomats, ordinary travelers?"

"And some not so ordinary." Dwyer nodded slowly. "Some are carrying information that could prove to be of great importance to the war effort. You've heard of prisoner exchanges? To have a successful civilian exchange…The daughter of a high-ranking Japanese functionary…" He circled one hand in a pathetic little flourish. "*Quid pro quo*—that's the name of the game."

Who in hell had been bending Dwyer's ear? Bending his arm more likely. "Last time I looked, this was the headquarters of the New York Police Department, not the War Office in Washington, DC."

"Well, look again, McKenna. With national defense at stake, New York can't afford an independent streak. Dammit, LaGuardia's even taking a beating over air raid procedures—the Feds are determined to organize them their way, not New York's way. We're all going to have to knuckle under for as long as this lasts."

Shit, McKenna thought again, detecting a flash of desperation in his captain's eyes, they've really gotten to Joe. Have they promised him big things after the war? Or is his job on the line?

McKenna felt a sinking sensation in his stomach. The New York City he was used to called its own shots, operating almost as a country within a country; the Feds' incursion into local authority was moving a lot faster than he was comfortable with. How long before New York coppers all turned into a bunch of mindless bureaucrats, filling out forms in triplicate before they could shake down a mug? He shifted on the wooden chair—nice time for the hip to start acting up—and asked carefully, "What is it you want me to do, Cap?"

"Wrap the case up. You've got enough evidence that the Jap lady is involved one way or another. Send what you have to the DA and wash your hands of it. Once Dragon Lady's charged with murder, she'll be worth twice what an ordinary civilian would be in an exchange."

McKenna replied very slowly. "And if Mrs. Oakley isn't Shelton's killer?"

Dwyer shrugged. "So she ends up in Japan. So what?"

"Are you aware she hasn't set foot in that country since she was a small child? A country on fire with hatred for anything associated with America?"

Another shrug. "Why should we care?"

McKenna swallowed, hard. "Let's look at it another way. If someone else killed Shelton, then we have a murderer running loose in the city."

"Hardly the only one—as you and I both know."

Yeah, McKenna thought, guys who kill each other over a craps game or a sleazy dame. But this was different. Shelton's murderer was uptown, smart, daring—a killer who knew how to manipulate an opportunity to the hilt—a dangerous person who needed to be put away. McKenna sighed. He knew he was outgunned, but he asked anyway, "What if I keep working the case?"

Dwyer didn't miss a beat. "Then we'll have to reconsider that retirement."

A vision of Shinnecock Bay, sparkling in the sunlight, again sprang to McKenna's mind. He was surprised how easy it was to push it aside. "Give me two more days, Cap."

Dwyer hesitated. Then, "Monday morning—nine o'clock sharp—your report on the DA's desk." He checked his neatly trimmed fingernails, then looked back up. "And not a minute later."

Chapter Sixty-nine

Miss Gardner's classroom had six tall windows set into the concrete-block wall. The low afternoon sun illuminated battered student desks in rows so straight they might have been aligned with a yardstick. Cabby stood in the doorway, her wrist still aching in its cumbersome sling, watching the teacher erase diagrammed sentences from the long blackboard. The smell of chalk dust pervaded the air, taking Cabby back to Hunter College High School. Once she'd gotten a taste of the larger life that school's vibrant teachers had offered, she couldn't wait to leave her family's cramped apartment, and even more cramped minds, behind. Was Howie feeling like she had? Is that why he'd run away?

Over burned toast and clotted oatmeal that morning, Helda's boarders had agreed to do whatever they could to help find Howie. "That little squirt," as Ruthie called him. "Otherwise," she said, "we're gonna have to move out of here before we starve to death."

"I'll go over to the school, talk to his teachers," Cabby volunteered. "That's what my cop friend suggested, and there's no way Helda would have the know-how to finesse the system."

"Finesse the system?" Mousie asked, frowning. She'd looked worried ever since she'd come downstairs this morning.

"Yeah. The New York City school system. Those teachers are tough dames, even tougher than the kids. They won't give student information to just anyone, but I had thirteen years of them—I know the drill."

"The drill?" Mousie looked even more worried.

"Yeah. Leave it to me." Then she grinned. "I should be able to wriggle a couple of hours off work this afternoon—once my editor gets a gander of the Stork Club story I'm gonna hand him." Cabby picked up her coffee cup and sipped at the bitter brew. Soon, she was reveling in envious questions about her nightclub escapade.

As she left the breakfast table, she snapped back to reality. Thank god, Lieutenant McKenna had offered to check juvenile hall and the hospitals, even the morgue. He'd have more pull at those places than she would. She shuddered at the thought of Howie laid out on a slab. Surely—surely—if there was any justice in the world, Helda would never have to face that.

Now, watching Miss Gardner's eraser sweep the board in precise arcs, Cabby felt oddly paralyzed, as if she were once again the frightened tot her mother had coaxed into Mrs. Costigan's kindergarten. After all that braggadocio at breakfast, she kind of wished one of her housemates had joined her on this errand. Alicia or Louise. Louise hadn't even been at breakfast. She'd blown out of their room first thing, as if Cary Grant was waiting downstairs with a diamond ring.

"And just who are you?" Miss Gardner's abrupt tone jerked Cabby to life. Howie Schroeder's homeroom teacher was tall and thin with salt-and-pepper hair, bushy eyebrows, and a long face just like the llamas Cabby had visited in the Bronx Zoo. She looked impatient. With her students gone for the day, Miss Gardner clearly wanted to straighten up the classroom and get home for the weekend.

Home to her cats, Cabby thought unkindly.

But when Cabby explained about Howie, the teacher sat down at a student desk and gestured for Cabby to do the same.

"This is bad news, indeed." Miss Gardner folded her hands and nodded primly. "Howard, you must understand, is an extremely promising young man. His Intelligence Quotient is in the top percentile nationwide. I have great hopes for him—some field of science or mathematics, perhaps."

Cabby opened her mouth to say something about the boy's attempt to enlist in the armed forces, but Miss Gardner kept going.

"Now I do understand that his mother is alone, struggling merely to support herself and the boy. But, nonetheless, with a New York public education Howard Schroeder can go anywhere he wants in life. The City College system is outstanding—and free."

"I know," Cabby inserted, wanting to tell Miss Gardner that she, herself, had gone to a public college, but the teacher blabbed on.

"So, when I saw the state he was in on Monday, I was alarmed. But then, of course, all the students were dismayed—overnight we'd been plunged into war, and the attack was all they could think and talk about. Howard's distress, however, was excessive. The first half of the week he seemed lost somewhere in his own head. Then yesterday and today he didn't show up at all. I was just about to report him truant."

"Miss Gardner." Cabby put considerable emphasis into articulating the teacher's name. Once she had her attention, she rushed on, prevaricating only a little, "Howie's mother was wondering if I could take a look in his desk. She's gone through his room at home and found nothing to indicate where he went. If he didn't take his notebooks home, they'd be in his desk. Right?"

Miss Gardner was pensive for a moment. Then, pointing a manicured fingernail at an ink-inscribed oak desk halfway back in the room, she said, "Howard sits right there. I suppose, under the circumstances…"

Cabby didn't wait for her to finish. She whipped back to Howie's desk and raised the lid. It was stuffed. Working one-handed, she pulled out discarded homework papers, a crumpled-up sports magazine, a publicity photo of Lana Turner, a couple of maps, and three worn notebooks. When she saw a copy of

Adventures of Huckleberry Finn, Cabby gave a little shriek and snatched it up. "This is the most important book I ever read."

"Really?" Miss Gardner raised her eyebrows. "Why?"

Cabby gave her a wicked grin, but she was dead serious. "Huck taught me that it was okay to break the rules. I wanted to be just like him."

"Hmm. Is that so?" Miss Gardner assessed her with a veiled smile. "But, remember, it's also a story about running away."

"Oh, yes." Cabby nodded vigorously. "And I bet Howie loved it."

"He did." Miss Gardner reached for a notebook. "Are you looking for anything specific here?"

Cabby shook her head. "Just anything that might tell us what's been on Howie's mind."

They worked in silence for a while, Cabby sorting loose papers and Miss Gardner turning pages.

The teacher broke the silence abruptly. "Maybe this is something." She turned the notebook toward Cabby. "These are simple arithmetic problems. Howard started Algebra this year—why would he be doing these exercises?"

Cabby studied the page. A short column of additions and subtractions ended with the following problem, boldly circled.

$$1941$$
$$-18$$
$$1923$$

"Eighteen!" she said. "That's how old he'd have to be to join the armed services!"

"Surely he's not thinking about that." Miss Gardner put a worried hand to her cheek.

"He's already tried once, but the recruiting officer sent him straight home. What if he decided to try that stunt farther afield?" Cabby eyed the maps she'd removed from Howie's desk. She picked up the one that showed the most wear. "Does he study geography?"

"No, not until tenth grade."

Awkwardly, Cabby unfolded the map. Howie had drawn a heavy ink line next to a row of what looked like chicken tracks. They petered out somewhere around Huntington, West Virginia. She turned the tattered sheet over and checked the legend. Railroads.

She studied the map. Ran a forefinger over the train line. Damn! Had that crazy kid taken to the rails? And why West Virginia, of all places? With lightning clarity a memory surfaced. A couple of days ago at breakfast. Marion's words taunting Louise. A newspaper article.

Cabby checked the map again. Yes, West Virginia bordered Kentucky. She grabbed the map and her bag. Scooted out of the desk. Sprinted for the door.

"Where are you going?" Miss Gardner cried.

"Home." Cabby yelled. "If I can get to the trash before the garbage truck comes, I'll know where Howie Schroeder's gone."

And I'll be able to set Lieutenant McKenna looking in the right direction.

Chapter Seventy

"Oh, no," Cabby groaned, as she turned into Helda's street. The dented garbage cans at the curb in front of the boarding house lay on their sides, empty, lids tossed haphazardly on the sidewalk, one leaning against the brownstone stoop. Her heart sank. It was the coldest day of winter so far, and she stood there in the darkening afternoon, shivering in her boots. She looked down the street in the direction she knew the truck would have gone. So much for Marion's discarded newspaper. So much for the article to which Howie had paid such avid attention at breakfast the day he disappeared. Now, if only Marion, or maybe Louise, could remember the name of the town in Kentucky that was reportedly enlisting underage boys.

Chapter Seventy-one

Dodging suicidal taxicabs and heedless redcaps with baggage-laden carts, McKenna loped painfully across the Pennsylvania Station carriageway and entered that sprawling temple of transportation through the grand archway of the main door. The place was jumping. Every resident of New York seemed to be on the move—determined, tense, cocky, confused—all scurrying along as if the newly declared war could only be won by sheer hustle. He elbowed his way through the crowd, determined to reach Concourse 62 before the 3:30 to Muncie left the station.

This visit to Penn Station was a last-ditch effort for McKenna. The medical examiner had released Arthur Shelton's remains, and the train to Indiana would carry his casket back home for burial. Every minute counted, now that the Cap had delivered his ultimatum. And McKenna wanted to see who, if anyone, would show up to say goodbye.

He made a practice of attending the funerals of homicide victims, alone, or with one of the boys. Yeah, it showed respect for the families, but there was another reason. Something about the enforced solemnity of the final rites made people easier to read; unexpected emotions could flash across the face of a mourner like blue-white lightning against a midnight sky. For Arthur Shelton, this send-off at Penn Station would be as close to a funeral as McKenna was gonna get.

A fat woman in a cotton-print dress planted herself in his path. "Where's the lockers?" she demanded in a transplanted hillbilly twang. A bulging suitcase, strapped around with a worn leather belt, weighed her down.

There was no getting around this insistent obstacle. Impatient, McKenna thumbed her toward a side corridor, and she stepped in that direction.

But a tall boy in a sailor's uniform stopped her immediately. "Can't go down there, Ma'am. They got the lockers all closed up. Some Kraut or Jap might plant a bomb."

"Bomb?" repeated a passing soldier sporting sergeant's chevrons on his dress khakis. Everyone in earshot paled and stopped dead in their tracks.

McKenna rolled his eyes, pulled out his badge and spoke in his most confident police baritone. "Nothing to worry about, folks. Move along. Move along." He hurried on, searching for a sign that would point him in the right direction. Glimpsing an arrow that pointed to Concourses 60-100, he headed in that direction.

An old woman's voice quavered, "…war planes…spotted over the city. I heard it on the radio."

"Old news, granny," said a gum-snapping boy, "and dead wrong."

McKenna limped on. It'd be squadrons of Messerschmitt 110s bombing Coney Island before the gossip mill was done.

Another arrow. Oh, great—Gate 62 was still the equivalent of a block-and-a-half's walk away. Better be worth the effort. He passed a huddled family saying goodbye, a small boy strutting around in his father's garrison cap.

When he finally reached the steps down to the trackside platform, McKenna started looking for familiar faces. Who would come to see Shelton off? For sure, his boyfriend, Lawrence Smoot, and maybe his assistant, Desmond Cox. Robert Oakley wouldn't be there—Dolan had reported Oakley was in the hospital, in an oxygen tent. And his wife, she was locked up tight on Ellis Island. But, Lillian Bridges, that professor, she was part of the Shelton/Oakley circle of friends. If Bridges didn't show up track side, he might just look her up.

Women have big ears, he thought, they always know the dirt.

Something had better pan out soon. Unless some Veronica-Lake-type blonde threw herself at his feet and confessed to hiring Herman Rupp to picket the gallery, he was just about at rope's end.

It was early yet; the rush that accompanied every departing train wouldn't kick in for another ten minutes. So he slowed down, sauntering along the platform, past passenger cars and Pullman sleepers painted in the Pennsylvania Railroad's signature brick red. Next came the diner, with its tables set in white linen, then more passenger cars. Looking in windows, he caught brief vignettes: a gentleman in a gray fedora sat leaning forward, his chin propped on his hands, his hands propped on a mahogany cane, apparently lost in thought. A white-haired woman stowed a straw picnic basket in a rack above the seat, while three little girls in satin hair bows squabbled over who got to sit next to the window.

McKenna saw no one of interest in the case until he'd almost reached the locomotive. Among the redcaps lining up with cartloads destined for the baggage car stood a pair of men in solemn black overcoats and homburgs. They hovered over a velvet-draped rectangle atop a wheeled gurney. McKenna flashed his badge. "This Arthur Shelton?"

The taller one inclined his head. "It is, officer." The words seemed to rumble from subterranean depths as he introduced his firm—Munsch Brothers and Sons Funeral Home, established 1906.

"Anybody else come to wave bye-bye?" McKenna made way for a redcap with a load of pigskin suitcases.

"Not so far, but...perhaps..." the undertaker trailed off and gestured to a young man trotting along the platform, top coat flapping out behind him.

Desmond Cox came to an abrupt halt, nodding to McKenna without any visible surprise at his presence. "Looks like I've come to the right place," he said.

McKenna stepped aside to let the gallery assistant have a moment with his late boss. It wasn't a long one. Cox passed a few words with the men from Munsch, then laid a hand on the casket. He stood silent and composed for the time it would have taken McKenna to run through an Our Father and a Hail Mary. Cool, calm and collected. McKenna gave a mental shrug.

With a final nod, Cox turned and stepped back, toward the detective. "Life's funny. Isn't it, Lieutenant?"

"I don't see anybody laughing."

"You know what I mean. Last Friday—just a week ago—I left Arthur at the gallery hale and hearty. He was riding high. He'd gotten rid of the protestors, sold several of Masako's canvases, and had deals in the works for a few more." Cox swept his over-long hair off his collar. "We weren't at war yet, and the gallery was going strong—even though he'd decided to take the show down, it looked like we might finish the year in the black for once." He gave a short, ironic laugh. "Now Arthur's going back to his folks in a box, and the few pieces he actually owned will be sold to cover his debts."

McKenna nodded. The war had turned things upside down for him, too. But, at least, unlike Shelton, he had a future. Maybe. He asked, "Will there be enough left to cover Lawrence Smoot's investment in the gallery?"

"I doubt it—but that's all up to the lawyers, now. They'll jump on Arthur's inventory as soon as they're allowed."

They fell silent as the conductor strode along the platform announcing, "All aboard" in a foghorn voice. The remaining passengers scrambled to board.

Then McKenna asked, "Have you finished organizing things at the gallery?"

"Just about. There's one thing I do need to mention. I finally reached that San Francisco collector. You know—the one who purchased the brush pot? As you predicted, it never arrived. She's fit to be tied. Do you think there's any chance it'll turn up?"

Like hell, McKenna thought, it's probably at the bottom of the East River by now. He shook his head. "Would she want it—if it did?"

That brought a snort of laughter from Desmond Cox, quickly stifled. He thought a second, hand over his mouth, then replied, "Mrs. Cuthbert-Symes is one of the most avid collectors I've dealt with—she probably would."

"Well, tell her not to hold her breath."

Along the train, vestibule doors slammed shut. McKenna twisted around. A burst of activity on the part of Munsch Brothers and Sons signaled Arthur Shelton's last ride. The undertakers wheeled the casket up to the baggage car door and peeled off the velvet covering to reveal a mahogany box outfitted with polished brass handles. A porter, skin as dark as the casket, jumped out of the train to help with the transfer.

"What are you going to do—now that you're out of a job?" McKenna asked Cox.

The gallery assistant kept his eyes on the casket that spanned the divide between gurney and baggage car. His answer was barely audible, "I thought my future held a partnership with Arthur. Running a gallery like his was truly all I ever wanted." A tragic mask deformed his face for an instant, but he quickly transformed it into a wry grin. "Fuck it all! Maybe I'll just toddle down to the recruiting station before my number's called."

A deep voice boomed out from up the platform, "No, no. Please. Wait." They both turned.

Lawrence Smoot, red-faced, arms swinging, barreled toward them. He must have run out of breath at that very moment, because his mouth opened again but nothing came out. Following in his wake was a more dignified figure—Lillian Bridges, tall, slender, trousered. Holding a clutch bag close to her body, she moved in the long, graceful strides of a golfer or tennis player. She, at least, wasn't huffing and puffing.

McKenna took close note as the pair passed him. Miss Bridges was as cool and graceful as he recalled from meeting her at Smoot's office. If he wasn't mistaken, the lady had attended the opening party for the gallery show. He checked with Cox.

"Yes, Lillian was there."

"With a husband?" McKenna asked out of the corner of his mouth.

"Lillian?" Cox's eyebrows registered mock horror. "The only thing she's married to is her career. She came to the reception with Lawrence—he squires her everywhere."

"I see." McKenna nodded. Bridges was obviously one of those women who didn't mind providing cover for homosexuals. A thought uncurled at the base of his brain, like a tiny budding leaf. Did Bridges hope for more than friendship with Lawrence Smoot? A lot of these gals actually believed they could change a tiger's stripes.

Just now she stood aside as Smoot threw himself on one end of the casket with a wild wail.

"Please, sir," a Munsch intoned. "The train will be leaving in a moment." The porter tried, and failed, to suppress a sneer of disgust.

Cox recoiled, too. "Good god. I can't stand this." The younger man cursed under his breath and scuffed the soles of his shiny Oxfords on the cement platform. "I've got to get out of here."

"Yeah, you do that," McKenna said, now more interested in the coffin drama.

Lillian Bridges had stepped forward and was patting her friend's shoulder. She whispered something behind her flat purse, as if to shield her words from enquiring eyes and ears.

Smoot was undeterred. His fingers curled on the casket as if they wanted to penetrate the wood, and tears flowed in sloppy, hiccoughing sobs.

Cox retreated so rapidly he was almost flying along the platform.

McKenna lit a cigarette, his brain giving leaf to a new idea or two.

Chapter Seventy-two

Abe Pritzker opened the door of the Italian restaurant, a "little joint" he knew in Williamsburg, and Louise was instantly enveloped in the aroma of garlic, onions, and tomatoes. "Oh, my," she gasped. "That's the best thing I've smelled since Kentucky pit barbecue!"

"Oh, yes?" He smiled, crinkly-eyed, down at her. "Then I'm honored to bring you to my favorite hangout. Welcome to Mario's."

"Hey, Abie—*Goombah*!" A tuxedoed maitre d' rushed up, threw his arms around the lawyer and pounded him on the back. "Long time, no see!"

"Hey, Mario—*paisano*!" Abe, grinning like a fool, thumped him right back.

"C'mon in—c'mon. For you, Pritzker, and your pretty lady"—he bowed to Louise with an interested sparkle in his brown eyes— "the best table in the house! Roberto," he called, "show my good friend here to table twenty."

After the aborted attempt that morning to secure Masako's paintings, Louise had taken the IRT uptown intending to spend the rest of the day at Professor Oakley's bedside. Of course she'd expected to find him still in the oxygen tent but, even so, she was shocked at how weak and passive he'd become.

Through the tent's slick, transparent walls, Oakley's gray complexion, jutting cheekbones and suddenly wispy beard seemed not quite of this world. Louise heartened for a moment as he raised one finger and sent her a nod. She slid her hand under the tent to pat his shoulder, but his attention faltered and his eyes closed.

She'd been sitting with him for about three hours as he drifted in and out of sleep when Professor Lillian Bridges walked into the room. She nodded a greeting to Louise, but had little to say to her. Instead, Professor Bridges aimed an innocuous, one-sided conversation at Oakley. Feeling like a very uncomfortable fifth wheel, Louise had finally headed back to Brooklyn. At least that gave her plenty of time to get ready for dinner with Abe.

Now, as Louise followed the waiter to a table directly beneath a huge gold chandelier, her stomach clenched painfully. She really had to quit skipping lunch. Despite her sudden hunger, she couldn't help noticing that Abe looked different. His hair had been cut, and combed with brilliantine; his blue suit pressed. For me? she wondered.

Now he waved the boy aside and pulled out Louise's chair. "Sit down. Relax. Everyone here knows me, and the food is fabulous. Mario will order for us."

Nodding, Louise looked around. Abe's "joint" was classy, but noisy, and the thick cigar smoke didn't do much for her queasy stomach. It struck her that the men at other tables were stocky and swarthy and, to her, sinister-looking; the women looked like… dames? For a moment she wondered if, for some incomprehensible reason, Abe had smuggled her into a gangsters' hangout.

"How do you know Mario?" Louise asked in a low voice, her brow furrowed.

Abe flashed a grin. "We were in school together—good pals. Mario went into the family business. I went on to college. We keep in touch." The beaming waiter returned with red wine in a glass. Abe swirled it, took a sip. "Terrific, kid. Pour some for the lady."

He turned back to her. "How's Oakley doing?"

"Not good. Not good at all. I wouldn't be surprised if Masako's plight didn't kill that man—he seems almost to have lost the will to live." She looked up at Abe. "Is there any way you might be able to get permission for Masako to visit the hospital—on compassionate grounds?" She smoothed the napkin on her lap. It was one thing to have an old friend like Lillian Bridges by his sick bed, but nothing would give the professor a boost like seeing his wife.

"I'll look into it," he said, dubiously. "If I could find a precedent…" He trailed off as the waiter delivered a dish he called Clams Oreganato, and they tucked in.

The food was delicious and it kept coming. Spaghetti, eggplant rollatini, pork chops in a sauce with potatoes and green peppers. At the end of the meal, when they were presented with cannoli, Louise moaned, "Enough! Enough!" Then Luigi came over from the bar with a bottle of grappa, and Abe insisted, so she tried it. Liquid fire. She liked it.

They sipped in silence. It was as if a bubble—a bubble of quietude—had expanded around them amidst the strident conversation of the room. "Louise," Abe said, somewhat abruptly. "Something I've been wondering about. What brings a girl like you to New York City all on her own?" His gaze felt as tactile to Louise as skin on skin. Those deep brown eyes…

Maybe it was his eyes, or maybe it was the grappa. She couldn't help it—she told him.

"That. Son. Of. A. Bitch! He just left you high and dry?" He glowered.

"Well, he did offer to pay my train fare home." She clenched her jaw, lest the humiliation she'd felt that night swamp her again. "But I told him, 'No, thanks. I'll buy my own…goddamn… ticket.' But, after everything, you see, I just couldn't go back to Louisville." She knew a tear was forming and knuckled her right eye. "I'd expected to arrive home a married woman."

"Bastard!" Abe erupted again. Louise thought the lawyer was about to twist the silver coffee spoon into a handcuff.

She waved away his indignation. "It's okay. Really." She picked up the delicate cordial glass and took another sip. "It's funny. I would never have left Louisville without him, but now that I'm here…" Her head was spinning.

"You like it?"

"Very much. It surprises me to say that. Life is so much more…" She didn't seem to be able to find appropriate words.

"More what? Expensive? Noisy? Rude?"

She laughed. "All three. But also more…interesting. For instance, at home I would never have gotten to know anyone like you."

Now it was his turn to laugh. "They don't have Jews in Louisville?"

"No. No." She wafted her hands in front of her, palms down. "I don't mean that."

"What do you mean?" He was studying her intently.

"I mean someone so very…so extremely— Oh, god, I'd better shut my mouth. I think maybe I'm…drunk?"

Abe laughed again. He was looking at her as if it was all he ever wanted to do in his life. "You're not sure?"

"How would I know?" She shrugged. "I've never been drunk."

"Ha!" He clapped his hands once, leaned forward. "Oh, Louise, you are absolutely delightful." He reached across the table, squeezed her hand lightly, let it go. Then he sighed heavily. "I'm not a masher, you know, despite my behavior that night at the Battery. But you, I'm sorry, you've gotten to me."

"Abe!" She couldn't breathe.

He sat back. "I knew, of course, the moment I met you that you were a beauty, but I'm just now coming to realize what a sweet, brave, extraordinary woman you are."

She pulled back in her chair, stunned even through the liquor haze.

He cleared his throat. "But, listen," he continued, "before I say any more about *that*, there's something else I've got to tell you. This afternoon, on the ferry back from the detention center, I was thinking—"

"Wait a minute!" She jolted up straight in her chair, suddenly sober. Well, soberish. "You went to Ellis Island this afternoon? You went to see Mrs. Oakley without me?"

He tilted his head. "Well, yes, of course I did. She's my client. Remember? And I've wangled an early hearing date for her. Monday, the twenty-second."

"Why didn't you tell me?"

"I am telling you. Right now." He was back in brisk lawyer mode. "And that date really puts the pressure on. The goddamn Feds won't allow her to have an attorney present, so I had to try to get some crucial information from her so I could advise her on how to present herself. And you're so protective—I knew you'd only get in the way."

"In the way! Abe, Masako Oakley is my friend. She's in a perilous emotional and psychological state, and you go in there without me, blustering—"

"Blustering!" He scowled, and ran his fingers through his hair, leaving it tousled once again. "It's not like I gave her the third degree."

She regarded him intently. "You didn't tell her the studio paintings were gone, did you?"

"Of course not. She didn't even ask about them."

Whew! "Would she talk to you at all?"

"Not a word." Abe dropped his gaze to the red-and-white check tablecloth. "She was like a wilted flower."

"See, you should have taken me. I might could've perked her up."

Abe snorted with laughter at her Southern wording. Then, "Louise Hunter, Dixie Belle."

Stung, she shot back, "I told you I'm little tipsy—don't you dare mock me!"

"Louise!" Abe, straight-faced now, his brown eyes soft, "I wasn't...oh, well...maybe I was. But I'm so sorry. The way you talk sometimes—it's just so damned...cute."

"Cute! Is that what you think of me? I'm cute? My efforts to help Masako are cute?" Louise raised her hand to summon the waiter. "My coat please, Roberto. I'm leaving. And please call me a cab."

Abe rose and threw a twenty-dollar bill on the table. "Nix the cab, Roberto. I'll take the lady home."

The lady glared across the table at him. "No, Roberto," she said. Her tone left no room for argument. "Call me that taxi. I'll take myself home."

Chapter Seventy-three

Louise's footsteps echoed off the concrete surface of the shadowy Prospect Park subway platform. She should have taken that cab—she really should have. But Abe had slid in after her, and, seething with anger, she'd jumped out the other side, hurrying down the sidewalk toward the subway station she glimpsed in the distance. Her only goal was to put as much distance between herself and Abe Pritzker as possible.

Now, having spent far too long on the screeching, jolting El train, including an interminable wait to transfer from the Myrtle to the Brighton Beach line, her rage was spent. Already second-guessing her rash words, Louise paused at the foot of the double flight of stairs that led up to Flatbush Avenue. The lights had burned out. Or been broken more likely. Their rusty sheaths tilted at a sharp angle, and telltale glass slivers gathered in the corners of each step. Kids. Louise shook her head at the dark tunnel.

She looked right, then left. A man with a hatchet profile and a black overcoat seemed to study a faded poster hawking Folger's coffee. She'd noticed him earlier, sitting on the opposite end of the nearly empty car. He'd given her the creeps. Everytime she looked away, the back of her neck prickled as if he was staring daggers, but when she glanced back, his eyes were glued to a folded newspaper. At her stop, he'd jumped off behind her and strolled straight over to the poster. Right—coffee—never seen that before.

A scattering of other people had also exited the train. Like all New Yorkers, they were in a hurry, already up that steep flight of stairs and away. Or were they? Hesitating, Louise felt the prickling sensation of being watched deepen and spread until icy scalpels of dread pricked at each vertebra. She shivered uncontrollably.

Get a grip, Nurse Hunter, she told herself sternly. Even if the man in black was a G-man, what was he going to do? He could watch all he wanted. "No skin off my nose," as Cabby would say. Louise took a couple of steps forward, sketching a brave, Cabbyesque swagger.

The man wasn't moving, wasn't paying her the least attention. But still Louise shivered. Then she thought: Could somebody else be watching me? Someone who wants me to back away from helping Masako Oakley? Someone who doesn't mind clonking art dealers, and, presumably, nurses, on the head? One deliberate foot in front of the other, Louise started up the stairs. Her gloved hand slid along the filthy banister, only bouncing once on a wad of dried chewing gum. Inhale, step. Exhale, step. Repeat. Just keep heading for that rectangle of light at the top.

Good. The landing. Three steps across, maybe four.

She took a bracing breath. The landing's rubber mat softened her footsteps, but still Louise heard hollow clumps echo off the close walls. Someone else was on the staircase. The icy scalpels dissected along the nerves of her arms and legs, paralyzing her.

Suddenly, a tall, bareheaded man in a gray trench coat appeared in the light at the top of the stairs. He barreled down toward her as if his train had already stopped at the platform and he thought he just might catch it. As he passed, Louise caught a glimpse of his pale face, oddly familiar.

He ran on, and the moment of terror was broken. But who else was on the stairs? Looking down Louise saw an anonymous trousered, coated, hatted figure turn and disappear toward the platform. Not the man in the trench coat. Or the man in black. It had been someone thinner, lighter, in a camel-hair coat. Oh, well—gone now!

Louise bounded up the second set of stairs, took a deep breath as the Flatbush Avenue traffic rumbled by. For no logical reason, she felt as if the man in the trench coat had rescued her from a terrible fate.

Chapter Seventy-four

Cabby's hands were deep in hot, greasy dishwater, and her brain was in a similar stew. At the dinner table, she'd quizzed the few women present about the Kentucky town that Marion had taunted Louise with—the one where the Army enlisted underage boys. They remembered the *Post* article, but not the crucial name of the particular Hickville she'd been reading about. Cabby had been sure that Marion would remember, but Marion had gone out to dinner with one of her gentleman friends—probably to avoid another of Helda's distracted meals. Jane and Irene, the quiet older women who shared the spacious front room, had also been absent from the dinner table. Even Alicia, present, but studying from a propped-up law book, had failed her. And nobody but Cabby herself seemed to have taken note of Howie's interest in the recruiting discussion.

That's when Cabby had really started kicking herself. Why hadn't she gone straight downtown from Howie's school? The *Post* had a morgue, and she had press credentials; she could have looked up the name of the town and sent word to McKenna right away. She could always run over to the Post building on Vesey Street in the morning, but terrible things might be happening to that silly, impulsive kid right this very minute. With her uninjured hand, she slapped the dishrag into a crusty pot, spattering the front of her dress in the process.

Before dinner, Louise had amazed her by not recalling the discussion at all. While her roommate changed into a nice dark-blue silk dress, Cabby pumped her for information. "You remember, don't you? Marion was teasing you about Kentucky's child brides."

Louise had merely looked blank and shaken her head.

Cabby was beginning to worry about her roommate. Louise was so tied up with her patient and his Japanese wife she didn't seem to be living in the same universe with the rest of the boarders. She'd been getting in late and missing meals; her eyes showed dark circles and her cheeks were hollow. Then, when Louise took up an atomizer and sprayed perfume behind each ear, it finally dawned on Cabby: she must have a date.

"Where are you going?" she burst out.

"I'm having dinner with someone," was Louise's response, as she shoved her arms into the sleeves of her flimsy southern coat.

Cabby was ablaze with curiosity. A new boyfriend? "With who—er, whom?"

But a car horn sounded dimly from the front of the house, and Louise was out the bedroom door without responding. Cabby clattered down the stairs behind her, but by the time she got to the parlor window all she could see was receding tail lights.

Now, at the sink, Cabby turned on the faucet to replenish the hot water; the warmth actually made her sprained wrist feel better. Grabbing a pot scraper she attacked the dirty pan. A pale, silent Helda had managed to cook a supper of chicken and dumplings that hadn't turned out too bad. Mousie had helped her, so Cabby felt it was only right to volunteer for cleanup detail. She'd ordered Helda to take a rest in her room, meaning, "Go cry your eyes out, but not in the same room with me."

By the time Marion waltzed into the kitchen in her full-length leopard-skin coat, Cabby had vanquished the heavy aluminum pot and Mousie had come in to help dry. "Darlings, I've just seen the most delightful film with Rosalind Russell," the actress gushed, twirling so that her coat spun out around her silk-clad legs. "She was absolutely divine. And, Don Ameche—"

"Oh, Marion, thank god you're home!" Dropping her dish-towel, Cabby grabbed the actress by her leather-gloved hand and pulled her toward the kitchen table. "I have to talk to you."

"Watch it, Cabby. These are kid gloves!" She pulled her hand free and began removing them.

"Forget the damn gloves. I've been trying to track down Howie. You know he's missing, right? I think he hopped a train somewhere, and I'll bet you know exactly where he's headed."

Marion's perfect brow furrowed. "Why would I know any-thing about that little squirt?"

Cabby realized she wasn't making much sense. "Okay, wait a minute. Let me explain. Remember that copy of the *Post* you brought to the table the other morning…" She pushed away the half-empty plate of sugar cookies that had constituted dessert.

As Cabby reminded Marion about the article, Mousie sat down with them, quietly wiping her damp hands on a dishtowel. She wore a cotton print dress with a round white collar edged with home-made tatting.

"And," the reporter continued, "I need to know the name of that town with the lax recruiting practices. Howie might have seen it as his one last chance to join up and fight the Germans. I asked Louise, but she doesn't even remember the conversation. She's so caught up in the drama of her patient's wife—"

"Drama?" Marion began to look interested. The whole time Cabby was talking, her housemate was toying with her gloves, laying them on the table, palm to palm, smoothing them out, folding them in half. Now she pulled a gold filigreed compact from her bag and checked her lipstick, as if the word "drama" had reminded her to look the part of an actress. Clicking the compact shut, she said, "It was some hillbilly town—they're all the same. I just wanted to get a rise out of Miss Scarlett, that's all." Turning to Mousie, she asked, "What about you, Ethel? You must have been there. You never miss breakfast."

Mousie's plain face was a study in concentration. She looked as if she were searching complex mental files for a scrap of information that had fallen between the cracks. "No. I do remember a conversation, but I was…" She trailed off.

Cabby thought she'd never known anyone quite so wet.

Jane Willis, still in the tailored suit she'd worn for her evening out, came through the butler's pantry with a bone china cup and saucer in her hand. "Tea time," she announced, taking the green enamel kettle from the stove to the sink and turning on the water. "Anybody else?"

The three women at the table shook their heads. "Could that town have been Plainsville?" Marion volunteered.

Mousie frowned. "I don't think so."

"Pittsville?"

"That's not quite right." Cabby sighed and reached for a cookie. She took one bite, and it showered crumbs all over her sweater. "Stale," she said, but she continued to nibble. "Helda hasn't baked in days."

"Pittsfield?"

"What are you trying to remember?" Jane asked, pulling out a chair.

"It's hopeless," Cabby said. "Some hick town in Kentucky we were talking about at breakfast the other morning, where recruiters—"

"Paintsville," Jane said. "Paintsville, Kentucky. You should have asked me—Mother always said I was blessed with the memory of an elephant."

Chapter Seventy-five

Howie Schroeder came to his senses all at once. Where was he? Face down on some hard, gravelly surface? Huh? Pitch black and cold. His head, two sizes too big.

As he pushed up and twisted into a sitting position, a wave of nausea washed over him. It was cold and darker than dark, and he had no idea where he was. The last thing he remembered, he'd flagged down a beat-up farm truck to ask if he was on the right road to Paintsville. Two men in faded overalls and broad-brimmed felt hats had offered him a lift to the next crossroads. They'd looked all right. They'd even said something about finding a sandwich for him, and, boy, was he hungry. But...

After that, it was all a blank.

He lifted a hand to his forehead. Oww! A trail of crusted blood led to a hard, swollen knot the size of a goose egg.

Shit, what a fool he'd been.

He'd done all right on the railroad—all the way to the Huntington rail yard—by never letting his guard down. Then he'd let exhaustion get the better of him, and look what he had to show for it. His jacket was missing. Rolling onto one hip, he made a frantic search of his back pants pocket. Of course, they'd taken his wallet, too.

Shaky, fighting dizziness, Howie struggled to his feet. If they'd left the pack with his blanket and extra clothing, it'd be around here somewhere. He gave his eyes a little more time to adjust. Peered around in the darkness. Still couldn't see his pack.

The only illumination came from a dim quarter moon riding high in the sky. No lights twinkled through the trees on the steep hill behind him or across the two-lane road where the land seemed to slip away to a creek or small stream. If he strained his ears, he could barely make out the sound of rushing water. Up and down the unfamiliar road, no headlights broke the velvety darkness.

Howie had never been in such a desolate place in his entire life. Never even imagined what it would be like. No cars. No street lights. Not even yellow lamplight streaming through windows. There were no windows. Not a house to be seen. He'd never imagined night could be so empty.

His breath caught in his throat and he took a sudden gulping sob. He could picture Ma in the parlor at home, surrounded by the boarders. They'd all be warm and comfortable, full from a good dinner. Miss Ward would be there, and that new Miss Ethel Furnish, who'd been so nice to him. They'd probably be wondering where he was and when he'd be coming back. Howie ran a hand through his hair, caught a finger on the goose egg, and winced. That's where he belonged—home in Brooklyn—not out here in the sticks.

It had been a mistake, he realized, a big mistake to come to Kentucky. He'd wanted to make things right—to prove that, even though Papa had become a Nazi, he, Howard Gerhard Schroeder, was a loyal American. But he was just a kid! A kid who'd bitten off more than he could chew. And, even if he did manage to fool some boondocks recruiter, how did he expect to fight Germans when he'd let two simple hillbillies take nearly everything he had? Even his map.

But they hadn't taken every last thing. Howie hitched up his jeans. He still had his feet and shoe leather to cover them.

The moon gave enough light to distinguish the blackness of the asphalt from the blackness of the brushy wood. Howie took a step, then another. He was heading home. To New York.

If he could only figure out which way was north.

Chapter Seventy-six

Saturday, December 13, mid-morning

"Not that coat, for god's sake." The voice came from the arched doorway of the mirrored alcove in Macy's Better Coats. "It makes me think of rubber galoshes."

Louise spun around, and the maroon wool chesterfield with matching velvet collar flared modestly at the hem. Abe! How had he tracked her down? Louise pushed a blond strand off her cheek. She didn't know whether to feel angry or flattered. After a glance at the carefully composed salesgirl in the crisp white blouse, she turned to the lawyer. Swallowing hard, she said, "Where did you pop up from?"

Abe came closer, his hair and overcoat shoulders damp with the cold rain now blasting the city. "I called the boarding house. Your roommate—Cappy, is it?—told me you were shopping for a coat at Macy's." He leaned on the curved handle of his large black umbrella, while water spread in a widening puddle at its tip. In the overheated store, the outspoken lawyer exuded a refreshing coolness.

Louise smiled in spite of herself. "Cabby. Her name is Cabby. And she ought to learn to keep her mouth shut." Louise hoped she sounded more severe than she felt. Actually, she wished she felt more severe than she did.

She'd lain awake until the early hours. Abe Pritzker's high-handedness in visiting Mrs. Oakley on his own seemed like small potatoes compared with her fright at the subway stop.

Somewhere around two, she'd realized it was Abe's heartfelt declaration that had bothered her much more than his solo Ellis Island stunt. His words had hit her like a bolt from the blue. Abe was so different from anyone she'd ever known. Could she possibly be falling in love with this intense, overwhelming man? Could she trust him? Could she trust herself? No! It was too soon after the debacle with Pres. And she was not the type of girl who could take on a man as a diversion. For her, it had to be the real thing. Could Abe be the real thing? She understood now that she'd stormed out of Mario's last night for one reason and one reason only—pure and utter stupefied confusion.

Oh, what was wrong with her? She needed to sort her emotions out. And she would. Just as soon as Masako Oakley was no longer under suspicion of homicide. As soon as the hearing board had released her to be back with her husband.

"I think you're being a little hard on your friend." Abe grinned, bringing her back to the present. "I'm good with ladies clothes. I can help you choose." He turned to the clerk. "Bring Miss Hunter that blue wool you have hanging on the rack over there, the one that's fitted at the waist."

"Abe—I don't know—" But the salesgirl was already unbuttoning the chesterfield and helping her into the blue coat with its black triangular Bakelite buttons. It fit perfectly and was deliciously warm. It even smelled wonderful, fresh and new. Louise made a proud promenade around the alcove.

Abe stood back, finger to his lips, assessing her. "Yeah, that's it. Striking. Look at yourself, Louise. Look what that coat does for you."

Louise turned slowly in the three-way mirror. Oh, my! That was becoming. But how improper of this man to think he could choose her clothing! She should be outraged at his audacity! Her mother would have a hissy fit if she knew. Louise's thoughts were confused, all over the place. But one thing was certain; she had to have this coat. "How much is it?" she asked the salesgirl.

"Thirty-seven-ninety-five."

When Louise cringed, the woman hastened to reassure her. "But it's of the highest quality for a ready-made, you can be sure. And while very few girls can wear that Lapis blue, it is certainly stunning on you."

Louise took a sharp breath. The coat would cost a full week's pay. But, then, she'd squirreled away some money her grandmother had left her. "I'll take it," she heard herself say, her eyes on the sophisticated young woman in the mirror. Every bit as stylish as someone like Lillian Bridges, she thought. Hmm. Maybe a pair of black gloves gathered at the seams and a black hat with a bit of a swoop to it...

"It's simply charming," the clerk rattled on, "classic, yet chic and elegant. And you wear it so well."

Abe's eyes were gleaming. "And, since you're not going back to Kentucky, you really need it."

She frowned. "Who says I'm not going back home?"

He wrinkled his brow, puzzled. "You did."

"Oh. I guess I did." She shrugged, and slipped out of the coat. Maybe she had made up her mind to stay, but she shouldn't have admitted it to him.

"Er, Louise," Abe said, flicking his gaze briefly toward the salesgirl, who was holding the blue coat. He seemed suddenly a tad uncomfortable. "Louise, I know how very little nurses are paid." Abe swallowed, and his Adam's apple went up and down as he pulled out a battered leather billfold. "Let me buy this for you."

"What!" She made three syllables of it, her voice rising on each. What did this insufferable man think she was? Some kind of floozy? "No, sir! I can buy my own coat, thank you very much!"

"Sorry." Abe backed away, hands up, palms out. "Sorry. No offense intended. I just thought—"

"Whatever you thought—"

The sales clerk cleared her throat and carried the coat out of the alcove, in the direction of the cash register.

"…you can just unthink it. I take care of myself!" She hoped the heat rising to her face wouldn't make her cheeks blotchy.

He regarded her soberly. "Forgive me, Louise. In the short time I've known you, I've never had any doubts about that. None at all." Then he flashed his big white grin and held out her old coat. "But, after you arrange to have your purchase delivered, will you at least let me buy you a cup of coffee so I can tell you why I'm here?"

◇◇◇

"So, two things," Abe said in Macy's tea room, as he lifted his cup of the steaming black brew to his lips. "First, I called you because I need your help again. I set my students to reviewing immigration cases, and they managed to find a few precedents for internees being allowed to visit critically ill relatives. Agent Bagwell wasn't as opposed as I'd thought he'd be, but he has to kick it upstairs for the final decision."

Louise nodded, still leery. Offering to pay for her coat! Really!

Any decent girl would've ordered him out of the dressing room right then and there, but here she was having coffee with him. Louise took a warm sip. Well, what else could she do? The Oakleys still needed his help.

Abe continued, "And, second, about last night…"

Louise thought his brown eyes had never been so warm.

"I had too much of Mario's good wine."

She nodded. So had she. But she kept her expression neutral.

His lips twisted. "And so did you, of course." He cleared his throat. "Nonetheless, I should have been more responsible and kept my feelings to myself. The last thing I want to do is scare you away."

"Uh," she said.

"So," he said, "I'll back off. You can rest assured that you will hear no more avowals from me—at least until…I've taken care of a few things." He nodded, as if he had satisfied himself of something.

"Oh." She received this enigmatic commitment with confused emotions.

"Okay?" The lip twist became a crooked smile. "Now back to Mrs. Oakley. What I need is the official lowdown on her husband's current condition. Then I'll know how hard I can lean on Bagwell. Can you get an update for me?"

She pushed her half-finished cup away. "I'm headed to the hospital, now."

"I really need to know immediately."

"Then I'll call Dr. Wright's office as soon as we find a phone."

He drained his cup and set it back on the paper doily that cushioned the saucer. Applying palms to the tabletop, he pushed to his feet. "Let's get moving, then."

As they stepped off the down escalator on the second floor, Louise saw a sign that read Foundations. On a sudden impulse she turned and headed in that direction. Macy's Foundation Garments—that's where Mousie worked. She wanted to see her frumpy housemate in the setting of this classy store.

Abe was right behind her. "I think the phones are this way, Louise."

"This will just take a second. One of my housemates works here. I want to say 'Hi.'"

He gave an exasperated sigh, but they'd already reached the displays of bras and girdles. Louise quickly glanced around, but didn't see Mousie. She approached a bored-looking clerk with a tape measure draped around her neck.

"May I help you, Madam? We've just received a shipment of silk panties, and it's hard to tell when there'll be another."

Panties! Louise looked anywhere but at Abe. What had she been she thinking, bringing him to the foundations department?

"N…no, thank you," she stammered. "I just wanted to say hello to Mou—to Ethel."

"Ethel? Do you mean Edith?" The blond smelled delicately of Shalimar.

"No. Ethel. Ethel Furnish." Louise thought back to breakfast. She was sure Mousie had said she was working today.

The woman frowned. She beckoned a passing floor manager and relayed Louise's question.

Touching the red carnation in his lapel, the man aimed a tight smile at Louise. "No one of that name works on this floor. Hmm. I think maybe we have an Ethel upstairs in Ready-to-Wear. Could that be she?"

"But—" Louise was confused. "But—she…"

Abe was restive. "Louise, I need you to make that call."

"Of course." Louise let Abe guide her away. Perhaps she did have the wrong department. She'd ask Mousie about it the next time she saw her. The important thing now was to get in touch with Dr. Wright. From a bank of pay phones by the restrooms, Louise dialed his office.

"Oh, Nurse Hunter," his secretary said, "I'm so glad you called. The doctor wants you at the hospital right away. Professor Oakley has entered the critical stage. I'm afraid the prognosis is grim."

Chapter Seventy-seven

Louise knew lurking death when she saw it. She'd been a fledgling nurse, graduation pin shiny-bright and starched cap sitting proudly, when the '37 flood devastated Louisville. That year, after an uncommonly rainy January, the Ohio River overflowed its banks to submerge nearly three quarters of the city. Louise's hospital, on high ground to the east, received boatloads of refugees, all suffering from exposure or pneumonia or scarlet fever or typhoid, or any combination of these. She worked around the clock. Throughout those dark days, death had become a familiar adversary, extinguishing the life spark in the weak, the young and the elderly.

Now, with Dr. Wright and three others—Abe, who had accompanied her uptown, and her patient's close friends, Lillian Bridges and Lawrence Smoot—Louise faced her old enemy again. Within the oxygen tent, Robert Oakley struggled for breath. With each inhalation, his nostrils flared, his neck cords bulged and deep hollows formed over the clavicle bones. His folded hands and closed eyelids never even fluttered; his body was conserving energy to fight the infection. As Dr. Wright moved his stethoscope over the professor's chest, Louise made fists of her hands inside her coat pockets. The professor's tortured breathing and the low hiss of the oxygen tank were the only sounds in the dim hospital room.

Dr. Wright straightened, pinched the bridge of his nose for a long second, then removed the silvery arms of the stethoscope from his ears. "Mr. Pritzker?" he asked.

Louise couldn't recall ever seeing such a solemn expression on the doctor's pleasant face.

"Doc." Abe pushed away from the wardrobe where he'd leaned his rangy frame.

"You mentioned the possibility of getting Masako over here." Dr. Wright came closer, lowered his voice so everyone had to shuffle over to hear him. "Now's the time."

Abe sucked in a deep breath. "Okay. I've got precedents for justifying an emergency pass, and I've filed a formal request. High priority. With a dying patient, it just might work."

Dying. Louise rolled her shoulders, straining at the tight collar of her blouse. Yes, she had been thinking the word, but she didn't want to hear it spoken. Especially by Abe. From his lips, it sounded like a done deal.

The attorney gave his cynical laugh. "Think how it would look in the papers if the FBI allowed a prominent man like Oakley to die without his wife by his side."

Lillian Bridges eyed the lawyer suspiciously. "How can there be precedents? It was only days ago that the FBI started rounding up enemy aliens." Her colleague, Lawrence Smoot, nodded in vacuous agreement. Louise thought his wrinkled suit and red-rimmed, baggy eyes made him look like John Barrymore playing the washed up, drunken actor in *Dinner at Eight*.

Abe crossed his arms. "Ellis Island is more than a gateway for immigrants. Ever since it opened it's been used for incarceration, too. Most of the precedents come from German merchant mariners held in the last war and—"

Dr. Wright cut him off with an irritated harrumph. "When I say now, I mean right now. The next two or three hours will tell the tale. Either the fever will break and the pleural exudate will resolve or…" His words hung in the air ominously. "And, who knows, Masako's presence might even help Bob rally his strength. I've known stranger things to happen."

"Abe," Louise croaked, throat tight.

"Calm down, sweetheart." Abe laid a hand on Louise's shoulder.

"Isn't there some way you can speed it up, cut through the FBI's red tape?"

The lawyer gave an exasperated sigh. "I could try to get the division chief on the line myself. Would you talk to him, Doc? Explain the urgency of the situation?"

"Of course."

"Good." Abe's hawk-like gaze lit on the professors. "Either of you got any strings to pull?"

Lawrence Smoot stood a bit straighter. His jaw line firmed. "I could call Dr. Butler. He carries a lot of clout."

Abe made a face. "Nicholas Murray Butler?" he spat out. "Columbia's president? The bastard who hung out the Jewish Students Need Not Apply sign?"

Louise put a hand on his arm. She didn't know this Butler from Dagwood Bumstead, but if he could help get Masako to her husband's bedside…"Abe, I don't care if he's a fully fledged, goose-stepping Nazi, you've got to let Professor Smoot try."

Dr. Wright cocked his head. "Sounds like a damn good idea to me."

"You're right." Abe slapped a hand to the back of his neck. "This is no time to stand on principle. Come on. Let's find a phone. First President Butler, then the FBI."

"We can use the phone in the doctor's lounge." With a glance toward the inert figure in the bed, Dr. Wright folded his stethoscope into his pocket. "On the floor just below this ward. Come with me." He hooked a hand under Abe's elbow and made for the door. The disheveled Smoot slouched out behind them.

For a moment, Louise thought Lillian Bridges would follow the men.

But no. Ignoring Louise, the professor commandeered the bedside chair and fixed an unwavering gaze on the sick man. With her hands clasped under her chin and light from the bedside lamp illuminating her head, she reminded Louise of a saint from some medieval icon.

Chapter Seventy-eight

Oops. Cabby bent to retrieve a garter belt that had fallen from her laundry basket. This windy, rainy Saturday afternoon called for chores like washing hair, tending manicures, and laundering unmentionables. She'd planned to see *The Men in Her Life* with Loretta Young, but, even with a good umbrella, walking to the pictures in a gale like this would leave a girl soaked to her skin.

As she started through the downstairs hall, the phone rang. Juggling her load in the crook of her arm, Cabby grabbed the receiver on the second ring. "Hello?"

A masculine voice, shot through with an odd mixture of elation and diffidence, stated a familiar name and asked if Mrs. Helda Schroeder was available to come to the phone.

"McKenna! It's me, Cabby." Her basket slid to the floor. Oblivious to the spill of dirty laundry, she gripped the receiver with both hands. "Have you found Howie?"

"I just got the call. The Kentucky Highway Patrol picked him up this morning."

Cabby took a deep breath of relief and nodded vigorously. "Then I was right. He was headed for Paintsville."

"Yeah. That's one plucky kid—almost made it all the way. He would've, too, if he hadn't tangled with some yokels."

"What?" Cabby practically spat questions into the mouthpiece. "Is Howie okay? What happened?"

"A couple of Li'l Abner's kinfolk knocked him around and took his wallet. He's got a headache, but don't worry, he'll be all right."

McKenna went on to explain the arrangements for Howie's return, but they were lost on Cabby. As she imagined telling Helda the good news, the detective's words became disjointed, as if he were talking at the bottom of a gurgling fountain. Cabby no longer saw the front hallway's shabby wallpaper and faded carpet. She felt like Judy Garland swept away into a Technicolor world, where Helda would smile ecstatically and the excited boarders crowd in like Munchkins to hug her, even the snooty Marion. In the coming months the war would doubtless bring tragedy to the boarding house, but today couldn't be better. Howie was coming home!

Cabby realized she wasn't paying attention. "What's that again? When does Howie arrive?"

"Open your ears, girlie." McKenna's words were clipped; he sounded more like himself. "Tonight. Grand Central. The Midnight Express."

"Great. I'll let Helda know right away."

"Uh…hang on a minute." McKenna was suddenly meek as a boy asking for a date to his first school dance. "I, er, I'd like to tell Mrs. Schroeder myself."

Cabby got it. She pressed her lips together to keep from giggling. "Okay, I'll get Helda right now. But first…I gotta tell ya…well, thanks, McKenna. This means the world to all of us."

He answered with a muffled cough, then: "Yeah, girlie. Anytime."

Chapter Seventy-nine

If only they'd allowed her to bring her palette knife from home, she would have been spared this latest baffling shame.

They had come to the women's side of the holding pen, two men in dark overcoats, told her to get her jacket and gloves; she was going for a ride.

"I am going home?" The first words she had spoken in two days.

"Fat chance, lady." The taller one wound a wool scarf around his neck and straightened his fedora. "Hurry. There isn't much time." A hand like a vise clamped her elbow.

She had been thinking about the palette knife, the asymmetrical one, the one with the pointed tip. Yes, she'd been thinking about it. She'd been dreaming about it.

The hand squeezed her arm. Off the ferry they loaded her like worthless garbage into the back of a black car. She sat there, flanked by the two tall men, small, and hot with pain and shame. She smelled her prison stench—only one shower allowed during her captivity and that without soap or rag. The men spoke with each other over her head in that brutal American way. As if she were not there, hot with shame. *Haji.*

Before they'd snatched her from the apartment, she had been painting in earth tones. The palette knife was sharp. It would do. If only they would bring it to her. An artist, she had studied anatomy. She knew the human body. She knew you didn't cut across, but up and down the veins.

They sped uptown. More questions, she knew. More accusations. More bare ugly rooms. More men in suits. More men
in uniforms. She would avoid, evade, elude, escape. She took
herself into retreat. At least she had that power now. She could
become invisible.

"We're here," they finally said. "Get out of the car." But she
was in the hiding room again, and the words bounced off her
ears. The strong hand on the arm.

They hustled her out of the car like a limp, cloth doll.
Through the cold, bitter rain, up the steps, into the elevator,
down a long green hall, into another room, a whitened room.
But she kept herself secure. She was not insane; she knew that.
She was simply—invisible. And she would stay invisible. Safe.
At least she had that right.

People spoke. She did not listen. Then, a familiar voice.
"Masako." Another hand on her arm. Gentle. She allowed her
eyes to see.

"Masako." The arm around her shoulder. "Masako, look at
me."

The doctor. Robert's friend. Franklin Wright.

The smell of medicine. The hiss of oxygen.

"Masako"...A weak, ill voice.

Robert? Robert! Robert is alive!

"Bob needs you." Franklin gestured toward the bed.

She felt the world flood in on her. Too bright. Too loud. It
hurt her head. The humming of fluorescent light. The sighing of
some big machine. The smell of antiseptic. The gleaming hood
a nurse had pulled back from Robert's face. A face slumbering
now, as still as a death mask.

"Oh, Robert, I'm here," she said, skimming forward and
half-falling across the sheets. Her husband was so thin, his skin
so pale, like a wilted plant, etiolated. And yet he was fighting to
move air into his lungs. She brought one of his white hands to
her lips, whispering. "My love, I thought I'd never see you again."

She recalled hearing from the Christian Bible a story about
the scales falling from a blind man's eyes. That was how it felt to

her. In an instant she had been jerked back into the real world. And Robert, her beloved—so ill, so very ill. But she was touching him, stroking his hands. His eyes were closed now, but they had seen her. He had called her name, and that one word had begun her life anew.

Franklin pulled the folded tent forward, then he positioned a chair for her at the bedside.

"What can I do?" Masako forced her gaze away from her dear one, searched the doctor's solemn expression. "What can I do?"

"Bob's fighting for his life. We've given him medicine, oxygen, but it's his struggle, now. All you can do is let him know you're here."

Her arm ached from the heavy grip of the men who had brought her. She whirled her head around. Yes, there they were, flanking the door like the hangman's minions.

The doctor caught her look. "Don't worry. You'll be allowed to stay as long…as long as you're needed."

"How?" she asked wonderingly. "Who has arranged this miracle?"

Nurse Louise spoke up from the other side of the bed. "Your lawyer, Abe Pritzker. Somehow he rammed it through the FBI."

"The scrawny one with the eagle's eyes who asks so many questions?"

"That's him." Louise nodded.

Masako bowed her head. "I may stay until I am no longer needed." She shuddered, as if someone had stroked her back with the tip of an icicle. Until I am no longer needed. She knew what that meant.

She raised her chin and stared at her husband through the glistening folds of the breathing tent. The days of dull apathy—of shame, yes, shame and apathy—were behind her now. The long muscles of her arms and legs contracted reflexively. Fingernails dug into her palms. She had become a tiger. Ready to fight. Fight for Robert. Fight for herself.

"Nurse Louise," she said, not taking her eyes off her husband. "This lawyer? Will you bring him? I must talk with him. Now."

Chapter Eighty

Pritzker's call had been a surprise, a real corker. "Lieutenant," he'd said, "Mrs. Oakley is now prepared to answer questions. Meet us in the doctor's lounge up here at Columbia-Pres, a.s.a.p."

That Jew lawyer was a smart one. McKenna didn't need to ask why he was extending the olive branch. The little Jap was caught in the crosshairs of some real big guns. If the fire from the homicide division could be silenced, Pritzker would have a better chance of neutralizing the Feds.

McKenna, with Brenner in tow, showed his credentials to a burly federal marshal and entered a lounge furnished with much-used leather club chairs and coffee-ringed wooden side tables. The cold rain battered tall windows draped in a dark-green woven fabric. The room seemed to have been commandeered by the lawyer for the exclusive purpose of this interview; other than Pritzker, Nurse Hunter, and Mrs. Oakley sitting in a corner, it was empty. The lawyer was tapping the ash from his pipe into a chrome ashtray stand.

McKenna couldn't help but gawk at Mrs. Oakley. The tiny woman who'd been so silent and lethargic at Ellis Island had suddenly come to life, her face animated, her dark eyes gleaming. She held the nurse's hand in a tight grip, causing the young woman to grimace. The hovering lawyer eyed the Japanese woman as if she were a wild mustang that, at any moment, might snap its halter and make a break for the mountains.

"Mrs. Oakley," McKenna stubbed his cigarette out in the white sand of the ashtray and sat. Brenner got out his pen and notebook, leaned against the windowsill. The lieutenant took a deep breath and got right to the point, "What were you doing at the Shelton gallery the night Arthur Shelton was killed? And don't give me any guff about it not being you in that cab—we have witnesses."

"Inspector…Is that what I call you?" Mrs. Oakley asked, in a high, fluting voice.

He grunted. What was this? An Agatha Christie novel? "Lieutenant will do. Well, Mrs. Oakley?" Trying to keep cool, McKenna made himself relax into the worn leather armchair. He thought of Joe Dwyer's order to have the Shelton case wrapped up by Monday morning. Would the information he hoped to gain from Mrs. Oakley nudge things into place? Or set him off on another wild chase? He knew that his continued presence on the force hung in the balance.

"Yes, Lieutenant, I was there that night—for a short time. My show had been up for a week only. Imagine, an entire year's work—one week only! My heart was broken. I said to myself, I must see my friend. I must talk to him.

"So I went to the gallery and Arthur was very kind. He told me of demonstrators and people yelling. He told me about nasty letters and articles in the newspapers. He said he had risked too much money, he could take no more chances, but when things calmed down, he would put up the show again." She grew silent, twisting intertwined fingers.

McKenna waited. Brenner's pen remained poised. The nurse patted Mrs. Oakley's hand. Pritzker tamped down fresh tobacco in the bowl of his pipe. He hadn't said a word since McKenna had entered, had just sat there with his pipe stem in his mouth, watching and listening, taking it all in, looking wise.

"And, then?" McKenna asked.

"And then I left. It made no sense to stay. He would not change his mind—I could tell."

"Did you believe him?"

She lifted her eyes to the detective and frowned.

"When he said he would give you a show at a later time."

"Oh. I knew there would be no 'calmed-down' time. I did not expect my father's country to attack just two days later, but things, I knew, were not to be…amicable…for a long time. I was resigned that the paintings would go back to my studio. I could show to one person at a time. But…"

"But, what?"

"But, I did not hurt my friend. I say goodbye and leave. I did not wish to stay away from Robert any longer."

It had the solid gold ring of truth. Nothing exaggerated, nothing defensive, nothing that smelled like a lie. McKenna had felt all along that this lady was innocent. "Why didn't you tell me all this when I asked before?"

She lowered her gaze to her thin, twisting hands. "I was in the Slough of Despond."

"Huh?" He caught Brenner rolling his eyes.

"Did you never read *Pilgrim's Progress*, Lieutenant?"

He shrugged, scowling. "Way back in high school…"

Nurse Hunter turned to McKenna. "I understand her. It's very clear that, during her detention, Mrs. Oakley experienced a severe depressive episode. Depressed people often withdraw from an unbearable reality to the point where they are unable to function."

"Yeah." McKenna knew about depressive episodes. Taking a deep breath, he let it out and sat back in his chair.

"Okay, Mrs. Oakley. Do you think you could take yourself back to that gallery, back to those moments?"

"My memory?" she asked.

"Yes, your memory. You're talking to Mr. Shelton, okay?"

She closed her eyes and nodded.

"You realize any further argument is futile. Okay?"

She nodded.

"You gather up your things. You rise. You head to the door. What can you tell me about those moments? What did you see? What did you hear? What did you—"

"Footsteps. Someone is moving in the upstairs gallery. Very quiet. But I had the sense all along that someone was in the gallery. Arthur seemed…I do not know…antsy? Is that a word?"

"Yes. He seemed nervous?"

She nodded. "Then I could swear I heard the sound of metal on metal, like someone wearing a ring touched the banister of the circular stairs. I looked up and saw the sliver of a shadow, retreating. I asked Arthur, 'Who is up there?'"

"And?" McKenna was aware that his hands were tightly clenched.

"'No one,' he said, and I thought—what business is it to me?"

"But you're sure someone was there?"

"Yes. The sounds. The shadow. And an aroma. Very light. Like jasmine or some flowery scent."

Hmm. Sounded feminine to McKenna. "A woman?"

"Perhaps," she answered, seeming not at all certain.

"Okay. I got one last question for ya. Do you know what a brush pot is?"

She gave him a wide-eyed stare. "Of course, I do." And, before McKenna could reply, she rushed on. "And Arthur had one. Very old. Very precious. Jade, I think. Edo period. It sat in a case on the reception desk. Ugly and beautiful at the same time."

Yes! McKenna nearly hit one fist into his palm. "Was it there that night?"

"Of course. No. Wait. He'd taken it from the glass case. He must have been going to pack it, because there was a wood box and those…how you call? Curly shavings?"

"Shavings?"

"What you pack breakable things in? How do you call it?"

"Excelsior?"

"Yes, that's it. And—"

The door to the doctor's lounge flew open. As if a mighty wind had disrupted the room, everyone rose or stepped forward.

Dr. Wright rushed in past the guard. "Masako," he said. "Robert has turned the corner. He's very weak, but he's asking for you. Come. Come quickly."

Chapter Eighty-one

Several hours later

The taxi raced back toward Brooklyn, one refrain echoing in Helda's mind: My son is safe.

Howie sat on the jump seat across from her, keeping up a joking conversation with Fraulein Furnish, who had offered to accompany Helda to Grand Central Terminal to meet the late train. The boy was making light of the bump on his head and describing the men he'd met along the railways as if he'd set off on a vacation excursion, rather than on a quest to become a soldier.

Helda put a hand to her forehead. The pain Howie had caused her! Did he have any idea?

It was well after midnight, and Lexington Avenue was almost completely free of cars. Store fronts were brightly lit, and Christmas lights shone in apartment windows. But Helda couldn't dredge up any Christmas spirit. What was she going to do about her wayward son? Even now he was bragging to Fraulein Furnish about how he'd made it all the way to Kentucky on five dollars. The girl responded by smiling and widening her beady eyes in admiration, like Howie was some kind of big shot. For some reason, *die Maus* seemed to get along with the boy better than any of the other boarders.

But for all Howie's big words, the boy couldn't meet his mother's eyes. He is ashamed, Helda thought, as well he should be, but—she let out a tremendous sigh—that was all right for now.

She'd seen her husband again that morning, out the back window as she'd dressed. He'd been standing by Mr. Lampton's shed across the alley, smoking a cigarette, hat brim shading his face so completely that she almost hadn't been sure.

It was the set to his shoulders that had convinced her. People who took pains to hide eyes, nose, and mouth rarely thought to change the way they stood. Ernst had a habit of hunching up his sloping shoulders to make them appear broader. *Jah*, that was him.

Helda lowered her chin into her rabbit fur collar. Why hadn't she called the police, right then and there? There was no love in her heart for the man she'd married—his betrayal had extinguished any remaining flame. No, the problem was the police themselves. They would not understand. Even if she informed on Ernst, he was still her legal husband, Howie's father. Her call might get them all in trouble, like that poor Japanese lady Nurse Hunter worked for. Helda needed to lay low, not come to the attention of the authorities. If they took her to Ellis Island, who would care for Howie?

On the other hand, Helda thought, not all police were bad in America. At Grand Central she'd been surprised to find that nice Lieutenant McKenna leaning up against a pillar near the track. "Just wanted to make sure the runaway made it home," he'd said with a kind smile. He even offered to drive them to Brooklyn. Miss Furnish seemed inclined to accept, but Helda had declined in horror. It was so late! By the time he got back to Manhattan it would be almost morning. The most she had allowed was for him to walk the three of them to the cab stand on Vanderbilt Avenue and give the driver her address. A nice man, that policeman—but he seemed so sad.

Fraulein Furnish's silly giggle pulled Helda out of her thoughts. She and Howie were both laughing at one of his jests. Helda leaned over to pat Howie's knee, and his ears grew red with embarrassment. It's all right, she thought, laugh and joke all you want, my son. I will not let Ernst get you.

Now they were downtown. In the darkness, Helda settled back against the seat and listened to the taxi wheels singing a wordless tune as they sped over the bridge. "My son is safe. My son is safe."

Chapter Eighty-two

McKenna draped his overcoat over the banister of the cork-screw staircase and laid his hat on top. The walls around him were bare of paintings, making the gallery seem both smaller and more impersonal. It reminded him of an empty house, a nice white Cape he and Gayle had once looked at, back when they'd expected to spend his retirement out on Long Island. All the things that made a house a home had been missing, and it'd been hard to imagine anyone living there, especially themselves.

Today was cloudy, the light coming through the arched windows of the front gallery dull and listless. It barely reached McKenna as he stood at the former site of the corpse spread out beneath "Lion after the Kill." But he didn't turn on the lights. He was looking for a ghost—the ghost of the presence Mrs. Oakley had described—and the raw brightness of the electric fixtures that had illuminated Shelton's display galleries might chase it away. What he needed was for the ghost to materialize and make its motivation known. Pronto.

In less than twenty-four hours a report would hit the DA's desk. It could either be his, or, he realized, someone's trumped up facsimile that would implicate Masako Fumi Oakley and further the careers of several G-men and police officers. If that's the way it went down, the report would be the last thing to bear his official—valid or not—signature before the Captain handed him his gold watch, slapped him on the back, and kicked his butt out the door. The last thing before an all-too-willing Brenner was promoted to his job.

Unless he could come up with the real goods.

McKenna made a slow circuit of the terrazzo floor, avoiding the stained traces of the winding blood trail where Shelton had been dragged from the front gallery to this one. His policeman's sixth sense told him Shelton had been a pawn, a means to an end, and that end had involved the fate that now stared the Japanese artist in the face. Light footsteps, Mrs. Oakley had noted on the evening of Shelton's death, a flowery scent, a slender shadow. A feminine ghost.

But a ghost solid enough to hire Herman Rupp to do its dirty work.

McKenna stopped at the windows and looked down out on the quiet, gray Sunday morning street. He pushed the heels of his hands into the window sill. Across Fifty-seventh, his idling squad car belched a wisp of exhaust into the cold air. Dolan was at the wheel, munching on a doughnut. Okay, he thought, a woman for his ghost and Rupp's employer. Perhaps.

But why not a man who was not quite a man?

McKenna heaved himself away from the window. He had to move.

He thought of a graceful young man who enjoyed weekend getaways where he dressed as a woman. Sure, Desmond Cox seemed to have an ironclad alibi, but McKenna had to wonder. Those fruits were thick as thieves—what if they'd all gotten together and concocted the story of the house party to protect him. Then he considered an older man who'd been a drama club stalwart in college, even taking women's parts on occasion. Smoot had no alibi at all.

Both men had had potential problems with Shelton. Cox seemed to want more out of his employer than Shelton was willing to give—in every way. Smoot had sunk a lot of money in the gallery and may have been cottoning onto the fact that Shelton was more interested in his wallet and influence than in his company. But what did either of the men have against Mrs. Oakley? Except that she made a damn convenient cover for murder.

Tiffy De Forest had plenty against the artist—she hated her for who she was, the tint of her skin, the blood that coursed through her veins. And speaking of alibis, Tiffy and Fairchild's was still up in the air. The couple who had gone nightclubbing with them in Harlem the night Shelton was killed had taken off for a winter vacation in Havana. No telling when they'd get back—what with the boat and plane schedules now on a war footing. But if they had visited the gallery that night, why would Shelton have hidden their presence from Masako Oakley? Why would he have opened the door to them in the first place?

McKenna ran a hand over his face, then peered into the dark corners of the third gallery as if the ghost he sought might take shape in the blackness. Show yourself, you bastard, so I can get this fucking case wrapped up. He realized he was straining his ears, but hearing only his own ragged breath. He patted his pocket, looking for a cigarette, then hesitated. There was another sound. A door had closed softly. Footsteps were coming up the staircase. Slow, dragging.

McKenna reached under his jacket, into his shoulder holster.

A gray fedora appeared at the top of the stairs. And then, in the dim light, a pair of massive shoulders.

"Who are ya?" McKenna demanded, tense fingers curled around the butt of his pistol, other hand holding his jacket out of the way. "Whaddya want?"

The hat brim tipped back. Patsy Dolan's wide face broke into a grin. "It's me, Lute. Didn't scare ya, did I?"

McKenna dropped both hands. Took a deep breath. "I thought I told ya to stay with the car."

"Yeah, Lute." Dolan shuffled his feet uneasily. "It's just that I found somethin' I thought you'd want to know about. Somethin' I was supposed to give ya."

"What are you talking about?" McKenna made his voice deliberately patient.

"This." Dolan fished in his overcoat pocket and brought out a folded pink square. He handed it to McKenna and moved to hit the light switch. "What have you been doing up here in the dark, anyhow?"

McKenna held the printed memo sheet at arm's length. In the sudden glare, he had to close one eye and tilt his head to make sense of Doris' hurried scrawl. "When did you get this?" he barked.

"That's the thing. Doris must've handed it to me on Friday— to give to you." The big shoulders hunched apologetically. "What with being so busy and pulling double duty for the guys who've joined up...well, it just slipped my mind. Sorry, Lute."

McKenna had stopped listening. He was looking at a crucial fact about his ghost. The pay phone Detective Perroni had asked the telephone company to run down? It was located smack dab in the middle of the Columbia University campus.

Chapter Eighty-three

Howie tossed in the last shovelful of coal, damping down the red-orange glare of the fire. He clanged the furnace door shut, dropped the shovel into the scuttle and suddenly realized he was smiling. He wouldn't admit it to anyone, especially not to Ma, but he was happy to be home, sleeping in his own bed without fear of being robbed—or worse. And eating Ma's cooking. She'd made waffles for breakfast, with stewed apples and heavy cream. She'd even let him drink a cup of coffee with the boarders at the dining room table.

They'd been nice, well, most of them, and made a big deal of his adventures. He'd come away from the table feeling a little glow, not red-hot like the fire in the furnace, but a good warm feeling in his heart. Or somewhere.

He rubbed his hands on his dungarees to get rid of coal dust, coughed, and turned around.

And jumped.

A man stood in the shadows. A tall man in a tan raincoat with blond hair that didn't bunch up as much as it used to.

"Papa!"

Papa put a finger to his lips, took Howie by the arm and jerked him over to an old bench by the coal bin. "Hush. Do not let your mother know I am here. She would not like it, but I must speak to you, my boy, my son." His blue eyes were busy, staring Howie up and down, as if he were taking inventory of four years' worth of growth.

Howie drew away, his heart racing like a fire truck. This man—so familiar, so strange—Howie didn't know what to say to him.

Papa continued, bending toward him. "I don't have long, son, so I must speak quickly. You are a young man, now. *Ach*! So big. So strong. No more the tiny boy I push on the swings."

"Papa, I—" Howie could feel himself shrinking even further back. What was Papa doing here? Papa was the enemy.

"Hush! Your mother mustn't hear. Women do not understand. You must come with me. We—my comrades and I—have a job for you."

Howie tried to pull away. The cellar air was dank and close, gritty with coal dust. It filled his throat.

"Don't say no. It must be. Important work is waiting. Crucial work."

Howie felt like he was going to be sick. "Do you think I would work for Hitler?" He choked it out.

Papa narrowed his eyes. His blond lashes were almost invisible. He looked dangerous. He looked, Howie realized with a sinking heart, like a real Nazi. The boy took a deep breath, but Papa wouldn't let him speak.

"All that propaganda you get in your schools? In your newspapers? In the films?" He shook his head furiously. "All lies! Think back to what you were taught at Camp Siegfried. Ours is the true cause."

The true cause? Howie took another breath. It hurt in his chest, but suddenly he knew what he had to do. It was a lot more important than lying his way into the Army. And much, much riskier. But he would do it. Okay. Now. He widened his eyes and tilted his head, as if he were waiting to be instructed. "I remember some things. Not all."

Papa seemed to relax. He smiled, and Howie's heart tore. He remembered that smile.

"How to explain when time is so short?" Papa's tones were quiet, but vehement. He glowed with zeal. "The Aryan people were lost for many years, and *der Fuhrer* helped us to find ourselves. He awakened our strength. He renewed our faith in *der*

Vaterland. Now, we are powerful! And we have a place for you. So young! So strong! So agile! You will be part of *der Fuhrer's* great plan."

Howie forced his face to remain interested. Papa took that as assent.

"Such a fine boy. Just look at you. You will be such a help." Papa seemed awfully proud of him. Despite his resolve, something in Howie's spirit felt as if it were rising to meet his father's pride. As if—

Bang! At the top of the stairs, the kitchen door hit the back wall. Howie's spirit fell with thud.

"What you doing, *liebchen*?" Ma called down. "Does it take so long to stoke the furnace?"

Papa's hand was over his mouth. His expression warned Howie not to give him away. Then he dropped his hand.

"Just cleaning up, Ma." Howie's voice cracked. "I'll be right there."

"Since when you clean up without I tell you?" But she closed the door.

Howie stared at his father. He stared and stared. This was Ernst Schroeder, all right. But it wasn't his father. All these years his father had been missing. No papa at his baseball games. No papa at the school concerts to hear him play trombone. No papa to help him with algebra. No papa to…The face might be the same. The sound of the voice. The hunch of the shoulders. The smile, even. But this man was a stranger to him. To bug out on him—and Ma! And for what? For an evil idea. For *der Fuhrer*!

A memory flashed through his mind: Papa at Camp Siggy in his uniform, goose-stepping with the other fathers and the bigger boys. They had been preparing for war—with Howie's country!

He should have known. He should have known, then!

Papa read his face, misunderstanding his intensity. "It is in your blood as it is in mine. I am doing my duty as every loyal German should. And so must you."

Duty? What was duty? It was Ma who had done her duty. Kept the house going. Kept him in clothes and comic books.

Fed him so well he was the tallest boy in the class. Through the grate in the furnace door he could see the warm red glow of the fire. The fire was the heart of the house. Ma was like that—the heart of the house. He could not let her know Papa was here. It would kill her.

Howie knew he had to convince Papa that he was leaning his way, so he nodded, lips tight to hide their quivering. "I will have to think it over." He could hear how oddly formal his words were. He looked this stranger in the eye. Man to man. "If I go with you…there are things I have to do…first."

Ernst nodded slowly. "I come back tomorrow. No—" He looked past Howie, thinking. "Must be later. Tomorrow we have serious business Who knows—may take several days. I will come on Saturday…*jah?*" He clapped both hands on Howie's shoulders.

The boy answered with a nod.

"*Gut, gut.*" More thinking. "When do the women here eat their supper?"

"Six."

"Do you and your mother eat with them?"

What was Papa getting at? "Ma always does. Sometimes I eat in the kitchen while I work on my algebra or something."

"Perfect. You see, fortune smiles on the brave. Saturday evening, you be on the kitchen porch at a quarter past six. You will see my cigarette glow over by Mr. Lampton's shed. That will be your sign." Papa nodded emphatically. "We have great work to do—you and me. I am counting on you, *jah?* You will be here? Ready to go, *mein Sohn?*"

"Howie?" The kitchen door opened again. Footsteps clattered down the stairs.

Too quick and sharp to be Ma.

Must be one of the boarders.

"We were worried about you," the voice said. Before he knew it, that nice Miss Furnish had entered the furnace room.

And Papa had vanished into the shadows just outside the cellar door.

Chapter Eighty-four

Alone in an interview room a few hours after he'd read Doris' memo, McKenna opened an eight-by-ten manila envelope and removed four photos. Spreading them in a neat row on the scarred tabletop, face up, he reached for the coffee Dolan had handed him as he'd left the homicide office. He was convinced that one of the individuals pictured had hired Hermann Rupp to picket Masako Fumi Oakley's show—not for patriotism's sake, but on some intensely personal matter. And that matter had ended with Shelton's corpse propped up artistically beneath the blood-streaked canvas.

McKenna blew on his mug and took one scalding sip. Damn, how did Dolan get coffee so hot? Blowtorch? Too bad Doris didn't work weekends.

As he fanned his open mouth with the envelope, the door to the interview room clicked open. Brenner swung in, one hand grasping the door frame. "O'Connell has Rupp downstairs. You ready for him?"

Using his fingertips, McKenna pushed the coffee mug to one side. "Yeah. Send 'em up." Then he took a last look at his photo lineup. Unlike a lot of guys on the force, he'd never been a betting man. Never backed a team in the football pools. Never played the ponies. But now, based on little more than a sense of unease creeping up the back of his neck, he'd be willing to bet a week's pay on the dark horse—photo number four.

He'd just turned that last eight-by-ten face down when the door opened again, and O'Connell escorted Herman Rupp to the opposite side of the table. McKenna half rose, made his tone formal. "Thank you for coming, Mr. Rupp. Have a seat."

A reek of rancid sweat accompanied the squat, muscular man. His every movement—jerking the seat out, dropping his lard ass onto it, depositing his elbows on the table with a clunk—screamed his reluctance to enter the cops' domain.

McKenna sighed. The man who could turn out to be his star witness looked anything but cooperative. To grease the union organizer's obviously rough skids, McKenna slapped on some flattering phrases regarding a citizen's duty and official appreciation. No surprise—Herman Rupp wasn't buying it. His thick lips remained set in something between a scowl and a sneer.

"We could find you some coffee," McKenna finally offered, ready to send the waiting O'Connell after a mug of Dolan's fire brew.

"Just get on with it, will ya?" Rupp fired back, sending uneasy glances over his shoulders.

Rupp must feel like a man with a big red target on his back, McKenna thought. As if some of the mob boys might materialize out of the walls to catch him ratting! It didn't matter that he would be fingering somebody from uptown, somebody who had probably never set foot on their Bowery turf. Ratting was ratting.

McKenna lowered his gaze to the four pale rectangles that punctuated the dark surface between them. While Rupp squirmed in discomfort, a familiar feeling swelled under McKenna's ribs, the sense of a case finally knitting together. The triumphant sense of impending justice.

"Okay," he said. "You're going to take a squint at four photos, one by one. Study each one carefully. Take your time. Then tell me whether it could be the person who hired you for the art gallery job."

McKenna flipped the first rectangle: a smiling Lawrence Smoot posed in three-quarter view, displaying his movie-star profile.

Rupp's expression went blank, then he pushed his stubbled jaw forward. "What kinda game is this? It was a woman that hired me—I told ya."

"You never heard of a guy rigging himself out like a woman? Word is, up in Harlem, they even have their own coming-out soirees, just like a debutante ball at the Waldorf."

"Hell, yeah—fairies. I seen 'em around. They're thick as fleas up on Forty-second Street." Rupp chewed at his lower lip. "But, Christ on a bike, doncha think I can tell the difference between some pansy boy and a real dame?"

"I need you to keep an open mind. Just picture the man in this photo dolled up like the woman who hired you." To give him time, McKenna sat back and laced his fingers over his belt. He traded a carefully veiled glance with O'Connell and Brenner down at the other end of the table.

Rupp stared at Smoot's photo for a good thirty seconds, then shook his head. "Nah, boss. No way."

"All right." McKenna leaned forward and turned over the second photo.

"Okay, this is more like it." Rupp's admiring gaze swept a head shot of Tiffy De Forest lifted from a *Town & Country* spread. Her lips were parted in a sexy smile, and blonde curls dusted her shoulders. "But...nah. My dame was older and not as jazzy."

"You sure?"

"Yeah. I know a dame what's past it when I see one."

McKenna flipped the third photo. Desmond Cox, full face, hair lifted by the wind blowing down Fifty-seventh. Snapped by a police photographer waiting across from the gallery just the other day.

Rupp heaved a sigh "Not another fairy?"

"Same deal." McKenna's stare remained implacable. "Imagine this face in a blonde wig, with a black veil coming down to the bridge of the nose."

Rupp burped, emitting a whiff of stale garlic. Then, focusing his gaze reluctantly, he said, "Nah. That dame was no queer."

McKenna lifted a corner of the last photo. This one had taken some doing. Dolan'd had to go all the way uptown to Columbia's library for a recent annual, and then the photo lab in Centre Street's basement had blown the postage stamp photo up to a slightly fuzzy eight-by-ten glossy. On a deep inhalation, McKenna turned the photo right side up.

Rupp narrowed his eyes and canted forward. When his chin tilted back up, his sullen expression had changed to a grin. "That's her—the snooty bitch."

McKenna released his breath. The triumphant feeling blossomed in his chest.

"So, can I go now?" Hermann Rupp scraped his chair back.

"Not just yet." McKenna stood, gathering the photos into a pile. "Not until Detective O'Connell types up a statement for you to sign."

"Aw, come on. Give a guy a break…"

Rupp went on, but McKenna wasn't listening. He was already out the door, taking long strides toward homicide.

He needed a car. And Brenner. She might be just a dame, but no way was he going to question Professor Lillian Bridges without some muscle on hand.

Chapter Eighty-five

"Do you think he believed her? Really?" Professor Oakley asked for the third time in as many minutes. "Is he really looking for the person Masako heard moving around the gallery?"

Louise smoothed the pea-green cotton hospital blanket. Then she enclosed his hand in hers. "Lieutenant McKenna seems like an intelligent man—honest, too—a very different sort than Agent Bagwell."

"So…McKenna must have believed her." The professor inched up on the bolstered pillows. "How could anyone look into Masako's eyes and not believe her?" He coughed, weakly, then squeezed Louise's hand. "You believed her, didn't you?"

Louise hesitated before answering, knowing she should attempt to fix the professor's mind on a quieter, safer topic. Pneumonia was a funny thing. After the crisis, the pulse, respiration, and temperature suddenly dropped to normal, leaving the body in a recuperating, but considerably weakened, state. If possible she should keep her patient from fretting about things over which he had no control. Just overnight, Professor Oakley had improved greatly, but he wasn't out of the woods yet. Before Louise had left Louisville, she'd nursed a mother with six children through a pneumonia crisis. The woman didn't trust the father, who "liked his pail of beer of an evening," so she left the hospital against advice and died of a secondary infection. She literally worked herself to death taking care of those children.

"Your silence speaks volumes." Oakley's gaze was bleak, worried. Only a hair less anxious than when Masako's guard had officiously insisted on transporting her back to Ellis Island.

"No. No. No." Louise shook her head. "I know Masako didn't kill Arthur Shelton. I've always known." *Despite everything*, she added to herself. "I just don't want you working yourself into a lather."

"Plato's ball—er, balderdash! What I need is to get back home so I can work on getting my wife out of the FBI's clutches." The blankets stirred as the professor tried to sit up. "Everything is there—address book, writing paper—"

Louise pushed him back and pinned him on his pillows. It was like subduing a kitten. "Do I have to call the ward nurse?" She gave the call button above the bed a pointed look. "If you need something from your apartment I'll go get it, but you have to promise you'll take a nap."

After a much huffing and growling, Professor Oakley told her where to find the stationery and the book with addresses of influential friends. "I also want Masako's photo from the desk top. And, oh yes, a clean pair of pajamas."

"And, Louise? Please hurry back."

"Why the rush? It's Sunday—I can't mail your letters until tomorrow."

He pursed his lips. His newly trimmed beard waggled back and forth. "Lillian Bridges sent word she'd be stopping by after church. She said she had something to tell me. I don't know what it could be." He sighed. "Sometimes she, uh…doesn't know when to leave…"

Louise laughed. "I see, you want me here to tell her when her time is up."

Professor Oakley nodded sheepishly.

"Don't worry. I'll be back before you know it."

◇◇◇

The apartment was dim and as quiet as the proverbial tomb. Louise didn't bother to remove her new coat, now spattered with spots from the light rainstorm that had blown up. She would only be a few minutes. A thin layer of dust covered the desk in Professor Oakley's study. She found the dove gray box of stationery and matching envelopes in the top drawer. After rummaging for the address book, she put the slim leather volume in the box and slid the whole thing into her large purse.

Now to find the photo of Masako—an eight-by-ten in a silver frame. Louise frowned. It wasn't in its usual spot on the desk. She switched on the brass desk lamp. Two small framed snapshots sat beside withered roses in an ugly vase, but no Masako. She glanced at one of the snaps and then quickly held it close to the frosted-glass lamp shade.

She'd seen a similar scene somewhere recently: the professor with a group touring some Middle Eastern country. She slapped her palm on the desk. Of course, in Lawrence Smoot's office! While he and Abe had been discussing the affidavit for the Hearing Board, she'd picked up a photo very similar to this one. Only Professor Oakley's first wife, Virginia, wasn't in the one she held in her hand. It was just the two men—Smoot and Oakley—with Lillian Bridges to one side. She grabbed the second photo, which showed just Oakley and Lillian. The urbane Professor Bridges, hair blowing in the breeze, was grinning like an infatuated schoolgirl, gaze fastened on Robert Oakley.

Louise put the photos down. She rubbed her stomach, trying to tamp down the sense of unease gathering there. Where had Masako's photo gone? She rifled the desk and finally found it in the bottom drawer, wedged beneath some old bank statements. The glass was shattered. Not just cracked, but shattered. As if it had been slammed against something hard.

How had the portrait been damaged? How had the snapshots come to replace it?

Louise's gaze traveled to the sagging roses in their green vase. How long had they been there? Louise ripped a bloom from its stem—wilted, yes, but the petals didn't crumble. They felt soft and smooth, like the chamois cloth Dad used to polish the Oldsmobile. The vase must have been on the desk no more than three or four days. Professor Oakley certainly hadn't placed it there. He'd been too ill to leave the bedroom.

The roiling in Louise's stomach increased as she reached for the vase. This seemed familiar, too. Green, squat, smooth. She traced the carved Asian characters with one finger and then recalled Masako's words to Lieutenant McKenna in the doctor's lounge. They resounded in her head, almost as if they were coming over a loudspeaker: Arthur had a brush pot. Very old. Heavy. Ugly and beautiful at the same time.

And after Masako had run to her husband's bedside, Louise had heard McKenna mutter, "I'd give a quart of the very best Canadian to find out where that brush pot's gotten to."

"Why," Louise had asked.

"It's the murder weapon."

In a swirl of dark red petals, Louise ran out of the study to the phone in the hall. She dialed the operator and asked for Police Headquarters. The desk officer there swore he'd radio the message to McKenna *toot sweet.*

Back to the operator. "Columbia Presbyterian, please."

After what felt like an eternity, she had the hospital switchboard. "Room 632. Hurry, please, it's an emergency."

Ring. Ring. No answer. Sweet Jesus!

Louise slammed the receiver down, rubbed a frantic hand over her cheeks. That green vase might be an antique brush pot or it might be just a cheap, ugly green vase—Lieutenant McKenna would have to sort that out. Even if it did turn out to be the pot that killed Arthur Shelton, what was it doing on Professor Oakley's desk? With flowers undoubtedly brought by Lillian Bridges?

Louise thought of the look on the woman's face in the photo. She'd been gazing at Oakley with absolute devotion. Now all the flowers made sense—Lillian Bridges was besotted with Robert Oakley. On one of her visits, she could have easily slipped in his study and replaced Masako's photo with her own. And earlier this morning, the professor had mentioned that his colleague had something to tell him. What was it? Certainly not a declaration of love? Oh, my god—no! How would Lillian react when Robert Oakley responded with the horror he'd certainly feel?

Louise hurled the flowers from the green vase and took off with it at a dead run.

Chapter Eighty-six

The elevator lurched to a stop on six, and Louise shouldered between an elderly couple and a sad young woman in a bedraggled hat. "Well, really," she heard the older woman exclaim as she hurried through the opening doors, "girls these days. No manners at all."

Louise had no time for niceties. During the stop-and-start taxi ride from the Oakleys' building, she'd imagined all kinds of scenarios. One ended in Professor Oakley laughing and telling her the vase she hugged under her coat was a dime-a-dozen special from Woolworth's.

The others weren't nearly so pleasant.

The nurse's station on Six North was deserted. Behind the counter, an array of patient records in metal folders stood unguarded. A glance down the intersecting corridor told Louise why. She could see all the signs of a medical crisis—an intern calming a distraught family, a nurse rushing a water suction apparatus down the hall, another delivering a sterile tray loaded with syringes and test tubes. A chest patient in distress, Louise thought. Even the ward clerk hovered outside the room, apparently taking down orders barked by a doctor inside. The full medical team would be busy for a while. Distracted.

The breath Louise took filled her lungs to the bursting point as she started down the corridor that led to the private rooms. She passed closed doors, some with bright red contagion warnings

on them, and open ones, with noisy families visiting recuperating patients. The professor's was at the very end. Faster she
walked and faster. With each step, Louise's worries multiplied
into pulsing sirens of alarm.

Did Lillian Bridges hate Masako Oakley? Had her deep
concern for the Japanese woman all been an act? Was Masako's
husband even now in dire peril from this woman he considered
to be a friend?

By the time she reached the professor's closed door, her heart
was pounding at her ribs.

Knock or burst in? She put an ear to the white-painted wood.
A sharp thump made up her mind. Louise turned the knob and
pushed.

Chapter Eighty-seven

"I'm weary—so weary with waiting, Robert," Lillian Bridges had declared. "With hanging onto your every word, decoding your signals."

"Signals?" She sat now on the side of his bed, far too close. He frowned, puzzled. Ever since his old friend had walked in the room, she'd been a tad off. Supremely satisfied, then petulant, by turns. Oh, where was Louise?

Lillian bent her frown into a smile. "You rush to pull my chair out at dinner, darling. You give my flowers pride of place. Why just before you became ill, you told Lawrence how much you appreciated me. I knew what that meant." She nodded, running her fingers through her black and silver bob.

Robert Oakley couldn't believe what he was hearing. He pressed fingers to his forehead, gritted his teeth. "Lillian, all that was over, decades ago. We were just college kids then."

Even in his wet-behind-the-ears, fresh from a missionary family naiveté, he'd known during those years that Lillian Bridges had been deeply infatuated with him. He'd taken her to the movies, a few dances, double-dated with a fraternity brother. Then they'd gotten more serious. The excitement of her confident swagger, her keen wit, and, yes, her sexual candor aroused him for a time. But the spark fizzled fast; Lillian was just so damned bossy. He tired of being told what to do, what to say, even what to think. By his junior year, he'd broken it off. But they'd remained friends.

College friends, part of a wider circle, he'd thought, and nothing more.

Now Lillian sat on the edge of his hospital bed, ready for romance in a silky blue dress with a plunging neckline. Her fingers descended to his thigh, stroking. She leaned so close he could smell her light scent, feel her breath ruffle his hair. "You don't have to hide it, darling," she crooned. "No more waiting. All that's over now. Masako will soon be back in Japan—where she belongs." Savvy fingers crept up his thigh. "We can be together now—like you've always wanted. We'll get a new place. You've always loved the Dakota." She threw her head back, lost in a bizarre fantasy that left Oakley appalled.

"When this war is over we'll travel. Explore the capitals of Europe." Her forehead puckered. "Good Lord, I do hope there's something left of Paris once the Nazis get through with it." She looked into his eyes and flashed a luminescent smile. "We must have Paris."

Oakley shook his head. "Lillian, stop this! I don't want any of those things. All I want is my wife back—Masako here by my side, out of that terrible prison, safe and sound."

She frowned, pushing out her chin in a parody of a thwarted child about to have a tantrum. Or was it a parody? Oakley was by no means certain. She said, "You love me. You know you do," then smiled.

Oakley's fists closed around the bedcovers. She hadn't said, "I love you." In that case he might have felt compassion for a vulnerable, lonely woman. Instead she'd said, with that secret, certain, even fixed, smile, "*You* love *me*. You *love* me." And that smile, mad.

Lillian was mad. How had he not seen this before? Meaningless, everyday politenesses—she'd taken them and woven a tapestry of romance. How long had this delusion—there was nothing else to call it—been eating away at her mind? All those years of his marriage to Virginia, and then to Masako? "You're a sick woman, Lillian," he croaked.

Her body snapped upright. "You don't mean that."

"But I do."

"No." She jerked her hand from his thigh.

"If you think I'd ever fall in love with you, you're totally barking mad." He hoped a disgusted sneer hadn't accompanied his words.

Lillian jumped up and whirled around, her hand sliding into her décolletage. My god! The woman was about to bare her breasts—right there in his hospital room! Where the hell was that goddamned call button? He looked around only to see it well out of reach. Had she moved it? Yes!

Could he summon the strength to get out of bed? He turned back to Lillian and immediately saw that the reality was worse than his fear. In her shaking hand she held a pistol, a mother-of-pearl-handled gun so small Oakley at first thought it was a toy. She held it in her palm, looking down, face full of indecision. The gun was pointed toward her own chest.

Then she met his eyes, seeming to read him, and her expression altered, darkened, became resolute.

Oakley felt himself shrink back against his pillows. Mad, he thought, completely mad.

Casually she turned her hand toward him, to show him the gun lying flat on its side. "When Columbia hired me on," she said, in a conversational tone, "Father gave me this—for protection in the big, bad city." She turned the barrel toward her face, now, staring into it, as if it held a message for her.

"'My life had stood, a loaded gun,'" she murmured. Then she smiled at him. "Do you know that poet, Robert? No, of course you don't. Not one of the greats—a little New England nobody. But she knew about passion; it possessed her, she wrote—'carried me away.' I know what that feels like."

As if he were being carried away, by a slowly moving nightmare, Oakley saw his old friend tightly grasp the pistol's pearl handle; it seemed to fit beautifully in her elegant, slim hand. As she raised her arm, light from the overhead fluorescent strip glinted off the bright nickel finish. She lifted the pistol to her head.

"No, Lillian," he yelled, attempting to heave himself off the bed.

She dropped the gun to her side. "So you do care, do you, Robert?" Lillian's tone was tender. She moved toward him, one step, two, her eyes pleading. "Then there's hope for us, is there not?"

She studied his stricken face for a long moment, and her expression hardened. "Make no mistake, Robert. If you won't have me, there's no future for either of us." Then she raised her lowered arm and stretched it toward him, pointing the gun's barrel straight at his chest.

Had he struggled for Masako's sake to recover from pneumonia only to succumb to this besotted woman's bullets?

Robert Oakley tensed his flaccid muscles, again made ready to spring. He intended to live to see his wife a free woman—not end as a sacrifice to Lillian Bridges' twisted delusions. Erotomania, he thought, that's what the Freudians call this. And, he recalled, it has no cure.

Lillian took another step, then another, in her red, high-heeled shoes. Red. Had he ever before seen decorous Lillian wearing red shoes?

Now, old man, he coached himself. Now, or never. Oakley leapt up. The blanket twisted around his leg, but he summoned enough power to shake it loose. He tackled Lillian at knee level, heard the pistol hit the floor as she fell backward. He, too, was on the floor, topping her. Now if he could just put his hand on that damn shiny toy of a gun.

But, no. She was faster than he. She had it. He was finished.

Chapter Eighty-eight

Louise burst into the hospital room to find the air reeking of sweat and overturned bedpan. And herself at gunpoint.

"Get in here and close the door." Lillian Bridges rose from her knees in one fluid motion.

Louise complied, then turned toward the professor, who was moaning and flailing on the floor.

"Don't touch him," Lillian ordered Louise in mid-step.

"But he may be hurt."

"It doesn't matter anymore." Using the gun, Lillian waved Louise around the bed, toward the room's one chair. "Sit down. Whatever you're hiding under your coat, put it there on the table. Then put your hands on top of your head. Keep them there." Her eyes were fixed and gleaming. Fanatical.

In that moment, as Louise placed the jade brush pot on the bedside table, she knew she'd been right about Lillian's erotic fixation on Professor Oakley, and she understood that Lillian meant to kill him. Because she'd stumbled in the door at the wrong time, she, too, would die. Then the woman would turn the gun on herself.

Bang, bang, bang. Three dead bodies in as many seconds, before anyone could come running.

Louise had only one hope: stall Lillian Bridges until the ward nurse finished with the emergency in the other corridor and came to check on Oakley. That would provide a distraction and maybe one of them could make a grab for the gun. Or—she'd left a message for McKenna, hadn't she? Any moment, the cop could burst in to the rescue.

Okay, keep this deranged woman talking. How? The psychopath wants to talk, her psychology books always said. Wants someone to understand.

Louise made her voice conversational, calm. "You see what I've brought?" She tipped her chin toward the brush pot, careful to keep her hands piled on her hatless head, one on top of the other.

Lillian gave it a careless glance, then drew up to full height. "So, you know about Arthur. Very clever, Miss Nurse. Much cleverer than that ox of a police detective."

Louise couldn't see Oakley on the floor, on the other side of the bed, but she heard him suck in a breath at Arthur's name.

Professor. Please, for once, just keep your mouth shut.

Louise went on, "I see why you must hate Masako, Miss Bridges, but why did you kill the art dealer? What did you have against Arthur Shelton?"

Lillian pressed her lips into a bloodless line. Steadied her aim. Louise thought she might shoot them right then and there, but after a moment's pause, the woman began speaking.

"Arthur was clever, too," Lillian said accusingly, as if being clever were the eighth deadly sin. "Somehow, he'd figured out that I'd hired some thugs to picket the gallery."

"No Go Jap Show," Louise whispered. "Masako was so stung by those words."

"I certainly wasn't the only one who thought she should pack up her precious paint box and go back to Tokyo." Lillian gave an anguished cackle. "Nigel Fairchild's floozy made a spectacular scene at the opening reception. When she hurled wine at Arthur and that beastly painting, I could have cheered."

"Yes, I heard about that, too." Louise forced an appreciative smile. "Did the wine incident inspire the picket line?"

An unruffled shrug. "I'll give credit where credit is due. Yes. When I saw red streaks running down that painting, I thought, why not a more public denouncement? Unfortunately, Arthur caught on—how I don't know. He called me into the gallery for a 'little talk.' He accused me of duplicity—actually threatened to tell Robert what I'd done. For his own good." She snorted. "What nerve! Arthur branding me duplicitous when he'd spent three years soaking poor Lawrence for cash."

Louise nodded, straining her ears. She couldn't hear a thing from the far side of the bed. What was Professor Oakley doing? Had he passed out? Lillian held her gaze. Not so elegant now, Louise thought, with her dress askew, hair falling around her cheeks. And that manic glint in her eye. And…that mannish camel-hair coat thrown across the chair…Suddenly Louise realized it must have been Lillian who'd frightened her that night on the subway platform.

And, at first, she'd actually admired this deranged female!

Must keep her talking. "Masako heard you moving around upstairs the night Arthur Shelton was killed."

"Did she, now? The little bitch! I stepped onto the top rung of the stairs to see who was visiting the gallery after hours. Her being there was a beautiful stroke of luck. With Masako and that unforgettable Jap face right there on the scene, not only could I make certain Arthur would never open his mouth to Robert, but I could provide a ready-made suspect. I'd already made sure the FBI had her in their sights—"

Lillian licked her lips and moved the gun from hand to hand. There was an animal intensity about her now. "Everyone assumed the FBI was interested in Masako because she was such an important artist—that they'd amassed piles of data—that they considered her Enemy Alien Number One."

"They knew about her father…the government post he holds…"

"That's because I alerted them. To her bigwig daddy and plenty more."

"More?"

"Her apartment overlooking the Hudson shipping lanes. Her mishmash paintings that could carry secret meanings. I even made sure they knew about the paintings stashed at her studio."

Louise felt her jaw drop. "That's why the studio was empty— the FBI had cleaned it out. All that shock and surprise! You were just putting on a big act for me and Abe."

Wide grin. "Robert and Lawrence weren't the only actors in the drama club."

Dimly, Louise heard a gasp from the other side of the bed. The professor must be stirring. She had to keep Lillian's focus on her, so she changed tack, gabbled out an accusation, "You must be the very devil. You marked that innocent woman with a big red X. Treason. Murder. Just so you could have the man you—"

Louise's heart gave a leap as Professor Oakley surged up to a sitting position. He bellowed and made a grab for Lillian's skirt. But he was simply too weak. Lillian scooted away and kicked him hard in the side. He sank down with a moan, once again out of Louise's sight. Damn!

Lillian's expression was frightful. She pointed the gun down as she spoke. "You think you can stop me, Robert? Save your sly little Jap?"

Another moan.

"Impossible. If they don't execute your precious Masako for Arthur's murder, she'll get a nice one-way ticket to Tokyo." Lillian Bridges stared down at Professor Oakley. She seemed lost in some private hell, the pistol held loosely now, barrel to the floor. "Not that we'll be around to see it."

Carefully, Louise looked toward the door. From the corner of her eye, she'd seen it crack open. A nurse or doctor would barge right in—it must McKenna. Right? But, oh, no. He'd come in only to face a pistol shot.

No more time for talking. She had to act. What to do? She looked around. She was a nurse, not a helpless ninny. Like Professor Bridges, she was a professional woman, trained to take things into her own hands. Trained to act. It was all in her hands now.

The brush pot—yes!—there on the table. Louise grabbed it with both hands, jumped up. With a banshee scream, she heaved it with all her might. She heard the satisfying thunk of stone on bone and saw Lillian's face contort in pain.

Then it all jumbled together. The door slammed open. "Drop the gun!" McKenna's voice. "Drop it! Do it now!"

But Lillian Bridges didn't drop the gun. She pressed the barrel to her temple and focused her gaze downward. "Oh, Robert, why couldn't you just love me?"

A shot, a rain of blood, and her body hit the floor.

"Shit!" McKenna again, groaning. "Oh, lady, it didn't have to play out like that."

Then, the room was full of police. Nurses. Doctors.

McKenna was at her side, his arm steadying her. "Oakley's okay, Nurse Hunter. Your patient's okay. Miss Bridges won't be hurting anyone any more. You done good."

Chapter Eighty-nine

Saturday, December 20

Christmas was in the air. Helda's fruitcakes had been wrapped in rum-soaked cheesecloth for weeks; today she was baking *pfeffernusse*. Ruthie had tacked mistletoe over the doorway in the front hall. Howie was in and out of the house on mysterious errands. All day long the aroma of cinnamon and nutmeg, vanilla and raisins, emanated from the kitchen. But Cabby couldn't get into the spirit.

It was only with the most sacred avowals of off-the-record confidence that Cabby had coaxed Louise to tell her and Alicia the details of what happened in that fatal hospital room. Bud Smallwood's curt article in Monday's edition of the *Times* had reported only the suicide of a Columbia University professor at the bedside of an ailing colleague. Cabby suspected that the university had a hand in keeping the story low-key in the *Times*. Of course, the daily tabloids were having a field day.

Louise had been having a rough time, tossing and turning in bed, crying out in her sleep. But she still went out every day to tend Professor Oakley and confer with the lawyer about his wife's case. Hearing the grim details of the shooting and watching her roommate soldier on, tight lipped, had given Cabby a new respect for the nurse. Earlier in the week, she'd offered Louise some advice for handling their fellow boarders. "Look, Louise. Ruthie and Marion will hound you to death—they both love dirt. Promise them one crack at the story and make it an expurgated version. You don't need to worry that I'll butt in and spill the lurid details."

So this evening, all the boarders had been hanging on Louise's tale in the parlor, only moving when Howie signaled the approach of dinner by fetching the plates and silverware from the butler's pantry. Now, at the supper table, Louise concluded with, "So Lieutenant McKenna has everything he needs to convince the DA that Lillian Bridges is the one who killed Arthur Shelton."

Helda passed the bread basket. "That Michael McKenna, he's one good police."

Alicia eyeballed the bread choices and took a slice of rye. "But it was Louise who kept Professor Bridges from killing them both—all three of them, actually—in the hospital room." She spread her butter carefully, a thin, even layer from crust to crust. "How did you know what to say to her, Lou-lou?"

All the girls had taken to calling her that now! Louise sighed, and shrugged. "A little psychology—and a lot of luck."

What a story! Cabby rolled a red beet around the plate with her fork, thinking back to the act of vandalism that had taken her to the Shelton Gallery in the first place.

Had it only been a couple of weeks since she'd read No Go Jap Show under Shelton's broken window? Maybe Louise could help clear up that little mystery. "I understand why Bridges hired the men to picket, but surely she didn't come back herself to toss that brick. There would have been no point. She'd already killed Shelton. The show was over."

"Lieutenant McKenna thinks the vandalism was just a random act—someone who'd noticed the protestors. Then, when Pearl Harbor was bombed, that someone took out their anger on the nearest Japanese target."

"Just think," Ruthie said, still focusing on the love angle as she reached for the butter-pooled mashed potatoes. "Loving a man for years, letting no one stand in the way of making him yours. And then killing yourself when you couldn't have him.

That lady professor must really be something." She plopped down with a passionate sigh.

Louise twisted her lips. "They also think it's possible she murdered Professor Oakley's first wife, Virginia."

"*Mein Gott*." Helda's hand flew to her heart. "A double murderess."

"How's that?" Cabby asked, eyes glinting.

Louise laid her fork down. "The lady died on a faculty tour of North Africa. Supposedly of food poisoning. Professor Oakley has his suspicions." She gave her roommate a straight look. "That's not for publication."

"Of course not." Cabby's big, brown eyes were guileless.

"W-e-ell," Marion drawled in her theatrical tones. "I've never met a man I'd risk going to prison for. Never mind the electric chair." She sent the prim spinsters, Jane and Irene, a mischievous look. "What about you two ladies?"

As Jane only put her head to one side and cocked an eyebrow, Alicia stepped in. "Louise, how will having identified the real killer affect the FBI's case against Masako Oakley?"

"That's the one good thing to come out of all this." She clapped her palms together soundlessly. "Abe believes Lieutenant McKenna's testimony will make a tremendous difference."

"The cop agreed to go before the Board?" Alicia again.

"You bet! McKenna actually heard Lillian Bridges admit to false accusations against Masako. He's determined to testify, even though he's had to fight his superiors on it. Along with Dr. Wright volunteering to supervise Masako's parole, Abe thinks the case is in the bag. The hearing is this coming Monday. With luck she may be out of detention by the new year."

Alicia scowled. "Well, Mrs. Oakley's only one of many. What about the rest of the detainees? And I hear scary things about government plans for Japanese on the West Coast."

Louise held up her hand. "I know—Abe has been fretting about that, too. But right now, just let me be happy for the Oakleys."

Cabby looked down at her plate. She was happy for the Oakleys, too. Happy for Louise, happy for Helda and Howie. Happy for everyone besides herself. She cut her tough cube steak into ragged, bite-sized rectangles, determined not to be a wet blanket. For once, all of Helda's boarders seemed cheerful, even jubilant. Louise's patient was healing. Even her own banged-up arm felt lots better.

It wasn't the fault of anyone in this house that Halper had given her another bum assignment. There was plenty going on. Bud Smallwood had covered Mayor La Guardia's address to the labor unions, inspiring workers to unite for the country's defense. And over at St. Vincent's Hospital, Archbishop Spellman had trumpeted plans to upgrade services for wartime emergencies. He'd even stretched out on a gurney to personally donate a pint of holy blood. Another one of the guys bagged that assignment.

What had Cabby done? She chewed morosely. Gone over to Queens to interview some dame who'd come up with the idea of giving war bonds as Christmas gifts. You couldn't argue with the sentiment, but, jeez, why couldn't Halper have sent her to the union rally instead of Bud? Wasn't she ever going to get another real news story?

Marion had started bragging about understudying some role at the Hudson Theater, but Cabby's gaze lit on Mousie, the only one who hadn't been paying any attention to Louise's story. She'd left the group several times, going through the dining room toward the kitchen as if she meant to help Helda, but each time she returned with empty hands.

Now Cabby watched as Mousie coughed deeply and balled up a fist to cover her mouth. She reached for her water glass, brought it to her lips and poured the contents down the front of her grubby pink sweater. "Oh, excuse me," she squeaked to no one in particular as she left the table.

What the hell? No one else seemed to have noticed, but in as obvious a ploy as Cabby had ever seen, the Mouse had spilled her water on purpose. Just what was that girl up to?

Cabby got quietly to her feet and pussy-footed into the kitchen. She intended to find out.

◇◇◇

The butler's pantry was dark. Someone had nixed the light that usually shone on the glass-front cabinets stacked with Helda's willow-patterned dishes. The fixture over the kitchen sink was off, too. The only light came from the naked bulb outside on the kitchen porch. Cabby steadied herself with a hand on the thick breadboard built into the counter. The glow from the porch light was enough for Cabby to make out Mousie crouched by the rear window. Her arm was extended along the sill. In her hand was…

Cabby blinked. Mousie had a gun?

And Howie was out on the porch. Cabby saw him pacing back and forth in his floppy-eared cap and outgrown bomber jacket. Each time he passed the window, his expression looked more worried, mouth tight, gaze furtive.

Cabby started to speak, "What's go—"

Mousie shushed her with a glare and a vicious hiss, then resumed her tense position. Her entire being seemed focused on the neighbor's shed across the yard.

Cabby looked back through the butler's pantry. No one. Good. Whatever was going on here, Helda and the boarders needed to stay away from the kitchen.

Cabby turned as the basement door creaked open. The fingers of a long white hand curled around the door's edge, scuttling upwards in a spidery dance. She recoiled as a man's blond head appeared, lips pulled back over clenched teeth.

He didn't see her. But he saw Mousie, and a silver pistol suddenly glinted at the end of his bent arm.

No!

He stepped through the door.

Quicker than thought, Cabby grabbed Helda's big knife, the one she used to slice her crusty loaves for the bread basket. She tensed her fist around the hilt. Twelve inches of serrated double-edged blade—that ought to do some damage. Fueled by adrenalin, she bounded across the kitchen, braced her feet, and sprang onto the intruder's back, knife firm in her grip.

The man bucked, arms windmilling, but he didn't drop the gun. Cabby hooked her left arm around his neck, slashed wildly with her right. He screamed. Blood spurted. Cabby held on, slicing at him again. His gun fired, and the explosion made Cabby's eardrums ring.

Suddenly, bright headlights lit up the back of the house. Half-blinded, Cabby sensed Mousie pointing her gun straight at them. "Drop it," she ordered. The man's gun hit the floor and so did Cabby. She kicked the gun away from him, as hard as she could. It skidded across the floor and lodged beneath the refrigerator.

Cabby crawled away from the bellowing man, then used the counter to pull herself to her feet.

Mousie still had her gun on the stranger. Blood ran down his neck in a steady rivulet. As if the gun didn't exist, he yelled something in German, charged Mousie and locked the smaller woman in a tight bear hug. She went limp, but, with a swift flick of her wrist, lobbed her gun in Cabby's direction.

Cabby bent, swept it up, pointed it at the intruder. The man froze, arms still around Mousie, hatred flooding his expression.

"He's in there!" A rough voice yelled from outside. Howie flattened his nose against the windowpane.

The women of the boarding house had come to life and poured into the kitchen through the butler's pantry. Ruthie started shrieking, ripping the air like a demented opera soprano. Marion slapped her. Ruthie slapped her back. Louise and Alicia pushed around them.

Just what we need, Cabby thought, more people to get hurt. Moving her focus from the gunman to the women, she ordered them back.

Taking advantage of her moment of inattention, the wounded man slammed Mousie to the floor and kicked her in the stomach. Then he burst through the back door and leapt off the porch. Cabby saw Howie run out after him, grabbing at his coattails.

A blur of activity followed. Running men crisscrossed the back yard. Flashlight beams sliced into dark corners. A big engine roared to life. More shouting, none of it distinguishable.

"Get back, kid!" A man's voice, deep and insistent, separated itself from the chaos. "Stay out of it."

Sputtering, but now upright, Mousie seized the gun from Cabby and sped outside.

Cabby couldn't keep the other women back any longer. Helda broke through first, calling for Howie. Then Ruthie. Then Alicia. The rest spilled out of the pantry in a knot, stumbling, questioning, bumping into table and chairs. Howie's neglected dinner plate crashed to the floor. Red beets rolled everywhere.

Helda made for the back door but slipped on one of the slimy beets. Cabby caught up with her as the landlady pushed up from one knee. "Helda! They have guns. Don't go out there!"

Try telling that to a hysterical mother bent on retrieving her son.

Helda gave Cabby a heroic shove and opened the door.

The landlady froze. Two men in dark overcoats marched a limping, bleeding handcuffed man across the now brightly lit yard. "*Gott im Himmel!* It's Ernst!" Was that horror in Helda's voice? Or was it triumph?

Cabby watched as the men put…Ernst?…Ernst Schroeder?… in a big black sedan. Helda had found Howie. With arms folded tightly around her struggling son, she watched the sedan as if transfixed.

Other agents ringed the yard. One of them shook Mousie's hand. Another clapped her on the back.

As quickly as the incident had begun, it was over. Cabby's head was reeling. Except for a few gawking neighbors on the sidewalk, the street returned to quiet as soon as the tail lights of the black sedans disappeared down the block. The boarding house residents, still shocked and bewildered, clustered around Helda and Howie. Louise, in particular, appeared absolutely stunned. But then, she'd already suffered a bout of life-threatening violence this week. Poor thing.

Alicia led Helda inside and handed her a glass of water. Cabby was dimly aware of Louise rousing herself to take the landlady's pulse.

While everyone was sorting themselves out, Cabby pulled Mousie through the butler's pantry and into the dining room. "You're not just a Macy's sales clerk, are you, Ethel?"

Mousie shook her head. "No. And I'm not even Ethel. Never was." She squared her shoulders, smoothed her baggy sweater and lifted her chin. Her gun was no longer in evidence. Had she hidden it in her waistband? In some indefinable way, Cabby realized she wasn't talking to Mousie anymore.

"And I don't work for Macy's at all," the new, confident woman answered, fluffing up her unfashionably cut hair.

"Who are you?" Cabby forced herself to be calm. She was a journalist: composed, detached, professional.

"Can't tell you, except that I'm with the FBI."

Whoa! Cabby felt the rush of a truly great story barreling toward her at sixty miles an hour. "Really?"

This new Mousie gazed at her soberly. "When the Bureau needed an insider in this all-woman boarding house, Director Hoover himself promoted me from secretary to Special Agent."

"You've been looking into Howie's father? The man you just nabbed?"

"Right. We expected Schroeder to approach the house from the alley. His coming up from the basement was a surprise. Must have been lurking there for some time." She narrowed her eyes at Cabby in professional assessment. "Lucky you were there, Miss Ward. You did a swell job."

A tickle of pride took over Cabby's throat for a moment. This time her usually trouble-making curiosity had actually helped.

"Yessirree," Mousie went on. "And it's fortunate you're a reporter, because I'm authorized to tell the press quite a bit. The Director believes it's of utmost importance for the general populace to be vigilant concerning homefront security. A story in the *Times* would go a long way toward raising public awareness of the peril we're in from spies and saboteurs."

"Sabotage!" Cabby grabbed Helda's grocery pad and pencil from the pantry. She began to write even before this…gosh!… this FBI agent continued on.

"Ernst Schroder has been on the Bureau's list of suspected Nazi collaborators for a long time—ever since the German-American Bund began holding secret meetings. When he disappeared in '38 with a few other Bund leaders, we began keeping an occasional eye on this house. A few weeks ago, one of our men in Yorkville got a tip that Schroeder and a couple of others had illegally reentered the country."

"So that's why you're here, and why you've been cozying up to Howie. You thought he'd be easier to get information out of than Helda."

"It was easy to determine that neither of those two were Nazi supporters, but Howie really turned out to be a brave boy. He helped prevent something that could have resulted in a major tragedy." She chuckled. "He actually asked me how he could get in touch with an FBI agent. Was he ever surprised when I explained he was talking to one.

"It turns out that Ernst Schroeder and his gang were planning to target a dam at the Croton Reservoir. Schroeder tried to enlist his son's help, but Howie wasn't having any of it. So, with the boy's help we stopped this particular cell of saboteurs, but there are surely more out there. We expect attempts on electric plants, on shipyards, bridges, on who knows what. It's crucial for citizens to keep their eyes and ears open. Like Howie did."

Cabby had a sudden, scintillating vision of dropping this bombshell on Halper. "Uh, all of this is on the record, of course," she would state, for once feeling ninety-nine and forty-four one-hundredth percent pure confidence.

The new Mouse eyed her soberly. "You're in luck with this one, Miss Ward."

They both glanced into the kitchen. Howie was talking a mile a minute, Helda hovering like a mama bear with her cub. Baby bear was red-cheeked and excited as the boarders clustered around. Cabby had to wonder how long his smile would last—after all, Howie had been smack dab in the middle of an operation that ended with his father's arrest. But for now, the kitchen was brightly lit. The coffeepot was percolating on the stove. They were all home, all safe. For now, at least.

And Cabby Ward had the story of her life.

Chapter Ninety

Tuesday, December 23

Louise walked at least a mile on Flatbush before she found a drugstore with a phone booth secluded enough for her purpose. This one was tucked in a nook at the back of the store, past the soda fountain and just behind the pharmacist's counter. She sat, closed the folding glass door, inserted her nickel into the coin slot.

"Mr. Pritzker, please. It's Miss Hunter calling. Yes, thank you. I'll wait." Louise tapped her toe, glanced around. An Amos 'n' Andy poster grinned at her from the booth's back wall—a Pepsodent advertisement. She ran her tongue over her teeth.

Yesterday evening, outside the hearing room where the Board was considering Masako Oakley's case, Abe had asked her to spend the holiday with him at a country inn in Vermont. He'd gazed at her with knowing eyes, and butter wouldn't have melted in his mouth. "I'm mad about you, Louise. And as for you? Well…" He smiled that crooked smile. "I think I can tell…"

She'd been so darn tempted, but something more than worry over the outcome of Masako's hearing had stopped her from giving him a definite yes or no. Now, after a troubling midnight talk in Alicia's room…

"Hello…Abe? Yes, yes, I think the hearing went well…Right, I have thought about your…invitation. But, listen…I know something now that I didn't know then…

"What? Well, I know that you're married—"

She held the phone away from her ear. "It doesn't matter who told me." Louise crossed her fingers, hoping Alicia's revelation wouldn't get her in any serious trouble at Brooklyn Law.

"But it does make a difference!…well, it does to me!…an understanding? Just when were you planning to explain about this understanding?" She came to her feet. Suddenly the booth seemed very small.

"Well, that's all very civilized, I'm sure…oh, Abe—stop it! You are so…so goddamned…disarming…you could talk me into anything if I let you…the answer is still no…I'm sorry, but I won't be going away with you this weekend…or any weekend…please, no…no…I'm going to hang up the phone now. Goodbye, Mr. Pritzker. Thank you for everything you're doing for Mrs. Oakley. But, goodbye. Goodbye."

The click of the phone in its cradle was like the period at the end of a long, incoherent sentence. No more messy love stories for Louise Hunter, RN. From now on, she was in control of her emotions—sadder but wiser.

As Cabby would say, "Never trust a man. That's the ticket, Lou-lou—never trust a man."

Oh, yeah. Good luck with that, Louise thought. And sighed.

Chapter Ninety-one

Late January, 1942

Sheets of snow assaulted the French doors leading to the winter-bare gardens of the big Tudor house just outside Bedford Village. A newly laid fire crackled in the brick hearth, and, although it was belated by over a month, a Christmas tree with bright lights and sparkling tinsel graced a windowed alcove.

Masako huddled into one corner of a chintz-covered sofa, shivering despite her green cashmere twin set and tailored wool slacks. She held her porcelain teacup as if it were the only reality securing her to this new safety, this new freedom. It was the first morning after her release from the Ellis Island detention center. Last night, George Wright had driven her and Robert up the Saw Mill River Parkway to his family's estate in Westchester County.

Sanctuary. She took a sip that warmed her mouth and throat.

The Alien Enemy Board had considered her case just before the holidays. The hearing at the US Courthouse in Foley Square dragged on for hours, lasting well into the night. Special Agent Cyrus Bagwell had fired off charges, one after the other: the Japanese national Masako Fumi had familial ties to a member of Tojo's cabinet; her residence was positioned to allow surveillance of US naval fleet activities in the Hudson River; Japanese characters and other traditional Asian elements in her art work gave her the ability to encode propaganda and sensitive military information. Said Japanese national thus posed a threat to the security of the United States and should be detained in Federal custody for the duration of the war.

Determined as she had been to keep her composure during the hearing, each charge burned its brand on her heart.

Her lawyer, Mr. Pritzker, had been a godsend. Thanks to his preparation, she was able to present herself to the gentlemen of the Board as a grateful refugee who had long since repudiated all ties to her war-mongering land, especially those to her militant father. Robert was the first witness called. The three board members had listened carefully as her weakened husband described their quiet life at home, her single-minded focus on her art.

One by one, George Wright, Lawrence Smoot, Nurse Louise, and various members of the New York City art world had also testified on her behalf. The most surprising support had come from that dilapidated police lieutenant who'd investigated poor Arthur's murder. His testimony had clinched the ruling: he had heard Lillian Bridges, the confessed killer of Arthur Shelton, admit to making malicious, unsubstantiated accusations about Masako to the FBI.

"Viper!" Robert had whispered into her ear.

Amid the cigarettes and ashtrays and the notepads and shuffled papers, the proceedings seemed to have gone well.

Still, it had been weeks—nerve-racking, soul-ravishing weeks—before the word came from Washington that Masako Fumi Oakley, Japanese national, could be paroled under the supervision of her family physician, Dr. George Wright.

Paroled? Why paroled? She had been completely cleared of any crime. But Bagwell had made the successful argument that, as the daughter of a high-ranking enemy official, she would always be vulnerable to pressure from the Japanese. It was in the best interests of the war effort for the American government to know where the Fumi woman was at all times.

Now, in the safety and comfort of this beautiful room, the fire was dying down. Robert rose from the armchair where he had been reading the *Times*. He chose a birch log from the antique-copper wood carrier but stumbled as he went to lay it on the fire. Masako jumped up, her heart suddenly constricted in anxiety. "Oh, Robert, you're still weak—and so thin."

"I'll be fine, darling," he said, coming to her. "What matters is that I've got you back—that you're safe." He encircled her shoulders with his arm, and they sat together on the sofa.

Driven by the wind, the snow formed shifting, ghostly outlines on the glass doors. Despite herself, Masako shivered. "Am I safe?" She reached out and straightened a spray of white orchids in a slender ruby-glass vase. Even now she didn't know if she would ever stop shaking.

She looked into Robert's eyes. "Am I really safe? When I'm so afraid I don't think I can ever leave the house? When I'm terrified to show my face in the streets? Will I ever be able to shop in a store—or be welcome in a gallery?"

Robert held her close. "Give it a while," he replied. "I'll get the apartment back in shape, hire a new housekeeper. That whippersnapper, Pritzker, is working on recovering your paintings. We still have your studio. People will calm down. Life will go on."

Will it?" she asked, clutching his arm. "Will it?" She found it difficult to share her husband's optimism. Maybe she could just stay here, in sanctuary, until the war was over. If it ever was over.

Right now, she couldn't imagine ever leaving.

Motionless, they sat together as the snow slowly abated and a sudden ray of winter sun illuminated a maple's dark branches sagging under fluffy blankets of white. Birds began to venture forth, one by one. A male cardinal streaked across the cold, dazzling gardenscape. Masako's fingers began to yearn for a brush, her heart for a dab of cadmium red.

To receive a free catalog of Poisoned Pen Press titles, please contact us in one of the following ways:

Phone: 1-800-421-3976
Facsimile: 1-480-949-1707
Email: info@poisonedpenpress.com
Website: www.poisonedpenpress.com

Poisoned Pen Press
6962 E. First Ave. Ste 103
Scottsdale, AZ 85251